dawg towne

a novel

alice kaltman

word west press | brooklyn, ny

isbn: 9781733466349

published by word west in brooklyn, ny.

first us edition 2021.
printed in the usa.

www.wordwest.co

cover & interior design: word west.

Also by Alice Kaltman:

Staggerwing, collected stories
Wavehouse
The Tantalizing Tale of Grace Minnaugh

For Ollie the Wonder Dog

summer

Y ou wouldn't know me now, if you knew me then. After a fury of volcanic spewing and glacial upheaval I settled into a verdant, hilly area of scruffy saplings and gentle streams. The sun liked me, but not too well. There was snow in the winter, and enough rain to keep my vegetation happy through the growing season. Eventually invasive vines came, as did vociferous insects that sucked greedily on anything with chlorophyll or a pulse. No habitat is without its problems, and my aggravations were minor. Mine was a respectable ecosystem, and if only the fittest survived, everything was the better for it. I had the most pleasant wildlife: bears, wildcats, foxes, all manner of rodent. And the birds! So spectacular of wing and symphonic with song.

My smells back then: pine sap, wet loam, river-tossed pebbles, pond scum, decaying carcasses, honeysuckle, trampled clover, crushed acorns, putrid feces, overripe blackberries, damp fur, blood.

Eventually humans arrived. People have always found me attractive, what with my workable soil, easily cleared forests, and manageable climate. They've stuck around now for centuries. Who can blame them? They've stayed through plagues and blights, endured my blizzards, made do through my occasional heat wave or cold snap.

They planted corn, cultivated fruit trees, raised cattle and poultry. They wove blankets from the fluff of sheep. After a time, they developed a new kind of species-to-species relationship when most interactions had previously been the kill-or-be-killed sort. But now, pets. Dogs and cats mostly, and an occasional chicken or pig deemed too special to slaughter.

This pet relationship fascinates me. The chosen animals offer simpler social exchanges than the fraught bondings my humans engage in with each other, the ridiculous kerfuffles that reek of hurt feelings and regret. Pets work thusly: the humans feed them, provide shelter, occasionally scratch them behind the ears, or rub their stomachs. In exchange, the pets, especially the dogs, love my humans unconditionally. Each pet gets a special name, chosen for mysterious reasons, monikers often arbitrary and disconnected. Tiny for a large, fat cat. Flora for a dog, when a dog is pure fauna. But then again, what do I know? Nomenclature is not my forte; I communicate through rainbows and erosion, humidity and drought.

People, what a puzzle. Befuddling since they first arrived. Mine are greedy. They have always wanted me to themselves. Early on, they had skirmishes with other humans from other habitats. Sharp objects hurled.

Screams, fires, torture. Murder. They've gotten better at sharing, but there's room for improvement. They continue to act in gruesome, horrific ways unlike those of any other species, which make no sense to me at all.

At first they lived in small domiciles built of earth and wood from their environment. Centuries passed and they began to cook over fires and read by candlelight. They traveled to and fro on foot paths and dirt roads. Their houses became grander, built of imported brick or stone, lit by gas lamps and later, electricity. They traveled in horse and buggy, disappeared to distant habitats on smoke-spewing, noisy snakes they called locomotives.

And oh, the Now. Presently their homes are obscenely large, constructed out of boulders and synthetics, or "reclaimed wood" which come from distant and dominated habitats. They drive cars. They still take the locomotive, but they now call it "the train." Walking seems to be reserved for pleasure or bare necessity.

There are, however, some humans who cling to the past. To which past, I'm not really sure. People use a word, "nostalgia," which sounds like a word they might use to describe a fatal disease. Nostalgics travel by bicycle. Their hair and beards remain untrimmed. They restore crumbling, old buildings through a process called renovation. They grow their own food in tiny backyard patches, even though there are large emporiums selling every kind of fruit, vegetable, or other foodstuff one could possibly need.

My smells now: exhaust fumes, sugar, lighter fluid, perfumed cleaning products, rancid cheese, singed meat, wet cement, mowed grass, hot tar, chlorinated water, roasted coffee, rotting vegetables, human piss, dog poop.

Welcome. You can call me Towne.

Chapter One

Nell: Nell's Playmate

Nell was a sickly child, sequestered often in her bedroom, surrounded by toys that only intrigued for so long. Labeled "gifted," the result of exceptionally high scores on a highly unscientific battery of tests performed at age three, Nell's parents treated her like a precious doll, but one who could perform in a brainiac manner at dinner parties they held for their City friends at their charming, if somewhat disheveled, former farmhouse on the outskirts of Towne.

Her father, Professor Laurence Delano, an eminent legal scholar, took credit. His genes must've been the reason Nell could multiply six-digit figures in her head by the age of five. But a gifted child was a restless child. Nell needed constant stimulation, higher hoops to jump through, more complex word jumbles to grope and order. Nell the seeker and finder of the answer, the key, the golden nugget. She was always successful in the end.

Nell's head was too big for her body, a scrawny frame kept that way by her preference for foods on the spectrum between blue and purple. This meant lots of blueberries, blueberry-flavored yogurt, blueberry-flavored yogurt dribbled over blueberries, a bit of blue corn, red cabbage, the occasional beet, and blue cheese smeared on purple potato chips. And though adults might find her beautiful in an ethereal, wood nymph-y way, other kids thought she looked like a wizened troll, what with that long mane of unruly rust-colored hair, all those freckles and those spooky, all-knowing eyes. Nell had a way of looking at you with a gaze that unfurled. Suddenly you were caught in her spotlight. Held there, examined. Potentially discarded.

It was hard for Nell to maintain friendships. For one, she lived three miles from the gridded suburban center of Towne, so any spontaneous hopscotching or ball tossing with other children was out of the question. More so, however, was Nell's innate oddness, and all those sick days when she stayed home and out of the school yard loop. Up in her pink canopy-bedded, ruffled room, she would exhaust all the imaginary games it was possible to play with twelve Barbies, a full set of building blocks, and collection of plastic stallions. If she had the energy, she'd wander downstairs, and poke her head into her father's study. If he was there, she'd skitter away. She had no desire to answer questions about Cicero or Scalia, when all she wanted to maybe do was watch some of those cartoons the other kids talked about at recess. But if her father was out, and if her mother, Beverly, was busy throwing impossible pots in her ceramic studio in the basement, Nell would sneak into the study and turn on the one and only TV in the gargantuan house.

SpongeBob was for sure her favorite.

By the time Nell turned ten it became harder and harder to conjure imaginary friends, and the few real live kids who might play with her on occasion were now fully ensconced in way cooler cliques. A pet seemed a sensible move. There were provisos, however. Nell's father claimed he was allergic to cats, but really it was his tyrannical need for order that kept their household feline-free. Nell's mother was scared of dogs, regardless of breed or size. Bunnies were out of the question; too many wires to chew. Guinea pigs, hamsters who lived in cages lined with cedar chips seemed like barely domesticated rodents. What if one got loose and caught Nell's parents unarmed? Ate Beverly's begonias, or left pellets on Laurence's heirloom Persian rug?

The answer was Jumbo, the box turtle. A slow pet, one who seemed mostly content to reside in his plastic terrarium. Nell loved Jumbo, but there were constraints to engagement. Jumbo was a shelled reptile with limited physicality. He was no puppy trickster. Fetch was an impossibility. Roll over even more so. Catch was doable, if there happened to be a fly hovering near Jumbo's mouth.

Nell was allowed, weather permitting, to let Jumbo roam around the spacious yard, as long as she kept her spooky, all-knowing eye on him. One day Nell let her mind wander. Her gaze floated upward to the sky where she watched clouds form and dissolve; bulbousness and wisps, shapes nonsensical and serene. She wondered about the exact location of heaven, and if angels really existed, how could they sit on condensation formations? Only a few moments later, when Nell looked down, there was no Jumbo, just a matted path heading toward a distant corner of the large backyard and thick expanse of boxwood. Nell saw a flash of brownish green shell glisten for a moment in a splinter of sunlight. And then Jumbo was gone, burrowing deep under the shrubs, en route to the large sprawl of untended farmland that lay beyond, onward to another life.

Nell sighed. Thoughts flitted through her head at warp speed. Games were over before they began. Answers instantly seen, clues discovered. The stupidity of it all. Tears as deep as lakes formed in her child eyes as a realization struck, a morbid truth that would hound her for many years to come: Nell might never be able to keep anyone or anything close by for more than a blink.

Abe: Everything and Nothing

"To each his own penis," Abe whispered to Milo, as his toddler son lay spread eagle and oblivious on the changing table. Milo diddled his pink nubbin and stared up at the cars, trains, and planes mobile hanging over his head while Abe wiped away the carrot-infused poo.

Milo was only three days old when Abe had first uttered this private benediction, so tiny Abe could cradle his son's sacred skull in his palm while Milo's body slumped like a hacky sack along Abe's forearm. There had been no mohel, no ceremony, no double-edged knives. After two sleepless nights, Abe and his wife Claire had laid the issue to rest. Abe could care less if his son had a penis like his own. He was fine with something unsculpted—less Yid, more Euro.

His rose- and cream cheese-scented boy. His sweet, alien creature. The first diaper change, executed without the hovering intervention of Claire who, sleep-deprived and sore nippled, had finally conked out in a face plant on the couch. Abe's beloved pit bull Gordon was curled up at her feet, also asleep and deeply invested in a whimper-filled, paw-twitching dream. Usually Claire would disallow Gordon any furniture snoozing. But she had been too exhausted to care.

Abe had been en route to the rear yard-facing window of their then-new house. He wanted to show Milo his future domain. The move from City to Towne had been such a good idea. Such a responsible decision. Claire and Abe took the suburban leap right before Milo's birth. They found an affordable two bedroom home ten miles from the slightly more sophisticated Village, where Abe's mother Barbara had settled after Abe's father Mort kicked the bucket. So, not moving home, exactly, but almost. A real house with a yard where Gordon could galumph and shit to his heart's content, where Milo would eventually crawl, get green kneed and grass-stained, where Claire and Abe would vigilantly pull bits of mucky grit from both dog and baby's mouths.

But back on that first, momentous morning the infant's loaded diaper couldn't be ignored. Abe pulled back the taped tabs on Milo's disposable diaper as delicately as his cloddish fingers allowed. How was it possible for such a featherweight angel to create, then expel, so much? Abe tossed the soggy loaded diaper in the bin and tried not to think about the pollution, the waste, the synthetics.

First diaper change, guys only. Abe had gazed down at Milo's uncut nubbin. Such a sweet bump of flesh atop bulbous scrotum. A little rosy dollop. That was when Abe had first uttered the now-ritualized diaper change benediction: To each his own penis.

Confronted with his son's genitalia on a regular basis now for almost two years, Abe often wondered: how many days had his own penis looked like this, before it had been trimmed according to Jewish law? What had Abe's father Mort thought in the moments before Abe's circumcision? Did Mort reflect on his own splicing as Abe's bloody ceremony took place? Did he wince with empathy at newborn Abe's possible pain? Mort was dead, gone now for seven years, and even if the surly grump were still kicking around, it was highly unlikely Mort would ever have discussed his nether parts in such detail with anyone, least of all Abe. Mort had named Abe after his dead grandfather, the original Abraham Kaufman, a man who'd escaped pogroms, been generous to a fault to all his friends and relatives, a king of a guy who ended life a penniless but well-loved *mensch*. Mort gave his son a traditionally inherited ancestral name and a circumcision ceremony with all the bells and whistles, but that was the end of real Judaism as far as Mort was concerned. He was the poster child for assimilation, as Jewish as a cinnamon raisin bagel and as communicative as a paper doll.

During that first diaper change, Milo began to stir as soon as the air chilled his sodden junk. Milo wiggled tiny taloned fingers and noodled his hands towards his face as his lumpy peach body curled inward, searching for itself. Milo wailed; every muscle in Abe's body seized in response. The son's screeches called so deeply to his father that it was as if a sinkhole swallowed every bit of reason the man had left. It was impossible to think clearly, seemed futile to attempt a simple task—like changing a diaper.

Milo would wake Claire if he kept crying. And with that thought, Abe had been compelled to action. He'd managed to wedge his fingers between his son's writhing arms and legs, his bear-like hand ungainly and grotesque against Milo's willowy limbs. Milo's miraculous heartbeat like moth's wings, his papery eyelids so transparent and otherworldly. Abe's palm came to rest on the mound of Milo's smooth warm gut, his tiny pillow of a belly. Everything and nothing held right there.

Abe massaged Milo's tummy in gentle circles, easing

what Abe had come to realize, three days into fatherhood, was probably just a bit of irksome gas, an air bubble trying to make its way up and out as a burp, or down and out as a fart. Abe's fingers, large and indelicate, did the trick. A fart. Milo had calmed from the sense of skin on skin, of release.

It still worked almost two years later, this magic touch. The mobile still spun overhead. And while Claire had long since returned to her City finance world job, Gordon still snoozed in a glorious, whimpering slumber at the foot of the changing table. Milo babbled nonsensically, no longer shrieking when fresh air kissed his shit-covered tush. Diaper changes were now a favorite activity full of potential; urine fountains, maybe even shooting his father right in the kisser, ample opportunities to grab his feet and suck on his own toes, the joy of kicking the padded table with the gusto of a WWE heavyweight.

Abe tried not to inhale until all of the brownish-orangish mess was wiped from his son's silky skin, from every fold and bump and orifice. Father to son. Son to father. The end to the beginning. The beginning of the end.

Paddy: Old Chum

Paddy gripped the plastic handles determined not to fall overboard and crack his skull on a craggy monolith jutting out of the Salmon River.

"No worries, people. We can navigate this river in our sleep," Saskia reassured while she and the other brawny river runners trussed the retirees in puffy orange life preservers.

Everything about this trip was wobbly-geezer friendly. Rugs in the tents, elevated air mattresses, featherlight sleeping bags. Gourmet meals prepared on a blazing fire pit. Pre-dug latrines. Paddy, a car mechanic, a man used to dirt and grime and discomfort, found such coddling annoying. He'd owned the Towne Gas n' Go for nearly forty years. Pumped gas and worked round the clock on all sorts of cars in side by side bays. Abraded his back getting under rich folks' Caddies and Lincolns, ripped the flesh off his thumb at least once a week on Chevys or Fords.

His wife, Mariah, was reveling in the comfort of this rafting trip. He turned to look at her. Mariah sat on the bench behind him with that lesbian couple from Santa Fe who wore matching crystals around their necks. Paddy's heart did a little flip when he saw Mariah's beaming smile. At least that hadn't disappeared. Yet.

To look at Mariah you'd never guess. The doctor said not to worry, an outdoor vacation was a wonderful idea. Do it now, while you still can. Mariah wasn't that far gone. Yet. It wasn't as if she would wander off and try to befriend a rattlesnake. But in six months there'd be no guarantees.

Paddy was glad Mariah had found other enthusiastic sorts on this rafting trip to have a chuckle with. Paddy wasn't always a grump himself. Just sometimes. His entire life people had misinterpreted his basset hound look for sullenness, assumed he was angry when he was merely having moments of contemplation. He'd tried his very best to remain chipper on this vacation for Mariah's sake. But who could blame him for being less than jolly? Morbid thoughts were hard to avoid, with the whole geriatric lot of them heading downstream, wedged next to each other, encased in neon like a shipment of crash dummies.

Was this fun? He wasn't sure. He wasn't a fan of the stomach souring ups and downs, or the soggy slosh of his wet ass on the hard seat.

"Hold tight, folks," Saskia called out. "We've got a big one ahead."

The wave assaulted, lifting the raft and dropping it with a neck-breaking thud. Churlish white water plumed overhead, drenching everyone. Paddy glanced back. Mariah was soaked from head to toe. Her eyes had that look, that new look, the alarmed stare that reminded Paddy of a rabid baby squirrel he'd once almost stepped on in his backyard. He tried to grab her hand, but his damn life preserver and fat stomach kept him from achieving enough torque and reach.

"Mr. Toad's Wild Ride, eh friends?" Saskia cried, so forcibly chipper Paddy wanted to slap her.

That was when Mariah stood, though standing in the raft was strictly forbidden. She looked as sane and determined as she had the day Paddy first spotted her on that Brooklyn sidewalk, cursing like a sailor at the wad of gum stuck to the bottom of her brand new high heel. Back when he'd been able to lend a helping hand.

Mariah's eyes were steely and no longer demented. Here, now, on a stupid rafting trip of all places, she tinkled her fingers and smiled at Paddy for the last time. As he watched his wife pitch sideways, toppling herself like a cedar felled into the raging Salmon River, Paddy leapt out of his seat, life preserver and fat stomach be damned, and pushed his way towards the front of the raft. As he made to dive in after the love of his life, the hands of Saskia and an equally sturdy minion clamped him in place.

"No, sir," Saskia commanded. "Stay. We'll do everything we can."

In a matter of seconds, Mariah's life preserver floated downstream like an origami boat. Paddy watched the young river rafters scramble to do a proper save. But Paddy knew it was a waste of time. The world went dark as he cried, and silent as he screamed.

David: Little White Lie

On the morning of his *bar mitzvah* David Leibowitz stood in front of the bathroom full-length mirror. Balthazar, David's ancient wire-haired and wire-minded terrier, the only family member David would ever allow anywhere near him at times like these, sat on the damp bathmat with his pointy ears at full alert.

David turned sideways and swiveled from the waist up, like a starlet photographed on the red carpet. With pursed lips and his head in a come hither tilt, he imagined himself wearing a little black dress. His body was still a scrawny asexual thing, so the imagining didn't require much morphing.

Today David would become a man, yet he felt more like a woman than ever. The last year had really sucked, what with all the preparation: the Hebrew classes, the *Haftarah* tutorials, all the talk at synagogue of what it meant to be a man. Judaism mattered to David, more than his barely practicing, mostly distracted parents. He'd hoped the *bar mitzvah* studies would provide him potent clues, hoped that delving into faith and Jewish law would ground him on one side of the gender fence or the other. But all it had done was open up more questions. To top it off, his parents had finally pulled the plug on their shit show of a marriage and gotten divorced.

To cope, David's relief came in sneaky fantasies. Lately the one he returned to most often was of himself as herself on the dance floor at the Towne Manor House, the site of his approaching *bar mitzvah* reception, grinding up against Chucky Weintraub, a boy David had had a painful crush on since third grade. Fantasy David—who when David fully allowed himself to be all girl he occasionally liked to think of as Natasha—had hair that was waist long and professionally straightened. Natasha wore

mascara and coral lipstick. Her nails were French mani-
cured. She wore the standard *bat mitzvah* uniform: spa-
ghetti-strapped ebony sheath, Tiffany bracelet, and ballet
flats; because every prepared girl knew you needed a pair
to change into if you really wanted to dance: high heels
were only for the ceremony and photos.

What was David? He didn't know for sure, yet. Honestly, everyone turned him on. Girls, boys, women, men. Nell,
his twenty-something former piano teacher; she was lovely
and willowy, a bit disheveled, half-incompetent but smelling of lilacs. Rabbi Levinson, the youngest rabbi at Temple
Emanuel with his beautiful smile and hairy forearms. Gwen
Harris from Bio class, with her early boobs and bossy-pants
personality. David loved looking at boobs—all of them—
but was that because he wanted a pair himself or because
he wanted to squeeze someone else's? All David knew was
he wasn't a man, had no urge to be manly. David felt like an
un-man, if that was even a thing.

David had his *bar mitzvah* speech memorized, a
bland treatise on *Derech Eretz*, the moral law that says,
"We must conduct ourselves in a way that does not offend
those around us." In his speech David would spin *Derech
Eretz* to be about acceptance: letting people be whatever
they wanted to be as long as they didn't hurt anyone else.
He was hoping to plant some seeds.

David pulled himself from his confusing reflection. He
shooed Balthazar out of the bathroom. The dog whimpered
ineffectually, but obliged. He loved this boy unconditionally,
they'd grown up together, both almost thirteen years old, which
meant something entirely different in Balthazar's arthritic, aging
doggie bones than in David's, still elastic and growing.

David made sure the door was locked before he
reached behind the toilet tank and removed a Ziploc
baggie he'd taped in a deep hidden crevice. Inside were
a pair of underwear from his friend Lucas' mother's

lingerie drawer. He'd coveted this particular pair for months. Ivy satin bikinis, with a delicate little bow.

"*Emet*," David whispered to himself as he slipped them on. Truth. One must always tell the truth according to the Torah, although a little white lie is okay if it preserves the peace. For the time being, until truth was possible or even known, David would keep his little white lie comfortably hidden behind the zipper of his brand new *bar mitzvah* slacks.

Lucinda: There goes the neighborhood

Lucinda was glad someone had finally bought the old Kearny Mansion across the street. She knew that as wonderful as the Kearny place looked from the outside, the insides were decrepit, on the verge of total collapse. Lucinda was a lover of all things elegantly historical, one of the few qualities she'd inherited from her Southern belle of a mother that Lucinda hadn't tried to shed when she'd escaped Atlanta for the Northeast. It pained Lucinda down to her pinkies that a potential gem in the crown of Towne Landmarks might end up destroyed by the next snow storm, or worse, demolished by an over-eager, taste-less 'designer-builder,' like her ex-husband Dan, who'd had his greedy, beady eyes on the Kearny Mansion the entire time they'd lived across the street from the place.

Thank god Dan and his girlfriend/business partner Rachel had finally moved out of Towne. Lucinda felt their absence like fresh wind against newly scrubbed skin. No more worrying about awkward sightings at local restaurants. No more surprise visits to pick up Dan's boxes of hoarded nostalgia from the basement. Granted she did need to deal with Dan regarding their son David, and would have more than her fill of her ex and his puffball girlfriend later that day at David's *bar mitzvah*. But for the most part, Dachel Construction did all their wheeling and dealing further north now, sliming their way around Village, out of Lucinda's stomping grounds for good. On one hand she envied their broader minded, and more culturally interesting community of Village, which seemed to exude a whole different vibe than Towne merely by virtue of being ten miles closer to City. Village had its own Arts Center, a Restoration Hardware, and a Peruvian taqueria, whereas time-warped Towne merely had an annual Craft Fair on Main Street, Dot's Fabric Store, and a sleazy bar and grill called Schepp's.

But Towne was not without its charms. For one, there was that work of architectural wonder across the street. The Kearny Mansion. What a gem. Lucinda took a swig of wine and tugged ever-so gently at the loose skin under her chin. Thinking of Dan and Rachel she singsonged, "Nah-nah, nah-nah, poo-poo. No Kearny Mansion for you two," as she stared across her sizable front lawn to the even more sizable front lawn of the Kearny Mansion. Her grass was a patchy, straw-brown disaster thanks to lack of funds and her dog Balthazar's geriatric intestinal issues while the Kearny lawn was verdantly green thanks to a shaded northern exposure and a crew of diligent gardeners employed by Christie's Real Estate.

The cosmetic outdoor treatment had done the trick for that old diamond in the rough. Word had it that the Kearny place had been purchased, all-cash, by Brady Cole, the semi-famous former movie star—now TV actor—who'd most recently starred in *Signet*, a police procedural filled with blood, gore, and gratuitous sex. Lucinda only knew this because her best friend Denise watched the show religiously. Lucinda wouldn't watch that trash if you paid her.

"I watch it for Brady Cole's ass," Denise told her over the

phone, "Even now, he's what, our age, right? Like forty-five, fifty?"

"Don't remind me," Lucinda had muttered.

"Anyhow, he's still fucking gorgeous. And they show his ass in like every other episode. I'm hooked."

Lucinda wasn't interested in Brady Cole's ass. What interested her about Mr. Cole was whom he might hire to do the interior work on the Kearny mansion. She wondered if he'd keep the decor in line with the late Nineteenth Century exterior, or if he'd switch it up, maybe add a cool modern twist here and there. Maybe some Roche Dubois sectionals in the living room, an Aeron industrial steel table in the grand dining room with retro Belle Epoque chairs in blood orange or shocking pink floral from Scalamandre. That's what she would do. Not that anyone was asking her decorating opinions anymore. The last big job she'd done, or rather half-done, had been for a stuffy legal scholar and his ceramicist wife fourteen years earlier. Their house was a rambling catastrophe at the edge of Towne: a former farmhouse gone to seed. The scholar was distant and remote, the quintessential coddled genius. The wife was one of those artsy types who pretended to be laissez-faire about everything but her "craft," while underneath was a controlling bitch. They had one child, a then-ten-year-old, pouty thing named Nell who stayed in her room playing with a pet turtle whenever Lucinda came by to do measurements or talk about window treatments. The scholar and the ceramicist were perfectionists who could never make decisions. Nothing was ever right, nothing good enough for them. Eventually Lucinda quit, left with half her fee and a sour taste for decorating.

When David was born a year later, Lucinda embraced motherhood with the same fervor she'd previously attached to bathroom fixtures and kitchen counter tops. Her own mother had employed a series of nannies to care for Lucinda and her insipid younger brother Ted. Most of the nannies were black and understandably scared of Celeste Montclair, who claimed to be an equitable, fair minded woman, she was Jewish after all, and "knew from their plight," but really she was a terrible racist: condescending, demanding and blind to her own nasty shortsightedness. Celeste had been an amateur interior designer, dabbled in realist oil painting, and spent most of her free time at the Country Club or Hadassah of Greater Atlanta events. She wore motherhood as a badge, something to compliment a fabricated peachy demeanor and matching complexion. Her hands were never dirty.

Not one of Lucinda's nannies ever stayed for more than a year. Each time one of them quit she felt a fresh heartache, and a child's certainty that she was the cause of their leave-taking. Once David was born, Lucinda vowed to never leave him to have his heart broken by anyone other than her. From then on it was strollers, schools, meals, playdates, soccer games, and homework. Coincidentally, David even took piano lessons briefly from teenaged Nell, still pouty and odd, a mediocre teacher at best.

For Lucinda it was a time of many suppressed emotions. She managed spurts of frustration through juice cleanses, a vegan diet, Pilates, yoga, hot yoga, Yogalates, and lots of denial. And then, the divorce.

Now it was David's *bar mitzvah*, later that day. This would be a real challenge. Dan and Rachel sitting at her table, all of them palsy-walsy, putting on a good show for David, but even more so, for all the guests. Dan and Rachel no doubt in blandly tasteful outfits. Dan would probably choose that vapid gray pin-striped double-breasted suit he'd had for years to hide his ever-widening gut. Rachel would opt for an unoriginal, form-fitting sheath, and might tame her ridiculous Bride of Frankenstein frizz into some braided affair.

Lucinda had yet to decide what to wear, which would

be a challenge as the Donna Karan she'd bought for the event barely zipped up the back, even when she forced her flesh into her most constricting undergarments. And everything else in her closet was a size from yesteryear.

Lucinda took another slug of wine. As she stared out the large bay window of her living room, a schlumpy, bearded man wearing thick-rimmed glasses walked past with a pit bull and what must've been his toddler son. The dog pulled aggressively on the leash, causing the man to lurch forward while trying to hold tight to his son's hand. Why have a dog like that anyhow? thought Lucinda. It's ugly, clearly unable to heed commands, and possibly dangerous. It was one thing to have one of those creatures for protection in the City, probably where this hipster dad came from in the first place, but there in safe, serene Towne, pit bulls just didn't make sense. They didn't fit in. Plus, Towne residents rarely walked their dogs. They let their dogs scamper around large backyards or frolic freely at the dog run in Allenwood Park. And pulling a tiny kid along on a sidewalk? The poor little dear. It made much more sense to have a kid that age in a stroller.

Lucinda was back to studying the mansion, when a limo pulled up the circular driveway. The black suited and official looking driver got out and scurried around to open the rear passenger door. Out bounded a massive yellow Labrador retriever. The dog sniffed the new perimeter plantings, settled on a budding rhododendron and promptly lifted a leg to pee his deadly stream on a cluster of pink blossoms. Then, out stepped Brady Cole. Or was it? Lucinda had only seen him in that one movie, ten years ago, the one with Marion Cotillard, the one with lots of crying and thrown crockery.

No, it wasn't Brady. It was a woman, a very large woman, wearing a white dress and a strange little beaded beret. She hugged the driver and kissed him on the cheek fondly before hiking a large patchwork satchel over her shoulder and clapping her hands a few times to get the dog's attention. Once the dog was by her side the woman unlocked the gorgeous, carved oak front door of the Kearny Mansion and walked inside with her pet, slamming the door and causing a mini dust storm on the front stoop.

Maybe this was Brady Cole's wife, or girlfriend. Better yet, maybe this was a personal assistant who made decorating decisions. Lucinda drained the Pinot. Was her interior design license still good? She'd have to check.

Brady: Up the Tamago

Brady stood in his new backyard and scratched his ass as he watched his dog Angus take a dump by the back fence. The itchy sensation reminded him of how he'd felt grains of sand easing their way up his ass crack back in California, during the Beauteous Men's Retreat, how he'd shifted his weight to the left, trying to avoid any skin to skin contact with Harold, the hirsute, sweaty guy sitting next to him in Tamago's Beauteous Men's Music Circle. Brady remembered flicking out the grains hoping no-one noticed. The guru Tamago had made it very clear before the men sat on the beach with their dulcimers, zithers, triangles, piccolos, finger cymbals, and shaky eggs: Those who decided to make music in the nude would have the most evolved experiences, but they must take in all sensations without fidgeting. Tamago failed to mention the substantial sea breeze coming off the Pacific, the voracious mosquitoes, and at least for Brady, copious clumps of sand up the ass.

Brady had been eager to please, to show everyone—especially Tamago—he was just a regular guy in spite of his celebrity status. And thus, naked he be. He'd been accused by his ex-wife of being a soulless cypher. His manager had repeatedly threatened to dump him if he didn't clean up his act vis-à-vis, well, everything. His mother used words like "extreme" and "scary" and "embarrassing" way too often after reading about her golden boy in the tabloids. Brady had grown desperate to prove them all wrong. He'd sold the place in Topanga, and the satellite crash pads in Manhattan, Aspen, and London. He'd stopped fucking twenty-year-old production assistants and thirty-year-old yoga instructors. He'd sworn off booze and cocaine, this time for good, or semi-good.

His manager, Lois, had grown up in this uncool East Coast suburb, Towne. She'd been the one who'd found Brady this low-profile house to hide out in after he finished the Beauteous Men's Retreat. The bizarre giant rattrap of a house stood behind him now as he waited for Angus to finish his business. Brady had no idea what he and the dog would do with all that empty space.

"Towne is super cute and quaint," Lois had said, "Like, in a time warp. Everyone wants to know everyone else's business, but they get the dirt and go back to their safe little houses like turtles into shells. If you stay put—just stay put, Brady, for once—in the fab mansion I found for you and don't get into any of your usual trouble, you should be fine."

Now the Beauteous Men's Retreat was finished, and Brady could fidget and scratch his ass whenever he wanted. But he was still committed to change. He would go full-guns on this inner-self thing. It would just be him and Angus. And some clothes.

He'd given fuck-all when those dudes on the Retreat saw him naked. He'd been showing his body off for over two decades. He still looked better than most of the fatsos sitting Indian style on the dampish sand, even with the 20 pounds he'd put on since *Signet* was cancelled mid-season.

Every man sitting in the circle had been desperate, even more than Brady, each more concerned with washing away their own sins than how well hung Brady might be, and how they might measure up.

The men on Tamago's Beauteous Men's Retreat had been a bunch of lost souls: assholes, wife abusers, legal cheaters, alcoholics, and cocaine addicts. Serial liars. Non-committals wealthy enough to stay that way. Brady's people, he hated to admit. He felt right at home.

Luckily Brady hadn't needed to worry about being caught cleaning his ass crack because everyone else in the music circle had their eyes closed, the naked guys and the ones who had wisely kept their white sack-like dresses on. Everyone recited in dull repetition, "No wine, no women, but plenty of song..."

Brady wiped the remaining residue of sand from his fingers on his upper thigh. He looked down at the dulcimer in front of him. What a dumbo Brady had been to let everyone else choose instruments first, trying once again to come off as Mr. Easy Going. He could've quickly chosen a marimba, or a shaky egg. But Brady thought not being grabby about instruments would show Tamago that he was already ahead of everyone else in Beauteousness. He'd ended up stuck with an instrument that actually required skill to play.

Brady resisted the urge to switch out his dulcimer and silently steal the shaky egg resting by the meaty thigh of cyber-scion Gary Links, while Links sat cross-legged, temporarily blind and oblivious. Links was an even bigger kiss-ass than Brady. No way he'd open his eyes and risk disappointing Tamago.

"No wine, no women, but plenty of song..." the Beauteous wannabes droned on and on. Resist the urge, thought Brady, as he eyed Links' shaky egg. That was the point of this whole thing, wasn't it? Resisting urges and making kinder, more conscious, less traditionally male decisions? Tamago's teachings sounded good on paper. But then again, everything sounded good on paper, including the final season of *Signet*, which had been trashed in the trades for being "clichéd and predictable," Brady's performance labeled, "dull and dusty."

Tamago abruptly stopped chanting. He opened his eyes and stared directly across the Men's Circle at Brady. The whites of the guru's eyes shone in the moonlight. His hair sprouted in ebony spirals from his skull, like a mass of writhing snakes agitated by the ocean wind. Tamago was a big dude, but not as big as Brady. Brady stared back at his Leader and had a niggling familiar feeling: here was one actor upstaging another. Like the annoying grit stuck to Brady's ass hairs, he attempted to sweep all suspicious thoughts away. Tamago is the real deal, he'd said to himself as he reached for his kinder, gentler, more compassionate self.

Angus finished pooping, and Brady had had enough of the thick, humid East Coast summer air. They went inside, where Angus settled by his feet as Brady picked up his dulcimer, closed his eyes, and started to strum, hoping that here, in this cavernous, shitty, gigantic house, he'd find the beauteousness within.

Chapter Two

Nell: Bones

Rather than replace Jumbo with another pet, Nell's parents got her a piano. At first, in an act of defiance Nell pounded the keys incoherently, without any discernible interest or talent. But soon, she couldn't help herself. The mathematical beauty and universal truth of music not only soothed her brain but also her soul. It captured her. She couldn't stop. She mastered all the Masters: Chopin, Beethoven, Bartok, Scriabin, Liszt.

Her parents wanted her to perform. It would've been the perfect feather in their artsy-intellectual cap. But Nell threw up all over the keys at her one and only attempt: a small, solo recital at the Village Arts Center when she was fourteen. After that, Nell refused to take the stage again. She shook like a wet, cold dog at just the sugges- tion. But she did record. At age sixteen her rendition of

Clara Schumann's Piano Concerto Op. 7 made it to the top 20 on the Billboard Classical listings. That was feather enough.

Given her obvious talents, Nell's parents deemed Towne's top-rated high school subpar. Nell commuted instead to a private high school for gifted and talented proto-geniuses in the City, where her teachers interpreted Nell's quirkiness as a fresh and novel form of brilliance. Nell spent most of her high school days curled like a pill bug in the furthest seat in the darkest corner of every classroom. At the last minute, usually after know-it-all Mark Kaminsky or fledgling Marxist Chloe Malloy shouted out juvenile insights, Nell would unfurl and raise her hand.

"Yes Nell? What are your thoughts?" a teacher might ask tentatively, as Nell was sure to offer a doozy. In a voice one decibel above barely audible, Nell shared bitingly candid and surreal perspectives, ideas no one else could've mustered, answers hard for even the most well-educated educators to argue with. They all wrote recommendations that obscured her oddness. And Nell did, indeed, look good on paper. Not only were her scores perfect and her grades impeccable, she was also a piano prodigy.

Nell was offered acceptance to every university she applied to. When it came time to choose, Nell, in a fledgling act of minor rebellion, chose a lesser Ivy, one known for its casual approach to grades and requirements. She got along well enough, kept a low profile. Nell spent much of her time alone, daydreaming. She showed up for classes, did a modicum of interesting work. She even managed to have almost-sex with a few gender-questioning and non-threatening young men and women. True love, however, remained a construct.

After graduating, she had dreams of a career in a vaguely literary or possibly cinematic field, but no such career ever crystallized. Instead Nell worked as a barista. She made terrible, milky cappuccinos. She spilled chai on aspiring writers' manuscripts. She was fired. Next she tried her hand at babysitting, but as an only child, and therefore the de facto baby in her own family, Nell found young children tiresome and boring. They found her the same. She had taught piano lessons briefly in high school but stopped after an unfortunate encounter with a pervy dad. Now a college graduate with a bit more savvy, Nell decided to take a stab at teaching again. This proved impossible. She had such a low tolerance for bad playing, she couldn't stand to be around amateurs, or worse: sullen, ungrateful kids.

Further options were limited, possible job leads through friends of her parents fizzled out. Nell filed papers for her cranky father and kneaded clay for her artistic, annoyingly upbeat mom. Her parents fed her. Provided shelter. They loved her and had been proud of her, once upon a time. Now they no longer mentioned her at cocktail parties.

After two years of tense cohabitation, Nell's father was offered a year-long fellowship in Spain. Off to Granada went Professor and Mrs. Delano, leaving Nell alone in the big house on the outskirts of Towne. Nell would have to fend for herself with a three-page list of home maintenance instructions and a generous sum to tide her over until her parents returned.

Without her parents around to push and prod her, Nell stayed indoors for long stretches of the stultifying summer days. After a few hours with her old friend the piano, she might take a dip in the leaf-strewn, scummy swimming pool. On occasion, she took out her old Sting Ray bicycle and rode the three miles to toodle around the gridded streets in the center of Towne. She wore her red raincoat, rain or shine, never knowing what the weather might bring her. She was also grateful for the raincoat's deep pockets, because she found herself sneaking into backyards when she could tell no one was home, climbing trees to steal apples, lifting vegetable garden fences to swipe tomatoes, zucchinis and green beans. It was the closest Nell had come to feeling excitement. But thievery was a limited high. If she was particularly restless, she'd stash her bicycle and go for a walk in Allenwood Park.

It was there, in the park, she found the bones. They lay in a fern glen, deep in the wooded area. The bones were bleached and lovely against the vulnerable green. Nell imagined the bones buried under suffocating December snow, pummeled with April rain, disturbed by August wind. Buried and hidden for months because of someone else's malice or neglect. Clearly, Nell wasn't the only one with problems.

Now the bones made a pretty pattern as around them life forced itself up through packed dirt, and the sun dappled everything with promise. Fronds uncurled and tickled the mandible. A crow pecked at a tiny bit of flesh remaining at the hip socket. Worms crawled through the jaw.

The bones looked peaceful. Their pattern so pleasing, indicating rest. The hind leg bones in slight stride, the front curled as if begging. The skull extruded and long. The canine teeth pronounced, declaring species alliance.

Around the non-existent neck a rusted collar and a tag with an illegible name. Something vague but significant percolated in Nell's soul as she knelt by the anonymous, long-dead dog. The unripe apple in her pocket seemed to throb. She left the Park and rode her bike up and down the streets of Towne until after sunset, hoping for clarity, feeling a directive might be just around the next corner.

Abe: *The Gist*

Abe's wife Claire was the earner, schlepping back and forth to the City every day via train, working at a venture capital firm while Abe stayed home with Milo—Mouse, as Abe liked to call him. It was what Abe's dad Mort had called Abe, back in the day, during rare moments of spontaneous affection.

Part of the plan was idealistic and naive: Abe would write while Mouse slept, somehow squeeze out literary gems that the fleeting moments of lucidity afforded the sleep-deprived father of a newborn, who two years later had become a solid and ambulatory little bruiser, waking daily at a painfully early predawn hour to demand that every impulsive need be met.

Abe barely wrote. In fact, Abe never wrote. Fuzzy toddler parent-brain and ambivalence were excellent collaborators. While Mouse napped, Abe would watch YouTube clips and live streams of extreme sports, wondering what it must feel like to take such risks of life and limb. To be an uber-jock, a visceral, blood-and-guts type dude who took no precautions. Abe had attempted other forms of procrastination first. He'd tried watching porn, but it gave Abe the creeps to wack off into a tissue, knowing that within minutes he'd be changing his son's diaper and wiping Milo's penis with another tissue. Not that Abe was turned on in any way by his son's blatant, splayed sexuality. But there was something overwhelming about so much attention to so many penises in so short a time. Watching sports was safer. Less perverted. Totally escapist and a way to fuel Abe's sloth. To feed his chronic low self-esteem without inklings of nasty, objectifying sex—or worse, pedophilia.

Abe was a good dad. He was a great dad. It's just that there wasn't any writing. No good, great, or even bad writing, which was fine in the beginning, when he and Claire were adjusting to new life in a new town with new baby. But it had become a problem, because now, two years later, he wasn't doing anything else either. The house was a pigsty. When he shopped for groceries, if he did shop, he bought all the wrong things. And then there was the laundry. The dirty, piled up, never done laundry.

Claire was annoyed. Maybe a bit suspicious.

"Should we get some help?" she asked one Saturday morning in late August. "So you can have even more time to work on *The Gist*?"

Ah, *The Gist*. The working title of Abe's supposed novel. The gist of *The Gist* was that all that existed of it was a title page. Nothing more.

"Nah," said Abe. He took off his glasses and wiped the lenses with his tee shirt. It was easier for him to lie when his vision was impaired. If he couldn't see it made him feel that he himself was unreadable, blurred. Life became one abstract pool of avoidance. "It's going great guns."

Great guns. What a joke. The few times Abe actually sat down and tried to write this supposed novel, he'd waste time Googling all sorts of inane stuff, kidding himself he was doing research.

Who was Mister Ed's trainer?

How many steps to the top of the Temple of Kukulcan?

What is the average life expectancy of a puma in captivity?

Who was the female lead in *Top Gun*?

How long can a person hold their breath underwater and hum at the same time?

When he'd exhausted all avenues of search engine procrastination, Abe would twist and writhe like a hyper-active third grader forced to sit in his chair. If Abe was honest, he would've told Claire he'd been whacked in the gut, the head, and the back of the knees with the sledgehammer of self-doubt.

There was no novel, but there was a deep, ongoing affair with their fifty-inch flat screen TV. Such an obscene and wonderful thing. A housewarming present from his mother. Could Abe blame his mother for his sloth and addiction? It wouldn't be the first time Barbara had been scapegoated by a buck-passing Kaufman. Mort had made a career out of financial duplicity; he fixed books, took bribes, "miscalculated" up the wazoo. Barbara was no dummy. She kvetched and moaned about Mort's shady doings, but like most women of her generation, she'd never had any power to change things. But now, at least, she had money to spend on a housewarming gift for her writer-son and financier daughter-in-law.

Bliss for Abe was Milo's two hour, late morning nap. Once his son was down for the count, Abe could grab a Snickers or two from his secret candy stash and watch uninterrupted sports porn on the massive screen, his feet up on the coffee table, his under-exercised ass spreading on the couch. If Abe and Claire got household help Abe would have to hide his sports addiction, secretly watch on his puny 13-inch Mac in the spare room referred to as his "office." Clearly this idea of household help had to be kept at bay.

"Really, Claire. I'm fine," Abe lied.

"Alright. For now. But when do I get a peek at *The Gist*?" Claire had always been Abe's first reader. In the past he'd shown her unedited, sloppy stuff, filled with plot holes and half-baked characters. Her feedback was always brutally frank.

"I want to show it to you when it's in a more evolved state this time around. Serve it to you clean and within bounds, okay?" Abe didn't usually use sports lingo to talk about his writing, but the Wimbledon Men's Finals had been live streaming earlier that day. With Gordon happily wedged and dozing between his legs, Abe had watched rackets wacking and balls whizzing for hours.

Abe worried that eventually Claire would figure it all out. That there was no novel. Not even a flimsy plot outline or character study. But for the moment he lied and as soon as she was out of the house he laid in front of the wide screen. Abe knew he needed help. But fuck if he wanted it.

Paddy: Afterwards

With no kids or grandkids of their own, there was no one Paddy felt compelled to tell about Mariah's corroding brain. It was easy keeping her slip-ups from snooping friends and neighbors because most happened at home. Paddy would find her sitting on the kitchen floor, legs splayed like a rag doll's, their toy poodle Barney running circles around her, intermittently whining and licking Mariah's hands, the skin above her anklet socks.

It snowballed fast. Soon, Mariah had no idea how she got here, there, anywhere. She'd forget not just the name but also the purpose of the key, book, or lipstick in her hand. Her eyes, so vacant at times Paddy wanted to collapse like a deflated balloon. Often out of nowhere she'd start laughing, a brittle rat-a-tat-tat that sounded non-human. She cried even more often, so Paddy grew to appreciate that creepy giggle.

One day, the week before they left for Idaho, before she floated downstream and out of Paddy's life forever, Mariah screamed the bloodiest of bloody murder from the kitchen. Barney was with her, barking clipped yip yips usually reserved for the doorbell. Paddy ran so fast to them he thought he might give himself a coronary, almost tripped over the damn dog, so tiny and brown he blended in with the dark tiles of the kitchen floor. Mariah stood by the sink staring out the window at the apple tree. That time of year it was loaded with almost ripe fruit, full of promise.

"I saw her," Mariah said, pointing into the branches. "She's back."

"Who are you talking about?" Paddy scoured the tree and the empty backyard. Barney stood between his legs scratching at the screen door. Normally Paddy would let the little bugger out, but he worried if he did, Mariah might have some other bizarre reaction. Instead Paddy picked Barney up and held him like a baby, rubbing his tummy, which the dog adored.

"Josie. She was climbing the tree," Mariah pouted like a child. "She's wearing her red rain slicker and it's not even raining. Mommy's going to give her a spanking when she finds out. Climbing trees is very, very dangerous."

Josie was Mariah's kid sister, a hippie-dippie seventy-year-old who lived in Vermont. Josie had always been jealous of Mariah, probably because Josie was a stringy sourpuss and Paddy's wife had been the epitome of beauty and kindness. Josie was no longer a kid, and she wasn't climbing any trees. She hadn't visited Mariah for years.

Paddy put Barney down on the floor, and took Mariah's hand, gently leading his wife to the living room. "Come on, Honey," he cooed. He was not by nature a cooer. "Let's go have a listen."

They'd gone to all the big shows in the City back in the day: Fiddler, Man of La Mancha, Hair, Cabaret. Paddy had bought every recording of every show. Now, when Mariah got agitated, he'd put a record on, and they would sit on the couch, a couple of nitwits holding hands, humming along for hours.

Dementia was no rosy path to intimacy. But for the six months before Mariah tossed herself off the edge of that raft, Paddy had never been more in love. All the stupid distractions of life fell away: Paddy's own bull-headed opinions, the world going to hell in a hand basket, rude customers at the station, Paddy's aches and pains, his hemorrhoids, insomnia, acid reflux, and unpredictable dick, his massive failures, and meager accomplishments. Poof—all of it. All that mattered was sitting with Mariah on the couch, breathing in her familiar sweet and yeasty smell, clutching her paper-thin, cool hand in his own.

The night before they left for the rafting excursion, Mariah was doing good. She was making sense and acting like her old self. As they lay in bed about to turn out the light, she turned to Paddy and cupped his fleshy jowls in her soft, trembling hands. "Paddy," she said, "This is going to be a barrel of laughs. We're gonna have fun. Just you wait."

Yeah, we'll see about that, thought Paddy. But he went along with her and kept up the charade. He croaked, "Life is a cabaret, old chum," thinking, this is far from a cabaret.

Mariah kissed his forehead and with what he now saw was a message of sweet foreboding she sang, "And when I go, I'm going like Elsie." Then she turned around as she had every night for the last forty-seven years; her rump wedged against his stomach, a pillow between her arthritic knees. Already on her way.

A few weeks after the funeral, Paddy got a beautiful hand-painted watercolor condolence card from the Lesbians. Inside was a photo of Mariah all trussed up in her life preserver, smiling at the camera like she'd just won the lottery.

Bless those gals, thought Paddy. He taped the photo to the cash register at the Gas n' Go. Mariah faced out towards the customers, not towards Paddy, who sat behind the counter, hiding his pain. Paddy liked knowing Mariah was there. It was just that her loveliness was still too much for him to take face to face, all day long.

David: Pros and Cons

David's *bar mitzvah* wasn't exactly the best day of his life. He could've blamed Chucky Weintraub, if he wanted to, but David's loyalty to Chucky was feral and intense. There would be no blaming Chucky for anything, ever.

Just before the *Hora*, Chucky sidled up to David and whispered in his ear, "Laura DeSousa is so fucking hot I want to do her," and gave David a hard-on. Not because Chucky was talking dirty about Laura—David could give two shits about Laura; he hadn't even wanted to invite the dumb cow to his *bar mitzvah*. But Laura's mother Denise was best friends with David's mother, Lucinda, so he didn't have a choice. The reason David got hard was because Chucky talked dirty to him, with hot breath in David's ear, all gravel-whisper and sex. David imagined kissing Chucky, pressing his boner against Chucky's thigh, rubbing it around a little. But instead David shoved Chucky away causing Chucky to stumble into the chocolate bar.

Pro: The chocolate bar stayed upright, more or less. Only a few dribbles of semi-sweet sauce had to be wiped from the floor.

Con: Since the *bar mitzvah*, Chucky had stopped talking to David, even during Summer Art Camp, which used to be their time to goof around. He called David a loser. Which was truer than Chucky even knew.

Pro: David aced his *Haftarah*. Everyone thought his speech was kick-ass. His Aunt Beth said especially now, "in this era of social intolerance," it warmed her heart that a kid like David "could speak so eloquently to the issue of acceptance."

Con: David wondered if Aunt Beth would feel that way if she knew he stole her lipstick while she was dancing to "Uptown Funk." How could he resist? Everybody was on the floor except David and Great Uncle Harold, and Harold was legally blind, so the old guy was a great cover for David while he finagled his way inside Beth's Judith Leiber clutch.

Pro: David didn't steal the whole Leiber clutch, which was what he really wanted to do.

Con: He did take twenty bucks along with a tube of Sephora Matte Rose.

Pro: Everyone was still *kvelling* about David's brilliance, a whole week later.

Extra Pro: Even David's father Dan was weirdly proud, and before the event he could give fuck all about the *bar mitzvah*. He told David he was "wicked impressed," when they were sitting on the gross leather couch in his dad's depressing new house, a house his father now shared with Rachel, who was younger than David's mother but not hot at all. Rachel reminded David of a startled poodle, pou-fy haired with beady, bugged-out eyes. They had all been eating take-out Thai and watching America's Got Talent when his dad turned to David and said, "You know, Dee. That speech you gave was da bomb." Even though David cringed when his father called him Dee—and besides, "da bomb" had not been cool for years—David's heart soft-ened slightly, and his dad scored a few parenting points.

But in the end, David's life was still mostly always Con with a capital 'C': David stole things. He lied. His brain was jam-packed with the most perverted, gross-me-out thoughts at the most what-the-fuck-why-now? moments. No one knew what he really was, least of all him. Being a *bar mitzvah* didn't seem to have changed anything, any-thing at all.

Lucinda: Welcome to the neighborhood

The *bar mitzvah* was a huge success. David was amazing. What a little man he'd become. He stood at the ark like a real *mensch*, reciting his *Haftarah* and afterwards, delivered a wonderful speech about acceptance. So clear and eloquent. Lucinda couldn't have been prouder. She thought he was even better than J.K. Rowling giving that 2008 Harvard commencement speech everyone still raved about.

Even her mother was complimentary. Celeste sat at the edge of her seat at the reception, ankles demurely crossed, holding court, as if David were her own son. Lucinda kept her cool, let her mother engage in *bar mitzvah* banter, charming the guests with her Southern drawl. In reality Celeste barely ever came up north to visit, though Lucinda dutifully brought David to Atlanta yearly during *Chanukah*, so Celeste could bring him to their temple to play *dreidel* games and pretend to her friends that she was a real *bubbe*.

Even sitting with Dan and Rachel hadn't been so terrible for Lucinda. It helped that Rachel looked miserable, scowling at Dan the whole time as he shoveled pile after pile of food in his mouth. Lucinda couldn't help herself. While Dan was on the dance floor with his sourpuss, put upon, never liked Lucinda, older sister Beth, Lucinda leaned across the powder blue damask table cloth, snaking her hand past wine goblets and *challah* crumbs to gently clasp Rachel's wrist.

"All good, Rachel?" Lucinda said with buckets of fake cheer.

Rachel looked up from her silk and glitter lap. She stared at Lucinda with mascara dripping off the lower lids of buggy, watery eyes. Finally she blurted "Sure."

Lucinda removed her hand from Rachel's wrist and raised her recently replenished glass of Pinot. "*L'chaim!*" she chirped while thinking, Dan's your problem now, Rachel. Please make sure to take that formerly trim, currently fat fuck and his potential coronary with you when you leave.

With the *bar mitzvah* over and done with, Lucinda

could focus on getting her life back in order. Set her priorities straight. It was high time for some Lucinda time. First on the agenda: going across the street and introducing herself to Brady Cole. She hadn't seen many signs of life over there in the past two weeks. When word had first got out about Brady Cole moving into the Kearny Mansion, just about every female between the ages of eight and eighty had stopped by to gawk at the closed door and curtained windows. They'd stand on the sidewalk across from Lucinda's house in giggly pods, urging each other to go up to the mansion door and knock. They left cakes, bouquets of flowers, stuffed animals, and not surprisingly, the occasional thong. They yelled, "Brady! We love you!" or "Take me in!" But Brady Cole never showed his gorgeous, chiseled face. The most his fans could do was turn to take selfies with the mansion door as their backdrop. Eventually the women got bored and the crowds dwindled. Now there was just one woman who stopped by every day, driving up in her convertible, hanging over the door to cry, "Come out you beautiful specimen, you!" This was Gloria, an older woman who ran the local thrift shop, a peppy seventy-something with a bleach blonde beehive and the libido, it seemed, of a teenager. Gloria left the most undergarments on Brady's doorstep. Lucinda had watched her waddle up the walkway and leave lingerie almost daily; leopard print bras, candy striped panties–you name it, Gloria wore it.

Lucinda hadn't seen the woman in the ugly white dress and beret again. She supposed the woman came that first day with the dog to set Brady's house up, so maybe she was a personal assistant. The dog, however, was definitely still there. Lucinda heard the poor thing barking itself raw day and night.

Lucinda would not talk about the barking when she paid her visit to Brady Cole. She would not be the critical, kill-joy neighbor. She'd be the kind, can-I-be-of-assistance neighbor. The welcome-to-the-neighborhood buddy. Lucinda would only mention her interior design background if it seemed appropriate. This was going to be a friendly visit. Lucinda would bring a loaf of her homemade zucchini bread, which might lead to an opportunity to mention her vegetable garden, which might lead to her inviting Brady to come over any time he wanted to pick his own home-grown veggies. Though god knew what kind of crop she'd have this year. Already a rabbit or squirrel had gotten past the chicken wire and nabbed most of the unripe tomatoes and made a mess of the green beans. It was a miracle she had enough zucchinis left to make the bread.

Should Lucinda wear something elegant and understated, that clearly showed she was a woman with taste, or go casual and show up in dusty gardening clothes? Give off an air of "just in case you were looking for some decorating advice" or "I'm so down to earth I wear it?"

Definitely the gardening gear. The last thing Lucinda wanted to do was come off as a desperate design poseur. She was better than that. Really, she was.

Brady: It Comes to This

Brady first learned about Tamago from his sort-of friend Cal, a guy who had played the supporting role of Travis, the alcoholic snitch, on *Signet*. One day, seemingly out of the blue for Brady, but not for those who were paying attention, Cal landed the lead as a closeted gay father in a edgy cable sitcom that became an off the charts critical and commercial success.

They were at Brady's Topanga hideaway, sitting pool-side with Brady's dog Angus. "Tamago changed my fucking life," Cal claimed over drinks. This was right after Cal had been nominated for a Golden Globe. *Signet* was headed for the trash. A few weeks earlier Brady's third wife, the model Webeke Handke, had left him and Angus to move back to Copenhagen, a city where she claimed "all men appreciate a powerful woman with strong, big bones."

Brady nursed his third bourbon while Cal sipped iced chai through a straw. Angus was happy, as usual, to lay his big muzzle across Brady's hairy toes.

According to Cal, this dude Tamago had originally been a hedge fund manager named Ted Moskowitz who'd escaped indictment in '08.

"Tamago is totally honest about how dishonest he used to be," Cal explained. "He high-tailed it to Indo, where he planned to hide out until he could return to Wall Street. He was gonna hang out, smoke weed, get laid by smooth skinned native chicks, maybe learn how to surf."

"Sounds good to me," Brady said. He wiggled his toes under Angus' jowls the way the dog liked. Angus had been especially needy since Webeke's desertion. Now instead of sleeping at the foot of the bed, Angus burrowed deep under the duvet and laid diagonally across Brady's torso with his grody dog butt close to Brady's face. Brady didn't have the heart or energy to move Angus. Plus, most nights he was too hammered to care.

"Yeah, but that's not what went down," said Cal. "Instead Tamago met a shaman who imparted the wisdom of the Beauteous Man, the teachings Tamago now shares with us all."

Beauteous Man, thought Brady. It sounded like the name for a new cologne. Or a dildo.

"The basic rules are: no sleeping around, no watching or playing any sport that involves a ball, no red meat, no cursing at anyone but yourself. And above all, live a life of beauteous compassion."

Brady had no one to sleep around with at the moment,

so that was an easy sacrifice. It was baseball season, and Brady was a football guy, so not watching sports would be easy for the moment. But for the occasional game of tennis ball fetch with Angus, he hadn't actually played any ball sports for years. Red meat would be hard to give up, but as long as he still had Yolanda to cook his meals, amp up the chicken and fish with her Mexicali spice blends, Brady could live without his burgers and steaks. Compassion? He could muster some of that up, probably. Not cursing, however, would be fucking hard.

"How long does this all last?" Brady asked.

Cal shook his head. "Dude, it is for, like, forever."

Forever, thought Brady. Permanence was not a concept he had much experience with.

"Saved my marriage and my job," Cal sucked the last bit of chai. "My offers are off the charts, Bro."

Signet was kaput. Brady had no offers of his own. Webeke had filed papers, soon he would no longer have a wife. All he had was Angus, the Topanga place—which he'd probably lose in the divorce—and a dwindling liquor supply.

"How much is this going to set me back?" Brady asked. This Tamago was a former Finance guy after all.

Cal quoted a sum that might have once seemed absurd to Brady, but after years of cushy living it was a mere pittance.

"Okay. I'm in. Sign me up, dude," Brady poured the icy dregs of his bourbon on to the pool deck. Angus took a few licks and then settled back atop Brady's foot.

"Welcome, Beauty Bro," said Cal as he leaned in to give Brady a full-on bear hug. Brady would soon learn there were none of the usual non-committal dude-to-dude displays of affection among the Beauteous. No one-armed, tap-tap on the back type hugs, domination handshakes, or the ubiquitous fist bump. It was full frontal hugging only, as if every Beauteous man was someone's Italian mama. Cal continued. "First you'll have to attend an initiation retreat. There's one starting next week up in Montecito. After that weekly meetings and drum circles are mandatory, but Tamago knows at times some of us have busy schedules, so we're allowed to Skype in on occasion. T's a decent guy."

Brady thought he could use some decency.

"Oh, and Brady, you're gonna love this: Once you've been through initiation you get to wear a really cool outfit. A white caftan with a really excellent little cap. Wait till you see it. It's outrageous."

And now, here he was in this tent of a dress, in this rattrap of a house in this pathetic little town. No furniture, no cook, no video games installed on the TV, no fun. The only thing he had to keep himself buoyed at first was to peek out the upstairs window and spy on all those women outside, his adoring fans, each one of them wanting him, or at least, the former him. The high perch provided him with some great views. Lots of cleavage, and lord knew he'd always been a boob man. An everything man, really. Eventually most of the ladies left. How could he blame them? He couldn't even so much as open the front door and pose for some harmless selfies with the teenage hotties, lest he be instantly banned from Tamago's program and on Lois' permanent shit list.

It was late in the evening, the blazing summer sun finally setting behind the house across the street. The only fan who kept coming by was that old lady with the terrible hair, and she didn't even get out of her car anymore. Just sat there with her engine running, took a quick peek at the mansion before driving off. He missed the cheap lingerie she'd left on his doorstep only days ago. Days that felt like months that he expected would eventually feel like years. What he wouldn't give for a bit of polka-dot polyester to pass the time.

Chapter Three

Nell: Catch a Whiff

In the dead of night Nell would ride through Towne without fear of discovery. The grid of empty streets became a predictable maze; North-Souths named after trees: Elm, Hickory, Beechwood. East-Wests more arbitrarily a mishmash of surnames and flowers: Collings, Lilac, Sherwood. She'd wobble her way in an obsessively north-east-south-west-north-east-south-west constricting pattern, eventually ending up in the middle of things, the intersection of Kearny and Pine, where the famous Kearny Mansion stood with its green pelt of a lawn and perfectly blooming bushes.

Now Nell felt like a huntress, though she wasn't quite sure yet, what she was hunting for. Her approach relied on instinct.

This led to zig-zagging. This led to trespassing, which led to thievery, to tiptoeing barefoot and soundless. This led to more and more ravaging of backyard vegetable gardens and fruit trees, to shoving discarded household items in the deep pockets of her raincoat, piling all her finds in two large shopping bags she would hang from each extruded Sting Ray handlebar.

Nell's chain was a wee bit rusty, but no one ever woke. No one ever opened their front door, or heard her rummaging through their zucchinis. No one ever yelled at her as she shimmied up their apple tree. No one ever startled as Nell pressed her moony eyes up to windows with mossy breath fogging the glass, curious to catch a whiff of normal.

Abe: Losing

Abe was shackled, pulled in two directions.

Gordon's leash twisted around his right wrist in a double loop, his hand wrenched and rubbed raw as the beast bounded forward. In Abe's left hand was Milo's sugar-sticky hand, flaccid, like a boneless bit of meat. It was a quiet, late summer afternoon, spiked occasionally by bird song and the slick rumble of car tires on smoothly tarred streets. Abe and Gordon had done this walk many times at a nice clip, the dog setting the pace, always more enthusiastic to get anywhere than the man. Abe had also gone this route with Milo, but those times Abe had been the only ambulatory one, Milo attached to Abe's chest in a harnessed holder, facing outwards, bleating in excitement at the slightest shift of sunlight on any surface while his moccasin-ed feet pounded Abe's gut.

But never had dog, man, and boy traveled this path all together. This was a test.

Early life with baby and dog had been a smelly, lovely fever dream. Gordon had been great with Milo when the boy had been a newborn noodle, when all Milo did was burp, cry, poop, or sleep. Gordon licked the baby's feet and cuddled next to him during family naps. But once Milo began crawling, the dog seemed confused. He curled up in the corner of the kitchen with his snout buried deep under stumpy front paws, one eye on alert while Milo thump-thumped around the house trying to open safety-locked kitchen cabinets and bopping his head against the baby-proofed, padded corners of the coffee table.

Then Milo started walking. Gordon growled at the toddler whenever the boy careened towards him, Milo shrieking, loving Gordon just because Gordon existed, Gordon's dog-ness an irresistible magnet. Milo's hand-eye coordination was abysmal. He'd lunge at Gordon, grab for inappropriate dog-body parts. The dog would push Milo over with gentle nudges or air nipped warnings when Milo reached to pet him. But when it was Gordon's eye socket that fascinated the child, or his stubby pull-able tail, the nudges got less gentle. Air nips were accompanied by guttural warnings. It was hard to blame the dog. Harder still to protect the child. Abe knew if things didn't change, Gordon would have to go.

Could Abe blame his son? Of course he could. The child was a havoc-wreaking menace with relentless enthusiasm and a monumental lack of boundaries. A pint-sized frenzy of distractions. He made it impossible for Abe to write, impossible for Abe to focus on anything, really. It was so easy to blame Milo: his cuteness, his neediness, his sleep-sapping schedule.

But the dog? Gordon never distracted. He only encouraged and supported. Gordon, so different now from the emaciated puppy Abe rescued seven years earlier in his premarital City dwelling days from the marginally functional white Rasta squatting in the apartment below Abe's own. Gordon was Abe's longest-term relationship, maybe his most functional. The dog preceded Claire by a year. Gordon, the scrappy and inspirational puppy-urchin had been there when Abe got his first, so-far-only story published in a journal that was considered a literary gateway to bigger and better things. They'd toasted together, Abe with a Maker's Mark and Gordon with a bowl of chilled Poland Spring.

What a conundrum. What a mishmash of love, loyalty, protection, and resentment. The last thing Abe wanted to do was get rid of Gordon, so now this walk. An attempt at triangular bonding. The Father, The Son, The Holy Pit Bull. To prove things could get better. Abe hoped Gordon's aggression would lose steam in the great outdoors, that the dog would be overwhelmed by the birds and smells, by his canine appreciation of fresh air. Milo would become a mere blip on Gordon's screen, what with all the distractions Towne's natural wonders had to offer.

As usual, the evenly paved sidewalks were deserted. Abe rarely saw anyone else when he walked around Towne. Occasionally a pony-tailed, spandexed woman would hurry past pushing a gigantic stroller on BMX wheels. On lucky days, she'd give him a smirky smile, maybe a breathy "hi." Abe might sneak a look as she loped away, take in the rear view, appreciate the form. Now that's an attractive alien, he'd often think.

But there were no attractive aliens that morning. Meanwhile, Abe needed a break after a half hour of stops and starts, Gordon sniffing every curb and bush, and Milo touching every dirty piece of leaf or litter. Abe was ravenous, parched. Before leaving home he'd fed the toddler and the dog, but had forgotten to feed himself. Now Abe craved a sweet, a real confection. Abe wanted bad chocolate with bad nuts and oodles of corn syrup, not an agave sweetened cardboard strip or serving of fresh fruit. Not anything he might find in his own home pantry.

There was a gas station and convenience store a mere half block ahead. He would dash in and grab a treat.

The trio bounded, wobbled, and leaned their way onward in the direction of sugar. It seemed the father might get something for himself after all, but in the store window, "NO DOGS ALLOWED" warned in large, determined, handwritten lettering.

Abe spun in a loop of self-pity. His life was fenced in by a baby and his sleep habits and bodily functions, by a wife who looked at Abe as if he were her pathetic younger brother, a guy she might love, might have once, but for right now she merely tolerated. And now, no treats. Abe was a man who couldn't even walk to a crappy gas station store and buy a candy bar without constraints.

Milo was utzy, bleeping like a rodent, indicating fatigue. If he had a meltdown, Abe would have to carry him home. Abe's flaccid, underused biceps and non-existent abs made it perilous to hoist Milo too far, especially while being yanked hither and yon by Gordon. And if the boy began to shriek his blood-curdling, over-the-edge cry, well, what would the neighbors think? To prevent that scene from playing out, Abe gave up his candied dreams and turned his motley crew back in the direction of home.

They traveled a block before Abe reconsidered. Who am I, he thought, to so easily give up on a goal? I exist. My needs matter. Screw the ponytailed joggers and hushed housewives. They can think whatever they want. The least I can do is get myself some chocolate. Abe untwisted Gordon's leash from his rope-burned wrist and looped it around a nearby street sign.

"You be good," Abe commanded. He looked down into Gordon's slitty eyes. The dog's tongue was hanging like a salmon filet out the side of his sharp-toothed mouth. Abe really had nothing to worry about. No one would mess with Gordon, who looked like an urban killer to suspicious suburbanites. Abe had already noted the nervous sideways glances given to Gordon in the local vet's waiting room. He'd heard them call for their cockapoodles and golden labs at the Allenwood Park dog run to "Come back!" when all the dogs—male and female—flocked to Gordon like he was a canine rock star, each one of those dogs wanting to hump Gordon's muscled butt. But the owners? Forget it. Gordon was profiled according to breed. Here in Towne folks preferred their dogs floppy-eared and sleek-coated. Pedigreed breeds, or designer mutts. Nah, no one would come near Gordon, and while searching for sweets, that suited Abe perfectly.

"I'll just be gone long enough to grab a Snickers, pal," Abe said as he scratched Gordon roughly, the way the dog liked, at the crown of his solid head. Or a Twix, thought Abe. Or maybe both. Abe scooped Milo up and ran the short distance to the gas station with his son wedged against his side like a battering ram.

"Wee...wee...wee! All the way home," Abe sang to distract Milo from his fatigue. We are headed to chocolate, thought Abe, my chocolate, a delight which, according to your mother, you're not allowed yet. For now I'm sworn to hide how divine it is from you. But no worries. When you get a bit older and wiser you'll figure it out yourself.

Milo started to fidget as soon as they entered the store, so Abe set him down on the grimy floor. Milo teetered like a drunk then plopped butt-first, his puffy diaper absorbing the shock.

There was an old guy perched on a stool behind the counter. He stared blankly across the store at a closed circuit TV set high above Sun Chips and Smart Food Popcorn. Abe glanced at the TV to see what the man was watching. The screen was dark, image-less. Out of order or just plain off.

Abe had bigger concerns than what was wrong with the man or the TV, or both. Abe needed to buy the chocolate, grab his temporarily abandoned dog and get his son back home before Milo became The Nap-less Demon. But unlike most places of its ilk, which kept treats by the cash register for predictable impulse buys, all Abe saw were protein bars and 5-hour Energy shots. True confection was nowhere to be seen.

Abe approached the cash register, which had a photograph of an older but attractive woman wearing a life preserver taped to the customer-facing side. The photo had been taken outdoors, near tall pine trees and some kind of water. The woman had long, curly white hair cascading over her shoulders. She grinned at the camera, open-hearted, guileless. She seemed lively and buoyant while the man seated on the other side of the cash register was as animated as a cinderblock.

"Excuse me, sir. Where do you keep your candy?" Abe asked.

The man hiked a thumb towards a shelf of car supplies. "Other side," he said.

Abe glanced down at Milo. His son was content on his built-in cushion. Milo's thumb plugged his mouth as he stared off to space in a rare state of self-soothing, providing a rare opportunity for Abe. He left Milo on the floor and went around the corner to explore the sweet options awaiting behind the motor oil and windshield wiper fluid.

What a disappointment awaited Abe. Only a meager collection of Mento's, Life Savers, and Skittles on the other side of the shelf. The slimmest of slim pickings. Way back in a dusty crevice Abe spotted a lone Nestle Crunch of questionable age. It would have to do.

Abe scrambled back to the cash register ready to pay and go, but stopped short, suddenly consumed with panic. While the old man hadn't moved, was still staring at the blank screen in the same beleaguered posture, Milo, his sweet boy, the reason for everything, was nowhere to be seen.

A torrent of unthinkables flooded Abe's brain: kidnapping, perversion, murder, dismemberment. Time—Milo-less time—was taffy. Abe's personal torture would never end. It felt like ages before he found his voice.

"Where's my son?" he gasped, trembling in a palsy, both hands on the counter, his face inches from that of the old man.

"What son?" The man looked at him, as blank as he'd been when staring at the imageless screen.

"My son, my baby boy. He was here, right on the floor a minute ago." There was no end to Abe's desperation.

The man shrugged. "I haven't seen any kid, sir."

Abe was still shaking, felt as if his heart would punch its way out of his chest. He looked left, he looked right. He screamed, "Mouse! Where are you?" There were no little bleeps in response. Abe raced outside, again screaming his son's name. All was sprawling emptiness. No cars, no people, no nothing. Panic heightened each of Abe's senses. The blue sky seemed unnaturally turquoise, the clouds mocking Abe in their perfect, cotton ball collectives. Every leaf on every tree was outlined in crystal clarity. Every tarred crack in the gas station's asphalt a shining river of black. The humid air pressed against his body like the steady squeeze of an invisible, slimy god. He smelled everything; exhaust fumes, sugar, lighter fluid, perfumed cleaning products, rancid cheese, singed meat, wet cement, mowed grass, hot tar, chlorinated water, roasted coffee, rotting vegetables, human piss, dog poop.

A girl rode by on a stingray bike, slicing the silence with the squeak of her banana seat springs and the rattle of her rusty chain. She was a giant of a kid, wearing a shiny red raincoat even though it was an assaultingly sunny day. The bike was way too small for this odd creature, looking like a giant predatory insect, her knees splayed out and her elbows wide as she pedaled. She slowed as she approached, coasting but not stopping, ignoring Abe, a man so clearly distressed and trying to grab her attention. The girl seemed more interested in what was inside the gas station store. She leaned over her handlebars with her neck craned, chin jutted forward, nose up, as if she were sniffing the air for goodies. And then she moved onward.

"Hey! You! Have you seen my son?" Abe screamed after her. "He's a little brown-haired kid. He's wearing a—" Abe hesitated, having to recall which of the food-stained tee shirts and puffy elasticized pants he'd dressed Milo in that morning— "blue and white striped tee shirt and red pants!"

She pedaled around the corner as if Abe was invisible, his cries not even a whisper.

Abe raced back inside and scoured the store, up one short aisle and down the next. Panic built to an intolerable level. Horror quicksand. Claire would never forgive him, he would never forgive himself. Life, as he'd know it, had ended.

Paddy: They Call the Wind

The faces people made were the worst, so Paddy stopped looking at people. The things people said were well-meaning but stupid, so Paddy stopped listening to people. Horrific reports of world events, or fabricated disasters, were easier to stomach, so Paddy kept TV news shows or bad cop-good cop shows on all day and night. Frozen refugees, tyrants, tenuous economies. Bank heists, serial killers, crimes of passion. The flat screen at home was set at a constant mumble while the old portable at the station conked out on occasion, temporarily a blank black screen. There could be ten-minute stretches at the Gas n' Go when all Paddy had to distract himself with was the possibility of one of Towne's old timers wanting full service at the pump. Otherwise Paddy sat at his perch, stared at the TV, and waited for the thing to light up.

Before Mariah's brain went on the fritz, she wasn't much of a TV fan. She called it the Idiot Box, preferred the radio for news and live theater for visual entertainment.

After the dementia set in, Mariah could sit in front of the TV for hours. Game shows, reality disasters, sit-com reruns, right wing news, left wing news, cartoons, music videos, home improvement shows, motorcycle repair shows; you name it, she'd watch it, mesmerized while misunderstanding most everything. Paddy worried TV made her dementia worse, all those fast talkers and ricocheting images bombarding his wife's feeble mind. As it was, some of the stuff, commercials especially, made his own head spin. But the doctors said if Mariah seemed content, TV was probably fine. Therapeutic, perhaps.

Probably. Perhaps. Fucking cop-out words, Paddy thought. All those experts with their vague diagnoses, offering false hopes right up to the very end. Until Mariah tipped herself over the side of that raft and floated away from him like a feather on a breeze. Mariah; his golden beauty, his always queen, out of his reach forever.

The house was a landmine of triggers, so Paddy spent more and more time at the station, where memories of Mariah were easily dulled. At first he tried to bring Barney with him, but the dog hated leaving the house. Barney would snarl whenever Paddy picked him up. He'd wriggle from Paddy's grasp, run to the back door, and bark incessantly. When Paddy let him out, the tiny poodle would run to the apple tree and continue barking up towards the branches as if it was chock-a-block full of squirrels. But there were no squirrels. There were barely any apples either. They'd all disappeared.

Paddy assumed the squirrels had gobbled the fruit whole from the branches. But the lack of apples or squirrels didn't stop Barney from non-stop yapping. Paddy was waiting for the neighbors to call and complain. Once the clock ran out on his recent widower status the phone would ring off the hook and the grievances would start pouring in. Some mornings Paddy could lure Barney back inside with a tasty bacon-flavored treat. Then Barney would settle in his favorite spot next to Mariah's needlepointed ottoman, pressing his itty-bitty body against the familiar, Mariah-scented wool. His sides heaved, he panted, he whined. He grieved.

"She's not coming back," Paddy told the dog over and over again, but it did no good. Barney would stare at Paddy blankly, bark once, then curl in on himself and pretend to be asleep. Paddy left the dog home, food and water bowls filled, with the back door ajar. "Bark yourself silly, pal. And do me a favor; do your smelly business outside," Paddy warned. "Ass to the grass, or your ass is grass."

Paddy went through the paces at the Gas n' Go. He filled some tanks, changed some oil, and replaced an old battery now and again, but mostly Paddy sold newspapers and sundries. Towne had become filled with sleep-deprived professionals on the move so Paddy moved the candy to the back of the store, and the Kind and Power bars up in front of the cash register, along with little vials of 5-hour Energy. Once Paddy tried the magic drink himself, hoping for a boost. But whatever was in that stuff did zip for him. He remained in a chronic state of exhaustion, whether he slept three hours or thirteen. What had he expected? Everyone knew there was no elixir for a broken heart.

One humid, overcast summer afternoon, a few months after Mariah died, Paddy was pumping gas for Gloria Nevins, an unmarried busybody who lived around the corner from him. Gloria made it a habit of stopping by the station in her red VW bug convertible almost every day since Paddy returned from Idaho a widower. At first she tried to engage him in gossipy talk about some celebrity who'd recently moved into the old Kearny place.

"You know who Brady Cole is, Paddy. He made a big splash back in the nineties, in that gladiator movie, now, what was it called…" Gladys twisted a finger in her unnaturally blonde hair, "Oh yes! Hero of the Golden Sword."

"Dunno him," Paddy shrugged. All those famous Brads and Bradys and Bens blurred in his mind.

"And he was just in a TV show called *Signet* where he plays a very cute detective who wears a signet ring and catches all kinds of criminals."

Paddy thought he might've just seen that show on the Gas n' Go TV, but as usual, he hadn't really been paying close enough attention. Plus, he could care less.

"Sorry Gloria, no recuerdo." He wished she would shut up and leave him in peace. But instead Gloria began asking stupid questions about her car, about brakes, about clicking sounds, about strange fumes.

"I don't know, Paddy," Gloria said, leaning an over-tanned arm on the open driver side window, and gazing up at him with swoony eyes. "It makes this terrible screech every time I accelerate." Gloria's voice itself a terrible screech.

In order to avoid face-to-face contact, Paddy stared over Gladys' head. That was when he noticed a girl on a pink stingray bicycle riding slowly by. She looked vaguely familiar, but then again all kids in Towne looked familiar to Paddy. They came in waves, the younger siblings of ones who had left for college, each new set with glossy hair and urchin features, skinny legs and knobby knees. This girl was tall for her age, the bike too small for her gangly frame. Her arms bowed out to make room as she pedaled. Her skinny legs never lengthened, her knees circled and nearly touched her chest. Her hair was a matted mess the color of dried blood. She wore a shiny red raincoat, even though it was August, the sun glaring and hotter than hell.

"Maybe you can take a look under the hood for me?" Gloria persisted.

The girl and Paddy locked eyes. For a moment time suspended. The only sound a flappety-flap-flap from the sparkling streamers cascading off the handlebars of the girl's ridiculous bike. The only movement the girl's slow procession and slight nod as she rode out of Paddy's view.

Paddy finally looked down at Gloria. She'd pushed herself further out the window, her boobs and stomach hanging over the car door, ridiculous, like a cartoon clown in a circus car, trying to escape a fake fire. Nausea and resignation joined in the pit of Paddy's belly. He pulled the nozzle out of Gloria's tank, a few dribbles of gasoline on the hot asphalt on the way back to the pump, atypical of Paddy, who was a superior mechanic, a gas station owner and an expert gas pumper. But he was weary and wanted to be done with today's ordeal. "Pull her in to the garage, Gloria," he monotoned, "I'll see if there's anything to do."

Paddy's first mistake had been to let Gloria come into the repair bay while he checked under the hood of the VW. She wouldn't shut up.

"Paddy, you know those lovely blouses Mariah used to sew?"

"Yeah, what about them?"

"I was wondering what you planned on doing with them."

"I hadn't planned on doing squat with them."

"Paddy. Let me be blunt," Gloria's tone was as school-marm-y as Miss Grundy from an old Archie comic. "It's been long enough. I'm asking on behalf of the Animal Rescue Fund if you would consider donating Mariah's blouses to our thrift store. Someone very needy would be thrilled to own one of Mariah's gorgeous creations."

"I'll think about it." Would he? He wasn't sure. All he was sure of right now was that he wanted to get this tin can car and Gloria out of his garage as soon as possible.

"You do that Paddy. You do that. Just so you know, we do pickups every Tuesday and Thursday. You don't even have to come down to the store."

His second mistake was letting her stay there after he put the car up on the lift so he could take a better look at the wheel bearings and axle.

His third was paying too close attention to his work, both arms overhead as he dislodged the front right wheel nuts with an automatic nut-wrench in one hand as the other hand held the wheel steady.

His fourth was never imagining Gloria would sneak around him, unzip his fly, wedge her hand through his boxers, whip out his penis, get down on her knees and stick him in her mouth.

"Jesus Christ, Gloria!" Paddy hissed, "What the hell do you think you're doing?"

It was a dumb question. Gloria obviously knew quite well what she was doing. "Think of this as my special thank you," Gloria paused. "For your future donation." Then she got back to work.

Paddy was in a state of shock. He was also incapacitated. All the lug nuts had been removed. There was a chance if he let go the wheel would tumble off the axle, possibly clocking both of them. He could've tossed the nut wrench to the ground, and then pulled Gloria off him, but throwing an expensive tool to the cement floor felt even more wrong than what Gloria was doing to him. Plus, Paddy was so unnerved he might accidentally smash Gloria in the head. Though maybe that wasn't such a bad idea?

In the few seconds all this occurred to Paddy, his dick had already begun—against Paddy's best intentions—to respond to Gloria's ministrations. Paddy looked down at the top of her bottle-blonde hair as it bobbed back and forth under his paunch. Gloria was quite possibly the last person on earth he'd ever want to have suck him off. But his penis was blind.

What choice did Paddy have? He'd never cheated on Mariah, though he'd had more than one occasion to do so. And now here he was with Gloria Nevin's coral coated lips sucking and squeezing the daylights out of him. God help me, Mariah, he said as he closed his eyes and came in a quick, quivering spew and heard the gulp of Gloria's swallow.

He also heard the sound of his store door open, and the rusty squeak of bicycle wheels racing away.

David: Consignment

When he was younger, one of David's favorite activities had been running errands with his mom. When he was in elementary school and still so small he wasn't allowed to ride shotgun, he made do in the back, happy to space out and, as he called it, "do my thoughts" while they drove from supermarket to shoemaker to dry cleaner to drug store.

David's thoughts were elaborate fantasies filled with talking animals, princesses, super heroes, and an occasional cowboy. A recurring storyline from age six to eight involved a fairy named David trying to escape from a slithery black-clad villain who had the same sour face as the old guy who ran the Towne gas station. David the fairy was always rescued by a handsome cowboy who looked like real boy David's assistant soccer coach Adam Lerner.

David the fairy had beautiful silver wings and a long

silk dress that flowed way beyond their delicate little feet. Their hair was Rapunzel's tone and almost as long. Aside from the hair and the wings and the dress, everything about David the fairy looked like real David. Yet real David couldn't quite let himself be the fairy, even when he shut his eyes and imagined the cowboy lassoing the fairy, pulling them in close against his strong body. Even while real David leaned sideways to sniff the leather seats of his mother's car and imagined he was inhaling the musty smell of the cowboy's leather vest and chaps. Even when the car went over a series of speed bumps and David imagined the fairy's wings fluttering as the cowboy leaned in to kiss them.

David's mother Lucinda was forever buying clothes she quickly decided she no longer wanted after wearing just a few times. Most of her impulse buys were way too tight on her, something she'd realize only after she'd gotten home and tried them on again. But Lucinda never seemed to learn her lesson. In order to justify buying more, his mother donated the barely worn clothes to the local thrift store run by the Animal Rescue Fund, better known as ARF. His parents had adopted Balthazar through ARF, back when Balthazar was a puppy—though not the cuddliest of creatures—and David was also a fussy toddler.

Little David loved going to the ARF thrift store. While his mother hauled shopping bags filled with clothes to the thrift store counter and waited for Gloria Nevins, the chatty old lady who ran ARF, to sort through the stuff, David would pretend to look at used Tonka Trucks and Super Soaker Guns. Then, while the women were examining and rummaging through Lucinda's giveaways, he'd sneak off to the Girl's Section and lose himself among piles of tiny pink sweaters and striped leggings, rabbit-fur muffs, and rows of patent leather Mary Janes.

David stole his first pretty thing, a tee shirt patterned with large-headed unicorns and a pink collar bow, when he was seven years old. From then on he couldn't control himself. Sometimes months would go by without David feeling the urge. But often there were week-long periods when he would seek out pretty things like a trapper looking for wild game. By age ten, David expanded his search area beyond the used girls clothing at ARF, hunting through his mother's discards or in her hamper. He would carefully scan the unattended makeup display at the Towne variety store, pocketing curvaceous bottles of nail polish or tiny phalluses of lip gloss. On playdates he'd venture away from backyard soccer games and *Star Wars* re-enactments, claiming the need to pee, to sneak into the bedrooms of his friends' older sisters and quickly grab a stray hair ornament or bra.

David kept most of his collectables in a plastic storage bin hidden behind his mother's gardening shed and safely camouflaged by overgrown weeds. Even Balthazar rarely ventured to that part of the backyard.

At age thirteen David was still swiping pretty things. His mother was distracted, and the cleaning woman had been let go for financial reasons, so it was easy to stash stuff behind the toilet, or in the back of his own closet for a few days before bringing them out to his storage bin. The lipstick from his aunt Beth's Judith Leiber clutch was David's most recent find. For a week he allowed himself to keep the lipstick hidden under his mattress, taking it out nightly to run fingers across the tiny shaft or hold it up to the light and watch it sparkle. He'd stand on his bed to get a view of himself in the small mirror above the dresser, apply a smooth coat to his lips and smile at his reflection.

"Hello, gorgeous," he whispered. Sometimes he thought of himself as 'Natasha'. But not always. Lately it didn't feel quite right. Nothing felt right these days. Nothing but prettiness and pink, and forgetting.

One summer afternoon, a few weeks after his *bar mitzvah*, David and his mother took a trip to ARF. They hadn't been there in months. In the back of the Volvo station wagon were two trash bags full of giveaways. David had already searched through the bags earlier that morning and pilfered two Victoria Secrets bras, size 36C. They'd work, if he stuffed the cups with a couple of pairs of soccer socks.

Balthazar was also along for the ride, sitting on David's lap, panting in a mostly happy, geriatric way. Lately if Balthazar was left alone in the house he'd pee on the front foyer rug or chew repeatedly at a spot on his left hind leg, leaving a spreading yellow stain on the carpet or a patch of red, raw flesh on his own little body.

David liked having Balthazar come along. This way David could avoid his mother's questions and converse with, or at least talk at, his dog instead. David cracked the window to let Balthazar feel the warm breeze.

"You like that, dontchya, Old Boy," David said as he scratched Balthazar behind the ears and Balthazar drifted into a canine trance. "Who's the best dog in the world? Yes, it's yoooou."

They approached the Towne Centre, with its mix of quaint shops and mediocre restaurants. On weekdays, Towne was a destination for pods of mommies with strollers, gangs of pimply, unintimidating high schoolers, Towne's three or four homeless guys, and blank-faced middle-aged women like David's mom. There were never many men around. It seemed the manly men of Towne didn't run errands. They spent daylight hours elsewhere, in the City, or in distant offices in industrial parks. What these manly men did was a mystery, or many mysteries. Probably stuff that meant the men had to wear suits. David liked suits. He liked the fussiness of lapels, and uselessness of the cuff buttons. He liked the silky feel inside a breast pocket. The vibe of the whole jacket, slacks and dress shirt, pulled together with the perfect tie.

They scored a parking spot right between Scotto's Pizzeria and the Calico Cottage Gift Shoppe.

"Sorry Davey, but Balzy has to stay in the car," his mom said. "No dogs allowed anymore."

"Since when?" David asked.

"According to Gloria they've had problems recently. A Doberman knocked a bunch of glassware off a table last week, and supposedly a Jack Russell chewed up a pair of barely-worn Topsiders the week before."

"Argh," David groaned. "ARF is a do-gooder place that saves dogs and they don't let them inside. That's so lame."

"It's not lame, David. They have to take precautions."

"But it's Balzy." David looked down at his benign, elderly pet, then beseechingly up at his mom. "Balzy won't do anything bad."

His mother nodded but her eyes said, come on kid, we both know that's a lie.

"Whatever," David sighed. He hoisted Balthazar off his lap and onto the backseat. "Don't worry Pal, We'll only be gone a minute."

David hadn't been inside ARF for at least six months. Practically an entire era. It was immediately obvious that Gloria had done some rearranging. The giant bookshelf filled with books no one wanted to read was where the musty, moth-eaten flannel button-downs of Men's Shirts had been. Those macho flannel atrocities were now where Women's Workout had been, a shit pile of greyed undergarments and slightly sweat-stinky spandex gear that had never had anything remotely attractive to offer David. All those depressing panties and jog-bras now replaced his favorite section, Girls Clothing. David surveyed the store. He didn't spot a single flash of petite calico or frill. Not a bunny-covered flannel nightgown in sight. He had no idea where the pink and pretty had gone. No way was he going to ask.

David's heart throbbed against the wall of his narrow chest like a hooked fish attempting to snap free. It was bad enough to feel like he was some sort of freak chameleon. But why did everything around him have to keep changing? If stuff on the outside just stayed the way it was supposed to, maybe he'd have an easier time figuring out his own shit. Who he was. What he was.

While Gloria and his mother were deep in a conversation about someone's somebody doing something, David managed to locate Toys. Perhaps Angora sweaters and taffeta party dresses would be nearby. If not, if worse came to worst, he supposed he might steal a Barbie. He could make do running his fingers along her absurd breast bumps, getting a charge from the smoothness of a miniature polyester halter top. Preferably a pink one.

Lucinda: The Stage Set

Brady Cole answered the door, wearing an embroidered skull cap with a strange insignia embossed on the front and a long white caftan with the same insignia stitched over his left pectoral. The logo looked like a cross between a palm tree and a dick.

Brady seemed out of it. His bright blue eyes couldn't quite focus and in spite of all sorts of attractive facial chisels, his skin was blotchy above his three-day beard. Lucinda thought maybe Brady was on drugs. Didn't lots of movie stars take drugs?

"FedEx, right?" He said. "Need me to sign?"

Definitely out of it, thought Lucinda. But she was determined to see her plan through. "Hahaha! No. I'm

Lucinda Leibowitz from across the street," Lucinda declared loudly.

Slowly Brady's gaze became less dazed as the here and now washed over him. He looked down at his feminized outfit and let out a manly howl.

"Ohmygod," he gasped. "I'm so sorry. I was expecting a package."

Lucinda couldn't help but stare at his weird costume. Brady Cole looked like an oversized rabbi or imam. Outlandish, really, but at least his get-up ended The Mystery of the Woman in White.

He noticed her noticing, and plucked at the fabric of his *schmata*. "I know. This dress is super weird. But there's a reason I'm wearing it." He pointed to the penile palm tree on his chest. "I'm a follower of Tamago, a guru who helps men locate their Beauteous Cores."

Lucinda nodded. Go with it, she told herself. "Beauteous core. How...fascinating."

Brady kept explaining. Supposedly his studies involved wearing the dress and cap, as well as meditating, chanting, and dancing in the least masculine way possible. On and on went Brady's mini-tutorial on the levels of Beauteous enlightenment, abstinence, further studies, workshops, personal sacrifices, financial contributions.

All this before Lucinda even passed the threshold of the Kearny Mansion. She shifted from foot to foot as this odd man talked on. Finally, Brady took a breath. She saw her chance and thrust her zucchini bread forward.

"Welcome to the neighborhood," she chirped.

"Thanks." Lucinda watched Brady examine the Towne Soccer League Logo emblazoned across her chest. "I love soccer."

"My son used to play," Lucinda shrugged, "But he's not very sporty anymore."

Brady shook his head sadly. "Tamago says organized sports are a woman's enemy and a man's worst friend."

Tamago sounds like a nut job, thought Lucinda, but she didn't say so. Instead, she smiled widely, showing lots of teeth.

Eventually they went inside where that gigantic yellow lab bounded towards them stinking of unwashed fur, tail wagging and head held high. The dog's snout and front paws were covered in dirt. Lucinda recognized the pitch of his bark. It had the same timbre as the incessant whelps she'd been hearing from across the street at all times of day and night ever since Brady and this dog arrived.

"Angus! Shut the hell up!" Brady's voice reverbed off the cavernous walls of the grand foyer. He turned to Lucinda and said, "I'm sorry. That wasn't very beauteous of me."

What did 'beauteous' actually mean, Lucinda wondered? She knew what beautiful meant, what beauty meant, but beauteous? It sounded like the kind of word her hairdresser Antonio would use to describe a volumizing hair product.

"What a great dog," Lucinda exclaimed, reaching her non-zucchini bread-holding hand out towards Angus, aiming for the clean top of his cranium. But Angus had other ideas. The dog slobbered all over her palm as if it were covered in liver treats.

Brady stood by and watched. His chiseled features went bizarrely agog. If Lucinda hadn't done due diligence before coming over for this neighborly visit and read every bit of semi-legitimate news about Brady in print and on the internet, she might almost have taken his slack-jawed, wide-eyed stare as attraction. But she knew all about Brady Cole's sexual sleaziness. He liked his conquests at least twenty years younger. It was widely rumored that Brady had cheated on every wife and girlfriend he'd ever had. The latest wife was a Swedish or Danish photographer or former model who filed for divorce after finding Brady, in bed or bathtub, with the dog walker or house-keeper. Whatever the case, there was no way in hell Brady found middle-aged, plumpish Lucinda Leibowitz attractive. No, he was definitely on drugs.

Eventually Lucinda took her hand away from Angus and wiped it on her cargo shorts. Men admired women who bonded with dogs and weren't scared of a little drool. And that was what Lucinda was after, admiration and a possible job. "Here," she thrust the zucchini bread at Brady once more, "It's zucchini bread."

"Excellent," Brady nodded. His hand slid over hers as he took the loaf from her. "I love zucchini bread."

"I made it myself from my own crop."

"Wow," Brady cried, "You grow zucchinis? That's amazing!"

Over the top, thought Lucinda. Every woman in Towne grew something edible in their backyards. But still she appreciated the compliment. Her life had been short on compliments lately. She shrugged. "Oh, it's nothing."

Then Lucinda did what she really wanted to do, she looked around. The stupendous grand foyer had five arched doorways off a central pentagram. Each doorway was surrounded by rococo carvings of birds, squirrels, and bunnies. At each apex a pair of cherubs frolicked with oak leaves covering their genitalia and daisy chains crowning their chubby heads. The wood—Late Nineteenth-Century Ecuadorian mahogany, no doubt—was in decent shape, only a few spots needed work. Stripping and re-staining it to a lighter shade would highlight the dimensionality of the original design. A glorious tiled mosaic sunburst inlaid on the hall floor peeked its way out from under years of grime. A few yellow sunbeams were chipped and undone, but this was something José, Lucinda's tile guy from days of yore, could definitely handle. And oh, that original chandelier! Aquamarine and turquoise frosted glass. If not a real Tiffany, it was a fantastic copy. She'd have to get Janice from Golden Glass Where to do a consult.

"You must be thrilled to own such an amazing historic place," Lucinda said, brushing her hand along the dusty plaster walls. Her old designer juices were flowing and it felt great.

Brady shrugged. "I guess. But if you ask me, it's sort of a dump."

Aha. Here was Lucinda's opening. "With a little TLC this could be a spectacular home." And another seed: "a showcase."

Brady shook his head. "Nah, no showcases for me, thank you. I'm trying to keep a low profile."

Uh oh, Lucinda thought. She'd gone too far. "Sorry. Occupational hazard. We interior designers walk into a place like this and we can't help ourselves."

"You're an interior designer?"

Score, thought Lucinda. "Yes."

"That's awesome," Brady was staring at her crotch. Had she wiped some garden soil there when picking the zucchinis? Or maybe he was looking for a hidden mike or camera. Who could blame him? Celebrities had to be vigilant. All those sex tapes and unflattering images of them on the internet.

Don't push, Lucinda told herself. Play it cool. She turned to admire the arched doorway leading to the living room, but also to let Brady examine her back for wires and suspicious bulges. She laughed to herself thinking, Look to your heart's content, Brady. All I have to offer is my slightly droopy ass.

"Maybe you could give me a few tips." Brady's voice was low and breathy behind her. "I'm clueless when it comes to couches and lamps and that kind of stuff."

Was this really happening? So quickly? Give him a few decorating ideas? Hell yeah. She already had at least five. Lucinda hadn't expected an offer like this to fall in her lap so effortlessly. She'd assumed she'd have to traipse across the street many more times to stroke Brady's movie star ego.

"I'd be happy to," she turned and said calmly. "You know, friend to friend, neighbor to neighbor." She was already calculating her fee in her head.

"Cool," Brady grinned. His white teeth gleamed as Lucinda imagined his floor tiles would once she got working. "Friend to friend. I'd like that." Brady was squeezing the zucchini bread. If he kept it up the loaf would be a crumbled mess. Angus sat by Brady's thigh looking up at the bread. His tail thumped the floor in a steady, excited beat.

"Here now," Lucinda cooed, speaking to Brady as if he were a child she needed to coerce gently from danger. "Why don't you just give me back the bread for the moment."

It was too late. Before Lucinda could save her bread, Angus nabbed it with a swift chomp.

Brady stood in his dopey cap and gown, unperturbed, with only a few crumbs left on his fingers. "Wanna see the rest of the place?" he asked.

Lucinda attempted an air of girlish insouciance, shrugging and lifting her hands with palms spread upwards. "Sure. If you've got the time." Her tee shirt rode up and exposed a muffin top of middle-aged belly. But who cared, really.

Brady: Rules of Attraction

Brady never thought he'd be attracted to a freckly, washed-out blonde his own age, or older. But there was something about Lucinda. He hadn't been able to stop thinking about her since she came over to visit in those dumpy cargo shorts and ratty Towne Soccer League tee shirt. A woman who put no effort into her appearance. A dowdy wallflower who baked her own zucchini bread.

He'd been expecting a package from Tamago, or rather, from the official Beauteous Man Store, where retreat participants enjoyed a 20% discount on all items. Brady had ordered a five-pack of scarves for his daily dancing ritual, and a half-dozen shaky eggs because he still felt deprived, not ever shaking any on the Beauteous Men's Retreat. Instead he got a better delivery; the gift of Lucinda.

Maybe it was because of Beauteous Man's Rule Number Two: All novices will remain celibate for the first three months of study, after which they shall practice monogamy only. You wanted something more when the something was forbidden. He hadn't been that close to a woman in weeks. Maybe anything with a pulse might turn Brady on. Still, Lucinda, or maybe it was just sex, was the only thing Brady wanted. Tamago said the first month would be the hardest, and Brady was only three weeks in. At least novices were allowed to wank off. It said so in the Beauteous Rules' annexed notes.

In the meantime, Brady had it bad for Lucinda. What a non-babe babe. So what if she had some junk in her trunk. Her skin could be smoother. The teeth were a bit horsey. Brady didn't care. Another cool thing about Lucinda was she didn't seem the slightest bit fazed by Brady's caftan and beret. How could he not be attracted to a woman who didn't freak out when a movie star like Brady Cole answered the door wearing a dress?

She was great with Angus. Really knew how to talk to him in a way that chilled the dog out. Angus was the calmest Brady had seen him since they'd moved into the broken down excuse for a house. For three weeks Angus had beelined to the back fence barking his head off, pawing in one spot like he wanted to dig his way to China. But since Lucinda's visit, the dog had let up, a bit. When Lucinda had scratched Angus' head and ran her fingers along his furry back, both man and dog drooled. When she'd knelt to let Angus lick her lovely face, Brady had to sit down, because the Tamago Caftan was mondo revealing and he had a boner that boinged like a spring-released tent pole.

Brady had worked really hard to ask Lucinda questions, to not talk too much about himself. Before she'd left him, his ex-wife Webeke accused Brady of being a narcissist, among other, less savory things. She complained that living with Brady had been like living with an "unoriginal, self-centered monologist." Fuck Webeke, thought Brady. But then he took it back. It was not beauteous to curse, and to curse women in particular, even if it was just in one's mind.

Brady would have to dive deep in his next one-on-one Skype session with Tamago. He knew he wasn't supposed to be obsessing over a woman. He was supposed to focus on his own inner beauty, to continue his journey towards a totally Pure Man Core. He was supposed to be hunkering down on drumming and chanting. If Brady were really honest with himself, or anyone else, this is what he'd say: you can't teach an old horn-dog new tricks. But honesty was elusive as ever. For now, he'd keep it in his pants—or rather, under his skirt. But that wouldn't stop him from wooing lovely Lucinda. Besides, he'd be doing her a favor. They'd get there, eventually. Everyone knew it didn't get much better than Brady Cole.

Chapter Four

Abe: Bye Bye Go Go

And then he found his boy.

"Pag a ba, ay cha ya," Milo said. Peek a boo, I see you. Just a temporarily abandoned toddler doing what toddlers do best. Play.

Milo sat between two precarious towers of Diet Coke. The soda display threatened to topple and shower him in cans if Milo were to move one of his little legs a few inches to either side. Abe's negligence hadn't led to abduction, but his stupidity could still result in his son's death or brain damage with one small gesture.

Abe lifted his son as if he were handling an explosive device. Once they were a few feet away he showered Milo in kisses.

"I'm so sorry, Mouse," Abe cried, tears streaming down his cheeks. "I'm so, so sorry."

Milo erupted in a fountain of giggles. He patted his father's flushed wet cheeks. He was adorable, demonic.

Nothing seemed funny to Abe. And he'd lost his appetite for sweets.

Father and son left the store, Abe holding Milo tightly to his chest. He inhaled the scent of his son's rose- and cream cheese-scented scalp and thanked a god he didn't believe in. He stumbled out of the Gas n' Go clinging to Milo like a life vest and wept. He wasn't going to let his baby boy out of his sight again for a nanosecond. They'd stay melded gut to gut until the boy was at least eighteen years old.

But when Abe looked down the street he saw something had indeed been lost. Not something. Someone. Gordon was gone.

The post Abe had looped the leash to stood unattended. For a moment Abe thought he'd made a mistake and left Gordon somewhere else, another post. Further up the street? In the other direction? Abe looked up and down the sea of green lawns and tarred sidewalks to further street signs, distant corners, all empty.

"Gordon!" He called. It was fruitless. He knew even then. "Come, boy!"

Everything hushed. Birds stopped tweeting. The wind died. All Abe heard was Milo's snory breath, a tinny rattle from a deviated septum Abe and Claire would have to make surgical decisions about when Milo was older but which, during toddlerhood, had a certain goofy charm.

"Gordon. Gordon. Gooooor-doooon." Abe beseeched the air. Seconds passed. No response, no dog pal waddling around the corner and galumphing towards him on linebacker legs.

For a split second Abe wondered if someone had stolen his dog, that they could tell Gordon would make an excellent pet. But Towne was not a place where things, much less dogs, were stolen. There were few burglaries, fewer serious brawls, no sexual assaults. Towne was a place where people left their doors unlocked, where neighbors handed out spare keys freely. They gave things to each other: baked goods, toys, books. They lent tools, cars, helping hands. The highest level of crime was the persistence of adolescents scribbling graffiti and wannabe tags on the high school facade. No, it was obvious. Gordon knew if he didn't run away, eventually he'd be given away. The smart dog chose his own destiny.

"Bye bye Go Go," said Milo matter-of-factly, with no sense of past, present, or future. For Milo, Gordon would be there, not be there, be there, just like always. Lucky kid, not yet fully comprehending loss.

Milo and Abe searched the neighborhood for a half an hour. Rather, Abe searched. Poor Milo was tuckered out, slumped like an emptied potato sack, his hot little cheek against Abe's shoulder, his drool and raspy breath Abe's only comfort. Abe knew in his deepest, saddest core that Gordon didn't want to be found, but this knowledge wouldn't stop Abe from searching. Gordon had seen the writing on the wall. The dog was smart, maybe too smart. Enough being relentlessly chased by Milo, his crazed midget fan. Enough of the boy's poking and squeezing. Enough wailing and screeching. And probably more than anything, enough playing second fiddle to that miniature human. Abe knew exactly how Gordon felt because he often felt the same way. The moment Milo pushed his way out of the birth canal and the midwife had laid his blood streaked body on Claire's exhausted chest Abe knew his days were numbered. How could Abe compete for Claire's affections with such a mesmerizing, slimy bundle of joy? They say there's nothing more beautiful than a mother's love for her child. Abe thought: Bullshit. The true saying should be, there's nothing more exclusionary than a mother's love for her child.

Still, Abe was smitten by Milo himself, and continued to be. Gordon knew Milo had usurped his role as Abe's main squeeze. He knew also that Claire, in particular, would tolerate only so much air snapping and growling. Gordon knew that in spite of their years together, he was still the lowly adoptee, a beast of sketchy heritage. Abe and Claire would never forget that their pet had a jaw stronger than a vise grip, and a bite that, if provoked, could end a life.

Gordon had had enough. Gordon had seen his chance and run away. But when has that kind of visceral knowledge ever stopped the brokenhearted from trying? Jilted lovers, accident survivors, parents of runaways or long ago kidnapped children? And now Abe, suddenly Gordon-less. Losers, all of them in the truest sense of the word.

Eventually Abe gave up and started for home. Claire would be back in a few hours. Abe had to prepare to tell her some version of the truth about this ill-fated outing. He'd tell her about Gordon but not about almost killing their son. She'd not be told about the almost avalanche of Diet Coke. That would remain a secret. Abe had gotten pretty good at keeping secrets.

"Bye bye, Go Go," he said softly to the air. Then he carried his son home.

Nell: Thanks, but no thanks.

Nell came upon him, abandoned in front of the Gas n' Go, his leash double knotted to a street sign. Nell saw the dog and the dog saw her. They locked eyes and it all changed. The pit bull barely flinched as she approached. He gazed up at Nell with beady but friendly eyes and cocked his head curiously askew. Nell had never felt more interesting in her life. Nell patted his blocky head. The pit bull smiled. She scratched him behind the ears and he leaned in to her hand like a pat of butter melting on to toast.

Nell wondered what kind of evil person would leave a precious, defenseless creature alone in this summer heat? The poor dog might die of dehydration. It could starve. It could be stolen and sold into pit bull slavery, forced to become a killer against its will. Nell was suddenly overwhelmed with the memory of the dog bones she'd found in Allenwood Park. The leg bones in their useless attempt at taking stride. The teeth, so perfectly aligned with nothing to chew. The collar, that damning evidence of human mistreatment.

She couldn't save that dear thing, but she could save this one. Nell's aimless wanderings and impulsive thievery began to make sense. The stolen food and the discarded clothes and old toys she found in backyard bins and plastic containers would become useful beyond their original purposes.

Up until that fateful moment Nell still cut a sad picture: this twenty-something-year-old girl with nothing to do but ride a bicycle too small for her up and down perfectly gridded, smoothly tarred streets. Nell scraped her knuckles bloody untangling the knot of his leash. Once loosened, she looped the leash around her sloping handle bars, tugged gently and whispered,

"Come on, boy. Come with me."

The dog happily obliged, trotting alongside Nell's bike as if she were leading him to a land of gristled meat and tennis balls.

She slowed her pace so as not to exhaust the poor dog once they were safely outside the Towne limits. Once they got inside her house, Nell unclipped his leash. While the dog sniffed every conceivable surface in the kitchen she filled one of her mother's ghastly clay bowls with water.

Nell placed the wobbly bowl on the floor and watched the dog slurp. Water sloshed all over the floor, possibly ruining the wood finish. Nell couldn't have cared less.

Taking the dog had been the right thing to do. It was a spontaneous, impulsive, and intuitively correct decision. Nell was heroic, saving this creature from a fate worse than death at the hands of a neglectful enslaver. Still Nell had no clue how to care for a dog. Jumbo had been simple; shake turtle food into the terrarium every other day. Change the terrarium water at least once a week. This Pit Bull, who'd finished drinking and now smiled up at her with a "So? What's next, human lady?" look on his face, was a more complicated beast. Nell needed to feed him, of course, but what else? What if this dog needed special medicine for special ailments? Did he need to be bathed regularly? His fur was short, so she doubted he'd need to be groomed in some fussy manner, but maybe there was something else she was supposed to do? And what about his nails? Or were they called claws on a dog? And his teeth? Wasn't there something special about dog's teeth?

"Oh boy." Nell sighed as she knelt down next to him. "What have I gotten myself into?"

The dog licked Nell's face as if it were a lollipop. After he'd tired of her face, he nestled on the floor with his head across her knees. Nell's entire body relaxed as he rested his warm body against her bare, freckled flesh. Nell combed her fingers through the pit bull's short fur and scratched his thick neck under the leather collar, an article of bondage she deemed unnecessarily tight.

The air was seasoned with the muskiness of dog dander, embellished with the sound of gentle panting. Minutes passed. Maybe hours. Nell felt no motivation to move from her spot on the kitchen floor with this magnificent creature resting in her lap. Waves of confidence washed over her, surging like Beethoven's Ninth. She could do this.

She would do this. Taking care of this dog would be like playing scales, something she could do in her sleep. Finally she glanced the little name tag hanging off the dog's collar.

"Gordon," she read out loud. He lifted his head and looked up at her. "Now that's a stupid name."

Gordon barked. It seemed he agreed.

The tag indicated Gordon "belonged" to someone named Abe Kaufman. It was a vaguely familiar name, but then again it was also a common one. There was a phone number to call, if one found Gordon.

"Fat chance," Nell said as she undid the collar and tossed it across the room. "Time for a new name."

Paddy: Sting Ray

"There's more where that came from, if you want it. You know where to find me." Gloria took out a tissue out of her purse to dab around her lips. "Now, how about I go sit on that bench you have outside the store while you figure out what's wrong with my car?"

Paddy gathered his wits. There'd been nothing wrong with Gloria's car that a little axle grease couldn't solve; the irony of charging Gloria for a lube job was not lost on him.

The following Tuesday, Paddy draped Mariah's favorite silk blouse across his forearms like a shroud. It had been her last sewing project before the downward spiral. Now Paddy stared at the limp thing and tried to make sense of the intricate pattern; bumble bees whizzing about but unaware of voluptuous red rose buds on branches nearby, each tempting twig floating against a cerulean sky.

Paddy remembered the day Mariah had bought the fabric, how she'd bounded into the den with the energy of a woman half her age. Paddy had been dozing in his recliner, wasn't in the least interested in patterns, weaves, or thread counts, but Mariah paid him no mind.

"Look at this, Paddy," she cried. "Isn't it just the most gorgeous thing you've ever seen?"

Mariah leaned over him and placed the folded fabric on his lap. She was still a knockout at seventy-five, snowy tendrils of hair framing an angelic face. Her breasts, still peach-like to the touch were buttoned up behind the fabric of another handmade blouse, one covered in a brown blobby print that reminded him of—he'd never tell Mariah—dog doo. And oh, Mariah's scent; lilac and sweat. Flowers and flesh.

"No, you're the most gorgeous thing," Paddy said. He felt himself harden, even after all those years, as he reached up to grope his lovely wife.

How had Mariah responded? Paddy couldn't quite recall now. She'd probably shooed away his hands with good humor and cajoled him to say something nice about her fabric. And Paddy probably had. He liked to please her, when it didn't require much work.

Now Mariah was dead, and the buzzards from ARF were due to come pick over her clothes within the hour. Paddy needed to get back to folding her blouses. He wanted to make a perfect pile, honoring her handiwork. A neat stack to boost his wilted spirit.

But this last blouse gave him pause. The futility of it all. Rose branches could never float like that, and bees wouldn't buzz around in the open air with all those blossoms blooming. Bees were driven creatures, hell-bent on their jobs. They'd have their scary little faces burrowed deep in the pollen belly of each scarlet bloom. They'd be relentless. They'd suck those roses dry.

Paddy was still staring at the blouse when the buzzards arrived. With just a slight relax of his elbows it could easily fall to the ground. Slippery, delicate. Such an absurd thing.

The stack ended one blouse short. The ARF buzzards whisked it away in their clackety clack van. Paddy had also tossed in a few of his old Woolrich shirts for good measure. Maybe his itchy plaids and Mariah's smooth silks would end up in the same hardscrabble household. Do some good somewhere together, again.

But one special blouse remained. The frustrated bees and the roses floating in that impossible blue sky would live with Paddy forever. No creases, no right angle folds. Instead the whole absurdity was rolled into a nice pillow, a perfect silken balm to hold against his aching heart every sleepless night.

A full week passed. So far Gloria hadn't shown her overly lipsticked and rouged face around his station again. One morning, while the store TV was on the fritz, Paddy noticed he was low on Kind bars and 5-hour Energy. He'd been lax keeping up with inventory in general, but it didn't seem possible he'd sold that much fake nutrition and pep in so short a period of time. Since he'd been serviced against his will by Gloria, Paddy was more wary of suspicious behavior than ever. When a guy who'd originally come in asking about candy suddenly called "Mouse!" as if there were a major rodent problem in the store (which Paddy knew, like he knew every part of a V-8 engine, there wasn't) Paddy was at full alert. Then the guy screamed, "Where are you?" and Paddy realized Mouse was a person. But Paddy hadn't seen anyone else come into the store. Then again, Paddy realized he'd been staring blankly at the TV screen, so maybe he wasn't as vigilant as he should've been.

"Where's my son?" the guy leaned over the counter towards Paddy, so close their noses almost touched.

Had this man's son come into the store without Paddy noticing? No. The man was over-reacting. Or crazy. Maybe there hadn't been any son at all. Paddy was annoyed. His quiet afternoon was suddenly filled with someone else's panic. He liked his days monotonous, no ripples. So this is how it's going down, Paddy thought. Paddy slowly reached for the baseball bat he kept under the counter, just in case the guy was a violent nut job.

"What son?" Paddy asked.

"Are you kidding me?" The guy was pissed. "My son, my baby boy. He was here, right on the floor a minute ago."

Now that Paddy was really paying attention, he could see that the guy looked desperate, sure, but not crazy. And it was possible Paddy could've missed the presence of a kid who was under-the-counter small. Paddy owed him the benefit of the doubt. Paddy had panicked like this in his own home when Mariah had gone out of his view for too long a stretch, even with all doors and windows locked, all sharp objects hidden, all slippery area rugs rolled, sound monitors in every room, an identification bracelet around Mariah's wrist, Paddy's cellphone in his pocket at all times.

"I'm sorry, Bud," Paddy said. "Lemme help you." He got off his stool, came around the counter to aid in the search.

That's when they found the little bugger. The kid had wedged himself in the center of the Diet Coke display, which was not a place for anything or anybody to be wedged. Luckily the dad got him out before the kid knocked a stack of cans on top of his little head. Talk about a disaster. Talk about a possible lawsuit.

The boy thought it was the funniest thing in the world, giggling in bubbly baby spurts. Crazy infectious laughter. His dad hugged him so hard it looked like he might crush the kid. Paddy couldn't even see the kid's face it was pressed so tight against the guy's chest. All that mattered was they were together. Paddy was invisible, which suited him fine.

When the guy first walked in he'd asked where Paddy kept the candy. He'd looked determined and ashamed. Now he left the store without buying anything, holding on to his son for dear life, mumbling in a daze. Paddy understood how shock could buzzkill any appetite. He had stopped drinking after Mariah died. He'd been a consistent two-scotch-a-night type of guy since he'd been old enough to shave. As Mariah's illness progressed Paddy became an unapologetic four-scotch-a-night type. Who was there to apologize to? Mariah wouldn't remember if the amber in his tumbler was his first or his fifth. But after she'd gone, Paddy lost the taste. The need was gone, but not fulfilled. A void replaced it. Was that better? Paddy wasn't at all certain.

Never let go of him, Mister, thought Paddy as he stood by the door and watched them walk past the gas pumps, heading towards the corner. Hold on to your son and never turn away.

Paddy went back to his perch. The one remaining bottle of 5-hour was in front of the photo of Mariah he'd taped to the cash register. The flaming orange bottle top positioned right under Mariah's chin. Hell if it didn't look as if his dead wife had been reborn as a tiny, arm-less caffeine shot. Strange times, thought Paddy. Strange times indeed.

David: Red Handed

When he held the Beachcomber Barbie he'd found at the bottom of a pile of hair-hatchet-ed Barbies in Toys, David knew she wouldn't cut it anymore. He'd outgrown dolls. Without any Girls Clothing and no Barbie urges,

David's last resort was Women's Blouses. He was still such a wisp of a boy, he'd have to roll up the blouse cuffs and tie the ends, but that wasn't such a big deal. It might actually end up looking cool.

David was running out of time. He made his way to an empty aisle and stopped midway to do a quick perimeter check. There were a few people scattered around the store. A schlubby, hairy guy browsed ugly lumber shirts à la Kurt Cobain in Menswear. A washed-out woman with thinning dull-brown hair, who probably worked in Towne but didn't live there, probably taking care of another woman's kids or cleaning her house, sifted through Women's Dresses. They both had their backs to him. His mother and Gloria were gabbing away about that movie star guy who'd moved in across the street, Brady Cole. David had seen him in some warrior movie at a sleepover at Lance Radison's house when he was about nine. He'd found the whole movie super stressful to watch; all that blood and gore, guys running around stabbing each other, falling off horses and breaking their necks. Lars thought it was cool, so David pretended he did too. Now, four years later, with everyone in Towne so pumped about Brady Cole moving in, David had looked him up on the web, to see if he thought Brady was hot. He didn't. He looked too much like a Ken doll, too perfect, as if he wouldn't feel it if you poked him in the face because he wasn't really real.

But Gloria obviously thought the guy was amazing, because she wouldn't shut up about him. This worked fine for David. He examined the blouses in front of him. The choices were lame: lime green polyester, ugly paisley print, unflattering red stripes. Blouses that dumpy old ladies wore. And everything was size Large.

But he had to swipe something. His fingers throbbed with need. There was one blouse shoved deep at the end of the rack, a brown blobby print that looked a little too much like dog doo. But it was hand-stitched and silk, and with the right accessories it might look less poop and more Prada. David slowly worked his way through the fabric to take the blouse off the hanger without any of his arm or hand showing. It was a technique he'd perfected over many years. With a minimum of rustling, the blouse slipped off the hanger. David rolled it into a ball one-handed and shoved it down his jockeys. He spread the fabric around to avoid tell-tale bunching.

When it was fully smoothed David turned. Standing beside him was his old piano teacher, Nell. He hadn't seen her in over four years. She wasn't lovely anymore, she was emaciated. She didn't smell like lilacs, she smelled like sour milk. Her hair, formerly a reddish wavy mane David wanted to rake his fingers through rather than plod through arpeggios during long-ago lessons, now looked like moldy spaghetti. Her eyes, a crystal blue he'd always admired, were filmy and bugging out over cheeks that jutted like rock cliffs.

Nell leaned towards David, hovering like a creepy praying mantis. If it had been the old Nell David might've liked it, but this Nell was like something from the Walking Dead. Her arm brushed across David's chest, and he wanted to scream, but the sound got stuck in his throat like a fireball. Plus he wasn't sure what she would do if he did scream. Would she rat him out? Completely destroy his life?

David braced himself as Nell's arm swept past him, and her hand took hold of the paisley blouse. Her gnarly, long fingernails had polish on them. OPI Flashbulb Fuchsia. David recognized the hue. He couldn't help but admire Nell's choice, even though most of the polish was peeling off, and she was disgusting, and possibly about to molest him. Without a rustle or sound, she swept the ugly blouse off the hanger. A split second later it was hidden deep in the pocket of her ridiculous red raincoat.

David and Nell stood staring at each other for what seemed like a quadrillion million years. Nell nodded slowly and threw David an air kiss. Ew, yuck, gross me out forever, he thought as he watched her creep out the door like an old tortoise.

"Davey," his mother called. "What are you doing over there?"

All eyes in the store were on him. The tired eyes of the washed out, downtrodden lady, the hairy hipster, Gloria's beady, nosy eyes, and the confused eyes of David's mother.

"Nothing," David's voice crackled like a half-dead toad's, "Just killing time." He shoved his hands in the front pockets of his jeans and slouched forward. He paused by Electronics and pretended to be interested in an old-school cassette tape recorder. He fingered through a plastic container filled with half-used batteries. After a carefully timed five minutes passed he called, "Hey, Ma, I'm gonna go out to the car and make sure Balzy is okay."

David walked out slowly, trying to control the urge to sprint. Once outside, he looked up and down the street. No sign of Nell. Thank fucking god. David couldn't wait to get back to the car, sit down with Balzy on his lap, smell his familiar old dog smell, scratch his hot little dandruffy head.

But then came the worst part of the already shitty day. There was no Balzy to calm David down. The car was empty but for the stench of Balzy's pee.

Lucinda: Sacrifice

The timing of Balthazar's disappearance couldn't have been worse. Lucinda had a schedule to keep. Earlier that day she'd accepted Brady's wet kiss on her cheek, and left the Kearny Mansion with a renewed sense of purpose. She'd ended up with the possibility of a real job much sooner than she had ever imagined she would. Now she wanted to go to the fabric and paint stores, get David home, feed him something vaguely nutritious, and get back across the street to Brady's for their first official meeting about the renovation. But clearly her plans would have to change.

Lucinda would never complain to David, but as far as she was concerned Balthazar had become a burden, a burden which she as the stay-at-home mother-slave had to bear. He snarled and nipped for no good reason. A piece of paper falling off a counter set him off in a torrent of phlegmy yelps. He smelled like the inside of an old man's shoe. He ate too fast then threw up immediately. He slept in inconvenient places: across the threshold to stairs, in front of bathtubs, on Lucinda's favorite chair. She'd had to throw old blankets over all the furniture, because Balzy shed bristly hairs like he was tossing confetti. And then there was the peeing. Incontinence? Maybe. Moodiness? Definitely. Accidents? Everywhere. Balthazar's aging was a direct assault on Lucinda's dignity. A way to keep her forever cleaning up after someone, or something. So when David came into ARF screaming hysterically that Balthazar was missing and she went back to the car, and saw that yes, the damn dog was indeed gone, for a fleeting moment she thought: whoever took you, Balzy, God bless them.

But while Lucinda was a bit self-involved, more so now than ever, she wasn't a total bitch. She could not deny Balzy's importance in their less-than-perfect little family back in the day when she still held out hope for perfection. She would always remember the day David found him, or maybe it was the reverse. Maybe Balzy was the finder.

Dan had insisted from the get-go: Only one kid. He claimed it was because of his commitment to zero population growth, but Lucinda knew better. After five years with the guy, she'd grown well aware of his persnickety ways, his need for order; above all, his inability to share a spotlight.

But Dan did want a dog, which was weird, given his dislike of sputum, vomit, and pretty much all other bodily fluids.

"I'm thinking a corgi," he announced one morning while Lucinda nursed eleven-month-old David under a modesty cape Dan had recently bought her because while he'd found beauty in the mother-infant bond, the slurp and suck of a nearly one-year-old child was a bit too much for him. Lucinda should've known then; this little family was doomed.

"No way," Lucinda said. "Their proportions freak me out. Those giant heads on sausage bodies and stumpy legs. Like someone took a German shepherd skull and screwed it to the torso of a dachshund."

"Don't be ridiculous," Dan huffed. "They are a well regarded breed. The Royals always have corgis."

Your father is fucking pretentious, she said silently to David, who was rustling under the cape, rooting his way from one boob to the other.

Out loud Lucinda said, "you're not a king, Dan. You're an American suburbanite. If we're going to get a dog I want to adopt one that needs a home. A shelter dog. Not one that's been bred to be bought by regal strivers."

Dan always needed to have the last word, a last word often delivered after pontification that bored her to tears. Not merely mansplaining, but Dansplaining. After a lengthy diatribe about the evolution of the domestic canine and the inherent "muttness" of even the most refined breeds, Dan agreed to go the rescue dog route.

Lucinda suspected an ulterior motive, because there always was one with Dan. If he couldn't have a fancy-pants dog, he could instead brag that he'd rescued a poor abandoned creature and thus elevate his virtuous status in the pet owning world. That was Dan; always going for the gold.

They went to the ARF shelter on a cold February morning. The sky was steel grey and dismal, as was the exterior of the shelter itself, an aluminum-sided quonset hut in an industrial park ten miles outside of Towne. David was fourteen months old and toddling by then, determined to walk everywhere, so Lucinda held his mittened hand as they made their way at toddler pace from the parked car towards ARF.

"Puppy," David said. Clearly. Two distinct syllables. A real honest to god word. His first.

"Dan," Lucinda called. "Did you hear that?"

Dan was ten paces ahead of them, as usual. He was wearing a red-checked L.L. Bean hunting jacket and a duckbilled cap. Lucinda suspected Dan would choose a dog that matched his apparel. A nice, outdoorsy dog. If Dan couldn't be royalty, New England WASP was the next best thing.

"Dan," she yelled louder this time. "Davey just said his first word!"

Dan turned back and waited. "He did?"

"Yeah," Lucinda said as she and David caught up to him.

"What did you say, Son," Dan knelt towards his son. Lucinda felt a brewing of excitement and joy she hadn't felt in a long time. To see David and Dan looking at each other so expectantly, maybe—she hoped—with love and deep father-son connection. This is a good moment, she thought. Try and remember it.

"Puppy," David said again. "Puppypuppypuppy!"

"Isn't that cute? And smart?" Lucinda said. "He knows where we are. He knows we're here to get the puppy."

Dan's expectant look had turned sour. "I guess."

The good moment gone. Poof.

"What's your problem?" Lucinda asked.

Dan shrugged as he stood, brushing bits of parking lot gravel from the deep grooves in his corduroy slacks. "Oh, I was just hoping for…you know…Papa, or Daddy."

Well suck it up you big selfish dickwad, Lucinda wanted to scream. And she might have, had David not been right there with his bird-boned arms hugging her leg as he gazed up at his father. Davey, her beautiful little angel, still expectant.

David would wait years for his father to come around, to be proud or, at the very least, satisfied. But that morning Lucinda's patience with Dan was already on the wane. She scooped David up in her arms and cooed, "Come on, my love, my one and only. Let's go find you that puppy."

The cacophony of ARF was migraine-worthy. Percussive barks and high-pitched whines threatening to break the sound barrier. Dogs scrambled around their pens, some happy, some stressed, some sick, old, and tired, some so young they looked as if they'd just been born. Each one a heartbreaker.

The stench was overwhelming; a combination of dander, piss, and poo embellished with orange scented disinfectant. Dan could barely stand it. He took shallow breaths through his mouth and walked the aisles without much notice of the creatures in their wired enclosures. Instead he fixated on the floor where stray turds and small puddles had yet to be cleaned up by the overwhelmed volunteer staff.

David ran forward, propelled by innate GPS, pulling Lucinda along with him, avoiding the messes, passing pen after pen of adorable puppies. Finally he stopped in front of Skipper, soon to be crowned Balthazar (one concession to Dan) who had his tiny, prematurely wizened snout poked through the fencing, his already knowing eyes fixated on the equally tiny boy.

David offered his hand. A slender, pinker than pink

tongue slipped through the interstices and licked David's palm.

"Pup-pyyy!" David's elated cry echoed off the aluminum walls, silencing every dog and human in the place.

And here they were almost thirteen years later, poor David a mess, crying like he hadn't since he was a toddler, snot streaming out of his nose, his face scrunched up like a prune. Lucinda harnessed her most caring mommy voice and comforted him.

"Don't worry, Sweetie," she cooed and patted, patted and cooed, "He might have just jumped out the window. Maybe he's still around here somewhere."

David sneered at her with pubescent distain. "Mom. The window was only open like two inches. No way he could've gotten out. Someone took him. He's been kidnapped!" David started bawling again. Lucinda grabbed a pack of tissues from her bag and handed them to him. She checked her watch. It would be impossible to finagle a trip to the fabric and paint store now.

"Let's look," she suggested. "I'll go up towards Orchard Street. You go down towards Elm, okay?"

David sniffed. "Okay."

"Text me." At least David would be using his *bar mitzvah*-gifted iPhone for something practical. Lucinda turned to begin the search, then added, "And use the tissues, Sweetie. Your face is a mess."

They didn't find Balzy, which came as no surprise because Lucinda really did agree with David; someone had probably stolen the dog. What did surprise her was that anyone would want an ugly, grizzle-muzzled, wire-haired terrier with the disposition of a constipated octogenarian.

Mother and son got home at six pm after a fruitless search. Lucinda was due at Brady's at six thirty. With no real samples to show him, she thought she'd create a Pinterest board of design ideas instead, but David claimed the laptop immediately. He sat at the kitchen table scanning photos of Balthazar for the LOST DOG posters he intended to plaster all over Towne. Lucinda put a plate of organic chicken nuggets and ketchup next to her son. It was the best she could do given the time constraints.

"David, I need my computer," she said. "I have a work meeting across the street and need to prepare images to show Brady."

"Mom. This is Balzy. Nothing is more important than our dog."

"Of course not. But life goes on—"

"No, it doesn't! Not until we find Balzy!"

Lucinda took a deep breath. Having the damn dog around until he croaked of natural causes would've been better. She didn't know how much more of David's drama she could stand and it looked like it wasn't going to end anytime soon.

"How much reward should we offer?" David dipped a nugget in ketchup and gulped it down in one bite. Crisis or no crisis, a thirteen-year-old boy will always eat.

"Reward?"

"Duh, Mom. There's always a reward. So how much?"

"How about a hundred dollars?"

"Are you for real? That's insulting. That's like what people pay to get back their sunglasses or something. Not a member of their family."

"Two fifty," Lucinda offered.

He shook his head.

"So? How much then, Davey?"

"Five hundred for information leading to his whereabouts. A thousand for his return."

At this point Lucinda would've agreed to anything because all she wanted to do was get her computer back. If she got the job with Brady she'd have money to burn.

She could get David his own computer. "Okay fine. But I need my laptop ASAP." Lucinda prayed whoever took the damn dog had travelled far, far from Towne.

"I can't stop now," David dipped another nugget. "I'm in the middle of designing. I want to print them out right away. Then I'm going to ride my bike and post them on every single lamppost and wall I can find."

How could a mother squash such determination? His tenacity is an attribute, Lucinda told herself, something she should support. Besides, she really needed to change into something more professional, yet stylish for the meeting. Her new Nicole Miller pansy print sundress would be perfect. Not too sexy, not too short. Summery and bright. "Alright. But don't under any circumstances ride your bike around after dark, you hear me?"

David smiled at her, for the first time in weeks. "Don't worry, Mom. I'm not stupid."

Brady: Keeping It Under Wraps

Brady stared out through the grimy window of his ridiculously huge living room, a room which would've made a bodacious place for some modified indoor ball sports, but for the precariously dangling chandelier crystals and matching wall sconces. He was waiting and watching impatiently for Lucinda. Lovely Lucinda gumming up the works. Lucinda with a doughy belly Brady wanted to test squeeze like a cantaloupe. Lucinda of the hee-haw laugh so deep and throaty it dripped of porn. Lucinda of the swinging breasts, a pair that begged to be gripped and nuzzled. Lucinda who smelled of some mysterious, over-ripe fruit. Lucinda who was middle-aged and dumpy and who Brady never would have noticed in his former life.

Lucinda, who for some unfathomable reason got Brady as hard as a fifteen-year-old horndog.

As he watched and waited, Lucinda's garage door opened and a kid with blondish hair wobbled out on a bicycle and rode away. He had to be Lucinda's kid. The coloring, the slightly weak chin. Brady had seen another kid on a bicycle earlier that day. A weird-looking girl on an old-fashioned Sting Ray bike. She was like something out of a low budget horror film, pale and scrawny, hair like a rat's nest, dressed for rain even though it was dry as the desert. They'd locked eyes for a second and then she took off. That banana seat, those plastic handlebar streamers brought back memories Brady would just as soon forget, flashbacks to riding his own Sting Ray up and down the Skokie streets, bored shitless, looking for something to do. Anything but go back to his cookie-cutter ranch house and listen to his father berate his downtrodden mother, or get cornered and shamed by the asshole himself.

Reginald Cole, dead now for five years, had had a chip on his shoulder the size of the Grand Canyon. A mid-level executive at a Chicago advertising agency, Reg never made it to the top, was forever passed over. The only upscale thing Reginald had was his pretentious faux-Brit first name, a gift from his unwed, illegal immigrant Irish mother.

"Your father is a burden you carry in your balls," Tamago told Brady in one of their first one-on-one tutorials. "He dominates you from the grave, points your penis in all the wrong directions."

Brady's mother Constance, according to his guru, was "like cotton candy, fluffy and of no substance." Momma Connie was a chubby conflict avoider who still adored Brady with unconditional love to near-suffocation. Before he'd become Beauteous, Brady and Constance Facetimed every day. But Tamago insisted Brady cut that shit out. "You need to stay away from that sweet pussy mama," Tamago warned.

"Enough with the everyday calls. Wear your own dress, Brady. Dance like a woodland nymph. Be a beautiful man."

Brady knew he was beautiful. He'd been working that angle for years. His beauty had gotten him his first modeling gig with Calvin in the '90s, and from there it was a bitchin', party-filled road to Hollywood.

But Tamago was talking about a different kind of beauty. A kind Brady was still trying to find, even after he'd sunk eight thousand bucks into the Beauteous Man Program. Brady needed to prove he was truly beauteous and capable of great things. So, once Lucinda finally came across the street to see him, Brady greeted her with Tamago's chaste but loving Holy Head to Headshake, placing his left palm to the left side of his skull, signifying support from the logical left hemisphere of his brain, while taking his right hand to the right side of Lucinda's head, encouraging a flow of creativity and love.

Her hair, if he was honest, felt like dry straw. But she wore an adorable pansy print dress that tested his Beauteous limits. They were supposed to go over design ideas for the Mansion, but it seemed obvious to Brady from the way she acted, the hints she dropped, that Lucinda wanted more.

"Great to see you again, Lucinda," Brady said. "You look incredible."

Lucinda blushed. "Aw sure. I bet you say that to all the old ladies."

How could he tell her he was turned on by her wrinkles and saggy kneecaps, when he was completely shocked himself by his attraction? Stay on the Beauteous Path, he told himself. Keep things from getting sexual. "Really you look stunning. I love your dress." Compliment the clothes not what's in the clothes, thought Brady. Even if it does make you sound gay.

Lucinda looked down at the giant pansy petals spreading across her chest. In all honesty, Brady thought the dress was sort of tacky. "Oh, this old thing?" she said. "Thanks. I love yours also."

There was nothing attractive about the stupid potato sack Brady was required to wear, but he appreciated Lucinda's attempt at humor. He laughed, but inside he thought, God damn you, Beauteous caftan.

Angus came running towards them. He passed Brady and went right for a look-see and sniff under Lucinda dress.

"Angus, no," Brady commanded.

Lucinda giggled and pushed Angus' head away. She knelt down so her face was level with the dog's. "Hello Big Boy," she cooed. Angus slathered her cheek with his giant tongue. "What a sweetie."

Lucky damn dog, doing what Brady wanted to do, and getting away with it. "Yeah, he's pretty great," said Brady. "He really digs it here. Especially the backyard. Literally. He digs it. He's back there for hours making a hole near the fence and barking. It's like he's having conversations with invisible friends or something."

Lucinda stood up and heaved a big sigh. "Our old dog Balthazar disappeared today."

"Whoa. That sucks. I'm so sorry."

"Thanks." Lucinda sighed. "My son David is beside himself. Fa-reaking out. Right now he's riding his bike all over town posting LOST DOG posters everywhere he can think of."

No wonder the kid seemed so determined, thought Brady. He didn't mention he'd seen David leaving because then Lucinda would know he'd been staring out the window waiting for her. The truth of that made Brady feel pathetic and needy. Even though access to those kind of feelings might serve Brady on his path towards greater authenticity. Brady didn't do pathetic and needy. Not yet, at least.

Luckily Lucinda was already on to other things. She looked over Brady's shoulder towards the kitchen. "I can't wait to show you my ideas for your countertops. Should we…"

"Oh we should," Brady said lifting the canvas bag off her shoulder. He couldn't help himself. He let his fingers trace a quick line down her bare arm. "We definitely should."

Lucinda shivered. "Alright then. Let's get to it."

Chapter Five

Nell: Seeing

Running into David Leibowitz at ARF had nearly undone Nell, who was already operating with loose wires. Then she saw him swipe the blobby brown blouse and forgot all the discomfort he and his family had caused her back in high school. It hadn't been David's fault. He'd been one of her better piano students. His playing was uneven, but he oozed passion and musicality. After completing some simple Schumann or Debussy, David would gaze up at Nell as if she were a goddess, melting Nell's brittle shell. She let David lean against her, sniff and stroke her hair. She hadn't minded this puppy-like affection. She relaxed considerably sitting next to David on the piano bench in his den while his parents bickered audibly in an upstairs bedroom.

Then there came that day when David's creepy father walked in on them.

"Hey, hey, hey," a knowing sneer spread wide on Mr. Leibowitz's tanning salon tan face. "What's going on in here?"

David pulled his head off Nell's shoulder and sat bolt upright.

"David is learning Für Elise." Nell's voice quavered. "He's doing really well."

Mr. Leibowitz glanced at David the way Nell's father glanced at articles written by colleagues he envied; eyes hooded, nostrils flared, jaw set in a vise grip. Then he looked back at Nell and his face melted like it was a wax candle, all goopy and unformed.

"With such a gorgeous creature for a teacher, of course he's doing well." Mr. Leibowitz walked up behind Nell, who turned back to sit facing the piano. "How about you give me a few lessons also."

Nell pretended not to hear. "Come on, David. Start again and try not to pause after the ritard."

David didn't seem to know what to do. He looked at Nell looking straight ahead at the sheet music, then up at his father, standing behind Nell. She could feel him looking down at the top of her head, could hear the man's breathing, ragged and quick.

Please don't touch me, please don't touch me, please don't touch me, Nell prayed.

Finally Mr. Leibowitz spoke. "Come on Dave. You heard your teacher. I want to hear what you've got." He put his dry, cold hands on either side of Nell's neck, so close if he turned his fingers towards each other he could choke her. Instead he kneaded the flesh of her shoulders in a slow, depraved rhythm, letting his fingers slip under the boundary of her flimsy cotton neckline, ignoring Nell's shivering goose-pimpled flesh, her rigid, ungiving posture, her blatant unyielding.

David played abysmally. He kept glancing sideways,

noticing his father touch Nell as if he were diddling with a toy. It sounded as if David had never played this piece before, when in fact he'd been playing it, quite decently, for months. When David finished, his father's hands did not. He kept kneading and plunging until Nell lurched her body forward, ramming her ribcage into the piano keys, which would leave a horizontal bruise just below her breasts that lasted for weeks.

"Bravo," said Mr. Leibowitz, his tone flat and noncommittal. Then he walked out of the room.

After that, David's innocent snuffling got mixed up in Nell's mind with his father's knowing leer and shuddersome touch. Confusion short-circuited Nell's already precarious framework. Nell felt sullied, exposed. She felt guilty for accepting David's affection. That was the last piano lesson she taught. Another avenue to normality, closed.

At the ARF thrift store Nell left a slightly older, but still gentle, David behind once more. She wished him well, even blew him a kiss. As she slinked up the sidewalk towards her bike, she passed a familiar station wagon, with an open window. The dog, David's dog, the one who had some pretentious name, now ancient, stared up at her through the slightly opened window, his ears propped excitedly, his desire for freedom clear. Here was one Leibowitz Nell could save.

Abe: Help is on the way

Two weeks since Gordon had run away, and Abe felt the loss as a constant punch to his solar plexus. He'd taken to wandering up and down the deserted Towne streets searching for hours. Abe trudged up bluestone paths to front doors and poked his head through side windows. He tiptoed past parked SUVs to peer over backyard fences. More than once Abe's uninvited appearance at garden gates, back doors, and front stoops led to a suspicious "Excuse me. Can I help you" or a misguided "Finally. UPS."

But there was no Gordon. No trace. More than once Abe caught a glimpse of "Freaky Sting Ray Girl," as he privately called her, that crusty-looking, wild-haired girl-creature on her bike. But the moment she became aware of Abe's presence she rode away as if he was the one who carried a curse or communicable disease. Unlucky Abe felt this was, perhaps, a wise assessment. Maybe he was the real freak.

After fruitless on-the-ground searching, Abe would sit at his computer and check the postings he'd done online: FindFido.com, the Facebook page for Lost Dogs of Allenwood County, Animal Control, and lastly, a sketchy site called PitbullPals.com.

No sign of Gordon anywhere. On the third Saturday since Gordon's exodus, Abe sat slumped on the couch like a retiree in a nursing home common room waiting for Bingo time while Claire ran a Swiffer cloth along the window sills. Relaxation for Claire always involved some kind of productive puttering.

"Your mother has nothing to do," said Claire. They'd been discussing child care. "We'd be doing her a favor by letting her come and help with Mouse. Your father's been dead almost eight years and she still acts like a grieving widow. She's stopped volunteering at the library. All her friends have moved to Florida full time."

Abe could hardly think beyond Gordon's absence. He'd been a muddle-brained mess. But the idea of his mother in his home, in his business, was like an instant shot of espresso, complete with the gastric distress. "No way," he grunted.

"She's family, Abe. And it's free."

It will not be free, Abe thought. With his mother there were always hidden costs. "How about instead we call that girl we had in to babysit Mouse when we went to the movies with Kate and Andrew?"

Claire groaned. "She was awful. She even told us herself she didn't want to come back, remember?"

It had been early on, when Milo was 9 months old. The babysitter had a poetic, Anglo name Abe couldn't quite recall; Neve or Norah. Maybe Nell. Whatever her name, she was clearly not cut out for the job. The girl had posted a "Local Babysitter Available" listing on the Towne Parents Listserv. Her credentials seemed fine at the time: born and raised in Towne, graduated from an elite East Coast Ivy, played piano, temporarily stuck in millennial quasi-unemployment.

The sitter was good on paper only. Abe and Claire had come home that night to a wide-awake poopy-diapered Milo, sitting next to the girl on the couch, both of them shoveling organic Cheerios into their mouths straight from the box. Abe remembered her having an Aubrey Beardsley kind of appeal. Not his type, exactly, but he knew plenty of aspiring poets back in the City who would have found her beautiful. She had mounds of unruly reddish curls and spooky green eyes that looked like she was processing information from two separate planets at the same time.

"I'm so sorry," the babysitter said. But she hadn't sounded sorry, she sounded impatient and ready to bolt, "I don't think I'm really cut out for this kind of work."

Claire had insisted they pay her anyway, and the well-educated ingrate left without even saying thanks.

"Yeah, you're right," Abe nodded. "She sucked." While Abe remembered Nell-Neve-Norah, it occurred to him that Freaky Sting Ray Girl reminded him of the babysitter. They could be sisters, though the girl on the bike was skinny and unkempt with a feral, desperate look, while the babysitter had been a space-shot, but neat as a pin in a violet colored, floor-length dress. Jailbait for those poets.

Abe glanced at Milo, sitting on the living room rug in a pretzel position only a baby or advanced yogi could achieve without major next-day regret. It was the same cross-legged position Milo had been sitting in when Abe had discovered him among the Diet Coke cans at the Gas n' Go. Now Milo was trying to jam a large oval lid onto a small square pan. Claire and Abe had about fifteen seconds to wrap up their discussion before all whiny hell broke loose.

Claire had a valid point. Abe wasn't functioning. He'd tried to write after the horrendous outing with Gordon and Milo. Talk about source material. Here was the meaty stuff of loss and mourning. His own trauma of near catastrophe should've provided literary, memoir-inspired gold. But the thoughts bubbling in his brain collided without coherence. Then they popped, disappearing with no trace of original idea left.

If Claire only knew how far from productive Abe was. But his mother? Every week? How did it come to this?

"My mother will make Mouse waffles every morning for breakfast. You want Mouse to eat all that fructose and gluten?"

Claire winced.

"Vat's wrong vith vaffles?" Abe added with a Yiddish twang.

"Don't be cute."

"Also, it's one thing to be Grandma for a few hours on a weekend afternoon. But every day? Who knows if my mother can handle that much of him." Abe pointed at Mouse whose face turned scarlet, brow furrowed like a weightlifter's as he wedged the mis-matched pieces of kitchenware together. "He's a monster sometimes."

As if on cue, Milo gave up, hurling the pot lid in a weak arc, letting out a cat-caught-under-a-hot-radiator squeal.

Instinctively, Abe glanced to the corner where Gordon had slept, knowing that this kind of cry from Milo would unnerve Gordon, and elicit a barking spree. But, oh yeah; No Gordon. Not any more.

Claire dashed over and scooped Milo up, cooing motherly comfort. "Alright Sweetmeat," she sing-songed as Milo buried his face in the lower regions of her chest, searching like a blind mole burrowing through darkness. Claire fiddled with child and clothing expertly, and while still standing she attached Milo to her left nipple.

It would not have been Abe's parenting choice, even if he had nursing capabilities. Wasn't there something he'd read about toddlers needing to learn frustration tolerance? Then again, what did that really mean? Who, at any age, could tolerate being frustrated? But all weekend parenting decisions belonged to Claire. She missed out on the precious and infuriating Milo moments weekdays, when she was busy analyzing figures and collecting data so the hedge fund's millionaire clients could take calculated financial risks.

"Barbara is coming, Abe," She said softly, so as not to disturb the Mouse. "You lost Gordon, for fuck's sake."

"I didn't lose Gordon," Abe snapped. "He ran away."

"Whatever," Claire hissed, trying to stay calm while Milo slurped away. "You're totally overwhelmed. You need help. You need to get your shit together and work on *The Gist*. Unless you no longer want to finish your novel, in which case it might be a good idea to think of some other way to use your time."

Abe, already drowning in a sea of inertia, weighed down in cement shoes of mourning, didn't have a choice. If push came to shove, if Abe really needed a fix, there was that sketchy bar near the train station he'd been to once that had ESPN playing 24/7.

"Call your mother and ask when she wants to start."

Claire glanced down at Milo's satin-brown hair. "We're busy at the moment."

Milo greedily nursed, making him the only truly happy person in the room. Before getting up to call his mother, Abe glanced once again to the corner, to the former domain of Gordon, Ultimate King of Contentment. If Gordon had been there he would've outdone them all in the happiness department with his slobbery dog brand of easy-breezy chill.

Paddy: Oodles of Poodles

The small colonial looked like a stage set that first warm April morning in 1958; crisp white shingles, glossy black shutters with quaint fleur-de-lis cutouts, flawless roof tiles, and bright brick chimney. The yard was impeccable; the grass crew-cut and uniformly green, the boxwoods along the slate walkway trimmed in a perfect horizontal, every daffodil a spurt of sunshine. There was a small apple tree in the back yard. Paddy imagined a future tire swing.

Paddy was a city boy, and Mariah a city girl. They'd both only lived in apartments. First in small tenement flats kept spectacularly clean by immigrant mothers, sharing beds with younger siblings and hall toilets with neighbors, using the corner payphone to reach the world outside their ghettos, neighborhoods that were in and of themselves entire worlds. After the war, Paddy made do in SROs, and Mariah found comfort and safety in all-female rooming houses. Then they met and fireworks filled the sky. After marrying, they moved to the last place, a cramped and dingy basement apartment where garbage bins limited their view of the pedestrian trudge and scurry, where the cockroaches were so large they spooked the mice.

Pennies were saved. Many, many pennies. Paddy was a

crackerjack mechanic and Mariah the fastest typist in her pool. They moved swiftly up their respective ladders. When suburbs sprouted like dandelions along new expressways spreading from city centers, Paddy saw opportunity and ran with it. All those new homeowners had cars, and cars, like people, needed looking after.

The house in Towne cost every cent they'd saved. Paddy worked his butt off for Schepp, who had the franchise on the Gulf Service Station. Schepp however, was a lousy mechanic. Better with booze than wheel bearings. Eventually he sold the franchise to Paddy and opened Schepp's Saloon, across from the train station.

Paddy ran his gas station like a well-oiled machine. His became the most successful Gulf franchise in the whole state. Things were so good Mariah quit her job in the City so they could make some babies. But the family Paddy and Mariah planned for never materialized. Five years of trying and not succeeding, and five more to get over the failure. Early on, Paddy was the one who felt it badly, while Mariah remained optimistic.

"Oh come on, Grumpy," she'd grabbed Paddy's calloused hand and put it to her cheek. "There's always next month."

And the next month, and the next. There weren't the new-fangled treatments back then, the harvesting of eggs in petri dishes, or tests on how robustly a man's tadpoles could swim. After the first year, tensions mounted. Mariah's brightness imperceptibly faded, Paddy's drinking increased. Paddy still remembered the day Mariah decided to put the kibosh on the whole thing. He'd barely walked through the front door when she marched out of the kitchen and announced, "I've made a decision, Paddy. No more trying to have a baby. I'm done. From now on sex is just going to be for the fun of it. You hear me?"

Her eyes had a brilliance he'd never seen before. Her jaw was set and her hands were clenched in fists. Paddy knew it wasn't him she was steeling herself against. It was her own resolve.

He would've kept going for it, but this was Mariah's call to make. So all he'd done was shrug and walk past her to the liquor cabinet.

Eventually they adopted a series of toy poodles. Buttercup, Tiger, Coochy Coo, Matilda, and lastly Barney. Smart little buggers, each and every one. Mariah's kick was back in her heels. Paddy loved the dogs almost as much as she did. He walked them, fed them, played with them. They all loved it when Paddy scooched his foot underneath their tiny bellies and with a gentle whoopsy daisy, gave them harmless, airborne rides. Each poodle gleeful while free falling, skittering back to Paddy over and over, wanting more.

The dogs all died, as all living things do. Buttercup—kidney failure, Tiger—distracted driver, Coochy Coo—chocolate overdose, Matilda—bone cancer. Now Barney was gone, though not necessarily dead. He'd been stolen, gotten lost, or run away.

Most days, Paddy returned from the station to find Barney in his spot next to Mariah's ottoman, or sleeping under the apple tree, his second favorite snooze location. But then came the day when the dog wasn't in either place. His food and water bowls were untouched. There were no tell-tale poops in his usual backyard spots.

Where was that little motherfucker, Paddy wondered. "Barney!" Paddy called into the thick humid air as he trudged through the overgrown grass of his neglected backyard. "Come on, you little devil!"

Barney had never ventured far before. Of all the poodles he was the most passive, a dedicated home-body. So which was it: lost, stolen, or run away? The pooch wasn't the brightest either. That would've been Matilda. Brainy little beast she was. If Barney had ventured past the boxwoods, he could've easily gotten lost. Barney was the color of melted caramel, easy on the eyes, a perfect poodle specimen, so someone might have stolen him. But maybe Barney had run away? Perhaps the dog grew tired of living with grumpy old Paddy, who'd long been a widower with a stone cavern for a heart, a geezer with a treasure trove of aggression stored in his rusty mind.

Whatever the case, it was Paddy's to solve. He felt Mariah's eyes upon him more than ever as he searched the yard and wandered into every empty room of his time-warped, calico-ed, doily-ed house looking for his dog.

Eventually Paddy gave up. He collapsed into his Laz-Y-Boy and mulled over the incident with Gloria, such a shameful betrayal borne out of his own stupidity. But this was worse. Losing Mariah's dog was a betrayal too grand to bear. How Paddy missed his wife. Paddy needed to blur the edges. Paddy craved fortification, deserved a nip. There was no booze in the house. Hadn't been any for almost a year. One trip to Schepp's. One scotch. That's all. After that he'd figure out what to do. After that he'd be right as rain.

Nell: Boris née Barney

After Nell saved Balthazar, she knew her quest had to continue. She attached a large basket between the handlebars of her Sting Ray, and a red wagon to her rear wheel when out on her search and rescue missions. Mid-mornings were best for central Towne searches, as most of the residents were out of their houses at jobs, or errands, yoga, or Pilates. Dogs were imprisoned inside crates in mudrooms or dens, easily accessible as most households left their back doors unlocked. Those that did have locked doors had hidden keys in places so obvious, Nell wondered if any of these dog enslavers had any sense at all. Some dogs were outdoors, harnessed to leashes attached to absurd wires that ran from one tree to another. Tortuous, Nell thought, for naturally free-ranging canines to run the same repeated line back and forth, back and forth with no variation, all day long. Dogs were sleeping on silly beds in shaded—but still hot—porches, crying in garages, scratching at windows, slobbering on sliding glass doors.

Nell did careful reconnaissance, casing out each home, recording schedules, noting human personal habits, sometimes waiting only hours, sometimes days till the coast was clear. Once all was safe, Nell put larger dogs in the wagon, smaller ones in the basket. Hiding them from sight under a lightweight sheet, she gave them meaty bones to chew on to keep them quiet, and after triple-checking that all systems were go, chauffeured them back to her retreat.

It was one late August afternoon shortly after she'd found Balthazar in the back of the Leibowitz' station wagon that Nell had the opportunity to rescue poor Barney, a fluffy toy poodle, abandoned in his backyard all day long, whining with heartbreaking relentlessness, only the occasional shade of an apple tree to give him comfort and rest from the blistering sun. She'd watched Barney for weeks, spying on him from a perch high in the apple tree. The poor little dog seemed so trapped and forlorn. Months earlier, there'd been a woman there, a sweet-seeming old fool who talked to herself and laughed at odd intervals. The poodle seemed happy when the woman was still about, but then the woman disappeared and Barney had been left with only that old grump from the Gas n' Go for company. Now the old man was gone and the timing was right. Nell swooped the dog up—along with a bagful of apples—and took him to her pup paradise, where he joined Raphael, formerly Gordon, and Pepe, once known as Balthazar, and six other pups.

Rechristened Boris, the lucky poodle's mourning days were soon over.

David: Searching for Balzy

God was punishing David for all his stealing. It was his fault, he knew it. God took Balzy. Or rather, God had let someone take Balzy, giving to them and taking from David. But David wasn't going to let God have his—or her—way.

David rode like the wind. His backpack was filled with freshly copied HAVE YOU SEEN BALTHAZAR? flyers, scotch tape, thumbtacks, a hammer, and nails. David was prepared for any and all walls. He'd plaster Towne's flat public surfaces with his dog's precious image. It was an old photo, but once David tweaked it in Photoshop, added some gray whiskers and red-rimmed Balzy's lower eyelids, it was a reasonable resemblance. His smelly buddy would be impossible to miss, impossible to forget.

David worked hard. The trash cans in front of the CVS demanded scotch tape. The telephone poles along Cedar Drive required nails. The bulletin boards at the Library, Bagel Bonanza, and Scotto's Pizzeria took the easy punch of thumbtacks.

David was starving, his chicken nugget dinner a dim memory after two hours of solid postering. Still, there was more ground to be covered. He wanted to put a HAVE YOU SEEN BALTHAZAR? poster up on the public noticeboard at the train station and on the boarded-up storefront next to Schepp's Saloon, across the street.

David coasted to a nearby corner and leaned his bicycle against a parking sign in front of Schepp's. Aside from being a place for alcoholic commuters and unemployed bums, Schepp's was notorious for not carding local high school students after 1 am on Monday nights. It was a rite of passage to sneak out on a week night while parents slept or pretended to sleep. High schoolers would meet at Allenwood Park to suck down pilfered beers first. After that they'd stumble towards Schepp's, a bunch of plastered lightweights with wads of cash saved from allowances, babysitting gigs, and lawn jobs. They thought they were cooler than cool. On slow Mondays they were Schepp's most reliable customers.

Chucky had once told David after soccer practice—which seemed like eons ago since David had bailed on the team this season—that he couldn't wait to get plowed at Schepp's and find some hot older woman to "do" in a booth in the back. David had nodded and said, "Totally. Me too," but really the idea of drunken sex in a creepy place like Schepp's with an old lady skeeved David out more than the idea of eating a plate of worms or having his fingernails ripped out one by one.

Before putting up his final posters, David peeked into Schepp's. The place was nearly empty. Through the grimy window David could see the TV above bottles of alcohol flickering like a light show. There were only two men sitting at the bar. David recognized one. The old grump from the Gas n' Go. David's former fantasy villain, the one that terrorized David the fairy.

The real gas station man inside Schepp's didn't look scary, he looked pathetic. He had an old man's lumpy and pale potato head plopped on top of a potato body. His hair was sparse and white. Rolls of flab spilled off the back of his neck over the collar of his olive green gas station guy work shirt. He leaned forward atop his stool, as if he had no backbone, as if he might face plant if not for the support of his ancient elbows on the bar.

The other man was from the City. David could tell. There was something about the way those guys dressed that differed from his neatnik father and everybody else who actually liked the suburbs. No faux-leather bomber jackets or smooth-fronted slacks. No squishy clean tennis shoes. No coiffed hair. The City dudes had a certain careless coolness that poseurs like David's father could never attain. They wore hoodies. Lumber shirts. Converse or Vans. David could tell them from the way they kept, or rather unkept their hair. This guy's wavy brown was a shaggy, gnarly mess. Imbalanced in a 'who the fuck cares' kind of way. He had a scraggly beard, and wore thick black-framed glasses.

Both the men inside Schepp's were far from any older version David might imagine for his future self. Plus there was no way he could imagine dressing, being, or existing like his own father in any way, shape, or form. Ultimately David couldn't see himself at Schepp's in any version of Towne manliness available to him. So when the time came in a few years, how would David stomach going inside that place? What would he wear to hide his true nature? To define his true nature? To protect himself?

David quickly taped a poster to the boarded-up storefront next to Schepp's and skittered across the street to the train station noticeboard.

When his parents were still together David and his mother would occasionally pick his father up at the station and David would check out the notices on the board while his mother waited in the car. He'd look at the desperate pleas about missing dogs, cats, watches, necklaces, and sentimental but worthless objects and feel little or nothing. He'd been a creeper, never truly concerned about anyone else, mostly just trying on other people's joys and pains like he did their skirts and sweater sets. Now, after losing Balzy he felt like a grown-up. His heart ached for everyone who'd ever lost anything, because now he knew how bad it sucked.

Lucinda: Not all it's cracked up to be

Lucinda was glad she'd slipped the bottle of wine in her bag before she left home. Though she preferred the slightly sweeter, fruitier buzz of a good Chardonnay, this tart Pinot from a reliably upscale winery was sure to make an impression on Brady Cole.

But now it seemed she was the only one drinking the stuff.

"It's against Tamago's rules," Brady shrugged with a coy little smile that matched the shrug perfectly. "But don't let me stop you."

He popped the cork like a pro and poured her a sizable glass. Brady lifted his tumbler of green gunk—a blend of kale-laden healthfulness he was required to drink three times a day—and toasted, "Here's to us."

They clinked. Lucinda took a hearty swig. The Pinot was vinegar-y. Totally off. It was good Brady was teetotaling. She was thus saved from bad wine embarrassment. Lucinda would continue drinking it though. She wanted the buzz almost as badly as she wanted the job.

"So, shall I show you some of my initial ideas?" she asked.

Brady responded with another shrug-smile combo. He stared at her all moony eyed. Once again Lucinda wondered if he was on drugs. She took another big gulp of the nearly unpalatable Pinot.

"Okay then. I'll take that as a yes." Lucinda reached in to her satchel and pulled out Post-it-laden copies of *Elle Decor* and *Architectural Digest* and spread them on the mustard colored formica counter top. The entire Kearny Mansion kitchen was a disaster of mid-70's tastelessness. The countertops, most offensive. "Since we're in the kitchen, I'll show you some cabinets and countertops that would work really well in here. I thought bringing back some period-sensitive original cabinetry combined with modern appliances and hardware would be stunning."

Lucinda flipped open to a full-page spread of a kitchen in a giant manor house somewhere in Cornwall belonging to a British rock star from the 60's and his fading beauty of a blue-blooded wife. Lucinda coveted this kitchen herself. She'd spent more time than she liked to admit staring at these pages imagining herself just like the wife, in the same diaphanous floor-length peasant skirt, bare-footed with a cluster of messy peonies in her arms.

"What do you think of this?" she asked Brady.

Brady glanced quickly at the rock star and his wife in their perfect kitchen then beamed back at Lucinda. "Sure."

"Sure what?"

"Sure whatever you think is best. You're the expert." The hand not holding his tumbler of slime inched over to cover Lucinda's. "I'll do anything you want."

This is weird, thought Lucinda. She wanted to move her hand out from under Brady's but if she did he might stop being so pliable. The best kind of design client was a flexible one, preferably someone like Brady with limited taste and lots of cash. "So you like the dark cherry cabinets with the cream colored countertops?"

Brady moved closer. His thigh pressed against hers as he leaned towards her and whispered. "I love cherries. I love cream. Cherries on top. Cream of the crop."

It had been a long, long time since anyone had come on to Lucinda. She'd been shrouded in the Middle-aged Matron Invisibility Cloak for at least five years. The UPS guy had stopped blatantly staring at her chest as she fingered her signature on his scanner, the old guy at the pizzeria no longer called her "Mi Amore" when she picked up a pie. Dan had stopped initiating sex at least two years before their divorce. That, at least, had been somewhat of a relief. Dan's perfunctory ass grab, pucker kiss approach had long ceased to arouse her. Another woman might've appreciated Dan's clean, minty breath, obsessively showered and shaved, deodorized body, his ability to keep an erection and come simultaneously when she did. Lucinda, however, felt a constant flicker of barely contained rage towards her control-freak husband, who could even master his libido, which was a thing men were supposed to be powerless to control.

Now dress-wearing, unruly Brady was coming on to her and it was beyond super weird. Not quite frightening, but definitely bizarre. "And what about those modern cabinet pulls?" Lucinda proceeded as if she hadn't noticed. "I happen to adore the geometric juxtaposed with the old heritage appeal."

"I'm down with geometry. I believe in symmetry. You know, when things align. Like you and me."

"Okay then..." Lucinda polished off the last dregs of Pinot. She slowly withdrew her hand out from under Brady's increasingly clammy one to grab the wine bottle and pour herself a second glass.

"Can I just say something?" Brady asked.

"Of course. It's your house."

"I love hearing you talk about design."

Another thing Lucinda hadn't heard for years. Back when she was designing and Dan had his newly successful contracting business, she'd hoped they'd be a team. But instead she'd sit and listen to Dan drone on about concrete pours and rebar and feign enthusiasm. When she would talk about damask versus linen Dan's eyes glazed over as if she'd crumbled a Klonipin into his Miller High Life. Which, as the years went on, she'd been tempted more than once to do.

"Why thank you," Lucinda blushed.

"You're like a real pro."

Now Lucinda was the one who shrugged. Hers, a sheepish sort of sluff up and down. "Well, I suppose—"

"No. Don't suppose. Own it. You are a pro."

"Okay…"

"Like, you could do anything you want."

"Well, I'm sure you have limits. I'd never go beyond your budget."

"I don't think I have any limits, when it comes to you." Brady came to stand behind her. He started kneading her shoulders. A little friendly neck rub. If it stayed like this everything would be okay. Then Brady spoiled it by saying, "I can't keep my hands off you. I want to give to you."

Or maybe he hadn't spoiled anything. Maybe it was Lucinda who was spoiling things.

"I want to make love to you," he whispered in her ear.

Brady Cole wanted to what? Sex. He was offering sex. Something she hadn't had in over a year, except with herself. Sex with Dan had always been so hygienic, a missionary fuck always punctuated at both ends by mandatory showers. Sheets were changed if there was any spillage. And here was Brady Cole offering to do stuff to her body that might feel good. He also wanted to pay her to fix up his house. And that felt better than anything, really.

Lucinda turned around so that she and Brady were face to face. His hard-on pressed against her belly. He was tall, handsome. Everyone said so. What did she have to lose? Even if he was on drugs and only wanted to fuck her because he was hallucinating. Even if she felt as turned on by him as a clock with a dead battery. Recently Lucinda had masturbated to the fantasy of the craggy old rock star screwing her on the granite topped island in the Cornwall kitchen from the *Elle Decor* spread. Humping away, next to the Bernard Leach ceramic tureen filled with garden grown radishes. Maybe she'd use that fantasy now.

"Okay." she said to Brady. "But not here. This kitchen is atrocious."

Brady: Everything and More

Pheromones, thought Brady. That's what it had to be. Lucinda must've been emitting those invisible whatever-they-weres and his whatever-they-weres were responding in kind. How else could Brady make sense of this insatiable attraction?

He'd slipped the bag off her shoulder, and immediately noticed the bottle of wine. Man, he longed to chug that whole thing down. But he'd already been having a hard enough time keeping the sex thing under control. If he broke down and drank, there'd've been no telling what he'd do. Instead he made do with his evening shake; a combination of kale, spirulina, beets, apples, and parsley. Good for the brain. Good for the soul. Good for the toilet.

Lucinda took hearty swig after hearty swig of the vinegary smelling wine. Her nose crinkled in adorable distaste. Brady liked a woman who wasn't picky about her booze. He'd been with his share of liquor snobs, women who only drank high-end vodka because of the lower calorie count, or organic wines from a specific "grape-friendly" winery in Mendicino.

When she'd asked him if he wanted to see her ideas for redecorating the mansion, all he could do was shrug. The spell she had over him was intoxicating. Who needed wine?

Lucinda spread all sorts of images out for Brady to look at, but all he could focus on was her. Her smell, a blend of mysterious, musky, sweaty odors seemed essential. She was essential. Lucinda was a magnet and he was a bunch of discombobulated iron shavings. The hand not holding his tumbler of slime inched over to cover Lucinda's hand. She looked up at him with the most inviting smile.

"I want to make love to you," he whispered in her ear. Tamago's Beauteous Rule Number Two be damned.

They ended up outside. They fumbled about at first, awkward like teenagers, too many dresses, too much fabric between them. Brady unzipped Lucinda's pansy-patterned shift and grocked at her freckled, hefty boobs, harnessed and held aloft by serious lace and wire girding. Brady undid her bra. Usually he preferred smallish breasts that stayed upright on their own, but these pendulous melons were epic beauties. Brady took this shift in his predilections as a sign. Maybe he was becoming less shallow, more dimensional. Someone who could see beyond the surface of things, could look beyond crepey necks, bulging arm pits, and hints of grey around the temples. Maybe his work toward beauteousness was paying off.

He did everything in his power to please her there on the chaise lounge, surrounded by the thrum of late summer cicadas, sweat pouring off her body, juices flowing inside and out, every lovely orifice attended to. When she came, she turned her head to the side—most likely overwhelmed by Brady's attractiveness—and shouted one single "Oh!" which caused Brady to collapse in his own spasms of wicked release.

Brady turned his own head sideways so they could rest cheek to cheek. It was then he noticed Angus at the far side of the yard digging a hole by the fence. Brady was impressed by his dog's determination; Angus rarely showed such drive. When the dog shimmied under the fence Brady's first thought was, wow, go for it Big A. But Lucinda seemed alarmed.

"Brady," she twisted underneath him, "Angus! He's run away!"

Brady leapt off the chaise and ran buck-naked

towards the pawed mounds of unearthed rubble and ruined grass that surrounded Angus' impressive hole. In that post-coital moment, if he was totally honest with himself, he was sort of glad the dog was gone. This way he'd have Lucinda's affections all to himself.

Brady turned back and walked towards the woman he was now convinced was the love of his life. She gazed at him as he approached, her brow furrowed as she admired his physique.

"No worries," Brady said. "He's my bro. He'll be back."

"I hope so," she said. "He's quite a marvelous dog."

Brady watched as Lucinda got dressed and imagined a future in which he got to play the toughest, meatiest role of his life; Brady Cole, the quintessentially decent guy.

Nell: Homeward Angel

Angus, a goofy yellow Lab, found his own way to Nell's compound, arriving one night covered in dirt like a determined pilgrim to Mecca. Nell wasn't surprised. What was growing inside her was a beacon shining a divine light across Towne, and maybe beyond. A psychic signal to all needy pups. Angus was all good humor and enthusiasm, if not that bright. He and Boris bonded immediately, such an unlikely pair, Angus so big and eager, Boris so petite and high-strung.

On the evening of Angus' arrival, after a sudsy rinse with the garden hose to remove the mud and dirt embedded in his golden fur, Angus leapt into Nell's swimming pool to retrieve an empty Doritos bag. He had most likely mistaken bag for bird. Nell sat poolside with her legs dangling in the cool water surrounded by Raphael, Pepe, and Boris, who had, in just a matter of days, formed their own little subpack among Nell's ever-increasing brood. The pit bull, wire terrier, and toy poodle cheered Angus on, their barks a cacophonous symphony. Angus laid the chip bag in Nell's lap and waited for her response.

"You will hereon be known as Eduardo," she said as she scratched Angus under his muzzle. Named after a kind but dim Junior from Chile she'd slept with her sophomore year at college. "You silly, sweet boy."

Eduardo shook his wet body as if electrocuted and a spray of pool water hit Nell right in the heart.

Chapter Six

Nell: Freak Fur Flying

And so, Nell had a mission. She detached the carelessly looped leash of a shivering puppy from a bench in front of a French café while its owner dashed inside for a café au lait. She scooped a panting grizzle-snouted oldster from the back of an overheated SUV parked at an expired meter. She tiptoed through the outskirts of Towne to rural farmland and lured a scrawny mongrel with tidbits of meat pinched between her fingertips. She traveled further away from Towne to find more and more dogs, always returning in the dead of night with her rescues.

Nell did not consider herself a thief. She believed the ever-growing brood of pups were better off in her care. How perfect, her large house with sprawling yard and swimming pool surrounded by a sturdy fence. The dogs frolicked freely: no leashes, no collars, no electric shocks. They pooped and peed wherever they wanted. They ate the stolen goods which Nell fed them to supplement the proper dog food she bought with the stipend from her parents. They swam in, and drank copiously from, the swimming pool which Nell replenished daily with fresh water from the garden hose. Freed from the bondage of family petdom, watch dogism, pocketbook canine arm candyness, all the dogs got along famously.

Overwhelmed with sudden understanding of dogs and their imprisonment, Nell grew keenly aware of how shackled dogs were by human expectations. Each domesticated pet an indentured servant forced to serve purposes they would never choose themselves. Sit. Lay down. Look cute. Kiss children. Kill rats. Don't bark. Well, bark at intruders. Never jump on Aunt Tessa, but prance about like a happy fool when Daddy comes home. Stop scratching. Don't eat that. Stay. Paw. Come. Play dead. If they didn't do as expected there were swift swipes on their snouts. They were threatened, berated, admonished, shamed. Dogs were banished to splintery houses, ratty floor mats, barren room corners. The dogs hadn't chosen any of it, any of it at all. Nell knew in her heart of hearts, recent visions told her so, new inner voices said the same; though born and bred to please, dogs—all dogs—were deeply, profoundly miserable.

Saint Nell removed choke collars and dog tags. She let floppy, curly, or bristly fur grow. She rechristened new arrivals with gentle, ceremonial taps on their noggins with a gymnastics baton left over from Towne Middle School. Though she cherished them all, she had her favorites.

Boris, formerly Barney, whip smart and a natural leader. Eduardo, née Angus, Boris' constant companion. What a pair, what a perfect union. They would lay spread-eagled in the shade of a weeping willow at the edge of Nell's lawn while licking each other's buttholes before focusing on their own.

There was Pepe, once Balthazar, so fat on first arrival that his callused stomach grazed the floor and picked up burrs from the grass. Thanks to Nell's careful monitoring, Pepe grew trimmer. He waddled along with the pack as best he could on stumpy little legs, jolly and no longer scraping bottom. A happy little trooper.

Nell had sweet spots too for Taliban—formerly Sunny, the shaggy Australian shepherd with the amputated tail; Cheseray—formerly Tupper, the ever alert corgi; Bingo the dopey, eager labradoodle, and the only one she already considered aptly named.

Her first and favorite would always be Raphael. His cloddish old name, Gordon, long forgotten. Now always and forever, Raphael. Her stalwart companion. The best of the brood. The leader of the pack. Her first disciple. Her truest friend.

She checked all the Lost Dog sites and created red herrings to protect her brood. If someone posted about one of her beloveds, she created a fake email address to lead them astray, posting messages like, "I saw a dog that fits the description of your Tupper at the lakefront park in Village last Saturday morning with a tall white man with long blond hair, wearing a blue ski cap."

Nell returned to the scene of each rescue she'd made and swiped all "LOST DOG" posters she could find. The posters for Balthazar (that stupid, pretentious name), were everywhere. His former enslavers, the Leibowitz family, most eager for his return. Fat chance, thought Nell. He's my Pepe now.

She kept all her posters in a folder tucked behind a bottle of Sentry Flea and Tick Shampoo. Every now and then she would browse through them to remind herself of the good she'd done. She marveled at the arbitrary value placed on each dog's life, the absurdity of their slave names, monikers that had nothing to do with each dog's true nature, whereas the names she'd bestowed were perfect and pure.

For the dogs in her care, life was a blissful puppy party. Even old timers bounded about Nell's compound as if they'd just been nursed and napped, tummies full of sloshy mother-dog milk. Every creature thrived, and Nell thrived with them, purposeful and contented as she'd never been before. She fed them, groomed them, kissed them. She scratched bellies displayed in supine stretches. She ran and tumbled and tussled. Fetch became as natural to Nell as breathing.

Nell serenaded her growing brood nightly with a varied selection of piano tunes, classical, pop, and a few original pieces she'd composed and never shared with anyone, man or beast. The hound breeds sang along, the others wagged tails in approval. At night they all hunkered together in a giant slobbering heap and slumbered on the cool basement floor. Nell slept among her charges, forsaking her upstairs bedroom with absurd canopy bed and reminders of childhood: Nell's math awards, dusty china dolls, and faded posters of floppy-haired teen boy idols from the previous decade. Instead Nell nestled her body against fur and muscle, inhaled dog farts and cellar mold, perfumed herself with canine breath.

Abe: Mother's little help

"I told her two days a week. That's it. Any more of my mother and I'll go fucking bonkers." Abe's mouth was yeasty from the four—maybe five beers he'd chugged. He stood close to Claire, keeping his voice down so as not to wake Mouse.

Claire's face morphed into Kabuki-like disgust as Abe breathed in her direction. "Ew, Abe. How much have you had to drink?"

The call with his mother had undone Abe. As soon as Claire had gotten home from work earlier that evening, he'd bolted out the door for a fortifying trip to Schepp's, the cavernous dive bar across from the Towne train station, with a sticky wooden counter, cracked red vinyl barstools and high-walled booths that hid all sorts of mischief. If Schepp's were in the City, it had all the makings of an ironic, hip destination. But in Towne Abe found only one other lost soul there, a sad sack drowning sorrows in a smudged tumbler of brown liquor. It took Abe a moment to recognize the old guy as the man from the Gas n' Go. Was this fate? Maybe this guy had seen someone or something after Abe had left, some clue to Gordon's whereabouts. Abe tried to strike up a conversation, first with "Hey, remember me? I'm the idiot who nearly lost his son in your store," which elicited a confused and hostile response: "whoerya callin anidiot?" After Abe finally convinced him that no, he was not calling the guy an idiot, Abe tried to find out more about Gordon, but that led nowhere. After that Abe stuck to friendly barstool type questions with this odd old duck; how long had the old guy lived in Towne, did he come to Schepp's often, who did he favor for the Super Bowl.

None of it led anywhere. The old dude was so sauced he could barely speak. He seemed so shrunken, so alone. Every few minutes his shoulders would shake as if he was having an epileptic fit. His cries were tearless, inward heaving sobs that erupted in sudden, glottal spurts. Abe gave up trying to connect. He moved one stool down to give the man some privacy and satisfied his own needs with another IPA and a rebroadcast of blockheads talking preseason NFL blather. But the gas station man was impossible to ignore. He stared deep in his glass as if it were a crystal ball, muttering "Mariah Barney, Mariah Barney," then pleading for forgiveness.

When the guy put his head down on the sticky counter and closed his eyes, it was clear the poor old codger was in no shape to get himself home on his own. Abe looked through his wallet and examined his driver's license. Patrick O'Halloran. 56 Bluebell Lane. It was just a few blocks from the bar. Patrick had no car keys on him. So he must've walked to Schepp's. In the end, Abe drove him home. After a fair amount of hoisting and stumbling, Abe got Patrick in his car and after that to Patrick's front door. Patrick had sobered up enough to stand on his own two feet and stagger inside. He'd already thrown up outside of Schepp's, so Abe wasn't too worried he'd choke on his own vomit. Hopefully there was someone inside to get Patrick to bed and to give him a hard but loving time in the morning.

Now Abe was home getting his own hard time from Claire. "I had a couple of beers," he lied, "Two. That's all. I swear."

Claire crossed her arms over her gorgeous, milk-filled boobs. Abe felt the inevitable woody, and wondered if he'd get lucky for the first time in two months.

"Okay, my mom can come three days a week." Abe was drunk and horny. He might regret the compromise later. "But that's it."

"Yay. A deal," Claire sighed. She tilted her head sideways. Her straight black hair fell over her left shoulder in a solid, well cleaned curtain. "You're going to be so glad, Abe. I know it. You'll make such headway on the book."

"I'm doing okay now," he lied. "But whatever. Sure. Maybe the extra time will help."

"You're sure you don't want to give me a sneak peek? You used to love my feedback. You said that without my shrewd notes you never would've gotten that story published in Tin House."

That lucky break story. The fucking one and only. Nothing that cool before, and nothing cool or uncool since. He almost wished it had never happened. Abe had to get off this topic. He pulled Claire towards him. "Not yet. Soon." Abe got a whiff of organic jasmine—or was it lavender—shampoo. He grabbed his wife around the waist and attempted to kiss her, get the party started.

"Whoa, Cowboy," she pushed against his softening belly, "No getting near me before some basic oral hygiene."

"Sorry." Abe released his grip and took a few gracious steps away.

"Meet you on the couch," Claire smiled. "Or the living room rug. If you take a shower first."

Abe scampered towards the bathroom. He was stoked. A suburban Kelly Slater at Honolua. Ridin' the wife wave.

Paddy: No dog hair, no hair of the dog

Dewar's double-edged sword. One night at Schepp's was all it took to remind Paddy that booze was a stupid way to clobber himself. He woke with blurry half-memories of someone with him at the bar, a youngish guy, one of Towne's newcomers. A City transplant. Or so Paddy assumed. Paddy's vision had tripled by the time the guy took the stool beside his so he didn't know for sure. Paddy did remember blabbing and blubbering about Mariah and Barney, how he'd failed them both. Paddy might've cried on this stranger's shoulder. The stranger might, or might not, have driven Paddy home.

Paddy's hangover was a doozy. He needed relief. There was no Alka-Seltzer or Advil in the medicine cabinet, but plenty of Preparation H. Mariah had been the one who kept tabs on toiletries. When she'd begun to lose her memory, she would buy the same items for weeks in a row. This was why Paddy now found himself with multiple packs of hemorrhoid cream and enough body wash to clean an entire army, but no painkillers. His own attention to domestic details had never been too swift. Now it had gone way down the tubes. He didn't notice things were missing until it was impossible not to notice. Like Barney. Was it possible the dog had been gone for longer than Paddy realized?

Paddy missed the little bugger more than expected, even though without Mariah around, man and dog had mostly ignored each other, each buried in their own miseries. They were like decorative tassels once at opposite ends of a lovely scarf, now snipped off, no longer serving any purpose. Without Barney, Paddy was a lone mass of unruly thread. He felt the dog's absence keenly. No more pitter patter of tiny toenails on the kitchen floor. No more fluffy brown creature dozing fitfully against the ottoman, one eye on alert as he waited for Mariah to come home. No more ever-hopeful creature, whose dog-bound ignorance of death fueled Paddy's own magical thinking, his fantasy of Mariah washing up downstream on the Salmon River alive and in one piece, her 'accident' knocking the sense back into her head.

There were many reasons to numb that morning's pain. Peterson's Pharmacy was closer to home than the Gas n' Go, where he had single-dose packs behind the register, but he needed relief soon, otherwise he might not make it through the day without killing someone. After a hot shower and two cups of black coffee Paddy drove to Towne Centre. He found a parking spot easily, it being 8 am and most stores not yet open. The air was humid and warm even at that hour, typical for late summer, when you're ready for something cooler but you still have to sweat it out for another few weeks to get a semblance of a breeze. What Paddy wouldn't do for a blast of cold air to the face, one of the most reliable hangover cures he'd ever discovered, long ago, in his checkered, boozehound past.

Everywhere he looked he saw posters for lost dogs.

Otis; last seen on August 17th outside of Carla's Café.

Butch; our precious child, taken from our backyard on August 20th

Gigi; bring her home now! She has a heart condition!

And many more. The pleas, the rewards, the tugged heartstrings. The dog that had the most coverage was named Balthazar. Taped to mailboxes, storefronts, and street lamps, thumbtacked to bulletin boards, nailed to wooden fences. This Balthazar was a strange looking little pooch, with a fuzzy grey beard and droopy eyelids. A canine Edward G. Robinson. Just add the fedora and cigar. His owners were offering a thousand bucks for his return. Whatever happened to the good old days when lost dogs were returned for free? What kind of cheapskate sleaze would take money anyhow?

Paddy wondered if he should make a LOST DOG poster for Barney also, but he didn't know how to get started. He wasn't good with the computer, which he assumed was how the more savvy managed to make flyers and posters these days. Plus he didn't have any photos of Barney. He had tons of snaps of Coochy Coo and Buttercup, which Mariah had arranged chronologically in padded photo albums. Like parents who take tons of cute pictures of their first born, and maybe the second as well, but by the time they get to the youngest there's only an occasional school portrait. Paddy supposed he could go to the print shop and ask them to make a poster for him. Maybe they could locate a photo of another brown toy poodle that looked enough like Barney on the interweb.

But what would Paddy have them write on Barney's poster? And how much money—if any—was he willing to fork over for the dog?

He'd give it another day, see if Barney found his own way home. The little guy was probably just hiding behind a bush to torture Paddy. In the meantime Paddy had left fresh bowls of food and water by the back door before leaving the house. Hopefully some raccoon or squirrel wouldn't get to it first.

Paddy skulked in and out of Peterson's, walking quickly back to the car with Alka Seltzer and Advil in hand, grateful not to run into anyone he knew, not to have to chit-chat about the unusually warm weather, the damn missing dogs, or that Bradley, or Brandon, or Brady So-and-so who'd moved into the old Kearny place and lived like some kind of weirdo hermit. But mostly Paddy was grateful not to have to endure any low-toned, "How are you really, Paddy?" or "Mariah was such a wonderful woman," or worst of all, "We're so sorry for your loss." He looked forward to the day when Mariah's death would be an afterthought in social exchanges, when her absence would blend and bleed into the giant repository of Towne's dead and missing. He couldn't wait to be left alone to grieve.

Paddy hit the road, on his way to recovery. He prayed for a slow day at the station.

David: The Beginning of the End

David rode his bike home in the bleak, still dusk. The roads were deserted, everyone in Towne inside living their boring stupid lives. Street lamps buzzed, emitting weak flickering light. Even though he was riding at a fair clip, desperate late summer mosquitoes seeking warm blood found him and made a feast of his neck.

Serves me right, he thought. The more punishment the better. David thought of the Hebrew word for repentance, *teshuva*. Maybe if David did a little *teshuva*, God would bring back Balzy. But to do real-deal *teshuva* meant repenting not just to God but also to the person you'd sinned against. David thought of all the people and places he'd stolen from. There were so many. It would take his whole life to list them all. By the time he was done, already ancient Balzy would be dead. Plus, that wasn't the point of *teshuva*. You weren't supposed to apologize to get something or someone real back. You did *teshuva* for other people, so they could feel better. You were supposed to put yourself last.

When David got home, he didn't have the energy to put his bike inside the garage. He let it flop over on the side yard grass, knowing the chain would probably get wet and rusty overnight, but he didn't care. He entered the kitchen through the back door and found his mom sitting at the breakfast bar, busy at work on her laptop. Her hair was wet like she'd just taken a shower, and she was wearing her pajamas. All of this was weird because his mother never took showers at night and only put her pajamas on once she went to bed.

"Hey Sweetie," she cooed. "I hope you got all the posters up."

Fake-y-fake, thought David. What a liar. He knew his mother secretly wanted Balzy gone for good. She complained about having to clean up after Balzy most of the time, and lately she went on and on about how she'd have to walk Balzy all the time once David was back at school in a few weeks, pulling the old dog like a wagon with stuck wheels until maybe Balzy decided to move.

"Who knows if anyone even looks at them," David grumbled.

"Oh, let's not be negative now..." His mother's

voice trailed off. She looked back at her computer. Probably at fancy couches for her Kearny Mansion Project, her new gig for that buff, hairy, over-the-hill actor Brady Cole, the sucky Tom Cruise wannabe. His TV show Signet was a joke, even more than that dumb gladiator movie. David had watched Signet once at Chucky's house, back when they hung out on a regular basis. Chucky's parents thought they were playing PlayStation in the finished basement when they were really searching for the Playboy channel, unsuccessfully. *Signet* was the raciest thing they could find. Chucky was super into it, thought Brady Cole's cop character was awesome. He giggled uncontrollably every time they showed Brady's big moon of a butt. For some reason Brady's butt just didn't do it for David, whose opinion was that the whole show sucked, and Cole sucked the most.

Brady Cole. Now there was someone David didn't find the least bit attractive. Thank god for that.

"Whatever," David snarked at his mother. He grabbed a granola bar and left the kitchen. Once upstairs he laid on his bed and stared at the ceiling. Normally Balzy would have wheezed his way up the stairs behind David, and scampered towards the bed. Back when he was an active little sprite, Balzy was able to jump onto the coverlet himself. Lately David had to hoist him up, careful not to break any Balzy bones.

Without Balzy's labored breath and unmistakable odor, David's room felt as hollow as a fully drained Coke can. All David had was a brain full of guilt. The Leiber clutch, Chucky's hot breath, the stolen blobby brown blouse. Balthazar abandoned, maybe shivering and starving somewhere miles from Towne.

Was lying as bad as stealing, David wondered? What would the ancient rabbis say? Did David even care what those old Jews thought anymore? Did one thing ever happen without the other?

And what about cheating? How did that figure into it all? David wasn't really much of a cheater in the board game sense of the word. But he'd cheated people by stealing from them, hadn't he?

And then there was that big question, the one that had been brewing in his brain, the one that he'd kept pushing away to the edges, which kept coming back like a bad allergy. Was he as bad as his father? That pompous cheating SOB? There had been a time, which seemed like another lifetime, when David had thought his father was perfect, thought Dan was an all-knowing god. Maybe Dan hadn't been the cuddliest or kindest god, maybe he was a god who criticized David's mother all the time and seemed picky about his food and who washed his hands after touching David, or scrubbed his face if David spontaneously kissed him, but still, younger David had adored him.

In Dan's world, boys liked kicking balls and jabbing each other with long sharp sticks. They competed. They were on teams. They came in after dirty rough and tumble and enjoyed a hot, bracing scrub in the shower. They didn't like tutus, or sneak off to play with their girl-cousin's dollhouse. They didn't steal American Girl Doll booties, hide them under their pillow, then suck on them like bonbons at bedtime.

David's adoration of Dan ended when he entered middle school. David, hormones raging and pubescent opinions aflame, realized how truly fucked-up Dan was in comparison to the other lightweight moms and dads. His dad was a pathetic, chino-wearing, white Reebok-shodden clean freak. David couldn't shake off his love for Dan, a love like hardened bubble gum cemented to the walls of his heart. But his admiration of the man was easy to shed.

David had returned home early from school one day

right before his parents' separation and walked in to the downstairs bathroom to find a woman braced against the vanity, tasteless maroon polyester skirt hiked around her waist, tacky red satin push-up bra pulled down to exposed strangely dark and elongated nipples. Her eyes were closed, her face was a mask of ecstatic pain. David's father stood behind this strange woman, pumping away, beige Dockers, leatherette belt, and tighty whiteys around his ankles, one hand yanking the woman's unnaturally pumpkin-colored hair away from her contorted face, while the other hand explored his own chin for a missed shaving spot or a zit on the rise. Dan and the woman— who six months later would be introduced to David as Rachel, Dan's "brand new girlfriend"— were oblivious to David's presence.

It took less than three seconds for David to take it all in. The scene remained seared in David's brain like a cattle-prodded tattoo. There was nothing more disturbing then the mishmash of betrayal, disgust, fear, and arousal that this event mustered in him. Even now, over a year later, it made him feel like barfing.

David lay on his bed and shook the memory from his brain, doused it with an imaginary hose. Instead David imagined Nell at ARF, how smoothly she had swiped the paisley print blouse. Her painted nails. Her nod and air kiss. Thief to thief. Partners in crime.

David had to stop. It had to stop. But what part of 'It' was David ready to let go of?

David had to find some version of truthfulness he could live with. He was a *bar mitzvah* now, a man who was supposed to do the mature, right thing. No question, he was something older. Maybe something wiser. But was David a man? Who the fuck knew? Did men steal? Did they lose their best friends?

He'd been brooding and stewing and fretting and worrying for over an hour. His mother was downstairs, but it felt as if she was a million miles away. She called to David, but he didn't answer. Poor Mom, David thought. Married to a cheater, mother to a liar and a thief. The sound of his mother's voice prodded David, told him what he needed to do. It might backfire, cause a shitshow, make him feel worse than ever, but it was the only avenue he could take. David got off his bed. He ripped open the wrapper of his granola bar and ate the crunchy thing in two determined bites. He tossed the wrapper in the trash and got to work. He was finally ready to dip his hot, itchy toe in the cool water of honesty.

On an unusually warm late August evening, a month after his *bar mitzvah*, David Leibowitz stood in front of the bathroom full length mirror. Balthazar, an ancient wire-haired and wire-minded terrier, the only family member David would ever allow anywhere near him at times like these, was not with him.

David turned sideways and swiveled from the waist up, like a starlet photographed on the red carpet. With pursed lips and head in a come hither tilt, he admired himself in the pansy print Nicole Miller shift he'd just found languishing, a bit sweaty and damp, in his mother's hamper. David's body was morphing in surprising ways. His shoulders felt broader than on the morning of his *bar mitzvah*. Though maybe he would've preferred hips? Regardless, David no longer felt like such a scrawny asexual thing.

David spread his lips to apply a film of Aunt Beth's Sephora Matte Rose. He draped Adam Kernbaum's mother's string of pearls over his head and let them rest against his flat chest. He slipped on Jeff Murrow's sister Julia's kitten-heeled mules. One last look and David walked out the door.

"Oh Davey," his mother called from the kitchen once

she heard him on the stairs, "Come in here. I have something amazing to show you!"

"*Emet*," David whispered to himself. Truth. Little white lies might be allowed according to Jewish law when someone's feelings were on the line, but not when they concealed bigger truths. David's truth. This truth.

"Me too Ma!" David called back as he sashayed, then paused at the top of the stairs. He felt nauseous, as if he were en route to his first prom.

Lucinda: Sex, Love, Money

Lucinda tossed the Nicole Miller shift and all the unsavory smells it carried into her hamper. She turned the shower on full blast and let the water pummel her like a scalding waterfall. Glopping a hefty dollop of body wash on to her loofah, she scrubbed every nook and cranny as if she could erase the stupid mistake she'd just made, *schtupping* Brady Cole. And while she was at it, maybe she could rid herself of all her other bad decisions along the way. Her thoughts tumbled backwards, thud-landing first on her failed marriage. Dan had been such an uptight SOB, obsessively lining up cutlery in perfect right angles to the edges of his placemat, scrubbing benign suburban dirt off his squishy, ugly Keen sandals and Mephisto lace-ups as if he'd been traipsing in forests laden with poison ivy and disease. She'd never imagined him capable of having an affair, much less with a messy ditz-brain like Rachel.

She'd considered divorcing Dan many times over the years, but stayed in it for David's sake. Rigid in her belief that it was better for kids, especially only children, to grow up in intact households, regardless of how well, or not well the parents got along. What stupid psychobabble, she now thought. Outdated advice akin to suggesting baby seals should swim in enclosed tanks with great white sharks.

Lucinda considered herself a damn great mother, even better now that she didn't have Dan breathing down her neck, criticizing or second-guessing her every move. David's hormones would soon be raging. The grueling torture of adolescence was about to storm the house. Slings and arrows would fly. Both mother and son would suffer. For now they were solid, even if David's attachment to Balthazar far exceeded his connection to Lucinda due to the current crisis. She fully understood. The smelly old creature had truly been David's best friend. And even though the thought of a stink-free, hair-free house was appealing, Lucinda was also going to miss Balzy if he wasn't ever found. While things had withered and died in her marriage, the dog had been her steady companion when David was at school or camp and Lucinda had hours and hours of empty time to kill. Balzy had followed Lucinda from room to room during the day and she had found herself talking to the dog more and more.

"Hey Balzy, I'm feeling like pasta pesto tonight. How about you?"

Grunt, whimper.

"Denise's daughter Laura is turning into such a little bitch. I'm so glad David is still nice to me."

Bark. Bark.

"So glad Dan got the last of his stupid exercise gear out of the basement. If I had to look at that fucking treadmill one more time I was going to coat it in Häagen-Dazs."

Slurp. Slurp.

"You're glad Dan is gone, aren't you Balzy boy?"

Tail thump. Happy yip.

Once David was asleep, Balzy would skitter into Lucinda's bed and lay across her feet, which was really nice because her feet were always cold and Dan had recoiled when she tried to wedge them under his warm thighs in the middle of the night.

Now Lucinda put her head back under the showerhead and let the water rinse through her hair. How the hell was she going to cough up a thousand bucks if someone actually found the dog? Ask for a loan from Brady? Lucinda already felt like a slimeball for sleeping with him, just so she could get her itchy decorator fingers all over the Kearny Mansion. Asking for help would make Lucinda feel even slimier than she already did. Plus, she didn't want Brady knowing how desperate she was for the work, the purpose, and the money.

There was only one solution. Dan.

Lucinda got out of the shower, dried off, put on pajamas, picked up her phone and stared at it. Dan still had prime auto-dial real estate, although he'd been completely erased as soon as Lucinda found out about his affair with Rachel. But due to the necessities of co-parenting Lucinda had reluctantly added him back in. Lucinda took a deep breath, made a fist, releasing her middle finger to push against her ex-husband's name.

"Yes, Lucinda?" Dan answered with his usual sprinkling of impatience.

"And hello to you too, Dan."

"What's up. Something wrong with Dave?" Dan was the only person who shortened David's name to Dave. It was so hail fellow well met, so not David, or the tender, more appropriate, Davey. David often asked Dan not to shorten his name. He boldly told him it was one thing if Dan didn't like to be called Daniel, but that David liked his real, full name.

Dan just smirked and said he'd try.

"No David's fine. I called to tell you that Balzy is gone."

"He died? Well, it is about time."

"No, he didn't die," Lucinda rubbed at a smudge of grime on the back of her leg that she'd missed in the shower, a reminder of Brady's yucky chaise lounge, and controlled the urge to add *you heartless bastard*. "He either jumped out of the window of the Volvo or someone nabbed him. Right in the center of Towne."

"Why in the world would anyone want Balthazar?"

Why in the world would anyone want you, is more the question, Lucinda thought but kept to herself. Not the time, with her big ask on the way. "I'm not sure," she said. "But all I can tell you is he's missing. David is out now postering the town with LOST DOG notices all over the place."

"Dear god, I hope he hasn't put any personal information on those posters. No "Leibowitz." No home address. No phone number. That sort of thing."

"Why?"

"Security purposes," Dan sighed in a classic Dansplaining style. "Stalkers, identity thieves, all kinds of other weirdos."

"I can't imagine anyone would use a LOST DOG poster as a tool for identity theft, Dan. I mean really."

"And come to think of it, I would rather people in Towne didn't know that my dog—"

"—Our dog," Lucinda interjected. "One you never took any real interest in by the way."

"Whatever. I was going to say, before you interrupted me; I would rather the people of Towne didn't know that a dog formerly associated with me was carelessly misplaced."

You miserable walking calculator of social standing, thought Lucinda.

"Dogs go missing, Dan. It happens to the best of them, to us. In fact, according to Gloria Nevins at the ARF Thrift Store there seem to be many missing dogs in Towne right now."

"Oh, good old Towne," Dan sighed. "I don't miss that claustrophobic, silly place."

Fuck you, you superior shithead, thought Lucinda. Watch out. Whatever's going on here might spread up to Village and that bitch-dog of a girlfriend you have might disappear.

She took another deep breath, reminding herself that

she needed money from Dan. And the only way to get it was to not take his bait. Instead she said, "Meanwhile your son is beside himself. You know how important Balzy was—I mean, is to him."

"Yes. Maybe a bit too important, but whatever."

"So because Balzy is so important we're offering a reward for his return."

"A reward? Oh boy. Now just wait for all the loony toons and con artists to start calling."

Lucinda should've known. She was tempted to end the call, but a mother will do what a mother will do. "I think in these cases it makes a big difference. So I'm asking for David's sake; if Balzy is returned, can you front me a thousand bucks?"

"You're fucking kidding!"

"No."

"For a thirteen-year-old, arthritic, stinky, nasty cur?"

Lucinda took yet another deep breath. "For your son's most faithful companion—who happens to also be a thirteen-year-old, arthritic, stinky, nasty cur."

"No. Definitely not. You're on your own with this one, Lucinda. You're over-indulging that kid. Giving him everything he ever wants."

That did it. No more Ms. Nice Guy. "Because you gave him so little."

"That is totally uncalled for in this situation."

"Oh shut up, Dan," Lucinda growled. "Go screw your idiot girlfriend. And make sure to put a towel under her unwiped ass. I know you don't like any messes."

How she missed the satisfying click of hanging up a real, old-school landline.

Lucinda was sitting in front of the computer browsing vintage chandeliers for the Kearny foyer, when David walked through the back door more forlorn than Bambi after the forest fire.

"Hey Sweetie," she cooed. "I hope you got all the posters up."

David grumbled, "Who knows if anyone will even look at them."

"Oh, let's not be negative now…" Lucinda stared at the computer screen, forgetting herself mid-sentence. She was distracted by a text pinging and popping up on her computer screen. Brady Cole. What the fuck? Back at the Mansion, he'd thumbed her "deets" into his phone and growled "goodnight Gorgeous" before kissing Lucinda sloppily with lips spread like a flounder's. Another woman might've found the moment disarming and sexy, but Lucinda felt slimed. And confused. Only a few minutes before the wet kiss, Angus had disappeared. The dog had dug a hole so deep under the perimeter fence he could squeeze his fluffy golden body through it. And so he did.

Brady rushed from the rickety chaise they'd been doing it upon, his bare ass shining like a spotlight as he ran towards the back fence screaming "Angus! Come back!" Lucinda took the opportunity to quickly re-dress. She was stunned at what had just happened there on that horrible patio furniture. As concerned as she was for Angus, his sudden escape was the perfect excuse to bolt from Brady herself. When Brady walked back towards her with his slick penis swinging back and forth, and a dopey grin on his Cover Boy face, she realized he had already all but forgotten his big, beautiful dog. The sooner she got out of there, the better.

Lucinda read Brady's text: hey babe. wrote a song for u.

She could run, but she couldn't hide. A song? For her?

In the meantime David stomped out of the kitchen, granola bar in hand. A potential bonding moment had been lost. Chasing after her son would only backfire. Adolescents needed privacy, but not too much. She'd heard horror stories about what could happen behind teenagers' closed doors.

Rediscovered Boy Scout penknives, stock-piled meds, inhalable aerosols, secret conversations with pedophiles posing as teenage girls. She would call him down in an hour. In the meantime she would postpone working on the Kearny project, and find something funny on the internet to share with David instead. A YouTube video of pratfalls or embarrassing karaoke. They'd laugh together at someone else's expense. It would be a balm for both mother and son's disturbing evenings.

But the *ping of Brady's texts kept coming.

titled it "Lovely Lou".

come over and I will play it for u.

oh yeah, u have a kid. forgot. maybe 2moro?

will I see u 2moro?

i have to.

i want more. do u want more?

A stress-related peri-menopausal hot flash beginning to percolate. Or maybe it was a panic attack. Lucinda should turn the messaging app off her computer and set her phone to silent. Keep Brady at bay, she thought. Perhaps another shower would help. But she still had to browse YouTube for something to share with David. So no shower. Not yet.

And then this:

hey, did i tell you money is no object? spend whatever you want on this place. i trust you completely.

The job, the job, the job. She couldn't forget the job. Her favorite lighting fixture website was up on her screen. Tabs were open for Overstock.com and always reliable Crate and Barrel. She'd located a vintage sofa on eBay that would be perfect for the upstairs foyer. Lucinda needed to nail down the kitchen color scheme before heading to the stone yard for granite countertops. There was an end-of-season sale on outdoor furniture at Design Within Reach and the Kearny back verandah begged for a retractable awning.

Whatever she wanted. He trusted her completely. When was the last time anyone had said anything remotely as generous to Lucinda? The most she'd ever gotten from Dan was, "It better be worth it," or "I hope you're right." Maybe she needed to give Brady a chance. Maybe the sex would get better. Maybe after some time Brady would reveal some unusual savvy or special brand of smartness. Maybe he'd eventually lose the dress. The least she could do was text him back.

looking at chandeliers. they're 2 die 4. think you'll love 1. She wasn't sure she was properly abbreviating.

if you love it, i love it. so tomorrow?

"Tomorrow," Lucinda sighed, resigned to her strange fate. Then she typed: 4 sure.

Brady: Oh what a feeling

Brady was super bummed about Angus. The dog had never run away before. But then again, he'd never really had the opportunity to bolt. Back in LA, Brady had a wall constructed to surround his entire Topanga compound to keep out the stalkers and salivating fans. No one, man or beast, could dig under or climb over that thing from either side. Angus had his own totally secure four-acre spread to explore, complete with birds, chipmunks, and slow, stupid squirrels he'd chase and kill. He'd bring them back to Brady as gifts once they were bloody, limp masses hanging from his jowls.

Brady knew Angus would return. That dog was the pure definition of loyalty. Maybe Angus was just bored and restless. As big as that back yard was, it didn't hold a candle to his previous domain. Brady figured the dog just needed to do a little reconnaissance, check out the neighborhood, and then return.

Brady had a one-to-one Skype scheduled with Tamago later that evening. Brady was set to talk all about Lucinda, how epically in love he felt, how she seemed to represent all that was good about his future, how her plainness was a beautiful thing. That loving her made Brady feel true beauteousness for the first time.

Tamago wanted to focus on the lost dog.

"I didn't lose him exactly. He ran away," Brady explained. "Dug a mondo-huge hole under a fence and bolted like a convict."

"So you feel as if you imprisoned Angus?" Tamago asked with the deep, hollow voice he used when Brady didn't understand something he said, which was more often than Brady liked to admit.

"No, no. Not at all. Angus and I were like for real buds. Honest. I let him do all sorts of stuff that most people don't even let their kids do. That dog gets treated better than me as a kid, that's for sure."

"Aha. So how were you treated as a child, Brady?"

Tamago's image was pixelating, the connection was iffy. The guy was totally harshing Brady's mellow. Brady didn't want to talk about his own messed-up childhood, the way his father terrorized him with threats of bodily harm that might or might not be delivered. How not knowing whether he'd get a crack across the jaw or not made it worse. Brady didn't want to admit his mother never had a spine in that obese body of hers. How she never protected him. How she was still just a weak, sweet, not terribly smart mound of flesh. Brady stared at the computer screen and watched his guru shift into tiny shards of black and tan, then reassemble into Tamago; overwhelming head of hair, sharp angular nose, big brown all-knowing eyes.

"It could've been better," Brady grumbled.

"Better how?"

The guru leaned in towards the screen, his beak-like

nose so close Brady felt the impulse to flick it with his thumb and forefinger.

"I dunno. I could've had more toys?"

Tamago harrumphed. "Brady, you must dig deeper, under your own fence and find the truth that lays on the other side. An animal you consider a 'bud' has deserted you. I can't help but think this isn't the first time you've been left."

I don't want to fucking go there, thought Brady. Please don't make me go there.

"Brady. I want you to do a journaling session about Angus as he relates to you now and to your own boyhood. Every thought and feeling you can access. You can share your findings with me in our next one-to-one. Until then, keep practicing your dulcimer and doing your dances. Be beauteous and all else will fall into place."

Tamago never said goodbye at the close of sessions. He just disappeared as the Skype jingle sounded. Done. Over and out.

There had been no talking about Lucinda, and she was the one Brady really wanted to think about, talk about, write about. But he wanted to be Beauteous, so begrudgingly he sat down at the kitchen table and set pen to paper about his *adios amigo* dog and his miserable childhood.

Angus was always happy. He loved pretty much everyone. He'll probably be fine with or without me. That makes me feel kind of useless.

Now childhood. Useless had been one of Brady's father's favorite words:

"Your mother asked you to take the trash out, Brady. Is that so difficult? Do it now, you useless sack of shit."

"Look at the two of you. Mother and son. Laurel and Hardy but useless, without any of the charm."

"Male model? My son is a male model? What a joke. What a useless waste of time."

What fun, thought Brady. He'd leave those memories for now. Back to the dog:

I mattered to Angus, but not that much. He always preferred Webeke. That made me a little jealous.

Now...back to Cole family disaster zone:

Brady's parents returning from a night out. His mother looking almost beautiful in a teal blue muumuu and matching head scarf, a sly smile on her kewpie doll lips. Reginald, sour as usual, walking in behind her and slamming the door. Connie's smile turning downward, her lips losing color as Reginald wags his finger in front of her face and warns:

"If I catch you yucking it up with George Bartlett at another dinner party, I can't be responsible for my actions."

Brady moved back to Angus:

Angus would slobber kiss me when I scratched his head or fed him table scraps.

Kisses...

Connie's sweet goodnight kisses on Brady's forehead every night making things seem almost fine. A good memory, finally.

Angus' dumps were not fun to pick up and without any staff here it was up to me to scoop the poop. So, no loss there.

Childhood association? There hadn't been any dogs in the Cole household so no poop-scooping. The only tangentially related memory was the sound of Brady's father straining on the toilet, his groans transmitting at a high volume regardless of the closed bathroom door. Brady secretly glad for Reginald's pain in the butt.

On to the dog, again:

No dog groomer stopping by to bathe him, so Angus was starting to smell. Another no loss situation.

Brady loved baths as a little kid. He'd push a rubber duck around soap-sud mountains, dive bombed for plastic coins.

His mother sometimes sat by the side of the tub and sang to him. Corny songs like "Bicycle Built for Two" or "You Are My Sunshine." Hallelujah, thought Brady. A positive memory among the muck. Another one he'd happily share.

Brady looked at his writing. All Angus. He couldn't bring himself to write down any of the childhood memories he'd recalled. Not even the good stuff, because on the tail end of anything good, came a mile long string of shitty. But he wanted desperately to please Tamago, so to end he added:

My father was a mean SOB and a real bastard, and I mean literally, who sometimes hit me and treated my mother like dirt. I'm glad he's dead.

My mother is a sweet woman. I wish she'd lose some weight and get a life. I mean, really; ding dong, the man-witch is dead, so some good times for her can finally begin.

Done. Finished. Brady pushed his pen and paper to the side and rested his head on the table. The whole deep-digging thing left him feeling like a rung out thrice-used paper towel. He got up from his seat and wandered up the creaky spiral staircase to his bedroom, in which the only piece of furniture was a king-sized mattress on the floor. Brady free-fell backwards, his body thudding gently against padded foam. He let his mind trip back to Lucinda, to the possibility of something better. Brady envisioned her on the other side of that imaginary fence Tamago wanted him to dig under. He saw her standing there, smiling at him with a design magazine in one hand and a zucchini bread in the other. Brady gazed up at the ceiling, at the web of cracked paint threatening to shower him with possibly toxic chips and whispered her name like an invocation: Lucinda. Soon enough she would magically transform this room and all the others. And Brady would be magically transformed too. Lucinda, Lucinda, Lucinda. Maybe she'd let him call her Lou. Brady thought guy nicknames for girls were incredibly sexy. Not that she needed to be any sexier for him.

Lou's dog Balthazar had disappeared the very same day as Angus. Coincidence? Maybe, but Brady liked to think it was a sign the universe was making room in their lives for each other. Without pets they'd have more time and brain-space for each other. They could be each other's pets.

Brady wondered when she'd want him to meet her son. When that day came, what would he do about the caftan? He couldn't exactly come off as cool to a thirteen-year-old guy if he was wearing a dress. And the beanie? Forget it. Total nerd-o-rama. Maybe Brady could wear the caftan like a long shirt with jeans underneath, like he was starting some new kind of fashion trend.

Would Lucinda want more kids? Could she even still have kids? Kids, or the lack of them, had been one of the coffin nails with Webeke. She wanted them, Brady hadn't. But maybe with Lou it wouldn't be so bad. A pack of little Lous and Bradys might be—dare Brady think it, a beauteous thing.

The cloud of Reginald and Constance had lifted. Brady felt so lighthearted he could sing. He picked up his dulcimer and even though it wasn't his scheduled time to practice, he felt a desire to strum.

Not only did Brady strum, he wrote a song. A song for Lucinda. Lovely Lou. He wanted to play it for her immediately, so he called to tell her about it to see if she could come back over to hear it, but she didn't answer. Brady texted her. Still no answer. She was probably nowhere near her phone. No doubt she was busy being a great mother, or friend, or person, so he just kept *pinging her until she was in range.

Conversations

Nell: La Madre

"How are you, Nelly darling? Do you miss us?"

"I'm fine, Mother. How's Granada?"

"Oh, it is divine. The university found us an amazing apartment right near the Alhambra. I'm there almost every day soaking up the Islamic influences. The mosaics are to die for. And I've found a ceramics studio where I can work to my heart's content."

"That's nice."

"Everything okay with the house?"

"Everything's fine."

"You must be very lonely there without us."

"Not really. I've had some friends over."

"Friends? That's wonderful!"

"Yeah, it is. It's really wonderful."

"Do we know these friends?"

"No. They're new friends."

"Oh. From Towne?"

"Yeah, more or less."

"Nelly sweetness, your father is telling me to tell you not to let anyone in his study. You know how he feels about his books and whatnot."

"Father doesn't need to worry. These friends aren't really voracious readers. They have different kinds of appetites."

"Well don't go having any crazy parties."

"Since when have I been the type to have crazy parties, Mother?"

"I'm just saying…"

"Well say no more. Anyway, these friends are more into music. They like to hear me play the piano."

"How fabulous. I couldn't be more pleased. Oh, hold on…your father is saying something again."

"Of course he is."

"Oh, sorry, Nell Bell. Got to dash. We need to primp for a dinner at Rodrigo and Elena's. Your father sends his love."

"Of course he does."

"*Adios* for now, Nelly dearest!"

"Woof. Woof."

"What did you say?"

"Goodbye Mother. Enjoy the chow."

Abe: So Not

"Abie! It's a Saturday. You never call on Saturdays. Is everything alright?"

"Everything's fine, Ma."

"Oh. Good. I saw your number on the Caller ID and I nearly had a heart attack."

"Sorry, Ma."

"Milo's good?"

"He's great."

"And Claire?"

"Also great."

"And you?"

"I'm fine. Actually, Ma, there is something I wanted to ask you."

"Of course Abie. You can ask me anything. You know that."

"Well, that's not entirely true, but—"

"Oh don't get started."

"Started on what, Ma?"

"All that mishegas about my withholding my true feelings from you growing up."

"Geez, this got ugly quick. No, Ma, that's not where I was going. "

"Okay. Good. Because you know I don't think it's appropriate for a son to muck around in his mother's private musings."

"Yes, Ma, you've told me that many times."

"So what did you want to ask me? Abie? Are you there?"

"Um, yeah, Ma. Sorry. So, how would you like to come help out with Mouse on a regular basis?"

"Please don't call Milo that. You know I have a phobia about rodents. I can't think of my grandson as one."

"Sorry. Sorry. How would you like to come here maybe two, three days a week and help take care of Milo?"

"Oh. My. You know I'd love to!"

"Fine."

"That didn't sound very enthusiastic, Abie. Was this Claire's idea?"

"No, Ma, it was both of our idea. And I am enthusiastic. I really, really appreciate you helping out."

"Oh. But there's one thing."

"Uh oh."

"That dog of yours. You know how uncomfortable he makes me."

"Well, Ma, you don't have to worry about Gordon anymore. He's gone."

"Gone? Really?"

"Yeah, really."

"I just heard something about dogs being stolen in Towne. There was a spot about it on the local news. A George somebody-somebody, he's the head of your town council, I believe. He was being interviewed. He's organizing a meeting to figure out this missing dog issue."

"I didn't know about that. See, Ma? You've already helped out."

"What else are mothers for?"

"But actually, Mom? Gordon wasn't stolen."

"Oh. So you finally got rid of him! Good for you. I told you that dog was a menace."

"We did not get rid of him. He, well, he decided to leave on his own."

"Oh come on Abie. Decided on his own. You always talk about that dog as if he were as smart as Albert Einstein."

"Well Gordon is exceptionally smart, Ma. And he isn't—or wasn't—a menace. Your attitude is really callous."

"Oh come on Abie. He was just a dog."

"Just a dog. Oh my god. I forgot how so not an animal person you are."

"What can I say? Dogs are not my thing. You know I'm more a cat person. But, Honey, I am sorry about Gordon."

"Sure, Ma. Whatever. Anyhow, you don't have to worry about Gordon bothering you because he's not around anymore."

"In that case, what days do you want me to come? I could come every day. It's not that long a drive."

"How about we start with Mondays and Wednesdays? See how it goes?"

"See how it goes? You sound like I'm a nanny you're testing out. Abie, I'm Milo's grandmother. I know how to take care of him. I took care of you, didn't I? You turned out okay."

"I don't know about that…"

"What did you say? You're mumbling again."

"How's next Monday, Ma? Come around 9?"

"9 it is."

"Love you, Ma."

"Love you too, Sweetie. Love you too."

Paddy: Belongings

"Paddy's Gas and Go. What can I do you for?"

"Hi Paddy."

"Who's calling?"

"It's Gloria, silly. Don't you recognize my voice? Hello? Paddy? Are you there?"

"I'm here, Gloria. Why are you calling? I thought I made it clear—"

"Oh, Paddy. What happened in the garage was lovely, but just a little whimsy."

"A whimsy?"

"Like the saying goes: what happens in the garage, stays in the garage. I've called to say thank you for the donation of Mariah's blouses. It seems we've already sold one of them. An unusual brown patterned one? I don't recall ringing up the sale, but, in any case, it's gone."

"Oh, well. Good, I guess."

"Also, Paddy; I've started seeing someone else."

"We were never seeing each other, Gloria."

"Silly man. I, for one, saw plenty."

"Please. Don't remind me, Gloria. So you've hooked a live one. I'm happy for you."

"Thank you, Paddy. I'm so relieved you understand. I was worried you'd be heartbroken."

"Are you kidding?"

"His name is George Takharian. He's the head of the Towne Council. You may have seen him on TV?"

"Can't say that I have, Gloria."

"Well, George has been on the local news a whole lot lately, talking about this missing dog situation."

"I don't watch the local news."

"Oh. Well. I can't tell you how many people have been calling the ARF shelter hoping against hope that their dogs are there. But it seems none of them are. I hope the meeting George organizes leads to some, well, organization!"

"That would be good, Gloria. But I really have to go—"

"And get this; I met George in the supermarket of all places! At the cheese counter!"

"Well, bully for cheese. It's a busy morning here at the station. So, is that all? Are we done here?"

"We could make you dinner sometime, Paddy. George is a gourmet chef! I'm sure you haven't had a home-cooked meal in weeks. Months now. It's been months since…"

"That's very kind of you Gloria. But no."

"How about tomorrow night?"

"I said no, Gloria."

"Next week, then?"

"Oh, gee, look at that. Someone just drove up with a smoking engine. Gotta go Gloria."

"Wait! Pad—"

David: Hey Siri

"Hey Siri, what does it mean if a boy likes to wear girls clothes more than boys clothes?"

"Okay I found this on the web for what it means when a boy likes to wear girls clothes more than boys clothes."

"Siri, I can look stuff up on the web myself. You're supposed to be like Jeannie on *I Dream of Jeannie* and be magically smart and helpful. Besides, those links are all about preschoolers. What about teenage boys?"

"What about teenage boys do you want to know?"

"What I just asked, you not-know-it-all app!"

"I'm sorry, David. I don't understand. Can you ask that question again?"

"Argh! What the fuck! Okay, again: "What does it mean when a teenage boy likes to wear girls clothes more than boys clothes?"

"Okay here's what I found on the web for what does it mean when a teenage boy likes to wear girls clothes more than boys clothes."

"Still not useful...Hey Siri, try this: Does wearing girls clothes mean a boy is gay?"

"I'm on it! Okay, here's what I found on the web about does wearing girls clothes mean a boy is gay."

"This sucks, Siri. Totally not helpful."

"I'm sorry I can't access information you find helpful, David."

"Okay. Try this: What if inside sometimes a boy feels more like a girl?"

"Coming up! Here's what I found on the web for what if inside sometimes a boy feels more like a girl."

"Do you ever answer questions without referring someone to the web?"

"I've never really thought about it."

"Well, you should. Hey Siri: What does transgender mean?"

"Transgender means denoting or relating to a person whose sense of personal identity does not correspond to the gender assigned to them at birth."

"Finally! A real answer. Hey Siri: Am I transgender if I feel more like a girl than a boy?"

"In my realm anyone can be anything."

"Well that's a lame answer. You're such a robot. Whatever. Okay. Here's one. Hey Siri: Which is worse, stealing or lying?"

"Checking my sources! Okay, I found this on the web for which is worse stealing or lying."

"Again with the web. Hey Siri, Is there an inherited gene that makes you a liar?

"I'm not sure I understand."

"Of course you don't. Hey Siri, is my father an ass-hole?"

"I don't know how to respond to that."

"Hey Siri: Am I crazy?"

"I can't really say."

"You're so wishy-washy Siri. Answer me this. Hey Siri: Will anyone besides Balzy ever love me?"

"Interesting question, David."

Lucinda: Ew Gross

"Denise, you're never gonna believe what happened."

"Is this about Balthazar, Luce? Have you found him?"

"No, he's still missing."

"Can you believe this? All these dogs gone? Karen Iverson's collie Mags was swiped from her mudroom while she was getting a mani-pedi. I mean, someone was in her house. In. Her. House! And you know the Kaufmans, that youngish couple from the city who moved in about two years ago to Poplar Street?"

"I don't know everyone the way you do, Denise."

"Well anyhow, the wife, Claire, gets her hair done at Tessa's. I met her there. She told me her husband's dog— one of those sketchy pit bulls? Well, he also went missing. It's creepy."

"The dog stuff is beyond creepy, but this isn't about Balzy. It's about Brady Cole."

"Ah. Your new BFF. What about him?"

"We had sex."

"Yeah, right. Very funny."

"No, seriously, Denise. We did it. All of it."

"Um, don't take this the wrong way Luce, but Brady Cole doesn't have sex with the likes of us. He only has sex with super models or rocket scientists who look like super models. Not saggy, sex-starved suburbanites."

"Well, I have news for you. He was all over this blubby body. And he claimed to find it irresistible."

"You're not kidding."

"I'm so not kidding."

"You're actually telling the truth."

"God's honest. I have the hickey to prove it."

"Ohmygod. How was it?"

"It was really, really weird and not that good."

"How is that possible? He's like a sex god."

"Well that's it. He was too good. It was like fucking a sex encyclopedia. He did all that picayune stuff men are told they're supposed to do. You know: 'Have sex with the whole woman, not just the vagina,' 'Pleasure her before yourself,' 'See her, really see her,' 'be attentive,' and blah blah blah. I felt like I was being groped by a giant Boy Scout."

"I can't believe you just fucked a People Magazine's Sexiest Man Alive and you're criticizing his technique."

"Denise, I'm telling you. I'm not into him. Also, he's kind of a wacko. He's in some men's cult where they wear dresses and dance with scarves and play finger cymbals. And he's not all that smart. I'd rather get myself off with my dildo and a nice rock star fantasy from some ethical porn site."

"So why did you do it if he's so unattractive? Though

Brady Cole and 'unattractive' don't belong in the same sentence as far as I'm concerned."

"Honestly? I'm so into redecorating the Kearny place, I just shut my eyes and thought, Whatever. Maybe afterwards he'll be able to focus on my ideas for the guest wing."

"I can't believe I'm hearing this."

"You're hearing this."

"Okay, so, tell me: Big? Thick? Long? Medium? Nice shape?"

"Ew gross, Denise!"

"Gross? You're the one who had sex with someone you're not attracted to because you want to redecorate their house. That's really gross."

"Okay, you're right. Um, average. His junk is totally average."

"Well, that's like, totally disappointing. I was imagining, you know, with David back at school, you'd have all the time in the world to just fuck and fuck and fu—"

"Enough, Denise. Anyway, I'm determined I won't do it again. I feel really guilty. The poor guy is totally into me. Sort of ironic. Me, the object of a movie star's desire after being dumped by Dan. Oh god how I wish I could rub his nose in this."

"Well, you could."

"No Denise. Definitely not…"

"Or I could."

"Denise, don't. Don't tell anyone. Seriously. You are sworn to secrecy. I can't jeopardize this job any more than I already have. I need the extra money, Denise. Dan's a miser; his child support is barely enough to cover my basic expenses. He's such a cheapskate. And if he got wind of my…my…whatever this Brady thing is, he'd yank every last penny away from me."

"Alright. But you owe me."

"Thank you. Oh, also, to make matters even worse, his dog ran away while we were doing it."

"You're kidding. What is with these dogs disappearing? There's like some kind of canine curse on our town!"

"I know, sort of bizarre right? We were on this chaise lounge on the back patio, the only semi-soft, semi-clean place to, well, you know, do it. I've turned my head sideways because, blech, like I told you, I wasn't into watching Brady all gaga above me, staring at me, pounding away. That's when I see Angus, his sweet yellow lab, burrowing under the perimeter fence. Angus disappears through the hole he's dug under the fence and I cry 'Oh!' Brady thinks I'm coming so he lets it all go."

"I hope you used protection."

"Denise, I'm not a fifteen-year-old idiot. Under no circumstances would I let that guy inside me without some latex between us. Anyhow, Angus running away was a good distraction. I feel really horrible for Brady, actually. That dog is quite wonderful."

Brady: Tamago Takes

"I'm disappointed in you, Brother Brady. You're only a month in, and a truly beauteous man waits three months before engaging in sexual activity of any kind."

"I know, Brother Tamago. But this is true love. I'm sure of it."

"True love does not necessarily require the fondling of another person's genitalia."

"I know, Beauteous Basic Number Two…"

"Beauteousness allows for private masturbation. We understand manly needs."

"I totally get it. I respect the Basics, I really do, but is there maybe, like, a fast track for guys like me? Who meet their soulmates, like, by chance?"

"Fast track? No, no, no, Brother Brady. Beauteousness does not require speed. It requires patience."

"Lucinda's amazing though. Not like anyone I've ever been with before. She's old. She's kind of dumpy. I used to only hang out with gorgeous power people, and she's neither of those things."

"It doesn't matter how you see her, Brother Brady. It matters how you see yourself."

"But Dude, I mean, Tamago, aren't I doing the beauteous thing by telling you this? Honesty and all that? Beauteous Basic Number One, in fact."

"Yes, honesty is quite important. But so is keeping in touch with our own feminine auras. And we prepare for this through celibacy in the early months of Beauteousness."

"I did it the beauteous way, Tamago. I really did. Lucinda was very well attended to."

"Maybe you're not cut out for our path."

"No, fuck no. I'm super into Beauteousness. I really am."

"Hmm. Have you been wearing your dress?"

"Every day. All day."

"Have you been doing your dances?"

"Morning, noon, and night. I'm getting really good with the scarves."

"Playing your instrument?"

"I'm like the dulcimer king. I mean queen. Or ah, dulcimer beauty."

"And you're planning on doing Level 2 work after finishing Level 1?"

"Totally."

"And you've paid the tuition?"

"Not yet, but I can today."

"Well Brother Brady, let me meditate on this. On occasion we have adjusted our expectations when true love enhances a brother's beauteousness, seeds towards his further growth. I will let you know my decision by end of business hours today."

"Thank you Tamago. Truly. I do want to stay beauteous, I really do."

"I believe you Brother. And in the meantime, alert your people that there is a new routing number for wiring funds. They can get it from Sebastian at the main office in La Jolla."

autumn

*L*ately, *most of my humans use me with a certain selfish survivalism. They extract fuels from me and burn them to warm their ridiculous houses. Some have large panels on their roofs, which has something to do with stealing the rays of my sun. They say this is environmentally correct, but I don't understand how stealing anything can be prudent.*

My humans drive outlandish, oversized vehicles. They shrug and blame their children. They blame their dogs as well. Large dogs require their own section of cars. Soft beds are needed in the rear of the vehicles. Trellises erected to separate dog from human. For privacy or safety. I'm not sure which.

The children have lots of needs, which the parents

fulfill with stuff. The parents blame after-school sports. Especially in these months when the temperatures are cooling. The energy of the young is boundless as leaves begin to color and dry, as they blanket the ground in crisped orange and yellow remains.

The parents blow the leaves with noisy machines, or scrape at them with fingered rakes. Anything to make it possible for the children to race around with sticks and balls, wearing strange headgear. Parents drive their monster cars to cleared areas. They huddle and sit on hard planks and watch the children run to and fro across large fields marked with white chalk.

My humans create heaps of trash while applauding themselves for their recycling efforts. Mounds of debris are piled in hillocks on my outskirts in an area referred to as the Dump. These trash heaps disturb my natural aura. They make me look like I have a rash, unsightly bumps on my northern edge. The stench is something nature never intended, like living death, hopeful poison, blooming wilt. Everything curdled.

In bygone eras my perimeters were flat and grassy. Untrodden, inhabited only by subterranean worms and microscopic fleas. Now, aside from the Dump, to the south I have the Mall, a giant sharp-edged monolith with bright shiny features, and an even larger area tarred over called Parking for all those aforementioned cars. Humans come out of the Mall hauling large satchels filled with material goods. I am starting to comprehend the purposes of some items. Food I understand: sustenance and survival. Clothing, also a must in changeable climates like mine; protection and thermal balance. Toys; distraction and pleasure. There's a category called Electronics, however, that is still an enigma.

When I'm this disappointed I need to remember every century or so a few special humans grow or settle in me.

I have a soft spot for the wrong-headed do-gooders who wreak havoc. I've watched their dramas unfold since the beginning of time, and I can tell you: they don't necessarily end well. But still I root for these unique if tiny specks who make it their mission to save the planet, save others, save the creatures, save themselves.

Chapter Seven

Nell: Downsizing

Nell's rescue missions continued into early autumn. By mid-October she had twenty-three dogs safely sequestered at her retreat. Nell would've taken in more if she could, she would've searched out and saved all the enslaved. Her house was only so big, her cash allowance only so generous, while her heart expanded continuously. Even saints have their limits.

If only the citizens of Towne could see how much happier and healthier their dogs were at Nell's perfect puppy paradise they might end their futile searches. Eventually they'd give up. Some amount of time would pass and they might get new dogs, dogs Nell might also have to save. But for now she settled for what she had. Grateful for every smelly member of her pack, reveling in their adoration.

Still, by mid-autumn Nell's funds began to dwindle. Calling upon her superior calculating skills, Nell estimated that if she pinched pennies at PetSmart and shoplifted the occasional can of Alpo from ShopRite the pack would thrive through the winter months. But she needed to cut back. And so, the dogs grew a wee bit hungry. The few that still had hunting instincts fared better than the others, supplementing with a bird here, a squirrel there.

Nell stopped buying human food for herself, so wasteful and expensive. She knew she could subsist on very little. There had been a period of time in tenth grade when Nell had flirted with anorexia. Even though Nell knew it to be a typically adolescent rebellion—so unoriginal, so girly, she was still intrigued by the idea of controlled deprivation as pounds of flesh left her body. And, of course, there was also the silent rejection of her parents and their combined love of food. Her mother considered herself an amateur chef, and her father considered himself a haute cuisine connoisseur. There had often been sumptuous feasts prepared even with only three mouths to feed.

Nell had employed many strategies to avoid meal time, often using music as an excuse.

"Oops. Sorry, Mother," Nell shrugged and rose from the table as cardamon and ginger infused the dining room from the sizzling curry her mother had just put on the table. "I totally forgot I wanted to practice the Bach before I get too tired. I'll grab a bowl from the fridge later." And off Nell would scurry.

She never forced herself to throw up. She never binged in order to purge. She ate just enough to survive. Her parents barely noticed when Nell's clothes started to hang off her bones like plastic bags stuck on the branches of trees. Her father once complimented her ability to eat so little.

"Wish I had your willpower, Nell," he said as he patted his belly. "But I just can't say no when it comes to food."

Luckily, it was a phase that ended before it got too dangerous. As with all things in her life, Nell lifted herself up and out of the mire. Now, her adolescent experiment in near starvation would come in handy for the sake of her dogs.

As the air grew crisper, Nell jumped fences in the dead of night to steal apples from neighborhood trees, the last dregs of shriveled tomatoes and softening squash from flimsily enclosed vegetable gardens. She was so slight she left barely a trace, tiny little tiptoed steps that could've been the paw prints of a bunny. She ate like a bunny also: greedily, cores and seeds and rubbery stems. She rode her old Sting Ray bicycle to the Towne Gas n' Go. While the old man who had run the place for as long as Nell could remember was pumping gas or inside the garage, Nell slipped in to the store and filled her pockets with the nutrition bars and tiny bottled drinks in easy reach by the cash register. She'd pedal away as swiftly as her weakening legs could carry her. Back home surrounded by drowsy pups, she'd twist off the bright orange tops of the tiny bottles and swallow the syrup-sweet elixir in a single gulp, waiting for the promised five hours of energy to arrive. But it never did.

Soon the gardens and trees were bare. Nell resorted to less savory forms of foraging. She snuck into the Towne Dump during the wee hours of dawn, searching piles of fetid garbage for edible scraps. In the evenings, under cloak of darkness she rummaged through the dumpster behind Scotto's Pizzeria, scoring the occasional pepperoni slice, which she would strip, saving the discs of questionable meat for the dogs, eating the stale crusts herself. She burrowed into the garbage pails behind the train station, where a commuter's hastily half-eaten egg sandwich, or moldy scone might await her.

While she searched for food, she also destroyed the

remaining LOST DOG notices posted all over Towne. She'd been ripping off signs for her most recent rescues— Bingo, mixed-breed hound; Chester, corgi; Morris, labradoodle; and Puffy, Maltese—when she noticed a new, disturbing sign on the train station bulletin board:

Special Towne Council Meeting:
Where Have They Gone?
Come discuss the missing dog crisis and possible strategies to insure their return.
7 pm November 12th Towne High School Auditorium

A sudden wave of heat coursed through Nell's body. Light-headed and flushed, her knees buckled and she collapsed to the rough cement. Nell leaned against the trash can, resting her forehead on the cool aluminum side. What had she expected? That these people would understand? That she'd done everything for their dogs, done these clueless humans a massive favor? Strategies to insure their return. What did that even mean? She'd been caring for most of the dogs for almost two months. Had it been careless to take in Chester, Bingo, Morris, and Puffy so recently? Had she inadvertently activated this sudden Towne frenzy? This call to action? Nell would have to be more careful. She would have to stop saving dogs, at least for the time being. Foraging was too risky, even at dusk and dawn.

And so began the season of less food, less sunshine, more lazy days indoors. The pack lounged around the piano as Nell played melodies to drown out the sound of her gurgling tummy. She chose easy-to-pluck pieces like Bach's Well-Tempered Clavier or Beethoven's Piano Sonata in G minor Op. 49, or his Dances for Piano. A little Schubert or Mendelssohn if she was feeling more energetic.

As her own mind grew restless, Nell took to reading aloud to the dogs, in a manner suited to her peculiarities. She'd speed-read a book, then gather the pups in a circle, stand in the center and recite entire tomes by heart, acting out dialogue, gesticulating action. Certain dogs had fictional preferences. Raphael preferred Dickens. Boris was a fan of Sophocles. Pepe liked the racy avant-garde stuff by Bataille. Angus slept through most everything.

On the night of November 12th, Nell dressed herself in a costume; beige slacks, white ribbed sweater with a little anchor sewn in the general heart direction, and forest green colored quilted barn coat. It was an ensemble she'd curried from her mother's closet, clothes her mother hadn't even bothered to take to Spain, they were so drab, so American. So Towne. Nell piled her matted hair atop her head and covered the entire mess with a beret. She traded in her rain galoshes for a pair of nautical loafers. Nell left the dogs in a sleepy huddle and rode the three miles to Towne. For the first time in her life, she looked like she belonged.

Abe: Pacified

Milo sat on Abe's chest as Abe play-nibbled his son's toes while they waited for Barbara's arrival. Milo's giggles filled the air like soap bubbles, disappearing without consequence. There were always more to come. The kid was an endless fount of laughter, especially after a good night's sleep, a hefty morning poop, and a nice bowl of cereal. In this he was like his father, though the first two prerequisites were harder to come by as Abe approached his thirty-fifth birthday. Middle age was on the way. No stopping that train.

Playing with Milo was pure joy for Abe. Abe felt invigorated and energized and decidedly not middle-aged while faux-chasing Milo around the living room, tossing him skyward and catching him, reading aloud as the still illiterate kid tried to gnaw the pages of his ABCs board book. Even Paddy Cake or Peek-a-Boo provided Abe with a sense of purpose and intense love.

Pure joy, until it became excruciatingly boring. Eventually Milo's endless demand for repetition, the limits of conversational exchange, his tyrannical "more, more, more," whined as "mah, mah, mah," would grate on Abe's nerves. In reality, the best Abe could expect was a bit of relief courtesy of his mother. And the jury was still out as to whether this would be a better or worse turn of events.

On the first morning, Barbara had arrived at ten am with her usual bundle of passive aggression.

"Abie, you look tired. Have you been getting any exercise?"

Translation: Abe, my formerly fit son, you are now fabulously fat.

"Claire sure has the pantry chock-a-block with so many interesting items!"

Translation: What is this organic dreck your wife calls food?

"Milo looks so adorable in that jacket. Where did you get it? Was it a gift?"

Translation: Why isn't my grandson wearing any of the clothes I bought for him? At full price, mind you?

"The house smells so fresh."

Translation: It's a good thing that stinky dog of yours ran away.

Abe tried to write. He holed himself up in the office with the internet off while Barbara took Milo and the requisite supplies of water bottle and baggie of whole grain kibble to the playground with written directions and a well drawn map, impossible even for Barbara to screw up. A blank word document beamed cool grey light towards Abe. He tried to respond. He sat for a long stretch. He shifted in his supposedly comfortable ergonomic chair. He tapped out a few words. He formed a few tepid sentences. It led to something, but the something was miserably weak and contrived. He deleted it all after an hour. Not surprisingly, he missed Gordon. In Abe's more prolific times Gordon would lay under the desk while Abe tapped out far more interesting sentences. Abe would be comforted by Gordon's occasional twitch and whimper, his doggie dreams. Both man and dog were productive back then.

With no original thoughts and no Gordon, the temptation to switch on the flat screen and watch a cricket match in Islamabad was so strong Abe felt it like an electric shock up the spine. But he wouldn't. There was something about sneaking sports behind not only Claire's back, but now Barbara's back as well, that would coat Abe in a world class wash of shame. Abe still had flashbacks: Grade school, when he got caught stealing a stuffed animal seal covered in real sealskin from his cousin Ralphie. The look on Barbara's face could've melted Kryptonite. Middle school, when his mother discovered Abe's stash of pre-Internet lightweight porn magazines shoved carelessly inside his trombone case. Barbara's scowl, the epitome of disgust. And then the lectures. All those lectures. The hour-long diatribe about respect and dignity Barbara gave him after Abe arrived at his father's 50th birthday party high as a kite on E. Really, Abe hadn't thought anyone would notice.

The shame list was lengthy. Abe's mother had the memory of an elephant. If Barbara caught a whiff of Abe doing anything that hinted towards self indulgence, had inklings of the illicit or looked like sloth, Abe would feel instantly slimed, like Mouse's pacifier, covered in drool and needing a good rinse.

It continued like this for many weeks. At first Abe

forced himself to sit and stare at the blank screen. Okay, he did take naps, but only short ones. By late October, the naps got longer, the shame got deeper, and the gap between real-Abe and imagined writer-Abe got wider and wider.

One chilly early November morning he was roused by a light rapping on the door.

"We're home," Barbara sing-songed. She'd become particularly cheery since taking on babysitting duties. Abe almost didn't recognize her. But only almost. Around every nicety lay a tazer ready to zap him.

Abe cleared the sleep out of his throat. He quickly opened his laptop and pretended to type. "Come in," he said.

Barbara poked her head in. "All good in here?"

"Great. I got a whole chapter done."

"Oh Abie," she cried. "That's wonderful!"

"How was the playground?"

"We had a marvelous time, as usual. Milo fell asleep in the stroller. Should I take him out or just let him be?"

"Ah, just let him be. Why wreck a good thing?"

"He ate his whole bag of, ah, whatever those snacks are, and drank all his water."

"That's great, Ma."

"His diaper may be sopping when he wakes up."

"No worries, Ma."

"Milo is quite the daredevil on the slide. You know, he prefers to go down on his tummy head first with his arms out in front of him like Superman!"

"I know Ma."

"He wants to do it over and over again and again. Do you think he might be obsessive compulsive?"

"It's called Toddlerhood, Ma. They all do that. Fixate on one thing obsessively until they master it. I was probably like that also."

"I don't remember you sticking with anything with such continued regularity."

Was the steam rising out of Abe's ears visible?

"Oh Abie; Some of the mommies at Allenwood Park were talking about the Towne Board meeting coming up. The one about those missing dogs."

"So?"

"Well I told them that you wouldn't be going."

"Why did you tell them that?"

"Well, you seem fine without Gideon around."

"Gordon, Ma. My dog's name was—is Gordon. Gideon was the name of Aunt Harriet's Chihuahua. He died about a century ago."

"Oh. Sorry. That little ratty dog. Geesh. I'd forgotten all about him."

"And for your information I still miss Gordon. A lot."

"Really? Everything seems hunky dory around here without that creature, if you ask me."

Abe snapped the lid of his computer down and walked past his mother towards the bedroom. He paced. He mulled. He stewed. He was his own worst enemy. He needed distraction badly. But not sports-watching. Not with his mother hovering outside the door, ready to pounce on every imperfection.

If Gordon had been there, Abe could've used walking him as an excuse to get out of the house. They'd set out at a steady clip, Gordon's pace, faster than Abe's natural lumber. Abe could've talked to his dog, complained to him about Barbara, Claire, writing blocks, suburban isolation, the doldrums of Daddy-dom.

Gordon, Gordon, Gordon, thought Abe. I need you, man. Where the fuck are you? Maybe if you came back, I could make things work. I could control Milo. Get rid of Barbara. Convince Claire you'd be chill around the Mouse.

Maybe Abe would go to the Towne meeting. What did he have to lose? In the meantime, Abe felt compelled to escape, desperate for purpose, confused as all get out. And out of this distress came a decision. Why wait for a fucking meeting? Since when had he become such a passive putz? He would start the search for Gordon again, this time with more range, more mileage, more motivation. Abe put on old sweats and his underused Nikes. He did a few rudimentary, useless side stretches.

"I'm going for a run," he called, quickly closing the front door behind him, so as not to hear his mother's potentially withering response.

The outside air had cool undertones, the sun was midday low, red-tipped leaves scattered on the pavement. The clock had just been set back and all would be darkness by 4 pm. Abe huffed and puffed down the sidewalk at the speed of a rusty tricycle. In no time he'd be wearing a down jacket and cursing his Northeastern existence. But this first autumnal run he was guaranteed some other rewards. He'd sweat, he'd ache, he'd struggle. He would run. Run to find Gordon. Leave no avenue un-explored. No rock unturned.

Paddy: Lost and Found

Mid-morning in September, just as the TV went on the fritz, a woman approached the front entrance of the store. She struggled to open the door and get a stroller inside at the same time. Most young moms and babysitters master the dual push and shove, but this older gal didn't get the mechanics of it. Normally Paddy would've sat behind the counter and pretended not to see what was going on, let the potential customer figure it out on their own, but this lady was no spring chicken, and in serious need of assistance, so he got up to help.

"Here. Let me get that for you," Paddy said as he pushed the door open with one hand and guided the front of the stroller in with the other. There was a little boy, probably about two years old, sitting in the stroller. Pretty damn cute, with springy brown curls around his head and a face like one of those pudgy angels in a fancy painting. He stared up at Paddy like Paddy was the most fascinating, door-opening, stroller-guiding machine he'd ever seen. Paddy was about to walk away when the boy blurted out, "Bye bye, go go."

Bye bye, go go? What the heck did that mean? Paddy looked at the woman for some guidance. She wasn't one of those older gals who tried too hard and ended up looking like a pinched lizard, like Gloria with her canary-colored hair and painted face. The woman had short grey hair, almost as short as a man's but stylish. Feminine. Her clothes weren't fancy, but looked expensive. She had a gigantic scarf, all purples and reds and oranges, tied in a complicated knot around her neck. She wore glasses, big round black-rimmed spectacles. Behind them it looked as if her clear brown eyes didn't miss a thing.

"He's been repeating that bye bye, go go nonsense since we got near your store," she shrugged and lifted her eyebrows. Her forehead wrinkled up the way a woman in her seventies forehead was supposed to. "I was wondering if it meant he didn't want to come inside, but he seems totally fine now."

Paddy looked down at the kid, who lifted his right hand and scrunched his fingers down and up slowly like he was working out some kinks in the joints.

"That I've figured out," she said proudly. "That's how he waves."

"Oh," said Paddy.

"And he likes it if you do it the same way back."

"Huh. Okay." Paddy scrunched back. The kid burst out in hysterical chuckles.

The woman started laughing too, which made sense because the kid's giggles were pretty infectious. Even

Paddy felt a little gurgle welling up. For the first time in months, he smiled.

"When he does that, he reminds me so much of my son at that age." From the way she said it Paddy could tell; the son was no longer so endearing.

"So I guess this little guy is your grandson?" he asked.

"Yes. This is Milo. I'm Barbara, by the way."

"I'm Patrick. But my friends call me Paddy." You liar, Paddy thought. You have no friends. He reached a hand towards her, and she shook it. Her palm was warm and smooth. Paddy's was a calloused, dry nightmare. Mariah used to cringe if he got too enthusiastic and ran his hands too roughly along her bare flesh. "Nice to meet you Barbara."

"Same here, Paddy," said Barbara. Barbara didn't seem to notice or mind his sandpaper grip.

Nice smile, Paddy thought. Straight teeth, a little yellow maybe. Probably a former smoker.

"So Paddy. I'm wondering if you can help me."

Paddy stood a bit taller, puffed out his formerly broad chest, and sucked in his flabby gut. "Sure Barbara. How?"

"Well, Milo and I were on our way to Allenwood Park playground and I seem to have gotten lost. Can you tell me how to get there?"

"Sure. Let me draw you a little map."

"Oh, I have one of those already. My son made me one." She handed him a piece of paper. It was a perfectly legible, easy to follow map to the park.

"You're right here," Paddy pointed to a spot on the map. " So, all you have to do is go three blocks south from here, turn right and go two more blocks east."

Barbara looked worried. "I don't exactly have the best sense of direction. So, south is that way?"

She pointed west.

"Ah, no, it's that way." Paddy pointed south.

"Oh my..." she looked even more worried.

"Ya know what, Barbara? Why don't I just walk you two there." The words came out before Paddy even knew he wanted to make the offer. A little catch in his heart cried, what the fuck are you doing, you old idiot? You're not allowed to do this, whatever it is you're doing. But that didn't stop him.

"Really?"

"Yeah. No big deal. Happy to help." That catch in Paddy's heart kept mewling; it's too early you fat blowhard, too out-of-the-blue. But he grabbed his keys anyway and hung the "Back in Ten" sign on the door, the one for when he locked the door to use the crapper and didn't want some passing hooligans getting any ideas.

"Thank you so much, Paddy. I told my Abe I knew how to get there. He treats me like I'm an idiot, and then of course because he does that I get flustered and act like an idiot. Honestly? I am completely and totally lost."

Me too, Barbara, thought Paddy as he helped her get the stroller outside. Completely and totally.

David: To Be Real

Things weren't cool. Things just kept getting harder. Now that school had started, it was impossible for David to concentrate. His mind wandered constantly; his eyes, too. He examined each and every student, trying to decipher who they were, what they were. Was he the only gender-confused kid in the entire seventh grade? There had to be others. Or maybe not. Plus, he had no friends anymore. It was like he exuded outsider weirdo-ness without even trying. Chucky might smile at him every now and then, which was better than calling David a loser, but they never hung out. All the girls were nauseating and phony; all the boys were awkward assholes. The only place David felt comfortable was in the new Afterschool club that had formed since all the dogs went missing. They called themselves The Puppy Pals. Mostly they were a bunch of nerds, other kids who liked animals better than humans. Lately David felt pretty much the same. The Puppy Pals hadn't really done much yet, other than choose the doofus club name and hold a bake sale to raise money for tee shirts. They planned to all sit together at the upcoming Towne Council Meeting and chant things like, "Save Our Dogs!" and "People Need Pups!" The Puppy Pals might end up being super embarrassing, but at least it was something to do.

Whether at school, home, or elsewhere, David was falling apart emotionally. He had to at least finally reveal himself to his mother, even if she did freak out and cart him away to some loony bin for kids like him. So one night in early November, after chickening out a bunch of other times, he finally took the plunge.

"So what do you think?" David stood in front of his mother and tried to control his shaky body. As soon as he saw her expression, he knew this was a big mistake. The Nicole Miller shift felt itchy across his chest. His feet slipped sideways in opposite directions out of the kitten-heeled mules. The lipstick. The pearls. How many times over the last two months had he put this same entire outfit on, gotten within inches of the top of the stairs only to bail and retreat back to his room? The first time he balked, he'd called down to her that he had something to show her. But he just couldn't, so he went back to his room, quickly changed, wiped off the makeup, and ran down the stairs. They had watched some stupid YouTube videos together, David faux-laughing in a way his mother had long since failed to recognize as a sham.

"So funny, right?" she asked him.

"Hysterical, Mom, hysterical," he'd lied.

"Now what is it you wanted to show me?"

David shrugged. "Ah, nothing. I thought I had a bruise, but it was just a smudge of dirt. I'm good. All's cool."

Now a very uncool David stood in front of her, finally, dressed to impress. Loony bin here I come, he thought, as his mother stared at him.

"Davey," Lucinda said with a blunt tone that sounded as if maybe she wasn't sure it was really him. "What are you doing?"

"You—didn't—answer my—question," David's voice was a quivering mess. "How do I look?"

His mother's mouth opened and closed a few times, like a fish out of water, gasping for breath. Finally she said, "You look like a girl, David. Is that what you want me to say? Is this some kind of joke?"

"It's not a joke."

"Then what is it? What are you playing at?"

"I'm not playing, Mom."

"What's going on here?" She got up from her seat and grabbed David by the shoulders. He was almost as tall as her now, especially with the heels on. "Where did you get those pearls? Who's shoes are those? Are you wearing... lipstick?"

"This is my truth. I'm showing you my truth so I can make things right."

"Make what right? Jesus, David. You're scaring me." She let go of him and went back to her wine. She downed the stuff, and poured herself another glass. David had never drunk wine except for Manischewitz at *Pesach*, but his mother drank wine all the time. Maybe not as much as she had when his father still lived with them, but she still had at least one massive swig of the stuff every evening. He almost asked if he could have some too. But he didn't.

"This is me, Mom. I like to dress up in girls clothes."

She stared at him as if he was Freddy Krueger. "How long has this been going on?"

David shrugged. "Like, um, forever?"

"What?"

"I don't know if I'm supposed to be a boy or a girl. I feel like a girl inside sometimes, but not always."

"Of course you're supposed to be a boy. You are a boy. You have all the boy parts, remember?"

She wasn't getting it. "I want to kiss everyone," David said. "Not you—ew, gross—not that way. I mean, I do like to kiss you, but you know what I mean. Everyone else."

"Have you kissed people, David? Girls? Boys? Oh my god, men?"

"No. I haven't kissed any men, Mom. I haven't kissed anyone, but I want to. I'm a fucking freak."

"You're not a freak," his mother was crying now. "Don't ever say that about yourself. Ever."

"I steal things, Mom. I stole all of this," David plucked the pearls, pointed at Jeff Madden's sister Julia's kitten-heeled mules. "I steal things from you."

"I need to sit down." Lucinda grabbed the wine bottle and veered towards the living room. David hadn't seen his mother this way since the first night he'd heard her ranting at his father about Rachel. And the second, and the third, and the tenth. There'd been a lot of rant-filled nights back then.

David stood still, unsure what to do next. He wanted to rip off his outfit, scrub his face clean. He wanted to erase it all. He wanted to erase himself. Leave a blank space where David Leibowitz used to be, and start over as a different kid. A girl or a boy, he didn't care which. Just one who only wanted to kiss someone of the opposite sex, who was their own age or close to it. He was about to run back upstairs when his mother called, "Get your ass in here right away, young man," then slur-mumbled, "Or young whatever-you-are."

David slipped off the mules and walked more sure-footedly into the living room. His mother was sprawled like a beached whale on one end of the sofa, her head against one gigantic throw pillow, another pillow clutched to her stomach like a shield.

"Come," she commanded. "Sit."

David did as she asked. He wedged himself as far from her as possible at the other end of the couch. His bare legs stuck out from under the dress like a couple of pale, speckled twigs. The hair on his calves had darkened recently. And there seemed to be more of it. He wanted to shave it off.

"You never told me," his mother said in an almost whisper. "You could've, you know."

David thought how that was bullshit. Telling his mother anything personal or serious always led to an endless blah-blah-blah, back in my day-type lecture. "It's hard to tell you things, Mom. You don't really listen all that well."

She sniffled. "Now you sound like your father."

"Thanks. That really helps." David got up to leave.

"Sit down!" his mother yelled. "Please!" She started sobbing.

David should've guessed it would go this way. What an idiot he'd been. He sat as commanded, but didn't know what to say or do. His mother kept crying. Finally after what seemed like hours, but was probably only a few minutes she stopped blubbering and said, "You're right. I am a terrible listener. I have to get better at that. I'm not perfect, David. I know that." She stared out the window across the street towards the Kearny Mansion. Then she turned back to look at him. "Believe you me."

His mom's face was all blotchy. Her nose was running

and her eyes were so red they looked like someone had rubbed dust in them. David Dust, he thought. I am toxic.

"You're okay, Mom," he said. "You really are. Like, in the mother category I'd give you a solid B."

She laughed. That was a good sign. Maybe he hadn't completely poisoned their life together by showing his true self.

"Okay. A solid B-plus/A-minus," David said.

His mother reached up and touched his hair. Then she combed her fingers along his scalp, which was what she used to do when he was little and couldn't get to sleep.

"Oh great," she sighed. "Just what every perfectionistic mother wants to hear. An almost, but not quite good enough grade. I appreciate your honesty. So now, as I work towards a solid A-minus, you have to explain: what the fuck is going on with you?"

David did as best he could. He talked about his dreams, his love of pink, his desire for silk and satin, his many, many crushes, his stealing habit, his unending confusion. The whole time his mother stroked his hair, or squeezed his hand, or rubbed his back. But she didn't say a word, didn't interrupt or instruct. Which, for his mother, was a big deal. When he was done, she only said two words: "*Oy vey.*"

Then she wrapped her arms around him and said three words: I love you.

They snuggled on the couch for a while, not talking, just like they had when David was little. Eventually his mother got up and said. "More about this tomorrow. I'm a mess. Not just because of you. It's late and you have school in the morning. We'll talk more about it when you get home in the afternoon. I'm going to sleep. You should too." She kissed David on the forehead. "And FYI, that dress looks way better on you than it ever looked on me."

Lucinda: Blindside

Sleep. That was a joke. The minute Lucinda laid down she knew it was a lost cause. How could she possibly sleep with her head spinning in this alcohol and adrenaline stew? Lucinda got out of bed and stumbled to her bathroom. With the cold spigot turned full blast, she alternated slurps with splashes, swallowing to dilute the contents of her high-proof stomach then slapping her face with the icy water like a hearty Norwegian after a sauna.

"You're a terrible mother," she said to her dripping wet reflection, an ugly woman with blotchy, wrinkled skin and bloodshot eyes. How could she not have known about David? Or what was it about her that made it impossible for him to let her know? Either way, it sucked. She sucked.

"And you're a terrible person." Her stomach gurgled and her heart pounded. Lucinda sat on the closed toilet seat with her head in her hands. She'd move quickly to reposition herself if this percolating nausea turned into dry, or not so dry heaves.

Lucinda was such a liar. The worst kind. The kind that lies to themself first, and everybody else after. She had known. She'd known when he was a toddler. When all he wanted was to wrap himself in her silk scarves, the pinker the better. When he'd enviously eyed the girls playing tea party at the playground. When he'd innocently asked to wear dresses, always out of earshot of Dan, always just to her. But Mommy, I want that, he'd say pointing to a tutu or a Disney Princess nightgown.

She ignored him. Or pretended it wasn't happening. Or distracted him with something else. She bribed him with food, money, more TV time.

Worst of all, she'd let Dan run the show with his macho masculinity. His fine-tuned brand of obsessive control. The color-coded storage system for his tools. The polished shoes and ironed polo shirts. The perfectly balanced meals he demanded with foods that never touched, sauces that never bled. The competitive nature that oozed into every activity. Everything a contest. Everything had a prize.

By the time David entered Kindergarten all his girly tendencies had disappeared. Or at least seemed to have. He played soccer—as Dan had insisted—and became a little star. His friends were all boys. He acted boyish. He looked boyish. And so what if he'd become more distant as he grew up? Didn't all kids? Lucinda had told herself that the sullen withdrawal, the closed doors, the blank stares off into space were all part of basic childhood development. Like any good conflict avoider, she focused on what looked, smelled, and felt normal. She shoved everything else under the proverbial rug. For almost ten years she'd not once again thought about David's girly phase. And now here it was. And from what he'd told her, it had never gone away.

Lucinda rose and steadied herself, white knuckling the edge of the vanity. She looked again at the harridan in the mirror. "You blind idiot," she hissed. "Over there fucking cray-cray Brady Cole." She should've been home, taking care of David, really helping with the Balthazar search. Really paying attention. From now on, that was what she'd do. David first. David only. Whatever David needed. She would go back to the Kearny Mansion now and tell Brady it was all over. The renovation. The fucking. All of it.

In spite of being drunker than an off duty Irish cop on Saint Patrick's day, Lucinda managed to get downstairs, out of her house, and across the street. She rang the doorbell, an old style, sonorous, alto-toned DING DONG which she'd admired on her first visit to the mansion, back when she'd begun this mess, making note that this bell would not need to be changed.

"Lou," Brady gasped when he saw her. "A surprise visit. Wow, loving this—"

Lucinda actually saw two Bradys. She lurched across the threshold past them. "Can you make me some coffee?"

He followed Lucinda as she teetered towards the kitchen. She found a stool to sit on and suddenly felt very, very weary. She lay her head atop crossed arms on the ugly yellow formica—which would be replaced in two weeks by stunning ebony granite—and closed her eyes. She could hear Brady opening cabinets, scooping coffee, pouring water. She couldn't wait to taste the hot, bitter brew. It would be just the thing to give her the sanity, clarity, and courage to say what she needed to say. Until then she'd just lay there and wait.

"Hey Lou, you look like you could use more than coffee. How about I do something else to cheer you up?"

Lucinda managed to raise a halting hand in front of the Bradys. "No sex. No."

"I was thinking of something else, babe."

Lucinda put her head back down and mumbled into her armpit. "Whatever."

"Stay right here. I'll be right back."

There was a long moment of silence, but for the final blurps of the coffeemaker. Lucinda was on the precipice of nodding out when Brady returned. All of a sudden the air was filled with clumsy, jagged music; tinny notes from what sounded like a guitar on steroids. Lucinda opened her eyes just in time to hear Brady begin to sing.

Ugh. That terrible song. His love song for her. "Lovely Lou." He whipped out that stupid dulcimer at every opportunity, playing the song, revising it, adding and subtracting ever more inane verses. That night, Brady's voice was particularly gravelly and off-pitch. Lucinda let this strange man continue his tune, while reconsidering her original reason for being there. Calling it quits might not be the best idea after all. Brady and his money and his house. All of it could help her. She'd still be able to give David what he needed. Maybe even more so. Who knew what might be down the road for her gender-confused, wonderful angel of child. Who knew how much being David was now going to cost?

Brady gave the dulcimer a final strum, then looked up at Lucinda with needy, pleading eyes. "So, what did you think?" he asked.

Lucinda forced a smile.

Brady's song: Lovely Lou

Verse 1:
She came through the door,
and I couldn't have asked for more.
Oh Lovely Lou,
what should I do.
She offered me her hand,
and though it wasn't what I had planned,
I fell for Lou,
what could I do.

CHORUS:
And now it's as clear as day,
that my love is here to stay,
it's not something to wash away,
she's a goddess to who I pray,
Lovely Lou, Lovely Lou, Lovely Lou.

Verse 2:
She came through the door,
this woman who I adore,

Oh Lovely Lou,
what should I do.
It was clear from the start,
when she offered me her heart,
Our fates were sealed,
My soul revealed.

CHORUS:
And now it's as clear as day,
that my love is here to stay,
it's not something to wash away,
she's a goddess to who I pray,
Lovely Lou, Lovely Lou, Lovely Lou.

Verse 3:
My life was such a mess,
then I saw you in that dress,
Oh Lovely Lou,
I wanted you.
We had ourselves a time,
our love is not a crime,
there's so much time for more,
you're a shock to my core,
Lovely Lou, Lovely Lou, Lovely Lou.

CHORUS:
And now it's as clear as day,
that my love is here to stay,
it's not something to wash away,
she's a goddess for who I pray,
Lovely Lou, Lovely Lou, Lovely Lou.

Chapter Eight

Nell: Of All the Places

Nell stood in the shadows, as far to the rear of the auditorium as was possible while still being in it. With her back against a display case of dusty trophies, her arms hugging her torso, she tried to keep her gaze downward as Towne residents piled into the auditorium, loud as a murder of crows. She caught snippets of conversations, inane statements she wished she could respond to. But she knew better. In her mind she had much to say.

"How many dogs are missing now?"

Not enough.

"I think it's over twenty."

Twenty-three to be exact.

"My Puff Puff has been gone for over six weeks. She's just a tiny delicate little thing."

Puff Puff is now Gaia, Ma'am, and she feels more powerful than ever.

"I'm not a dog owner myself, but I think it is my civic duty to help any way I can."

You can help by minding your own business, Mister.

"The kids are beside themselves, still, even after all this time. I can't imagine what's happened to Tillie."

Tillie was a stupid name for such a huntress, so now she's Artemis, and she's fabulous and never thinks about any of you at all.

"David, are you going to sit with me and Denise, or with your friends?"

Nell snuck a peek. There was David Leibowitz and his mother, Lucinda. Lucinda looked different than she had the last time Nell had seen her, at ARF talking to the clueless older woman who ran the place and never noticed when Nell, or David for that matter, stole things. Or maybe it wasn't that Lucinda looked different, but that she exuded a different energy. Nell had always felt cognizant of other people's moods and attitudes. She had an even keener intuition for human auras since forming her canine pack. She could sense their emotional pulse in a very dog-like way. This Lucinda exuded a combination of determination, hope, fear, and regret. The Lucinda Leibowitz Nell had known when teaching her son piano lessons had been a clueless, vapid, glosser-over.

David also gave off a different vibe. Softer than he'd been when he'd swiped that blobby brown print blouse off its hanger at ARF, but less afraid. This David was fiercer but more forgiving. Nell watched as he squeezed his mother's hand.

"I'm gonna sit with them if that's okay, Mom?"

"It's more than okay, Davey. Go on. We'll meet up when the meeting is over."

Nell looked down quickly as David rushed past her

towards a bunch of giggling middle schoolers holding homemade signs that read, "Puppy Pals Persist" and "Power to the Puppies." Most disturbing was "We Will Find Our Dogs!" These mini-vigilantes worried her. Kids had instincts. Kids had wiles. Kids had energy. She'd have to fortify the entrance to her compound, put up a better, kid-proof gate.

Nell kept her head down as more people filed in. The place was packed. She sensed someone else come to stand against the back wall to her left. She could hear them breathing heavily. Their scent was overwhelming: sweaty, cheesy, and distinctively male. She scooched further away, still not looking up, hoping this man would keep his distance and that the dreadful meeting would soon be called to order. She wanted to get the vital information she'd come for and then make a hasty and well-informed retreat home.

"Attention, attention," a voice called through a crackly microphone. "We'll be getting started now so everyone settle in, please."

A slow hush descended on the crowd. Nell raised her head to watch once she sensed everyone was seated with their attentions directed towards the stage.

"Welcome fellow Towne residents and dog lovers. For those of you who don't know me, I'm George Takharian, President of the Towne Town Council. I myself have a wonderful pooch named Ollie, who luckily is still with me, safe at home."

Nell had always thought pooch an obscene, offensive term. It made a dog sound like a flabby, flaccid genital, not a regal, respectable beast. George Takharian was himself flabby and flaccid. An old man with a dyed brown combover and the physique of a giant mound of Playdoh.

"We're here to discuss the horrible and perplexing disappearance of twenty-three dogs, who were, or rather are, your companions and true canine citizens of our fair town."

Citizens, thought Nell. Slaves would be more apt.

"Before opening up the floor, I thought it would be great for us all to hear from an expert on this kind of situation, so I've called in Hector Moore from the Missing and Lost Dog Division of the City Animal Care Center. I'm sure Hector will have boatloads of valuable information for us out here in the 'burbs and hopefully some guidelines for action. So, take it away, Hector!"

Hector Moore was a scrawny man who couldn't have been much older than Nell. Up until then he'd been sitting on a folding chair, nervously biting his nails. Nell braced herself for Hector's message, wanted to spit at this member of the enemy camp as he stood and walked uncomfortably to the mike.

"Hey folks. First off, super sorry about this situation. It really blows, for all of you. But right off the bat, you need to know; the likelihood is that given the amount of time that's passed the dogs are probably all far away from here by now. Most likely living in new homes scattered all over the country."

The audience got restless. Somebody cried out "What the fuck?" Nell, however, could not have been happier. Hector's doomsday message was perfect: all far away from here, all over the country.

"Don't get me wrong," Hector shrugged, "I'm happy to brainstorm some alternatives to what you've all been doing already, but with this number of abductions, and the lack of any clues or leads, this looks to me to be the work of a very well-organized dog-napping ring. These guys know their stuff. They keep shifting locations, players, email accounts, websites, the works. It can be years before we've located missing dogs and by then most dogs and new owners have bonded and the whole situation gets really complicated."

Nell felt so relieved she could kiss him.

"Put the knife in deeper why don't you?" cried out a woman sitting near the former enslaver of Mags, now Malala, a beautiful, compassionate collie who'd been abandoned for hours and hours, hungry and stressed, while this woman indulged herself in all sorts of useless spa treatments.

"What the hell are we doing here then?" asked a man in a suit sitting near the spa woman.

Hector shrugged. "Honestly? I don't know."

The audience was a rumble of this is bullshit, what the fuck, I could be home watching *This Is Us*, I told you we should've kept that dinner reservation, and on and on.

"This is a total waste of time," bellowed someone who had been sitting in the last row of the auditorium not far from Nell. "I'm blowing this popsicle stand." He stood in indignation. It was the old grump from the Gas n' Go.

"No shit," said the stinky man who'd been leaning against the back wall near Nell, "Total waste."

Nell forgot her caution and glanced over at him. He was large, hairy, dressed in running clothes. She knew this guy. She'd first seen him months ago, around the time she'd happened upon Raphael, chained to that street sign. Lately she'd seen this man running around all over town. She'd always been careful to avoid him, riding her bike up alternative streets, staying out of view.

Now in the dim recesses of the Towne High School auditorium, their eyes locked. Nell should've looked away, but she hesitated. She hadn't looked eye to eye with a living creature not covered in fur for many months, and while this guy was hairy, he wasn't a dog. The novelty of it wooed her. Caught her off guard. She took in his aura: kindness, confusion, impatience, desperation. She realized her grave mistake when the man's expression tightened and he said, "Whoa! Freaky Sting Ray Girl. Of all the places."

Nell did not hesitate a moment longer. She bolted from the auditorium, raced to her bicycle, and fled the scene, pedaling as quickly as her weak and worried legs could manage.

Abe: She Was the Way

Abe had been running almost daily for over two weeks. He'd started with a paltry one mile jog on the days Barbara invaded his home, but quickly amped it up, adding evening runs on non-babysitting days, handing Milo over to Claire the minute she walked through the door. Claire didn't mind. She was glad that Abe was getting in shape, but mostly, she loved bonus alone time with her baby boy.

Abe hadn't found Gordon yet, but he'd run up and down every street in Towne searching. At first he'd only been able to manage a mile or two before returning home a wheezing, shin-splintered basket case. But gradually Abe grew stronger. Two miles became three became four. On good days, maybe five. He'd become an amateur cartographer too, mapping out his morning routes in a notebook before leaving the house. Perhaps four blocks north on Mulberry, six east on Grayson, three south on Forest, ending with zig-zag northwest on this tree, that person, this tree, that person, cutting a jagged route home.

His gaze would shift from side to side, eagle-eyed at open curtains. Ears tuned for Gordon's familiar bark. Abe stopped to examine unscooped turds, hoping he'd recognized the shape and general color. But none of the stray shit ever bore Gordon's signature. Still, it had been over two months and it was likely Gordon was eating different food. It was possible the shits Abe stared at were Gordon's shits. There was no way of knowing.

The running and the searching kept Abe from

sliding too far down the slippery slope of moping. It kept him manly, made him feel almost virile. Even if his search for Gordon proved futile, who could fault a guy who worked on increasing his mileage? Who got out there, rain or shine to increase his serotonin levels, got his endorphins pumped, his metabolism tweaked? He'd pound the pavement, loving the deep squish of his Nikes in the occasional puddle, felt like a racer when he dodged twigs, slippery leaves.

By the end of the first week Abe was clocking three to four miles at a decent clip. His legs felt like pistons, his breath a purring engine. By the end of week two he was running a solid five daily, his belly jiggled less and he could sing along with the Gordon-searching playlist he'd compiled titled "Hi Hi Go Go." It must've been true what they said about endorphins, because in spite of there not being even a hint of his old pal anywhere in Towne, Abe still ended his runs feeling better than ever. His post-run sense of wellbeing came as close to optimism as he'd ever experienced without the aid of some kind of drug.

He'd almost forgotten about the town council meeting on the night of November 12th until Claire reminded him when she came home that evening.

"Aren't you going to that meeting about the dogs tonight?" she asked as she sat at the table feeding Milo his dinner.

"Ah, oh yeah, that," Abe said. He'd been so focused on running lately, and when not running himself, watching the pros on TV, that he'd lost track of the days. "I'd like to. You cool with me heading out?"

"No Mouse. Poke, poke, poke, not scoop, scoop, scoop." Claire was attempting to get Milo to stab his tiny broccoli florets with his spork.

Abe didn't need to ask again. Obviously Claire was cool with his going out. Sometimes it felt like she didn't even really care if he was there to begin with. Whatever,

Abe thought, this way I can get in another couple of miles.

The meeting was scheduled to start at 7 pm. The high school was about a mile away. Abe left his house at 6:52 pm, which meant he had to clock an eight-minute mile to get there right on time. If he sprinted he might make it.

Panting and heaving the last quarter mile, Abe plodded up the walkway to the school. After a hearty slurp of water from a stained porcelain water fountain outside the auditorium door, which brought back memories of the same metallic smell of the water fountains from his own high school days, Abe bounded inside. The place was packed, not a seat left in the house. Abe took a spot against the back wall, still breathing heavily, the sweat covering his body doing its naturally-intended job, cooling him off, if also stinking him up. Luckily there wasn't anyone too close to him, but for one woman, a scrawny specimen dressed like all the other Towne women dressed in the autumnal months, as if she were some cross between a yacht owner and a dairy farmer. Abe could tell by her body language—shoulders hunched, arms crossed and face averted, that she wanted him to keep his distance. And so he did.

Abe didn't have high expectations for this meeting. He still held onto an unfounded presumption that he had better instincts and higher intellect than the average Towne resident. He'd spent his formative years in the gritty City. He'd had his nose in all sorts of intense, critical urban stuff. He'd seen things, read things, done metropolitan things. Abe knew it was unfair to think this way, but he couldn't help himself. He thought most of the people in Towne were a bunch of nincompoops, that their bland, suburban lives meant they weren't capable of creative solutions, or proactive strategies. He knew he was an awful snob, but had chosen not to do anything to shift his perspective for the two-plus years he'd lived in Towne. Now in the quest to find Gordon, he'd have to give these people the benefit of the doubt. He'd do anything, even stand in the back of this auditorium waiting for something, anything to begin.

"Attention, attention," a voice called through a crackly microphone. "We'll be getting started now so everyone settle in, please."

The man at the mike reminded Abe of Mr. Potato Head. Once people had shut up he continued.

"Welcome fellow Towne residents and dog lovers. For those of you who don't know me, I'm George Takharian, President of the Towne Town Council. I myself have a wonderful pooch named Ollie, who luckily is still with me, safe at home."

Geezus, thought Abe. Rub in how unlucky the rest of us are, why don't you. From then on, things got even worse. George called an expert up to the mike, some guy who came from City who had a lot of experience tracking lost dogs. Or rather, not tracking lost dogs. The guy confirmed all of Abe's deepest worries: that given the amount of time that had passed, the dogs were all far, far away, that they'd probably been swiped, carted and sold to new owners. In Gordon's case, Abe imagined, life in some pit bull fight ring, being forced to battle, getting mauled to death—or worse, mauled over and over and over again.

The audience's uproar matched Abe's inner turmoil. What was there left to discuss? They might as well all give up. A man stood up from the last row, right in front of Abe and yelled, "This is a total waste of time. I'm blowing this popsicle stand."

Abe would recognize that raspy voice and bulbous bald head anywhere. It was his old pal Patrick from Schepp's.

"No shit," Abe said, "Total waste." As he turned to leave, he looked at the woman who'd been standing nearby. There was something odd about her. She was younger than he'd imagined. While she was outfitted like so many other women in Towne, the clothes hung off her frame as if she were an unwilling mannequin. Her face was pale and nearly cadaverous. A few matted tendrils of hair had come loose from under her jaunty beret, clearly not a hairdo coiffed at Tessa's, where Claire got her severe bob chopped and glazed every month. The woman's gaze unnerved him, the blue eyes blazing with a certain insanity, or maybe brilliance. The mouth set in a rigor mortis grimace. She stared at Abe as if she were seeing through to his soul. He felt a shiver run up his spine. It wasn't from sweat cooling on his skin, it was from recognition.

"Whoa!" he said, "Freaky Sting Ray Girl. Of all the places."

She fled immediately, not looking back. Not realizing as she pedaled away on her absurd bike that Abe was hot on her trail. He had a feeling she was the way.

Paddy: A New Wrinkle

Paddy doubted much would come of it. An auditorium filled with desperate dog owners, searching for answers when there probably were none. But he felt he owed it to Mariah to at least show up. If she'd been alive, no question she'd have been there in the front row making her opinions heard loud and clear. Then again, if Mariah had been alive, Barney wouldn't have disappeared. The little guy would've been glued to her side as usual, happy as a pig in shit as long as Mariah was nearby. And Mariah, for all her confusion in those final days, would've known the minute someone was anywhere near the little critter.

Paddy missed Barney in particular because the dog was the last living vestige of life with Mariah. There was no next generation of O'Hallorans to see her aura in, her genetic imprint, her incredible spirit. No children or grandkids to look at to be reminded of how and who she loved aside from Paddy himself. But there had been Barney. Paddy could comfort the dog, share grief with the dog. He could see in Barney's shaggy brown face the results of adoration from a mistress who showered him with kisses and treats and patience and affection galore. So maybe, just maybe, this meeting would offer some fresh possibilities.

When he got to the auditorium, there were still plenty of seats towards the front, but Paddy chose a spot at the rear, as far away from Gloria Nevins as was possible. There she was, holding court by the foot of the stage, dressed in some get-up that seemed more appropriate for a ballroom dance competition than a pow-wow about dogs. Paddy assumed the man by her side was her new boyfriend George, the head of the Towne Town Council, the guy who would be running this meeting. George reminded Paddy of a Pep Boy from the old insignia over each of the automotive shops; the one in the middle with the creepy little mustache and beady eyes. Gloria kept stroking the shiny fabric of George's flashy, striped shirt as if George were a dog himself.

Woof, Paddy thought. Good for the two of you. Glad you found each other. Paddy settled into his small, wooden seat made for slimmer, younger bodies and reflected on his own state of semi-romantic affairs. Because there was a new wrinkle in his life also. A wrinkle named Barbara.

The second time Barbara came to the Gas n' Go, after the exchange of dollar bills and quarters, an invitation, of sorts, was delivered.

"I'm not exactly sure if I can find that playground," she started, "But I think I can manage. Unless you'd like to show me again."

Paddy put the "Back in Ten" sign in the window and led her to the park. He even sat for a spell—a spell much longer than ten minutes—with Barbara while Milo toddled with the other toddlers.

The third time she was more direct, "Milo and I were heading to the playground. Would you like to join us?" And so he did.

After that no verbal invitation was needed. Every time Barbara and Milo came by, the door was locked with Paddy's new, improved, time adjustable "Back at (whatever) pm" sign on the door, and off they all went.

It helped that Barbara was easy on the eyes, or at least, Paddy's slightly nearsighted eyes. It helped that she arrived at the station every Monday and Wednesday like clockwork. There was nothing Paddy had to do but wait. At 11:30 am he'd look out the window and see her pushing Milo's stroller on the sidewalk, walking at a nice clip for an old gal, her sturdy but not too-hefty legs propelling without a limp or arthritic catch. Paddy would rise from his stool and open the door.

"Hello Paddy," she'd say. "How's your morning been so far?"

Paddy would shrug and say, "Same old, same old. How about yours?"

At which point Barbara would start a narrative of the morning's events: how the traffic had been getting out of Village on her way to Towne, cute Milo anecdotes, what she'd eaten for breakfast, weather-related aches and pains, complaints about Abe, her difficult son, perceived slights by her workaholic daughter-in-law Claire. Paddy usually didn't like Chatty Cathy types. But when Barbara talked— and she talked a lot—it was like listening to a soothing melody. It almost didn't matter what she said. The sound of her voice mesmerized him. It called to mind the plucking of gentle strings. One of those guitar-ish things. A dulcimer, perhaps.

Paddy knew Barbara wouldn't be at the meeting. For one, she lived in Village, not Towne. Secondly, Barbara was not a fan of dogs. She had mentioned earlier that day, when they'd taken their customary stroll to the playground, that her difficult, non-communicative son Abe might be at the meeting.

"He's a big man," she'd said. "He takes after his father, my Morty. Neither one of them a natural athlete. Both of them natural eaters. Maybe you'll see him there. Dark bushy hair, which he may have up in one of those silly man buns. He wears glasses. He'll be dressed like a schlump."

Paddy scoured the audience for someone with these very un-Towne-ish characteristics. None of the men in the audience fit Barbara's description. Paddy twiddled his thumbs, eavesdropped a bit, suppressed a belch. Finally, once the place was packed like a giant can of sardines, Gloria sat down in the front row, like she was the First Lady at the inauguration, while George got up on the stage and spoke into the mike.

"Welcome fellow Towne residents and dog lovers. For those of you who don't know me, I'm George Takharian, President of the Towne Council. I myself have a wonderful pooch named Ollie, who luckily is still with me, safe at home."

Christ, thought Paddy. What a stupid opening. Read the house, George, read the house. After that, it all went to shit, really. George had called in this guy from City who knew all sorts of depressing facts about this kind of missing dog situation. The basic message? Fuggedaboutit. The dogs were gone. They'd never be found. He might as well have told everyone to go home and drown their sorrows however they chose. Bourbon, beer, marijuana, fudge.

"Put the knife in deeper why don't you?" cried out a woman Paddy recognized. Forest Green Subaru Outback 2014. Catalytic converter on the fritz in 2016.

"What the hell are we doing here then?" asked a guy who drove a sweet little beige Carrera when he was on his own. A gas-guzzling silver Denali when he was with the family.

Hector shrugged. "Honestly? I don't know."

That's when the shit hit the fan. It was pandemonium.

George's guest speaker had turned his big hoopla into a total disaster. George stood on the stage while the audience went apeshit, looking like a nauseated ape himself. Paddy wondered if George had even bothered to talk to this Moore beforehand. Gloria, meanwhile, sat in her seat, craning her head this way and that like a panicked ostrich.

A bunch of kids, not yet fully teenaged, but with all the pimply, awkward signs of trouble ahead, began to cry. The kids wore brown tee shirts and held signs reading Puppy this, and Puppy that.

"This is a total waste of time. I'm blowing this popsicle stand," yelled Paddy, shocking himself as the words bellowed like a police siren from his mouth. He'd meant to just think the thought. Oh well. He stood to leave. What was done was done.

David: A Little Niggle

The day after his big reveal, when David came home from school he and his mom talked and talked. There were tears. Lots of tears. There was pacing, and stormy trips in and out of the room. But in the end, decisions were made. David's mother would buy him pretties and pinks, as long as he stopped stealing and agreed to therapy.

"Someone reputable," she said.

"Someone cool," David said.

His mother rolled her eyes. She couldn't help it. And David couldn't really blame her. "Coolness doesn't matter, David. They can be gay, straight, transgender, cross-dressing. Whatever. I don't care. As long as they know about this gender and sexuality stuff and can help you figure out yours."

Towne wasn't exactly a hotbed of LGBTQ resources. It took a couple of weeks to find the right shrink. After an expanded search, his mother found someone highly recommended two towns over. David was scheduled to meet with the guy the day after the big Towne Town Council Meeting. Meanwhile, David and the other Puppy Pals spent every afternoon in the Art Room making posters and flyers, planning to find their dogs in what they all knew was a mostly powerless pubescent way. There was comfort for David, however, in chatting and sharing stories with these kids who all bordered on misfitting, some more transparently than others. None more in hiding than David himself.

Among the motley crew: Benji Morrison wore thick glasses that made his eyes look like pinheads and had a perpetually runny nose. Danesha Cole was the only black kid in the entire grade. David couldn't even imagine what it must feel like for her to be in such a white and uptight town. Chloe Barnsworth had always been pathologically shy, quivering in fear if anyone so much as established direct eye contact with her. Hyperallergic Paul Shack wore his Epi-pen on a lanyard around his neck, just in case of an allergic reaction. Samantha Borstein picked her nose and ate it publicly without any reservations.

"I'm surprised to see you here," Benji had said to David at the initial meeting.

"Why?" David asked. "My dog Balzy was one of the first to go missing."

Benji shrugged. "I dunno. It's just that you usually hang out with Chucky and all those guys, don't you?"

"Not so much anymore," said David.

"Plus you're, like, a jock. I'd have thought you'd have

some sports practice thing that was more important to you."

David looked at Benji through Benji's smudged glasses and placed both hands on Benji's skinny shoulders. "Morrison. Let's get one thing straight. Nothing is more important than our dogs. Am I right?"

Benji smiled. "You are so right."

They cut out construction paper signs, Sharpie-d bubble lettered slogans. They slathered Elmer's Glue on ripped out media images and created canine collages. They practiced their chants. Even Chloe added her mouse-like squeak to their cause.

The afternoon before the big meeting, they all had high hopes.

"We need to convince the grownups that we can help," said Beth Eastman as she combed her nail-bitten fingers through her greasy hair.

"Totally," agreed Danesha. "We need to make sure they give us something to do."

"Power to the Puppy Pals," cried David as he stood from the work table. He lifted both arms high and pumped his fists.

"Power to the Puppy Pals," everyone else chanted. Everyone but for Matt Tishman, who'd been sitting next to David. Matt was staring at David's waist. David looked down and saw the frilled edge of a new pair of panties his mother had just bought him peeking out from the waistline of his jeans. Immediately he dropped his arms.

David cringed as Matt stood up slowly next to him, expecting a horrible end to David's brief respite of belonging in Puppy Pals.

David's whole body stiffened. David turned to look, expecting inevitable middle school cruelty; but instead, Matt smiled warmly, awkwardly, a full set of railroad track braces across his pokey rabbit-y teeth.

David held out a tentative fist. Matt bumped.

Once David and his mother arrived at the auditorium, he left her to join the Puppy Pals. He sat between Paul and Beth.

"You haven't eaten anything with peanuts today, have you?" Paul asked.

"No Paul," said David. "I'm clean."

David noticed other non-Puppy Pal kids scattered around the auditorium sitting with their families. Lance Radison glued to his phone in the fourth row. Dumbo Laura with her mother Denise, who was sitting next to his own mother, Lucinda. Chucky was there with his parents. The Weintraubs' Australian shepherd Tillie had been swiped from the back of their Denali when they'd left Tillie alone in their driveway, supposedly for less than five minutes. David knew this secondhand from overhearing the news in the school lunchroom. It wasn't like Chucky told him directly. It wasn't like Chucky told him anything anymore.

People poured into the auditorium. It was like a rock concert or something. The rumbles from the audience got the Puppy Pals excited. They chanted. They sang:

"Oh where, oh where
Has my little dog gone?
Oh where, oh where can he be?
With his ears cut short
And his tail cut long
Oh where, oh where can he be?
I think he went down
To the building site
To see what he could see
And in his mouth
Was a globe so bright
I wonder what could it be

Oh where, oh where
Has my little dog gone?
Oh where, oh where can he be?
With his ears cut short
And his tail cut long
Oh where, oh where can he be?

Some of the people around them joined in, some looked annoyed. David noticed Laura rolling her eyes. Loser, David thought. He saw Chucky schlumping down in his seat. Who needs you anyway, thought David. But not really believing himself—not yet.

Finally a roly-poly old man dressed in a horrible shiny striped shirt that did nothing for his complexion got up on stage and called the meeting to order.

"Welcome fellow Towne residents and dog lovers. For those of you who don't know me, I'm George Takharian, President of the Towne Town Council. I myself have a wonderful pooch named Ollie, who luckily is still with me, safe at home."

David didn't see why the man had to tell them his dog was still with him. It seemed braggy, maybe even kind of mean. But whatever. David sat still and paid close attention, hoping the man might have something valuable to offer, some solutions that would bring the dogs home.

It turned out the man had nothing to offer. All he did was introduce another man, this one younger, and not quite as unattractive or old. His name was Hector Moore and he was a missing dog expert from City.

"Please, please," whispered David. "Help us find our dogs."

"Amen," Beth said as she patted David's forearm on the armrest between them, with her semi-greasy hand.

"Hey folks," Mr. Moore started, "First off, super sorry about this situation. It really blows, for all of you."

He understands, thought David. That's a start. Hector Moore had a nice, kind face. He looked concerned, like he knew how tough this was for all of them. David was sure Mr. Moore would tell them what to do, that David and the other Puppy Pals would leave the meeting with a plan of action.

But as Mr. Moore continued to talk, David's heart sunk. He could literally feel it plunging from his chest into his abdomen like a heavy stone. Dogs far away…years before they're located…dogs bonded…really complicated.

Denise stood up and yelled: "put a knife in why don't you?"

The audience exploded. David could hear snippets of frustration and anger as his own ears buzzed with disappointment; this is bullshit, are you kidding, what the hell, George, I want my Puff Puff back, I told you we should've kept that dinner reservation.

Beth began sobbing. Paul wheezed. Danesha wailed. Matt muttered fuck fuck fuck under his breath. Soon all the Puppy Pals were in despair, including David. Thick hot tears streamed down his cheeks.

"This is a total waste of time," yelled a voice that sounded like the Great and Terrible Wizard of Oz. David turned to see the old Gas n' Go man stand and shuffle out of his seat down a bit from David in the last row. "I'm blowing this popsicle stand." As the man passed the Puppy Pals he shook his head and muttered, "You poor little devils. Duped by the adults, once again."

By then all the Pals were crying, and their tears were contagious. David leaned against Beth, who had her head in Danesha's lap. Danesha was hugging Chloe who held hands with Matt. Benji had taken off his glasses and had his head in his own hands. Paul was leaning over Benji's chair and rubbing his shoulders while he himself wailed like a grieving widow.

David felt Beth's shudders against his cheek. He snuck a tearful peek at the rest of the Puppy Pals and felt a little niggle that wasn't all bad. Balzy might not ever return, but finding other outliers to love had started to ease David's grief at losing him.

Lucinda: No Backseat Driving

Two weeks after David came downstairs in Lucinda's dress, she was still in quite a state. It was no longer a state of shock, it was a frenzy of action, fueled by parental guilt. When not managing window replacements and radiant heat floor installations at the Kearny Mansion, while simultaneously dodging Brady's pleas and gropes, she was back at home reading everything she could about how to support David in his quest for gender truth. Was David a he? A she? A they? When she asked David directly, he started to tremble, then screamed, "I don't know!" before running away. Thank god she'd finally located a shrink for him to talk to. Dr. Thomas McQueen in the town of Burg seemed to have all the right credentials, and he'd been so kind and calm with her on the phone.

"I'm a terrible mother," Lucinda said. "I knew this was brewing and I just pretended it wasn't there."

"Mrs. Leibowitz?"

"Call me Lucinda, please."

"First off, I'm sure you're a wonderful mother. But most importantly, this isn't about you or your parenting."

"Oh, okay."

"This is about David. Exploring gender identity is a complicated journey. You will be a passenger. He will be in the driver's seat."

"Got it. Passenger. I can do that."

"Good. No backseat driving, Mom. And put on your seatbelt. It is going to be a bumpy ride."

For the time being, David seemed okay as long as Lucinda didn't ask too many questions. He promised to stop stealing. As an incentive Lucinda brought home gifts for him; a three-pack of rainbow socks, pink frilled underpants, a lime-green angora sweater with sparkles. It also helped that he'd joined a group at school who called themselves the Puppy Pals, all kids who'd also lost their dogs. He came home after Puppy Pal meetings animated in a way he hadn't been for years. David had never been part of any group before, other than the obligatory sports teams Dan had wedged him into.

"Wait til you see our signs, and tee shirts," he'd told her at dinner the night before the Towne Town Council meeting, as he shoveled mash potatoes in his mouth. "We're like, legit."

"I bet you are," Lucinda beamed at David. He was growing like a weed, or rather a gorgeous flower.

"We're totally stoked to hear what the Council has planned and we're ready to help out however we can, as kids, obviously."

Lucinda was not as stoked as her son. She really couldn't imagine what, at this late date, could be done to find all those missing dogs. But she was not going to rain on David's parade, especially not now. "Me too, Davey. Ready to help for sure."

Lucinda spent the bulk of the next day at the Mansion. She was grateful the place was crawling with subcontractors, making it harder for Brady to corner her, asking for blatant reassurances or subtly for sex. She felt a little guilty for not telling Brady about the Towne meeting. He had, after all, lost a dog like the rest of them. In the beginning she had been his source of information; what did people do around Towne for fun—not much; where could he order the best sushi—nowhere; did she have the name of a good masseuse—nope. But ultimately Brady didn't seem to care very much about what went on outside the confines of his Beauteous domain. So she told herself that if anything significant came out of this meeting, she'd let him know after the fact. Besides, the last thing she wanted was for him to glom on to her in front of everyone, exposing their relationship to every voracious gossip in town. And to David. *Oy.* She couldn't imagine David and Brady together. Not yet. Maybe never.

"Lucinda! Over here!" Denise had spotted Lucinda as soon as she and David entered the auditorium. Denise waved her arms from the fifth row of the auditorium as if she were directing traffic on an airport runway. Too much, already, Lucinda thought. Too much.

Lucinda asked David where he wanted to sit, with her and her loud friend, or with his Puppy Pals. Of course she already knew the answer. But he'd been so affectionate lately, holding her hand in public even, so a small part of her hoped he'd stay glued to her side. Lately he'd seemed softer and less afraid; fiercer, but more forgiving.

"I'm gonna sit with them if that's okay, Mom?" He squeezed his mother's hand.

"It's more than okay, Davey," she said. "Go on. We'll meet up when the meeting is over."

Lucinda watched David run towards a ragtag group of kids wearing brown tee shirts over their regular clothes. A girl Lucinda thought she recognized from David's second grade class—Chloe Something-or-other, who had the same shrunken posture, the same terrified eyes—handed David one of the shirts, which he put on without hesitation, even though Lucinda was sure it did not jibe with his burgeoning fashionista sensibility. My little trooper, she thought as she made her way down the aisle towards Denise. Then she wondered if calling David a trooper was too sexist? Too all-male? Too gender-stereotypical?

"Where's Brady?" Denise asked loudly as soon as Lucinda's butt hit her seat.

"Keep it down, Denise." It was a miracle Denise hadn't yet told the entire town about Lucinda and Brady. Lucinda would kill her if this meeting became the accidentally-on purpose event when Denise finally cracked.

"Sorry. My bad." Denise whispered, "So, where is he?"

"I didn't tell him about the meeting."

"Didn't you tell me that he had some fabulous dog that ran away?"

"I did."

"So he'd want to know there were people here, in his very own town, doing something to find these dogs."

"I don't think Brady considers Towne his town."

"Oh. Too cool for the likes of us?"

"I'm not sure it's that snobby-specific. It's just, well, Brady is sort of in his own world. I don't think any town is, or will ever be, his."

"Still, a missing dog is a missing dog, Lucinda. I think it is pretty harsh that you kept this information from him."

"Gimme a break, Denise. You just wanted to see Brady Cole up close and personal. If I left you to your own devices, you'd pull his dress up and take a photo of his butt."

Denise gave Lucinda a withering look which quickly morphed into a wide grin. "You're probably right." She laughed.

The two women bumped shoulders. All was forgiven.

"Honestly?" Lucinda said, "I don't have high hopes for this meeting. I mean, really. It's been months. Balzy is probably happy on some old lady in South Carolina's lap right now. Or dead."

"Lucinda! That's harsh."

"I know, but let's face it. Balzy was already on borrowed time back in August. Besides, why are you even here? You guys don't even have a dog."

Denise pointed at her daughter, two rows in front. "Laura has a major crush on Chucky Weintraub, who does have a missing dog. So I'm the schlepper. God forbid I sit anywhere near her."

Lucinda watched Laura writhe in her seat, tossing her hair as if it were covered with head lice, and batting her eyes at Chucky, who barely looked in her direction.

"Poor girl," sighed Lucinda. "Middle School crushes suck."

An older man in a garish striped shirt got up on stage. He reminded Lucinda of Elmer Fudd dressed for a night out at an 80's disco.

"Welcome fellow Towne residents and dog lovers. For those of you who don't know me, I'm George Takharian, President of the Towne Town Council. I myself have a wonderful pooch named Ollie, who luckily is still with me, safe at home."

Lucinda couldn't tell if the dark shaggy mass on the top of George's head was a shredded hat or a bad toupee. She really should wear her eyeglasses more often.

The meeting was over almost before it began. Lucinda didn't need eyeglasses to hear the bad news delivered. Within minutes, George called up an expert who told the expectant, hopeful crowd: Don't bother. Your dogs are probably long gone. Suffice to say, the message didn't go over well.

Lucinda turned to Denise and said, "see? I told you. On an old South Carolinian's lap."

But Denise wasn't having it. She bolted upright from her seat and cried, "put the knife in deeper, why don't you?"

Leave it to Lucinda's drama queen best friend to start the flurry of epithets, curses, and demands hurled at the overwhelmed, unsuspecting, and quite young dog expert from City. How embarrassed she was to be part of this irate, entitled bunch. All the guy was doing was stating facts. Lucinda wanted to crawl along the sticky auditorium floor and slither out the fire exit. But there was David to worry about. Her poor son must've been devastated by this no-dog doomsday proclamation.

She stood and turned to search for him, which was hard because half the audience was now standing and waving their arms while yelling at George and his young expert. She could make out a the mass of brown jersey huddled over an expanse of seats towards the rear. David was in this mosh pit of Middle Schoolers, leaning his sweet freckled cheek against the back of a heaving, greasy-haired girl. And he was smiling.

Will you look at that, thought Lucinda. Best bad meeting ever.

Abe: Simplicity

Freaky Sting Ray was riding slower than other times Abe had seen her, and Abe was running faster than he'd ever run before. He made sure to keep a full half block behind her, worked hard at keeping his tread light, dancer-like, or as dancer-like as a two hundred pound thirty-four year old klutz could keep it. Sting Ray kept riding straight on Sherwood Lane, which lost its suburbanized name a mile outside of Towne and turned into Route 26—plain and simple. The dark November sky made it hard to keep her in view once she was riding past the last remnants of farmland in that part of the world, but every now and then a widely spaced streetlight revealed her. Three miles outside of town, she veered to the right onto a dirt road. Abe sprinted to keep her in view. For a brief moment when he got to the intersection he could hear the sound of tires on loose gravel but then the sound faded. It was pitch black and he couldn't see for shit.

Abe groaned as he doubled over in what felt like near-cardiac explosion. He hadn't realized how hard he'd been charging. As his breathing evened out, his will returned. He'd go forward into that dark abyss and see his search through to the end. He still had a feeling Freaky Sting Ray would lead him to something important.

The last thing he needed was to twist an ankle on some rural root or to fall into an unpaved hole. He took out his phone to turn on the flashlight and noticed four texts from Claire:

Stop @ minimart on the way home from mtg and pick up oat milk.

Then: Organic.

Then, finally: Thanks.

But then: Where are you? I thought the dog meeting was only an hour long.

Abe tried to text her back, but there was no cell service on this godforsaken road. He'd try later. Meanwhile he turned on the flashlight and continued forward.

The gated driveway was about an eighth of a mile down the road. Abe peered through the slats, and saw Freaky Sting Ray's absurd bicycle leaning against the porch of a large three-story, cedar-shingled, ramshackle house.

The gate was closed from the inside. But it wasn't the highest gate in the world. Abe hoisted himself up, and held himself steady with one arm while reaching down with the other to unlatch it. The gate swung open while Abe tumbled to the ground.

No broken bones. No twisted ankles. A sore elbow, but who cared. Abe tiptoed down the gravel drive and skulked around the edge of the house, past ravaged bushes, a collection of chewed-up dolls and stuffed animals, a pile of half gnawed bones. He came to a window and carefully peeped in, like Kilroy looking over his brick wall.

There had to be at least twenty dogs, grouped in three masses, like a series of hairy hills. Some were sleeping, some were licking, some were staring off into space. Gordon lay curled in a comfy crescent among a pile of equally comfy dogs, morphed to each other in a glorious heap of fur. Gordon looked great. He looked happy. He looked well-fed. Fit as a fiddle. He looked like he could model fancy doggie coats from Orvis.

Abe didn't see the girl, so he took a risk, and rapped on the window pane. The pack, including Gordon, looked up at him. None of them barked. None of them seemed all that interested. Not even Gordon. Abe was like a leaf grabbing attention momentarily as it flittered past Gordon's view, forgotten as soon as it landed on the cold, cold ground. Gordon turned away from the distraction at the window and started gnawing at a spot on his rear haunch. Abe's heart felt shattered all over again.

Though Abe's eyes began to blur with tears, he could see Freaky Sting Ray in an adjacent room. She'd taken off the faux-farmer jacket and snappy beret and stood, hunched forward with her face in her hands. Her waif-like form trembled. She bawled, as if she had suffered her own loss, felt her own heart-shattering pain. Then the girl stood upright, and Abe saw that she was smiling. Her tears were of joy, of relief. Freaky Sting Ray wiped her eyes with the sleeve of her sweater. She slipped her feet out of her nautical loafers and strode into the dog-filled room.

When the dogs sensed her, the room erupted into a blissful frenzy. They gathered round her, barking and pawing at her legs and licking her outstretched palms. Even the scrawniest, oldest mongrel transformed to a frisky and smitten disciple. The girl's pale face shone with love and light and pure selflessness. Among the dogs she no longer looked like a demented weirdo, she looked beatific, holy. Freaky Sting Ray; Saint Francis of Assisi reborn.

And there was Gordon, front and center, leading the pack. Alpha dog, by virtue of his gregarious, confident nature. The girl bent to kiss Gordon gently on his wet and wonderful nose. In that moment it was clearer than ever; Gordon adored and was adored in return. Gordon was surrounded by like-minded friends. Gordon had found something better. Gordon had found his true home. Gordon was never coming back.

Abe watched Gordon in all his glory and felt awash in gratitude; to Freaky Sting Ray Girl, and to fate for allowing Abe this glimpse into Gordon's brighter future. And then, as if she could hear Abe's thoughts, the girl suddenly looked up and stared straight at Abe with his nose pressed against the window like a kid lusting over rows of cupcakes in a bakery display.

The two humans froze, one on the inside, the other, forever on the outside. Interchangeable, though, and they both knew it. Something clicked. Something connected. The girl's panicked expression softened. Abe's tears dried.

Abe conjured a silent message. He brought a finger to his lips, then made the gesture of thumb to pointer finger for "okay," and ended with a hand on his chest. Your secret is safe with me.

The girl gazed at Abe as Gordon and the rest of the dogs surrounded her in a post-nap lazy mess; playing, ball-licking, ear scratching. Her brow furrowed like a shar-pei's. Finally, Freaky Sting Ray smiled and nodded slowly, signally Abe's time to leave.

"Where the hell have you been?" Claire hiss-whispered as soon as Abe came through the door. She was sitting on the couch, pedicured and scrupulously clean feet tucked neatly under her bum, iPad on her lap.

This was the moment. The moment Abe could come clean. He could tell Claire about the dog discovery, and be-ing Claire, she'd do the conventionally right thing: call the authorities, return the dogs, get Freaky Sting Ray locked up in prison or a psych ward. He'd considered this on his run home. It was a good thing that running cleared the mind and led to the best decisions because, no, he wouldn't tell her. Telling Claire about the dogs might lead to the other dogs returning to original homes and relative happiness, but Gordon would be doomed. No way he could come home, where Barbara the dog-hating mother, Claire the ever-more-persnickety wife, and Milo the rambunctious, impulse-driven child reigned as a triumvirate. Gordon had the perfect life now, and no way Abe was going to mess that up.

"I'm sorry. The meeting went later than I expected. And then I decided to put a few more miles in afterwards."

"Didn't you see my texts?"

Abe shrugged. "Phone died. My bad." What was one more little lie?

"Well that's great. Now we're totally out of oat milk."

Big deal, thought Abe. "Like I said, sorry."

"Well, I hope at least, you got some work done on *The Gist* today."

So many secrets. He wouldn't tell her about Gordon, but maybe this was his opportunity to tell Claire about his writer's block, and the sham of it all. Maybe a kernel of confession would make him feel closer to her again. "Well, about the novel…"

"Yes?" Claire was scrolling through the *Wall Street Journal* on her iPad. A good time to drop the bomb.

"It's proving more complicated than I first imagined." Spit it out, you coward, he thought.

"Oh, that's good, right? We like complex. Simple is for simpletons," said Claire without looking up.

Since when had his wife become such an intellectual snob? There had been a time in the not so distant past when they'd both enjoyed the same low-brow stuff: slo-mo videos of water balloon fights, Belgian fries smothered in gravy, reruns of the original *Starsky and Hutch*.

Now Claire was all PBS, organic foods, and financial flow charts. Would she understand if he told her the truth? Abe walked over to stand behind the couch. He stared down at the dark, smooth, fresh smelling head of his beautiful wife.

"I don't know. Maybe simple is the way to go," he said.

"Seriously?" Claire turned her head to look up at Abe. Silently and only for a second, husband and wife examined each other, stared at each other as if they barely knew each other, strangers possibly on the way to becoming enemies. He'd felt more of a bond with Freaky Sting Ray Girl in their one moment at the window. It hadn't been sexual; it wasn't even friendship. It was understanding; it was simple.

Nell: Safe With Me

Nell rode as fast as she could, but her mother's fashionably tight trousers slowed her down. If she hadn't felt the shock of recognition with the hairy man in the auditorium and felt the need to flee, she would've stopped to strip off the pants and tossed them into someone's yard. In spite of the cold, she would've ridden back to her retreat in her underwear. But a combination of comfort and fear kept Nell going. The meeting had been too much. Too much flesh, too much loudness, too much emotion. All she wanted was to be back at home with her pack.

What had the man called her? Freaky Sting Ray? Maybe he meant it to be complimentary, a super hero's moniker. But Nell couldn't take chances. There could be no further conversing. She'd had no choice but to flee.

When she finally got home, she was exhausted. Nell stripped out of her disguise while the pack slept in the living room; rolling, breathing, stinking hills of fur and hair. While thanks to Hector Moore she needn't worry about a search party coming to her door with torches ablaze, she continued to fret over how she would keep the dogs fed and safe through the coming months. But the dogs were safe. She was safe. She couldn't hold back any longer. She wept soundless tears of joyful relief into the palms of her hands, heaving like a silent earthquake.

There would never be enough time or tears to shed. Nell wiped her eyes with the sleeve of her mother's silly white sweater and slipped her feet out of her absurd shoes. She took a deep suck of dander-laden air into her lungs as she entered the dog-filled room. As expected, Raphael noticed her first. He instantly rose from his spot wedged between Daphne the dalmatian-terrier mix and Clio the ridiculous but gorgeous Irish Setter and scampered across the floor. Nell opened her arms. Raphael jumped upon his goddess with abandon, covering her mother's beige slacks with perfectly filthy paw prints.

Soon all the dogs surrounded her. Nell felt a calm settle in her bones, warmth quelling the shiver in her heart. Everything was as it should be.

And then she sensed it. Something new. A different energy. Not a bad one, but not a dog one, either. She looked toward the window and there he was: the hairy man, with his nose pressed against the glass. The light from inside the house lit his face as if he were a storefront display. She could see that he too had been crying.

They stared at each other for what seemed like centuries. She took in his aura as she had in the auditorium. Still there was kindness. But she didn't sense his confusion, impatience, or desperation here at her home with the dogs displayed in full glory, where she would've expected the man to feel all those things, and more. Where was the anger, the surprise, the disgust? Instead all that he brought was this kindness. And then also, gratitude. It didn't seem possible, but Nell accepted that this was how it was.

The man raised a finger to his lips, then made the "okay" sign, and ended with his hand to his chest. He seemed to be saying something about his heart, keeping quiet, and approval. Nell concentrated intently, furrowing her brow, trying to understand. And then she got it: Your secret is safe with me.

Nell nodded slowly and smiled. The big, hairy man understood her understanding, and backed away from the window, disappearing into the dark.

Conversations

Abe: Use Your Words

"So it's just you and me, Mouse. Finally. I thought Grandma Barbara would never leave."

"Bye bye, Ba Ba."

"Yeah, bye bye Barbara. So you hungry? Want a PB and banana?"

"Nana! Nana!"

"Coming right up. Your wish is my command, you little dictator."

"Paba a nana."

"Yeah, exactly, and I think I'll make one for myself as well. Crusts on for me though. I deserve it after the wild time I had last night."

"Run run."

"That's me. Run run. You said it."

"Run run, Go go."

"Yup Mouse. That's it. I ran for Gordon."

"Gogo! Gogo!"

"And guess what. I found him. But he's not coming back."

"No no no!"

"It's okay, Mouse. He's good."

"Go go Goo."

"Yeah, so we have to say goodbye to Gordon."

"Bye bye, Go Go."

"Yeah. Bye bye, Gordon. Do you miss Gordon?"

"Buffablubbablaaaaaaaah!"

"I agree. Buffablubba—whatever. It sucks, but he's living in a really cool place now with all sorts of puppy friends."

"Buffablubbablahblahblahbababaaaaaa!"

"No worries, Mouse. Gordon's happy."

"Go Go hap hap?"

"Exactly, Gordon's happy. Meanwhile, here's your Paba a nana. Let's try not to smear any on Mommy's couch. No booster seat at the table for this snack, dude. NCAA wrestling finals are on and Daddy's not gonna miss them."

Paddy: A Mess

"Oh Mariah, I've made a mess of it."

"*Well yes. A bit of one, I suppose. I've been watching.*"

"That's what I was afraid of. So you know then."

"*Know what?*"

"Well for starters, Gloria. In the garage."

"*Ah that bitch was always after you. Even when I was alive.*"

"She was?"

"*You men. The things you don't see. Anyway, honey. There was no avoiding that little episode. Gloria had you cornered.*"

"So you're not mad?"

"Paddy, I'm dead. Why should I waste any celestial time being mad?"

"What about my fall off the wagon? You hated it when I drank. There I was, feeling sorry for myself so I go and get plowed at Schepp's. Some young guy had to drive me home. I passed out on the kitchen floor."

"That was pretty horrible. I hated seeing you that way again."

"I haven't had a drop since. But still…"

"It wasn't your finest moment, but one fall off the wagon does not constitute a grievous crime."

"Oh Mariah. I miss you so damn much."

"I miss you too, Paddy. But I had to go."

"Yeah. I get that now."

"I'm doing great here. One nice thing about being dead is I have all my marbles back."

"Come to think of it, you do sound like your old self."

"I'm better than my old self. You wouldn't believe the things I understand. I could teach philosophy at Harvard!"

"If I could get anywhere near that school I'd take your class and sit in the front row and bring you an apple every day."

"You're too sweet."

"Speaking of apples. There's Barney. That's the worst thing. I guess you know I lost him."

"You didn't lose him, Paddy."

"Seems there's been an epidemic of missing dogs around this place. There was this bogus meeting at the high school about it which only made a bigger mess of things. Seems it was probably some organized group of hooligans stealing our dogs and selling them far away."

"I don't think you need to worry about that, Paddy."

"It was stupid of me to let him have the run of the backyard while I was at the station."

"*It's really, really okay.*"

"I just figured he'd sleep under the apple tree all day, or by your ottoman."

"*Really, Paddy. Don't worry about Barney. He's fine.*"

"You're sure?"

"*I'm sure. Trust me. And let it go.*"

"Well I guess you know better than me, Mariah. Come to think of it, that was always the case. Even when you weren't all there you were more there than me."

"*We were always there for each other, Paddy. Marbles or not. That's what mattered and still does. And that's the way it will always be.*"

David: Where Are You When I Need You Most?

"Hey Dave. How are ya, little man?"

"I'm fine Dad. Sort of."

"What do you mean sort of?"

"You know Balzy was stolen, right?"

"Yes. Of course I know that."

"Well, if you knew, why didn't you come to the Town Council meeting last night?"

"Dave. Now that I don't live in Towne anymore, or for that matter, with you and your mother anymore, I don't really consider Balthazar my dog to worry about."

"Wow. That's harsh."

"It's not harsh, Dave. It's just the truth."

"Well the meeting was horrible. Total bummer. The expert dude told us that the dogs have all been stolen and probably live in places far away now. So, duh. I'm pretty upset."

"Sorry Dave. I know that old dog meant a lot to you. But life goes on."

"Your life maybe."

"Don't be so dramatic. A dog is a dog."

"So typical."

"You're mumbling Dave. What did you say?"

"Nothing Dad."

"Dave, let's face it. Balthazar was ancient. And smelly. Probably better to have him out of your life now so you don't have to deal with the mess of his, um, demise, later on."

"Un-fucking believable."

"Mumbling Dave. Mumbling."

"Whatever, Dad. Why are you calling me anyway?"

"Can't a dad call his son just to say hello? Is that a crime?"

"No Dad, it's not a crime. But you never just call."

"Well actually I do have something to tell you. Big news."

"What is it?"

"Rachel's pregnant."

"That didn't take long."

"I suppose it didn't. Aren't you going to congratulate us?"

"Woot, woot for you and Rachel."

"You're going to be a big brother."

"Or something else big."

"What's that supposed to mean?"

"Forget it. You wouldn't understand."

"You're being very cryptic Dave. I really don't like it when you talk to me this way."

"Well, maybe if you called me David instead of Dave—"

"Oh, not that again—"

"Or better yet, why don't you call me Natasha."

"Very funny, Dave. Very funny."

"Not as funny as you think."

"What did you just say? You're mumbling again."

"Nothing Dad. It's just a bad connection. So are you going to do one of those useless gender-reveal parties?"

"We know the gender already."

"No you don't."

"Dave. Yes, we do. It's a girl. Isn't that great? Now I'll have one of both."

"Or two of a kind. Or many kinds."

"Dave, sometimes you make no sense to me. No sense at all."

"Whatever. Ta-ta for now, dahling."

Lucinda: Chablis

"I haven't seen you in here before, have I?"

"Oh, no. Definitely not."

"Geez Lady. You say it like my bar is cursed or something."

"Oh, I'm so sorry. I've had a rough few weeks. Are you Schepp?"

"The one and only."

"Wow. I wasn't even sure there was a real Schepp."

"Well here I am, in the flesh. Real as they get. What can I get you young lady?"

"Young lady. Ha. You're sweet. What kind of whites do you carry?"

"Chablis and Chablis."

"I'll have the Chablis then."

"Coming right up."

"I used to park across the street from here to pick my husband up at the train station. Back when I was married. I always wondered what it looked like inside."

"Well, now you know. Up to your standards?"

"I think it's marvelous, Schepp. You've got the perfect retro-noir decor working for you. Those cracked leather banquettes are classics and this old, solid-oak bar is weathered and scratched in just the right way. I love the frosted glass windows on the doors to the Gents and Dames. So Raymond Chandler. And this Chablis in a smudged, thick tumbler is exactly what I imagined. I'll take another, please."

"Sure. I'll try and find the dirtiest tumbler I can."

"Oh, I'm sorry. I didn't mean to offend you."

"It takes more than some gobbledygook about my décor and glassware to offend me, lady."

"I'm probably offending people left and right these days and not even aware of it. It's probably the shitstorm of a life I'm leading. Sorry for my French."

"French is all we speak in this shithole."

"I like you Schepp. Here's to you."

"And I like you…"

"Lucinda. Lucinda Leibowitz. Former wife of Dan Leibowitz, pretentious asshole. Owner of Balthazar, arthritic wire terrier, lost or stolen. Mother of David Leibowitz, beautiful, confused, brilliant boy. Or brilliant girl. Or brilliant something else entirely. Oh and then there's Brady. Mr. Wackadoo Big-Shot Cole. I suppose I'm something of his too."

"Are you talking about Brady Cole? Star of *Signet*?"

"The one and only."

"You know him?"

"Ha. Do I ever."

"I heard he was living in Towne. That's a for-real rumor?"

"Yep, he's here, in all his glory."

"Well I'll be a son of a gun. I loved his show *Signet*. The guys in charge are idiots for cancelling it. Best thing on TV for years."

"I wouldn't know about that, but I do know I want another Chablis please."

"Coming right up."

"Merci, Mr. Schepp."

"So how do you know Brady Cole?"

"Oh, how do I know Brady Cole. Let me count the ways. Let's just say I'm redoing his house. I'm his designer-decorator."

"Wow. You think you could get him in here? Drinks on the house."

"Unfortunately he only drinks green slime these days, Schepp, so I don't think that's possible."

"Too bad. I'd take one of those selfies with him and put the picture up there, next to the one of me and Mickey Rourke."

"I'll mention the opportunity to him, Schepp. But don't get your hopes up. Meanwhile, I'll take another glass of your fine Chablis when you get the chance."

"You might as well have bought the whole bottle, Lucinda. You on a roll, or what?"

"Oh, Schepp. What a shitstorm."

"And her French continues…"

"I let our dog be stolen."

"How does anyone let a dog be stolen?"

"Balzy was in my car, which was unlocked with the window open, right on Main Street where any dog-stealing asshole could walk by and nab him."

"Ballsy? As in gutsy?"

"No. Balzy, short for Balthazar. Dumb name. Don't ask."

"Well, no one locks their cars around here, so it sounds like the kind of thing that could've happened to anyone."

"You're too kind, Schepp. Way too kind."

"Well, I dunno about that. But I do like to keep my customers happy."

"My son is a fairy."

"Now, now, Lucinda. Even old-timers like me know that's not the right word for a gay person. Especially your own kid."

"No. I mean, he's a real fairy. A delicate, ethereal otherworldly creature filled with grace and beauty."

"I suppose you're gonna tell me he has wings like Tinkerbell."

"He deserves a much better mother than me."

"I bet you're an okay mother."

"Thanks Schepp. But I've been bad. Losing Balzy was just the tip of the iceberg. You don't know the half of it."

"I don't know fuck all—now you gotta pardon my French."

"Vous êtes excusé. My David may be gay, or transgender, or that other thing in between, what do they call it? Non-binary?"

"You're asking the wrong person, Lucinda. I'm not gonna even start to tell you what we called those kind of folks back in the day."

"Anyhow, it's hard to know what David is. And whatever he is will be totally fine, if a bit surprising. But it's all a bit more complicated than that."

"How so?"

"He likes to wear dresses. And skirts. And make up. And jewelry. He's been stealing women's clothes and accessories for years, hiding them around my house. And he never felt like he could tell me. It breaks my heart."

"That would be a tough thing for a young boy to tell anyone, even his ma, I suppose."

"There were clues, Schepp. But I was too wrapped up in my quest for a picture-perfect life so I chose to ignore them."

"Everyone wants a perfect life."

"Sometimes I'm so much like my bitch of a mother I want to scream."

"So scream."

"I'm screwing a movie star just so I can decorate his house."

"Wait a second. You're doin' the deed with Brady Cole? Holy shit, Lucinda. Now you've got me."

"My mother screwed my stepfather while she was still married to my father because he was rich and had a famous, historical house outside of Atlanta. I'm selfish and oblivious like her and it makes me want to throw up."

"If you really need to hurl Lucinda, do you mind heading to the Dames?"

"Just a figure of speech, Schepp. I was exaggerating. Sorry."

"So Lucinda, tell me; why are you getting sloshed on cheap white wine in my dive bar when you should probably be home with your fairy son?"

"That was harsh."

"Comes with the territory. I've been at this for over thirty years. I get to say whatever I want."

"No, you're right. I'm a terrible person."

"Oh stop with the moaning and groaning. Just get out of here and do your job."

"And what is my job, oh wise, mean old Mr. Schepp?"

"Stop fucking around. Listen and love instead, Lucinda. But first just get out of my bar, go home, and sleep it off."

Brady: The One

"Brady, sweetheart! I haven't heard from you in weeks!"

"It's only been a few days, Mom."

"Well it feels like weeks. How are you, honey?"

"I'm good, Mom. Really good."

"Oh, sugar, that makes me pleased as punch."

"I've got big, big news, Mom. I've met someone. A wonderful woman. I think she may be the one."

"Oh, darling. Again?"

"It's for real this time, Mom. I've never been with anyone like her before."

"I hope she's not too young, dearest. You made a mess of things that time with your friend's nanny."

"No, Mom. She's my age. If not older."

"Oh funny you. Trying to get a chuckle out of me."

"No, I'm serious."

"But precious, you're never with anyone your own age."

"Well I'm different now. I think my Beauteous studies are really paying off."

"Well I should hope so. I can't abide my son hiding away, wearing dresses, and chanting gobbledygook for something that's not worth it. Is that Timothy character still telling you not to talk to me so often?"

"It's Tamago, Mom. Not Timothy. And yeah, he is. But hey, I'm talking to you now, aren't I?"

"Yes lovey, I suppose you are."

"I can't wait for you to meet Lucinda, Mom. I think you'll really get along."

"Lucinda. What an unusual name."

"She's an unusual woman."

"I hope by unusual you don't mean she's into kinky things, Bray-bray."

"No, Mom."

"Because there was also that time they caught you in that club in Amsterdam with—"

"Mom, I'm done with all that stuff, remember? Lucinda's my age, and ordinary, but in an amazing way. She's not going to win any beauty contests, but she's beautiful to me."

"Well as the saying goes: Beauty is in the eyes of the beholder."

"Exactly Mom."

"I miss you Brady."

"I miss you too, Mom. I miss you too."

Nell: Getting down

"Who's the best boy in the world?"
woof...woof
"That's right, Raphael! Yes you are! Yes you are!"
thumpthumpthumpthump
"I know who wants a treat. Boris wants a treat."
pantpantpant
"Eduardo, stop licking Boris' privates, you silly dog!"
ruff, ruff
"Be nice Pepe. No nipping. We are all friends here."
grrr
"No, Raphael! It's too cold to swim in the pool. We only drink the water now!"
Laplaplaplap
"Okay, dinnertime. Everyone gets frankfurters tonight! Only two weeks past expiration. A delicacy courtesy of Carla's Café!"
slurp, chomp, slurp, chomp, slurp
"We're celebrating because tonight I found out that no one is ever going to take you away from me. We're safe. All of us."
Woof, yip, howl, ruff, yip yip
"So what special piece shall I play for you tonight to celebrate our freedom, my loves?"
woof...thump...pantpant...pant...thumpruff... grrr...woof...ahwoooo
"Good choice. Ode to Joy it is."

winter

I have no choice. I am where I am. I know there are other habitats with whom my borders bleed that have less changeable climes. And there are those further still, that have never had to suffer the indignities of frozen earth, barren branches, or fallow fields. Habitats never abandoned by their birds. Where bears never sleep. I envy those whose lakes never turn to ice, where life is visible in constant sprouts, not dormant like mine, hidden during harsh winter months, barely green nibs curled in on themselves deep, deep underground.

There are other places where humans aren't forced to endure the chill like mine in me, bundling up like unrecognizable rag piles in heavy cloaks, scarves, snow, and salt-speckled boots. There are other habitats where humans don't eat too much food accidentally-on purpose, blubbered up like their whale cousins, don't over-drink fermented liquids in an attempt to warmly numb their bellies and minds.

Where they don't curse. Or mope. Or sleep too much.

I can't blame my people. After millennia, winter is harder even for me. These are not pretty times. These are harsh, unforgiving times. I look terrible; gray, dry, spindly, weak. I offer no comforts, no warm beaches, tropical breezes, fields of flowers, or crisp, invigorating mountain air. The only smells I offer in winter are noxious fumes from relentlessly burnt fossil fuels. I can't even offer a warm rock to sit on this time of year. Who would want to be here with me? Who would choose me now?

Still, much is happening below my surface. I feel it like a chronic itch. Those aforementioned little nibs. The lake trout and river perch slowing their heartbeats and swimming in lethargic circles. The dull, persistent muffled human complaints. The sound of hands rubbing arms up and down so vigorously I'm scared some humans will shred their own dry, crackled skin. I can't get away from it, because I am it, much to my chagrin.

I must remember that contrary to bleak, harrowing appearances, winter is not a time of death. It is a time of rest. Some plants and animals won't survive these months, but most will come back with renewed vigor. Even the humans. They always do. At the first sign of spring they'll underdress and stay outside for long spells, unintentionally frying their skin to crisps, flitting around like their brethren bees, laying on cool, freshly mowed green grass that smells like hope.

But try telling that to them now, when temperatures plummet, when the sun barely gives me a second glance. I'm lucky to get a brief orange fizzle arcing over my horizon line. In this dark season there is no guarantee of a hot, humid future. There is only enduring this frozen stasis. I'll keep doing what I do, based on physics, gravity, and earthly rotation while my humans are left to embrace the thankless cold with tepid but unbeatable hope.

Chapter Nine

Nell: Sleep

By early December, Nell realized her calculations were off. She didn't have money to pay for anything, after draining the funds her parents had left to pay for household utilities. There'd only been a few other times in her life when she'd been so blindsided by her own mistakes. Still painful to think about was the time she lost Jumbo. The memory of her parents callous reactions was even more gut-wrenching than the memory of Jumbo's shell glistening in the sunshine before he disappeared under the shrubbery and was gone for good.

"Well that proves it," her father said, barely glancing up from the *Harvard Law Review* when Nell ran into his study to tell him. "Case closed. We are just not a pet-type family."

"Easy come, easy go," her mother had sighed, wispy and non-committal, while she poked random, artistic holes in a work-in-progress globular sculpture, "Maybe the turtle will be happier somewhere else."

The loss of Jumbo was as much a non-event for her parents as it was a crisis for Nell. She'd had no idea where to go with her feelings. Angry, bereft, confused little Nell spent the remains of the day in her room chopping at the hair of her Barbies with the scissors from her Suzy Home-maker sewing kit. Her parents puttered below, reading, cooking, pontificating, creating. Leaving Nell alone.

Now Nell could not, would not ask her callous parents for more money. So Nell became destitute; soon she would barely be able to feed her brood. She sacrificed everything to keep the dogs fed and moderately warm. Rations diminished and the dogs had to do with less. Pricier wet food was now entirely off the menu.

It helped that she now had a guardian angel of sorts. Every few days since her encounter with the hairy man, she'd find a bag of high end kibble and a few packets of bacon-cheese treats waiting outside the gate to her home. The first time, he'd left a note:

I won't bother you, I promise. But please let me help. These were, and maybe still are Gordon's favorite food and treats. I'm sure he'd be willing to share. Thanks for all you're doing, —Abe Kaufman

At first Nell bristled at the intrusion. She drafted a note to leave in return:

Dear Mr. Kaufman, I don't want, or need your help. Please stay away.

But then she looked at her brood, noticed the ribs starting to show on Bingo, the listless gait of Portia, and the filmy eyes of Thor. So she ripped up her note and let Abe Kaufman make his donations. The supplements helped, and the dogs endured, but Nell grew weak. Her hair fell out in mangy clumps. Her skin bruised at the slightest nudge. Her nails were soft and pliable as orange peels. She slept for long spells under a crochet blanket she'd stolen from the ARF Thrift Store. Boris and Eduardo huddled by her feet, too tired for frisky genital washing. Other dogs lay nearby, inert, panting, lumps of dusty fur.

Nell couldn't conjure a brilliant thought. Her mind was as barren as a dirt mound, bereft of insights. She hadn't the energy to play the piano. Reading hurt her eyes.

In rare moments of clarity, she wondered if saving the dogs had been a terrible mistake. She wondered if they were still happy to be there with her in this giant, unwelcoming, drafty house. It was hard to tell if their gazes were rheumy from hunger or adoration.

She recalled the day when she was a little girl and had looked skyward for an instant, losing Jumbo, losing faith. She would never take her eyes off her beloveds again. Never.

Abe: You Can Run But You Can't Hide

The weather was miserable. Still Abe ran almost every day, jogging through spitting rain or sleet, under a sky that was uniformly dull, like a much washed, lusterless bedsheet. Sudden gusts attempted to unnerve him, challenged him to keep going. Blustery ghosts delivered invisible slaps to his face. Harbingers of Nor'easters to come.

For the time being he could still make the three-plus

mile trip every few days to the Dog Sanctuary, as he'd taken to calling it, with a backpack loaded with food and treats. Careful to leave without his mother seeing him grab the empty backpack stored in the garage, Abe pit-stopped at Pop's Pet Emporium and bought dog food and treats with cash. Running with an extra ten pounds on his back was brutal work at first, but Abe figured it an even trade with the weight he'd lost on his actual frame. And it made the return trip feel like a piece of cake. In fact, sometimes he'd have a real piece of cake after he got home. Just rewards.

"Fuck you, Weather," Abe would shout as he zipped his brand new waterproofed, micro-fleece lined runner's shell up to his chin and stepped outside. The jacket was a peace offering from Claire, whom he'd continued to deceive.

"I'm sorry I said your running thing was obsessive," she'd apologized after her snarky comments the night of the Towne Council meeting. "It's great, Abe, really. It's just that I worry you're getting distracted from your real work."

"Don't worry, Babe. It's all good," Abe lied. He lied to himself also, telling himself that helping feed the dogs qualified as real work, even if it was work he couldn't tell anyone about, even if it was work no one asked him to do.

Abe and Claire were having sex again, sort of semi-regularly. Once a week at most, not back to their pre-Milo tally. It was mostly distracted, perfunctory sex, Claire barely lifting her hips to meet him, yawning on occasion, and mewling half-heartedly when she came. But this was pretty good given the two years of self-diddling that defined Abe's sex life since Milo's birth. Abe knew if he told Claire about his writer's block and about the dogs, he'd be back in the sexless Sahara for months, if not years.

Appearances were everything, and it appeared to everyone that Abe was managing to use his time productively, taking full advantage of Barbara's help.

Every morning Claire gave Abe a cursory peck on the cheek before she left for the City.

"Be brilliant," she said.

"I'll try," he said.

His mother would deliver a similar directive on her way out to the playground with Milo. "Get cracking on that next Great American Novel, Abie."

"I will," he said.

Thing was, there still was no novel, great, next, or otherwise. There was no writing. But there was running.

Abe timed his returns to coincide with Barbara and Milo's exits. Before coming back into the house, he'd stash his emptied backpack in the garage, behind the barely used lawn mower. Barbara took Milo out after his morning nap, regardless of the weather. It was quite impressive for a seventy-five-year-old widow. Abe had never known his mother to be so impervious and elementally hardy. She would bundle the Mouse up, put him in the stroller, flip the rain guard around the whole contraption like a space capsule, put on her own floor length mud-colored coat and rubber boots, and march out the door.

By mid-December they'd settled into a rhythm. A semi-peaceful co-existence. Abe returned from his runs and conversations would go something like this:

"Hey Ma, how'd he sleep?"

"Oh, like an angel as usual. You look flushed, Abie. I hope you're not pushing yourself too hard."

"Don't worry. I'm not running that fast. It's just the cold air."

"Because cardiac issues run in the family."

"I know, Ma."

"Your poor father. If only I'd known."

Abe wanted to say, you did know that Dad ate like a pig, smoked two packs of Camels up until the day he keeled over, raged silently against every machine his whole miserable life. Made the worst financial decisions a man of modest means could make. Nearly went to jail over tax fraud. But Abe controlled his contrarian impulse. Instead he summarized: "Hindsight is 20/20, Ma. Dad was hellbent on self-destruction. Probably nothing any of us could've done."

In the past, Barbara might sigh and wilt forlornly like a week-old asparagus spear. But lately she rebounded from Mort-centric ruminations with greater elasticity. "I suppose you're right. But please, Abie. For your mother. Be careful, Sweetie." Barbara zipped up her gigantic brown coat, looking like a five-foot-tall earthworm. "Now say bye bye to your baby. We're running late."

It was all about the playground for Barbara. She had found her place in the socio-political landscape of mommies and nannies in a matter of months. She'd return home sated with gossip. Barbara had opinions about everyone; this charming "ethnic" nanny, that wonderful attentive mommy, this horrible bully who was destined to become a criminal, that self-absorbed mother staring at her phone all the time, this shy, adorable, delicious little girl with the pigtails, etc. etc. etc.

"Are you really still going to the playground in this weather?" asked Abe one particularly frigid morning. Outside the freezing raindrops approached hailstone dimensions.

Barbara hesitated. "Well. No. We're actually going on an indoor playdate this morning."

"Wow. That's cool, Ma. Like, really. I mean it."

"I would hope you mean what you say. Otherwise, why say it."

Abe stifled a groan. "Who's the playdate with?"

Barbara tightened the toggles on her hood. Her face almost entirely disappeared behind the circle of faux fur trim. "Sonam and Lily," was her muffled response. "Sonam is from Tibet. Did you know there is a whole community of Tibetan women in this country who work as nannies?"

Abe did know that, but he decided not to know it right then. "Wow. No. That's super interesting. Well, have fun."

"We will," she said. "Happy writing!"

Abe grunted. 'Happy' and 'writing' did not belong side to side when directed at him. But once again; appearances. "Okay Ma. Thanks."

Once his mother and son were out the door Abe spent the remaining time consuming a mid-morning BLT on rye with college wrestling on the big, wide screen.

Paddy: Love in the Afternoon

He wasn't looking for a girlfriend. He couldn't conceive of a new wife. But Barbara was something. She was an opinionated shock to Paddy's rusty system, got him thinking, made him laugh. Made him want to put on a clean shirt and gargle with Listerine. Barbara was a breath of fresh air, and God knew the air around Paddy had been stale for months.

It wasn't until early December that Paddy learned of Barbara's deep mistrust of dogs. They passed by the dog run, a long swath of untended tramped-on dirt behind a chain linked fence, littered with half chewed basketballs and headless dolls. Dogs of all shapes and sizes made a chaotic ruckus while their owners threw neon green tennis balls for them and shouted clipped directives which were ignored as often as obeyed.

"These dog people pay more attention to their animals than to their kids," said Barbara, "Just listen to those shouts. My son's dog ran away a couple of months ago and you'd think the world ended. He moped for weeks. He's still testy about it."

Paddy thought of Barney. "Well, a dog can be a man's best friend." Where was that little whippersnapper, he wondered? According to that young guy at the disastrous Towne Meeting, Barney was probably in Seattle, or Cincinnati. Paddy hoped he had a nice warm lap to curl up in.

"I'm sorry. Not a dog fan," Barbara shook her head decisively. "They're unpredictable. All of them. Even the ones who are supposedly tame and sweet. Every one of them has a full set of fangs. Who knows what can set a dog off?"

Mariah had loved all dogs, even the ones who growled at her. "The small ones are okay," Paddy tried. "Those tiny poodles?"

Barbara shivered. "No. They scare me the most. They're like battery operated stuffed animals. With teeth."

The subject of dogs aside, things between Paddy and Barbara felt right as rain. When everyone at the playground mistook Paddy for Milo's grandfather, neither he nor Barbara did a thing to correct them. When Milo nestled against his chest while they sat on the park bench and fondled Paddy's droopy earlobe to soothe himself to sleep, Paddy felt a calm settling in his gut. When Barbara asked him probing questions about Mariah, Paddy responded with candor that even surprised him. When Barbara kissed Paddy goodbye on the lips, he blushed like a ten-year-old at a kissing booth.

It wasn't the deep unspoken knowing he'd had with Mariah for fifty years, that ancient primal merger long-standing married couples develop, whether they want to or not. He'd been lucky to cherish his wife to the end, to be bound to someone as lovely and tolerant as Mariah for so long. Being twisted up with someone you didn't love, or worse, couldn't stand, had always seemed like a living hell to Paddy. He knew couples like that; old cranks fused together, feasting on shared resentment like blood-sucking vampires.

This thing with Barbara was good. So surprising. Who expected such pleasant surprises at their age? They both marveled at this. As winter continued, and other playground denizens took to the indoors, Barbara and Paddy had the entire park to themselves. Bundled up and leaning into each other they'd watch an even more bundled up Milo waddle his way from the swings to the slide to the near frozen sandbox. Milo was happy to have the playground to himself. At his age other kids were mostly obstacles to maneuver around or shove out of his way. Barbara and Paddy were happy also. Eventually there was some gentle smooching. Paddy would tenderly push the fur hood away from Barbara's face and sidle up for a kiss, the flaps of his red checkered hunter's cap like hound dog ears, just barely keeping his own ears warm, while the rest of his body thrummed with newfound sizzle.

David: Dress for Success

David loved the black dress with silver threading best. The way it fit through the hips and flared slightly just under his butt. The sparkle of the silver when the light hit just right. He couldn't decide if it looked better with the open-toed booties or the strappy sandals.

The orange romper was also totally cute, with a wide-necked, slouchy collar and matching patent leather belt. So retro. So eighties.

"I had one just like that," his mother claimed as she watched David shimmy into the romper. "Back in my wild clubbing days."

They were in David's room, a pile of brand new

clothes on the bed next to Lucinda, who lounged against the pillows and watched David watching himself. She was in Balzy's usual spot, though she took up more room. Months had passed and still no one had found Balzy. The Leibowitzs had gotten a bunch of calls, from creeps pretending to have found Balzy, greedy assholes who were only after the money. One guy sent them a photo of a terrier that looked nothing like Balzy. When David's mother said, "Sorry, that's not our dog," the guy said, "So what? This one's cuter." David still wasn't ready to give up. He refreshed the posters in town ripped off of telephone poles by maintenance workers or covered over by newer notices on bulletin boards. David prayed to God every night to return his dog. In spite of the doom-and-gloom message at the Towne meeting, the other Puppy Pals persisted too, each member not ready to give up on their beloved pets. Sometimes David, Danesha, Chloe, and Matt would hang out after school and walk around town putting up their LOST DOG notices together. Occasionally they'd grab a slice or a doughnut afterwards.

Aside from hanging out with the Puppy Pals, David had embarked on a whole new adventure, one that involved shopping and the trying-on of lots of different looks. Lots of different selves. David hadn't allowed his mother to spend more than five minutes in his room before what they both now referred to as The Night of the Big Reveal. Now she was in there all the time helping him with zippers, clasps, tiny pearl buttons. She voiced opinions that were sometimes valuable, sometimes not.

The Night seemed so long ago, when David had walked downstairs in Lucinda's dress and almost given her a heart attack. But he hadn't given her a heart attack. Not at all. A shock, maybe. But she hadn't keeled over and died. She'd listened and then she'd helped. She found David a cool therapist, for one. Not exactly cool in a hip way, but Thomas was cool in a better way: the understanding, smart, helpful way.

In their first session, Thomas told David that once upon a time he had been stuck in the body of a really unhappy woman named Teresa.

"Your mom already knows this," Thomas said. "She's okay with it. How about you?"

Thomas looked like someone's nerdy uncle. He had a terrible comb-over and thick glasses. His sweater was multi-colored in rust, brown, and forest green. He had a pot belly and pale, pasty skin. He was like a scientist who barely ever left their laboratory. David was relieved to not have a crush on him at all. "I'm okay with it," he said.

At the beginning of each session Thomas leaned back in his black leather chair, patient and solid, while David sat upright and antsy, knees shaking, fingernails gnawed. They quickly learned the drill, knowing it would only take a few minutes before David relaxed and spread like a well-fed kitty on Thomas' comfy couch.

Thomas suggested David start privately, within the bounds of the house, with David's mother as his witness and even better; his personal shopper. While David explored his gender and sexuality, his mother explored the Junior's sections of every clothing store in a twenty mile vicinity of Towne. No more mothballed sweaters from ARF or dirty stolen underwear. David's mother came home with brand new clothes with price tags! Soon there were dresses, skirts, shirts, and flashy footwear. Every day David put something girly on as soon as he got home from school.

"I can't wait to hear how you feel when you're wearing something gorgeous without any shame," said Thomas. "Who you feel like. What you feel like. All the feels. Be prepared. You're bound to go all over the map."

And all over the map David went. Sometimes he felt

like a girl, sometimes like a boy dressed as a girl, sometimes like a gay man dressed as a girl, sometimes as a straight man, sometimes like a straight woman, sometimes like a ditzy teenager, sometimes like a wise old man, sometimes like the most bisexual person ever, sometimes like some ethereal, asexual angel who didn't need any body. It was confusing. Frustrating. It gave David headaches. But being David no longer felt scary, or dirty, or weird. It just felt difficult.

Finding killer clothes for David became his mother's newest passion aside from working as an interior designer for Brady Cole. She seemed like a different person to David. A kooky, but more interesting person. She no longer shopped for herself. All that retail focus went towards David's growing wardrobe. Actually, his mother started looking super dowdy. She'd stopped coloring her hair and had a stripe of grayish brown down her center part. Every day she wore the same pair of baggy, high waisted mom-jeans and a food-stained cardigan. Forget jewelry, or make-up. Sometimes David wondered if she even showered.

Yet his mother seemed happy and energized. Even with a little more pudge around her middle, with her hairy arm pits and shins. Clearly David wasn't the only one going through changes.

David liked having his mom in his room. Snuggled against his pillows, all fuzzy and unkempt, she was like a new pet. "You went to clubs?" David asked as he shimmied into the retro orange romper. "Like dance clubs?"

"A few," said his mother. "I know it's hard to believe."

"Not that hard, Mom," David said. He liked the way the romper cinched his waist, but he couldn't figure out what to do with the collar.

"Let it fall off one shoulder," his mother suggested. "À la *Flashdance*."

He hadn't even had to ask. She just knew.

Lucinda: Let It Go

Brady was sweet, but he wasn't all that bright. He claimed to adore Lucinda, stroked her like a precious, rare object, cooed sweet nothings in her ear, but really the guy hadn't a clue as to who she really was. She'd since noted an ironic coincidence; the night she first ventured across the emerald lawn of the Kearny Mansion in her pansy-patterned frock, she had undressed and ended up flesh to flesh with Brady on a rickety chaise lounge, her dress tossed atop Brady's own weird white dress. Later the same night David undressed to put on the same pansy print dress, and almost—but only almost—revealed himself to her. She'd learned in their first joint therapy session with Thomas that David had put on that well-worn item of clothing at least four times before working up the nerve to finally do the deed.

"I dunno," David had said as he squirmed on the couch next to her. "You've been out of it, Mom. Like not there. Distracted all the time by your big mansion project."

The sordid synchronicity was not lost on her. A man in a dress, a boy in a dress. And a woman in a dress, touched by all three of them, for very different reasons. Brady, David, and Lucinda herself, zipping and unzipping the thing. Purple blossoms parting, bodies slipped in and out.

After the Night of the Big Reveal, Lucinda had felt bombarded by inappropriate attire. Assaulted by fashionable jokes. For a few weeks she stumbled around her house in a daze. Dishes piled in the sink, beds went unmade. She told Brady she had a terrible cold so she wouldn't have to deal with his overwhelming energy. She day-drank, found herself guzzling cheap wine in that horrid place by the train station, confessing her sins to Schepp, the owner.

Lucinda hadn't expected the cranky owner of a dive bar to be the one to knock some sense into her. But he was.

Lucinda decided to go along with it. All of it. With David she made a wise and loving parenting choice, though there were moments of insanity and hysteria, when mother and son were as confused as they'd ever been. Recently David came downstairs outfitted as if he were headed to Cannes for a weekend of yachting and champagne-swilling.

"Um, excuse me?" Lucinda tried to keep her already high-pitched voice from crawling up the scale to shrill, "What are you wearing?"

David scowled. He plucked at the form-fitting rayon jumpsuit Lucinda had scored from the sales rack at Nordstrom's—a vintage hippie throwback in bold sunflower print with wide bell bottom flares, a halter top closure, and deep V-neckline. His hair was growing out, and he'd clipped it back on both sides with matching sunflower barrettes. Platform sandals and bangle bracelets completed the look.

"What? You don't like my outfit?" he said with age-appropriate thirteen-year-old hostility.

"It's not that, Davey," said Lucinda, "It's a great outfit. But remember what Thomas said? You probably shouldn't be wearing those clothes to school just yet."

"I'm not an idiot. I know that," David said. "I was just showing you, that's all."

"Okay. It looks amazing. Now take it off. You need to leave for school in ten minutes."

"I know, I know," he huffed. "I can change in ten minutes."

"But you haven't had your breakfast yet, and—"

"I'm not hungry." David walked over to the full length mirror in the adjacent mudroom to admire himself, turning, and posing, practicing various smirks and smiles.

"Get ready now, young man—"

"You're not supposed to call me that!"

"Sorry, Davey but—"

"Thomas said so, remember? No gender qualifiers! Just endearments and nicknames!"

"David. You need to eat some breakfast—now—then change out of that fabulous outfit."

"Whatever," he huffed. He came back into the kitchen and stuffed a piece of toast in his mouth, chewed it quickly, took a few glugs of orange juice, then left his dirty plate and glass on the table. "Thanks for the positive feedback," he yelled as he clomped like a Clydesdale back upstairs to change his clothes.

There were other scenes. The time David almost stormed out the front door on a chilly December morning in a pink bikini. The time he hurled a glass of milk at her and nearly gave her a concussion. The time she slapped him across the face and then cried for an hour while he locked himself in his room. But those splintery moments were rare. For the most part their home filled with new magic, fresh potential. They declared their love and admiration for each other; they fought bitterly. Lucinda was ready to do whatever he needed her to do. Whatever Thomas suggested. Bring it on. Lucinda was all game.

With Brady, well, that was another story. There, her motives were entirely ulterior. It wasn't the first time Lucinda had slept with someone for selfish reasons. She'd always considered her previous hook-ups and lead-ons the results of the narcissistic foibles of youth. In high school there'd been four months of back seat humping with Mark Krupinski because Mark was best friends with Greg Bass, who was the one she really wanted to be with. In her twenties, she'd dated a Belgian pharmaceutical salesmen with the personality of a tree stump because he had a very cool vintage Citroën she liked driving; it made her feel like a euro-sophisticate.

Right before she'd met Dan there'd been the six-month slog with a morose architect whose pretentious minimalist aesthetic she secretly abhorred, but whose father was a famous abstract expressionist, and wow, wasn't that cool.

And then there'd been Dan. She wasn't even sure anymore what the original draw had been. Was it because Dan smelled good and the morose architect had smelled like moldy cheese? She'd learn eventually, Dan's minty fresh manliness was a result of obsessive showering. Was it because Dan seemed like a nice guy, in the most bland sense of the term, and she'd just been through a string of neurotics and depressives?

Her biological clock had been ticking. Back then Dan had money. Back then Dan had a decent body. What else had been the draw? It was excruciating to chip through all the hardened gunk clinging to more recent memories. Harder to admit was how shallow and stupid she'd been. Hardest of all was to admit to herself that Lucinda didn't know what true romantic love really was. Maybe she was incapable of it.

She didn't love Brady, she loved his house. She loved working on the Kearny Mansion. She loved getting paid. She loved having a nearly limitless budget. She loved the big ticket stuff; the gutting of walls, the re-positioning of pipes. She loved the subtle details; the choice of knobs, pulls, and hinges. Paint colors were her candy, window treatments her crack. She was a home improvement junkie, and she couldn't stop.

Brady came at her as if she were a goddess—he often called her Goddess when he wasn't using the annoying pet name Lou—pulling Lucinda's shirt over her head as soon as she entered the mansion, fondling her saggy breasts, kissing her meni-pot. Lucinda was all in, as long as her daily decorating chores were completed. Then Brady could have at her. After summer turned to fall turned to winter, sex with Brady became more than an exercise in endurance. Lucinda almost began to look forward to screwing Brady Cole. Good, straightforward fucking. That's all she wanted, and she told him so. And Brady got less annoying, less Mr. Pleasure At Your Service.

He was dogged, in spite of the fact that Lucinda made absolutely no effort to be desirable. She stopped coloring her hair, had a skunk-like stripe down her center part. She never dressed up. She stopped shaving her legs and plucking her hag hairs. She packed on a few extra pounds. In the beginning she had hoped that if she really let herself go, Brady's hound dog adoration might die down. By the time she was deep into the renovations, he couldn't fire her, but maybe he'd stop jumping her bones like she was Venus on the half shell. Then Lucinda would get what she wanted. Less sex, but enough to satisfy, and more time to work on the house.

Now it was winter and a Brady slow down didn't seem to be coming anytime soon. Besides the sex, Brady claimed he wanted to know everything about her, yet when she told him stories about her life, she wasn't sure he was really listening. He went on loosey-goosey, touchy-feely tangents. If he wasn't entirely missing her points, he definitely went off the mark.

So while Lucinda grew fonder of Brady, she could never love him. Underneath his caftan lurked the heart of someone lost and searching. A baby—a sweet one, perhaps, beneath the folds of white fabric—inside the body of a stud. The thing was, Lucinda already had a baby. David, whom she loved with a ferocity that fired every crevice and every cell of her expanding body. She might be incapable of loving a man, but she damn well knew how to love the hell out of her baby. A baby she would die for, run in front of buses for, fall on swords for. And honestly? Her baby wore much nicer dresses.

Brady: Something

He couldn't put his finger on it. Maybe it was her scent: coffee, sour lemons, dirt, wet leather, old sweat. So powerful he could smell her the moment she entered a room. Other guys might find the scent off-putting, but he found it intoxicating. He found it cleansing. She walked through the door, bundled up now that it was winter, in an olive green puffy floor length coat that looked like a costume from a film about giant slugs, and a hat that looked like a dead rabbit was napping on her head, and still Brady found her to be the most enticing creature alive.

He imagined former Bradys leaving his body when Lucinda arrived. Vaporous sinners, they wafted towards the rafters and disappeared like clouds of smoke. Enraged high school jock Brady who probably date-raped more than once, but was too drunk to remember. Newly minted male model Brady who let a guy suck him off in the bathroom of a hip Indonesian restaurant because the guy was a big cheese fashion photographer, afterwards punching the guy and claiming he'd never done the deed in the first place. Up-and-coming Hollywood heartthrob Brady using and abusing anyone more vulnerable than himself. Rich and famous actor Brady using and abusing many more. Every one of those former Bradys had punched holes in walls in various locations, in various countries, passed bucks, cursed people for no good reason, found fault where there was none, when the only fault was the giant gaping void where Brady's heart should've been.

Though with Lucinda, he was like a hungry newborn. Pure and easily sated. Being with her filled that massive hole. Lucinda was a complete and satisfying meal, all the food groups, all the nutrients. He felt desire for her all the time.

She made him want to be generous. She made him want to be good. He wasn't sure Lucinda had a handle on the whole renovation project, there were still a bunch of things in shambles; the demo-ed guest room and exposed electricals in the ballroom for starters. But because Lucinda wanted it so badly, Brady assumed the best. So what if some of the colors she'd chosen for the walls struck Brady as garish, or that he would have preferred a squishy sofa to crash on instead of the space-age itchy board-like thing she'd selected. Lucinda insisted they gut the perfectly functional bathroom at the top of the stairs to replace it with just another functional bathroom, albeit with sparklier fixtures and a special ass-crack washing gizmo, and all Brady did was smile and sign the check. Brady would never complain to Lucinda. He'd never criticize his true love. Not in a thousand years.

Brady let himself dream. He imagined a glorious future and planned for it, secretly. With nothing much to do, and nowhere to go, he'd lay atop the silk duvet on his giant bed and let his fantasy play out like the final scene of a romantic comedy, a Nancy Meyers-type romp that ended with a flash-forward montage rolled out during the credits:

INT. KEARNEY MANSION — EVENING

Lucinda has finished the renovation project. Brady and Lucinda are celebrating with a bottle of expensive champagne (which Brady would drink also, it being a special occasion, whether Tamago approved or not). Brady asks Lucinda to get something out of the drawer in the granite everywhere, eight burner oven-ed, stainless steel applianced, multiple-sinked kitchen. The drawer would be empty, but for a velvet ring box.

LUCINDA

Brady, what the—oh my God.

BRADY

Lucinda. You're my everything. You complete me. You make me a better person. I can't imagine my life without you. Will you marry me?

Brady would think of more original lines. He had some time.

LUCINDA

(Overwhelmed. Tears forming in her eyes. A happy smile spreading on her chapped lips)

Will I? Of course I will. Oh Brady!

Close up, Brady and Lucinda in a deep embrace, kissing.

Cut to overhead shot, circling. Brady and Lucinda kiss passionately.

FADE OUT

SUPER: Credits

INT WEDDING RECEPTION — AFTERNOON

Lucinda's son David is the best man (In real life, Brady had yet to meet David. It was nearly Christmas. Brady and Lucinda had been together for almost four months. Lucinda claimed David was too busy with school, that maybe Brady could meet David in the Spring. Meanwhile, Brady had caught a few glimpses of David across the street, jumping on his bike, or scrambling into Lucinda's station wagon. Early on Brady saw David coming from a trip around the back of the house with that pile of pink women's clothes in his arms. Sweet kid, Brady had thought, doing laundry for his mom. Helpful the way Brady had been with his mom. Brady loved David already.) and some relatively attractive friend of Lucinda's as maid of honor. (Brady still hadn't met any of Lucinda's friends either. When he'd asked why, she'd been wicked cagey. Brady assumed it was because Lucinda thought her friends would feel envious of her good fortune, those women probably stuck in marriages with paunchy, boring dudes. It wasn't like he could party with them anyhow, and it would be super weird to hang out with a bunch of people from Towne wearing his Beauteous caftan and drinking his green beverages, so Brady stopped asking, respectful of Lucinda's boundaries, and somewhat relieved he wouldn't risk embarrassing himself.) Tamago officiates. Guests are a multi-cultural mishmash of good-looking, happy folks. No celebs aside from Brady. Or maybe celebs playing regular people. But wait! This isn't really a movie. Brady and Lucinda dance to "Lovely Lou," while everyone looks on. Gradually, the dance floor fills with other couples. "Lovely Lou" fades into a funky song and Brady breaks out in an impressive krump. Lucinda looks on, amazed. (Brady would take krumping lessons. He'd learned how to do lots of other physically challenging stuff for various roles. How hard could that kind of dancing really be?)

SUPER: Credits

EXT. BACK YARD — DAY
Brady and David are playing football. Angus has returned and chases after them. Lucinda relaxes under a retractable awning, on a neon green chaise lounge, drinking a glass of white wine.

FADE TO BLACK

If the renovation went according to the latest schedule, meaning twice as long as originally planned for twice as much money, Brady would be able to propose by April. In the meantime, they'd hunker in for the winter months. Brady would make love to Lucinda on the bearskin rug in front of the blazing fire, on the kitchen island, on his brand new horse hair-stuffed, hand-built mattress from Sweden, which cost more than a mid-sized sedan. He'd look down at her lovely face while she gazed over his shoulder, or closed her precious eyes. His attractiveness obviously overwhelmed her, even after all this time. But no worries. Once they were engaged, Lucinda would realize Brady Cole, in all his handsome fabulousness, and more importantly, all his newfound goodness, was hers to keep forever. After that she'd stare lovingly and happily ever after straight into his bright blue eyes.

Chapter Ten

Nell: No More

Nell made her way through the icy streets of deserted downtown Towne in the late evening one icy December night. The roads were slick with black ice and her bike slipped precariously, as if she were pedaling on Teflon. She parked the bike behind the train station and slinked along the sidewalks, hiding in the shadows of doorways when the occasional car drove by. Each store-front was an assault; lit and decorated for the coming holidays, all green and red and tinsel and joy. Bobo's Toy Shoppe had an electric train running on a track in endless circles, with tiny stuffed animals sitting in the seats wearing stocking caps, miniature tankards of eggnog glued to their paws. The mannequins in the window of the ARF thrift store paired gaudy, bangled, snowflaked Christmas sweaters with flannel pajama pants. There was a giant gold menorah and a Happy Chanukah sign flashing good cheer in the Scotto's Pizzeria window. Every lamppost along Main Street had a grinning elf climbing up its side, and in the center of it all, hanging high overhead, the traditional Towne stuffed Santa Claus in a stalled sled leading to nowhere by Rudolph and the rest of his crew.

There would be little holiday joy for Nell this year. Not that she'd ever enjoyed the season. Christmas had always been a dismal affair in her home. The only decorations allowed on the Christmas tree were gloppy, abstracted baubles her mother made out of heavy clay which caused the branches to bow downward in defeat. There was never a pile of presents waiting for Nell on Christmas mornings. Instead her parents gave her a single expensive item—one year it was the Sting Ray bike, another time Nell received a top-of-the-line computer, once she got a professional microscope with an attached camera. Probably the happiest year was when they got her the Steinway, though the unspoken expectation of payback that came with that gift was even larger than usual.

Cold, winter nights held promise of a different sort for Nell. Frigid temperatures meant all the refuse and leftover foods from Towne restaurants would be less likely to have gone bad, iced and hardened in the dumpsters and trash bags she scrounged through. Nell's chilled fingers clawed frosty mounds searching for half eaten hamburgers, pizza crusts so hardened they could poke holes in a wall, congealed brains of udon noodles, turkey slices as sharp as frisbees.

That particular night, Nell was disappointed by her meager findings. She'd expected more of a bounty, but it seemed the townspeople of Towne had hearty pre-holiday appetites, finishing up their hot meals served in cozy restaurants, coats and hats off, their tushes comfortable on leather banquettes. They'd licked their plates clean, leaving Nell and her brood little to eat.

Thankfully Nell still had half a bag of kibble back at the compound. Abe Kaufman usually left food every three days, but he'd missed the last delivery. Nell wouldn't, couldn't worry. She had enough food for the next week, whether he returned or not. Once the food from this latest haul had thawed and the dogs had been fed, Nell could still save one pizza crust, and half a tuna sandwich for herself.

Nell could tell something was amiss as soon as she got home and leaned her bike against the porch. Usually at least a few of the dogs ran up to the front door to greet her, regardless of the time of day. But not that night. She entered the house, fearing the worst: the dogs all gone, swept away in a horrid van, taken to a shelter, redistributed to their former enslavers where they'd be shackled and shamed, living diminished lives once again. Or maybe one of those terrible dog-stealing gangs Hector Moore mentioned at the meeting had discovered her sanctuary, had stolen her brood and was already on the road, taking them far away.

Then Nell heard a cacophony of yips and barks coming from the backyard. She'd re-jiggered the back door in early September so it swung open in both directions and the dogs could get out of the house and use the yard whenever they wanted. It was rare that they'd all go out at once in this colder weather. Nell trembled as she ran through the dark house towards the back door. While the dogs might still be home, something was terribly amiss.

Abe: No More

Abe blew his nose for what must've been the four hundredth time in three days. How could there be so much mucus in one man's body? He'd caught Milo's cold, a cold that Barbara informed him had been raging through the under-five set at Allenwood Park playground. Half the nannies had it, as did the moms. Barbara had been spared. Claire had been spared. Abe had not.

At least he no longer felt like a weak and useless wet rag. He needed to run again, not only for his sanity, but also because he'd missed a delivery of supplies to the Dog Sanctuary. It was a cold and miserable night, but a man had to do what a man had to do. So, when Claire got home, he told her he was going for a run.

"Are you crazy?" Claire asked. "It's miserable out there."

"It's not that bad, Babe. I've been laying around for days. I'm going fucking bonkers. Believe me, you'll be glad because when I get home I won't be such a grumpy asshole."

"Whatever. Just don't wake me up if I'm already asleep." Claire turned her attention back to her phone, where Twitter beckoned.

The weather report called for a light sprinkling of snow that night. Abe hadn't yet run in snow, and imagined he might slip on icy sidewalks, still somewhat of a clod, not the most sure-footed jogger in Towne. He already had a bag of food and a package of snacks ready in the garage. He shoved the supplies in his backpack, parka-ed up, Velcroed the fleece headband around his ears and hit the still-dry pavement at a steady clip.

With each significant seasonal shift, Abe's thoughts about Gordon percolated with obsessive fury. That evening, as the sky took on an aluminum sheen and the air felt like a towel drenched in ice, Abe remembered Gordon's first City snowfall, back in his puppy days. Gordon couldn't get enough of that white stuff. As Abe huffed and puffed along he hoped that it did snow that night, and that Gordon got to play in it, snuffle his blocky nose deep in crystalized piles, watery traces from exhaled hot air dripping from his magnificent nostrils. And then, as if someone, or something up there in the sky had heard Abe's wish, delicate flakes lightened the air around him, melted on his hot face, cleansed him. Something akin to happiness surged.

The snow-delivering clouds were so low they looked as if Abe could reach up and touch them. It was probably the cold propelling him at a brisker than normal pace, or maybe it was that happy feeling in his gut. Either way, some essence of purposefulness got Abe to Freaky Sting Ray's sanctuary in record time.

Abe was about to leave his delivery at the gate when he glanced through the slats and noticed the girl's bicycle, usually leaning against the front porch, wasn't there. He'd felt the urge to sneak another peek around the compound every time he ventured out to this place, just to make sure Gordon was still there, still happy, still thriving. Abe wanted to get a better sense of the property, where it started and where it ended. There might be a pool or a pond. He'd heard splashing once or twice. Gordon loved to swim. But each time Abe had almost snuck in, he'd stopped himself, knowing, even though she'd never said it, that the girl would not allow it, that if she caught him on the property again there was no knowing how she'd react.

But he could tell she wasn't home. The lights were all off inside the house, the bike gone, the dogs quiet. As the snow fell around him, Abe thought, why not? The snow would muffle the sound of his footsteps. He'd wander around like a ghost.

Abe hoisted himself up, lighter than before, unlatched the gate and ventured inside. He walked around to the opposite side of the house he'd not seen on his first visit. A bright outdoor light illuminated a sprawling expanse of lawn, overgrown and covered with dead leaves, ragged toys, and the unmistakably blended effluvia of piss and poo. The snow was starting to stick, filling the earth between weedy sprouts. As he'd suspected, there was a pool, now filled with frozen water. The place was a human disaster, but a dog paradise.

Suddenly, there was a rustling at the far end of the property. Two dogs, a large golden retriever and a tiny toy poodle, poked their heads out from under overgrown hedges. As soon as they saw Abe they ran towards him, barking like crazed sentries.

He knew from the quality of their barks they were a friendly pair. Abe wasn't scared of them, but he was scared of what he'd started. Almost instantly, all the other dogs inside the house began barking, and then, through a swinging door, the whole mess of them ran outside, plundering the earth, leaping towards him, filling the formerly empty yard with wonderful psychotic dog energy.

Gordon came right to him, jumped up and licked the snowy trickles on Abe's face. His buddy, with Abe again. It was slobbery bliss. But Gordon didn't linger. What mattered most to Gordon was the snow. Abe was a little heartbroken, but not as terribly as he might have been under different circumstances. Abe brushed off an old Adirondack chair and sat, watching Gordon and the other dogs run in crazy circles, trying to catch flakes, wrestling with each other, shaking their wet bodies, then starting the whole dance over and over. Every now and then a dog came up to him, sniffed his crotch, maybe licked his gloved hand, or the bare skin on Abe's cheek, then galumphed away to join the pack. Abe felt like a favorite uncle, tolerated and well-liked, but not adored. He was okay with this. He could've sat there and watched forever. But no.

"What are you doing here?"

The shrill cry seared the back of his neck. Abe turned to face Freaky Sting Ray Girl. She was as slender as a bamboo shoot, but her anger was as tall as a redwood.

One hand clenched a garbage bag, the other was balled into a fist. Her hair was tucked inside the hood of her ridiculous red rain coat, but tendrils fell out around her neck, like Medusa's snakes. Her eyes were Medusa's as well, filled with murderous rage. Abe had never been more scared of anyone in his entire life.

"I'm so sorry," he said as he stood to face her. "I never should've come in here. I promise I won't do it ever again."

"This is my house," she screamed. "My haven. You've spoiled it. Poisoned it."

"Like I said, I'm really sorry."

"Don't come back. I don't need you. Don't leave your stupid food and stupid treats. I throw it all away, anyhow. That processed stuff isn't good for dogs. Don't you know anything? No, of course you don't. You. Know. Nothing."

Abe nodded. "You're right. I know jack shit."

"That's why you left your dog in the hot sun, nearly dying from heat stroke. Who knows what would've happened to him if I hadn't saved him."

"Well, that's a bit extreme—"

"Find your own purpose, Abe Kaufman. Stay away from mine."

My own purpose, thought Abe. If only it were that simple.

"I just want to say," Abe began, "That what you're doing here is a wonderful thing. A *mitzvah*. You're lucky to have all this." He looked at Gordon, now sitting by the girl's scrawny leg, licking her scabby knee. "And these are some lucky, lucky dogs."

"Leave now." Freaky Sting Ray's bottom lip trembled with fury. "Or else."

Abe opened his mouth to say one more thing, but found he had nothing to offer. All he had left to do was run his ass homeward.

Chapter Eleven

Paddy: Caught

By the time winter truly set in it was clear Paddy needed to finally put Barney's doggie bed, squeaky toys, and food bowls in the basement. He couldn't throw them out, not yet. That would be too callous—and a final slap in Mariah's face. But he did want to make the house as hospitable as possible for Barbara and Milo, who were coming over to Paddy's place for the first time later that cold December day for a little pre-holiday cheer. God forbid the kid stuck one of Barney's slobbered toys in his own mouth, or worse, ate the dog's food.

The house had turned into a grimy, stinky, dust bunny convention center. That morning Paddy mopped the floors, vacuumed the rugs, wiped all the knickknacks. It was brutal, hard work. He talked to Mariah the whole time. Out loud, like a crazy person. It made the whole ordeal easier, imagining her nearby, telling him to lift the lamp and dust under it, to not only wash the mildewed bathroom towels, but to throw the bathmat in the machine as well.

"And don't forget the bleach, right?" Paddy asked.

"*Right,*" Mariah said.

"I think you'd like Barbara," Paddy said as he turned the knobs. HOT: Whites Only. FULL LOAD. "She's a bit talkative, but she's 'good people,' as you'd say."

"*I'm happy for you Paddy. I really am. You need love in your life.*"

"It's just a friendship, Mariah."

"*We'll see…*"

Paddy scrubbed Comet into the shower tiles, which had become a molding carnival of germs.

"*Well, if nothing else, Barbara's visit is getting you to clean up. I swear Paddy, you'd think an ape lived in this house!*"

"Yeah," Paddy chuckled. "A big, fat, hairy ape."

"*A lovable ape.*"

"Your ape, Mariah," Paddy sighed.

"*Yes, my ape. But I'm willing to share.*"

The visit started out fine. Barbara and Paddy sat at the table munching Barbara's Chanukah cookies shaped like dreidels, iced in blue and white, and drinking nutmeg-flavored coffee Paddy bought for the occasion, while Milo babbled nonsense at their feet. Barbara and Paddy had been talking about politics. The world had been going to hell in a hand basket since the 1980s as far as Paddy was concerned, and he liked to rant about it. Mariah would've rather discussed whether to cook pork chops or strip steak for dinner, but Barbara liked to chew political gristle as much as Paddy.

"She's here," Barbara said suddenly, out of nowhere. Her eyes made a wide arc around the room.

"Hilary?" They'd been talking about the recent election disaster.

"Mariah," Barbara said calmly. "She's watching us."

It was one thing for Paddy to go around the house talking to his dead wife. It was another thing for someone else to imagine Mariah was actually there. Paddy didn't think Mariah was really around, like a ghost or anything. He knew his talking to her was all inside his head, a private conversation. "Nah, I don't think so."

"It's not a bad thing," Barbara said. "It's a very nice energy, actually. Mariah has a wonderful aura."

This spiritual who-ha stuff coming from Barbara wasn't a complete surprise. Barbara adamantly insisted Mort visited her every now and then, leaving little gifts or signs. She told Paddy that several years earlier she'd woken up, overwhelmed by smells of tobacco and bourbon, Mort's favorite duo, even though he'd been dead for two years by then and she'd moved to an entirely new apartment. Recently, while Paddy and she were taking turns pushing Milo on the bucket swing, Barbara claimed Mort had left a bracelet she'd lost months ago on top of her bureau that very morning.

"She's calling us, Paddy." Barbara got up and walked, as if in a daze, in to the living room. "Come in here."

Paddy was confused. "What about Milo?"

"He'll be fine. We can keep an eye on him through the door."

Paddy wasn't sure if "we" meant she and he, or if Barbara was including Mariah in the eye-keeping. Paddy got up while Milo continued to play.

"Bye bye Pa Da," the kid said calmly with his little crunchy wave. Then he continued to clank a skillet against the table leg.

Barbara sat on the couch. She patted the cushion next to her. Was Paddy ready for this? To sit so close to Barbara on this couch, the couch he'd sat on for decades with his wife?

Where he'd held Mariah's trembling hand while Richard Kiley from the original cast of *Man of La Mancha* sang about destiny calling?

"I feel her," Barbara said, "Mariah. Sitting right here."

Close call. Paddy had almost sat on his wife.

"What a gorgeous home," Barbara said, sighing as she gazed around the room. "You must love it so much."

"I do." Paddy was glad he'd done his industrial-level clean up. Lemon Pledge, Swiffers, the works. He stood, not knowing what to do next, looking at Barbara looking at Mariah's stuff. The matching ceramic bluebirds, one with a hairline fracture in its wing, the empty glass vase Mariah would fill with hydrangeas from the garden, the seascape paintings bought on a long-ago trip to Cape Cod.

Barbara's gaze settled on a spot behind Paddy. Her eyes got wide. "Oh my! Will you look at that!"

Paddy turned, fully expecting to see Mariah's ghost, or maybe Mort's, or maybe some other spirit Barbara had conjured from the grave. But it was just snow, heaps of it, falling fast and furious outside the picture window.

"Like a thousand exiled angels," Barbara sighed. "I know, I'm a Jew. We're not supposed to believe in angels. But look at that. It's spectacular."

A spectacular pain in the butt, thought Paddy. The shoveling. The traffic snarls. The possible power outage. The digging out of his car, which Paddy parked in the driveway because his garage was filled with accumulated auto parts and other saved silliness from the past fifty years. The snowstorm wasn't supposed to start until 5 pm. It wasn't even noon and already it was piling up like sand in the Sahara.

"I'll give you guys a ride home," said Paddy. "Before the roads are impossible."

Barbara shrugged. "What's the rush?" She patted the cushion next to her again. "Come on. Sit."

"But I thought—"

"Oh, it's okay. Mariah's gone."

No she's wasn't. Mariah would never be gone. Neither would Mort. But that was okay. Paddy settled down next to Barbara, the cushion sinking with the weight of him. The weight of them all.

Abe: Caught

Abe arrived home from his morning run, a sweaty, heaving mass of man. Before heading to the shower, out of habit he clicked the remote and turned on the big screen. Slalom racing on the Motatapu Chutes in New Zealand. He stood for a moment and watched lunatic geniuses careen down sheer drops of endless, blinding whiteness. Abe felt his usual sense of awe, shortly followed by awe's cranky little sidekick, envy.

It had been two weeks since he'd been banished from the Sanctuary. The girl's words—don't you know anything—were on repeat in his head like an earworm. And more relentless: Find your own purpose, find your own purpose, find your own purpose.

Purpose still evaded, but Abe had plenty of awe and envy for what Freaky Sting Ray had. Really, for what everyone had. Would these niggling feelings of crapitude ever end for him? Abe kept the TV on as he showered. He raised the volume so he could hear the announcer's blow by blow, and with the bathroom door ajar he could tell who was placing, who was out of the running, and which unfortunate schmo tumbled perilously into avalanches of snowy madness.

While Abe scrubbed his left armpit, the sound of the TV went off. He quickly rinsed off, grabbed a towel, and walked into the living room. Claire sat on the couch look-ing at the blank screen.

"Hey Hon," Abe drawled. "What are you doing home?"

She turned and looked at him with what Abe thought of as her school principal about to reprimand a juvenile delinquent eyes. "There's a blizzard watch for later today. They sent everyone home early. Look at it out there. It's like the North Pole."

"Oh, cool. Snow day!" Abe cheered, knowing full well from her expression that Claire was in no mood for glee.

"Where are Mouse and Barbara?"

"Um, ah, they must still be at Sonam's. You know, her buddy the nanny."

"Good. I was worried." Claire narrowed her eyes. "Now what the fuck is going on here, with you?"

"What do you mean?"

"Why was the TV on full blast on some stupid sports show?"

Abe hesitated. A cold mix of shower and sweat lin-gered in the most unsavory places. "I reached a good stopping point in *The Gist* so I went for a run before get-ting back to work. Thought I'd watch something mindless before diving back in. What's the big deal?"

Claire got up and went into Abe's office. She came back carrying his laptop. "Why is this off if you were writ-ing earlier and planned to get back to it now?"

New sweat began to form on Abe's skin. Stress perspi-ration. The stinkiest kind. "It's good to turn the computer off completely every now and then. You know that."

"Yeah, I do. But why turn off your computer in the middle of a work session?"

"The computer was acting wonky. Thus I turned it off. Thus my run. Thus my break."

"Show me."

"Show you what?"

"*The Gist*, Abe."

"Claire, I told you I don't want to show it to you until I get further along."

Claire glared at him. She'd moved beyond the disappointed school principal phase to the Mommy Dearest where's my hanger phase. "Bullshit Abe. It's been over six months. Show me your fucking book."

"Okay. I'll show it to you, but you can't read it, you can just see it. A quick peek, a visual, that's all."

Claire sat by Abe's side as he turned the computer on. He positioned the laptop screen away from her, but she shifted her entire torso so she could still see it. Abe fumbled around with files, found an old story he'd written a few years back. He prayed lines of text, any text, would fool her.

"Here it is," he said as Claire squinted towards the screen in the split second Abe allowed her. He shut the laptop. "You saw it. Satisfied?"

Before he could stop her Claire grabbed the computer off Abe's lap and bounded to the bathroom where she shut and locked the door.

"What the—hey, Claire!" Abe ran after her. "Give it back."

She wasn't in there long. Not long enough to stalk all his files, or check his browser history. And anyway, there wasn't anything sordid or secret for her to find. The problem was there was nothing for her to find. Nothing she hadn't already seen including a title page for *The Gist* and nothing else but a big, fat void where there should've been a novel. Not even a gist of *The Gist*.

Claire opened the door and handed the laptop back to Abe. "I can't believe you've been lying to me this entire time."

The judgment. The failure reflected in her eyes. The

defeat, the crackle, the distance in her voice. Abe found it excruciating. He wanted to scream, "You see that? The way you're being? That's why I never told you I had writer's block as solid and impossible to scale as a fucking New Zealand monolith." Instead Abe stayed mute and duly shamed.

"And you don't even have anything to say. You're unbelievable." Claire walked away from him to the bedroom, closed and locked its door.

Abe paced the living room in his towel, like a pervert banished from a men's sauna. Outside, massive white flakes began to pour like packing peanuts from the sky.

An hour passed, and still Claire remained sequestered. The wind picked up, howling and bending tree branches, threatening to down power lines. The snow morphed into tiny icy pellets. It sounded as if thousands of rodents in high heels were skittering across the roof. When Abe looked out the window all was a white and dismal blur. At 3 pm his phone rang from where he'd left it on the coffee table. He'd been so distressed by Claire's discovery and his mute and passive response that he hadn't glanced once at the tiny screen of his phone which often functioned as a miniature brain-numbing time sucker when the big screen was off limits. A number he didn't recognize with a local area code.

"Abie, it's your mother."

As if Abe didn't recognize the voice. "Hey Ma. I hope you're safe inside."

"Oh yes, we're fine. Snug as bugs in a rug."

Abe heard a man talking baby talk in the background. "Who was that?"

"That was Paddy. My friend."

"I thought your friend was a babysitter, a woman from Nepal."

"That's right, but this is another friend."

"So this guy Paddy is also a babysitter?"

She laughed and said, "He thinks you're a babysitter, Paddy!" Her voice was all Doris Day, perky and bright.

"Mother," Abe said, "who the hell is Paddy?"

"Abraham. Do not curse. Paddy is a gentleman I met a little while ago. I've been meaning to tell you about him, but, oh, I don't know, it never felt like the right time. In any event, Milo and I are at his house. I know what you're thinking. Don't worry. We're fine."

Abe was speechless. A gentleman I met a little while ago.

"Abie? Are you there?"

"Yeah, Ma, I'm here."

"I think it would be nice for you to meet Paddy sometime. Maybe he can come over to your house some night and I can make us all a nice dinner?"

Abe thought of Claire locked in the bedroom. Not talking to him. Who knew what she'd say or do when that door opened? Who knew what would become of them? The idea of a nice dinner seemed quite remote. "Ah, well, maybe—"

"Wonderful," his mother bulldozed. "But for now Milo and I will be staying here until the storm passes."

"Ma, how well do you know this guy, really?"

"Abraham, are you questioning my judgement?"

"Well, sort of—"

"Well, don't. I've taken fine care of myself for all these years. I know exactly what I'm doing."

"Okay…"

"I suppose you now have Paddy's phone number because I called you and it is showing up on the app or whatever you call it. Or—do you need me to tell it to you so you can write it down?"

"No, Ma, that's okay. I have Paddy's number. Permanently lodged now. Right here, on my phone."

"Alright then Abie. I'll talk to you later. Stay warm.

Don't go outside. The weather out there is dangerous! I haven't seen anything like this since the blizzard of '78. Don't do anything stupid, okay?"

If only his mother knew.

David: Caught

The Principal let everyone out after fourth period, and the blizzard had already started once everybody got outside. Millions of tiny little flakes. David and his classmates stood in front of the school with their heads back and their tongues out, catching little icy treats. Coats, hats, hair all frosted in white.

David wanted to bolt home, change into a dress, make a cup of hot chocolate and maybe binge watch some Battlestar Galactica. But Thomas had told him not to isolate. David didn't have to say anything or do anything. He just had to be there, with other kids. He at least had to try. He found Danesha, Benji, and Paul over by the flagpole. Paul was trying to catch snowflakes in a jar.

"Dude," David said, "You're wasting your time. They're just gonna melt."

"Sometimes the journey is more important than the destination, David," Paul said as he held his jar skyward.

David patted Paul on the back. "Enjoy the trip, Shack Attack."

Danesha and Benji were scooping up as much snow as they could to make miniature snowmen.

"Snow people," Danesha said. "Wanna help?"

David knelt to gather snow from around the base of the flag pole, but he wasn't as good as they were at getting the stuff to form into little balls.

"I think I'll just watch," he said.

Benji smiled at him. "All creative artists need an audience."

"Whatever you say, B-man," David nodded.

David was shocked when Chucky walked over a few minutes later, like he was on a peace-keeping mission.

"Hey Lebo," Chucky said.

"Hey Wieno," said David.

They were a couple of awkward dumbasses staring at each other, flakes falling and coating them while other kids screamed like kindergartners, gathering snow to make throwable weapons.

"You look like someone's grandfather." Chucky touched David's hair and brushed the snow off.

David shivered, not from the cold. Then he did the same back. "Yo, Chucky the Abominable Snowman."

Chucky giggled. David giggled. They kept brushing imaginary snow off each others heads.

Eventually Chucky got called away by his new crew; jocky a-holes who were notorious drinkers, or at least claimed to be. Before he left he said, "We should hang out again, Leibo. I miss your sorry ass."

David watched as Chucky ran away, thinking, I miss yours, too. So much pretending. So much hiding.

Danesha winked at David. "I think somebody likes you," she said in a sing-songy way.

David looked away. "It's not like that. Chucky and I go way back."

"Way back where?" giggled Benji.

David gathered a handful of snow and threw it at Benji's face. Benji's glasses were covered in white. He just stood there.

"Oh shit," Danesha said.

David was convinced Benji would start crying, because that was the kind of thing Benji used to do all the time. But, finally after an excruciating number of seconds Benji shouted, "Dude! You've helped me realize my true calling! I'm Mr. Magoo!" Benji started veering around like he was that old, blind, dumbass cartoon character. It was actually pretty funny.

The snow started coming down harder. Paul had a jar full of slush and Danesha had a complete mini-family of snow people. Benji had slowed down his blind wanderings. David had done his job, hung out like his shrink wanted him to, survived it. Had fun even. He gave himself permission to leave.

When he got home the house was empty. David figured his mother was working across the street at Brady Cole's. He dumped his backpack, jacket, and soggy sneakers by the front door and went upstairs to change into something dry and more beautiful. Off went the stupidly about-to-fall-off-his-butt jeans and generic, boring black tee. Flung to the floor, the wide elastic-waisted jockeys. On went the ivory satin bikinis he loved so well. Now, what to wear. Something cozy and warm. His mom had recently bought him a white velour cowl-necked floor length dress. It was a dress-me-up or dress-me-down sort of gown. Half evening wear, half leisurewear. Perfect for this snowy day.

David slipped the dress over his head and thought: Dudes are so deprived. They don't get to cover themselves in head-to-toe luxurious softness. Maybe David could change that. He'd been playing around with fashion design, sketching his own creations; clothes for everyone, unisex to the max. Maybe one day he'd have his own clothing line.

Even though it was going to be a couch potato TV watching kind of snow day, David wanted to primp a bit. He brushed his hair, which was getting super long—chin length almost— side-parted it and clipped the longer bit back with a rhinestone barrette. Lastly, a light covering of lip gloss, for a barely there shimmer. David wished he could add a little mascara, maybe some silvery eye shadow, but Lucinda forbade it.

"When you're sixteen, we'll talk," she said. "For now,

no way, Buddy. No thirteen-year-old girl, boy, or anything in between is walking around my house looking like a hussy-kewpie doll-street walker."

Hussy-kewpie doll-street walker. That had cracked David up. It was nice to be able to laugh at, and with his mom. When had they ever had this much fun together?

David had just smacked his lips on a tissue when he heard Lucinda come in downstairs. She hadn't seen him in the dress yet, so he was super excited to show her how it looked.

"Ta-daaaaaaa," David sang as he skittered down the stairs. He had to keep his eye on the steps because the dress was long and he didn't want to trip.

"Wow, hey. Hmm… Okay then. Cool."

David looked up. It wasn't Lucinda uttering this string of stupid nothing words. They came out of the mouth of a man, a man wearing a terrible white dress. He also had on a big blue parka that did nothing for his figure. Here was Brady Cole, in the flesh, in David's house.

David was stunned. He wanted to run back upstairs and lock himself in his room, but he felt immobilized, like one of those super-isolated jungle tribespeople who have their photo taken and think their souls have been stolen.

"Uh," Brady stammered, "the door was open. I came over to make sure you and your mom were okay."

David blinked, like a big flashbulb had just gone off in his face, and he couldn't see a thing.

"It's coming down like an avalanche out there. I'm Brady, by the way. Are you, um, David?"

David wanted to say, of course I'm fucking David, you dimwit. Just because I'm dressed this way doesn't mean I'm not David. But he didn't say any of that. He just nodded.

"Well, I'm super excited to meet you David." Brady held a hand out. David shook it.

"Is your mom home?"

"Uh, I thought she was working at your house."

"No. I wish she were though." Brady smiled. He had perfect movie star teeth. Nothing like teeth David had ever seen. Not even Deborah Kaplan, his high school sophomore neighbor who'd had braces for a gazillion years (plus a rumored nose job) ended up with teeth like that.

"She must be shopping."

"Cool." Brady nodded. "So are you on your way to a costume party? You look great by the way. Like a real little lady. That hair thingie is a nice touch. The girls are gonna love it. You'll definitely get some action. Chicks always like it when dudes expose their feminine side. Show that we're not afraid to be, you know, a bit softer. Less macho."

"It's not for a party." David couldn't believe he'd said it.

It took a few moments to register with Brady. His Disney prince face went through all sorts of contortions while he was trying to figure David out.

"I like to dress this way," David blurted. The dam had burst. Later Thomas would suggest that it was a right time, right place sort of situation. That David was starting to gear up to show the world who he truly was. Plus, Brady wasn't a real person to David. He was a famous actor, which meant he wasn't real. He didn't exist in David's sphere, wasn't friends with any of his friends, or his mother's friends. Brady was an outsider. A weirdo recluse really, who lived across the street, an eccentric, dress-wearing income stream with hairy calves poking out of the top of fuzzy booties, which were drenched and looked like wet bunnies.

"Why are you dressed like that?" David pointed a discerning finger at Brady's ugly caftan.

Brady looked down at his dress. "Oh. Yeah. This."

"Yeah. That. What were you thinking?" David had recently been watching reruns of *What Not To Wear*. He felt confident in his fashion policing. "It's horrible."

"No, you don't get it. I didn't choose this."

"You're wearing it. You look like some peasant sheep herder. It does nothing for you."

"I'm Beauteous," he said. "I'm a follower of Tamago. We wear dresses. Well, this dress. Sometimes. Not always."

"Tamago? Sounds like some kind of pasta sauce." Good one, thought David. Maybe someday I really will be a witty style expert on TV.

"Tamago is a person. A guru, I guess. He's really great. He's totally into men harnessing the feminine. Especially guys who've been, well, not so great to women in their pasts."

David shrugged. "That's cool."

Brady looked relieved.

"But that *schmatta* is terrible. You should talk to Tomato about updating the outfit." David said tomato like a Brit. Tom-ah-to. "You hungry?"

"Sure. I guess." Brady was a big guy, like over six feet tall, but for some reason David found him about as intimidating as a helium balloon.

"You can dump your wet stuff over there," David pointed to the coat hooks where his smaller but equally sopping wet and ugly parka was hanging above sodden sneakers. Brady hung up his coat and slipped off the bunny booties.

"I can make grilled cheeses, if you want." David, the hostess with the mostest.

"Cheese is always good," Brady said.

"Well, follow me then." He strode past Brady towards the kitchen, the wide skirt of his velour gown swishing around his skinny legs.

While David made sandwiches Brady sat at the breakfast bar and rambled on in a nervous way about Beauteous Manhood and the tomato dude. It sounded like hippy music; dulcimers, and dancing, not to mention the terrible dress. David kept his mouth shut and let Brady blab on and on because it was obvious Brady was super uncomfortable talking to David about David. Even with all his guru bullshit he was still just a straight guy trying to make sense of a teenage boy in a dress.

And then things got really weird. And really wonderful. Lucinda came home with a gift. David knew what it was even before he heard the front door slam behind her. The skittering of toenails on the floor like castanets. The huffy puffy breath. And almost as instantly, the stench.

"Balzy!" David cried. "You're home!" David lifted his old pal up and didn't care if Balzy's paws left dirty marks on the white velour. Balzy licked David all over his face. Snuffled his wet nose in the boy's neck.

"Snow Day Surprise!" Lucinda called as she came into the kitchen. Her expression went from super stoked to super shocked when she saw Brady and David in their white dresses, eating sandwiches, both of them avoiding the crusts.

"Brady. What are you doing here?" Her voice wobbled.

"Hey, Lou," Brady got up off his stool and put his arms around David's mom. Weird. Then he kissed the top of her head, speckling her gray roots with bread crumbs. Even weirder. "I came over to make sure you were alright in this blizzard."

David stared at them. What was going on? His mother and the movie star? Like, together? Into his mind lurched the image of his father pounding against Rachel in the powder room, which morphed into Brady Cole doing the deed to his mom. No way, David thought. Incomprehensible. He wanted to hurl.

Balzy started to growl. Dogs. They got it. They knew when something's wrong.

Nell: Caught between a rock and a hard place

The week before Christmas Nell was down to zero. By banishing Abe Kaufman, she'd jeopardized the well-being of her pack. But she wouldn't renege. Nell had a stubborn streak as solid as a steel rod. This meant only one option remained. Nell chose Pepe, formerly Balthazar, who occasionally nipped at the others when seemingly unprovoked. While Pepe was still a lovable creature to all-loving Nell, he would be the least missed by the other dogs. Most importantly, his poster offered the highest reward. With that money the heating bill could be paid and all the other dogs could eat for another few months.

Pepe was returned to Lucinda Leibowitz in the middle of a blizzard. Nell hadn't seen this woman for years, and then over the course of the last few months, Lucinda Leibowitz seemed to be everywhere: at ARF, at the Towne Meeting, once while Nell was dumpster-diving by the train station, Nell saw Lucinda stumbling out of Schepp's Saloon. Dim memories of her earlier encounters with Lucinda percolated in Nell's fevered brain; Lucinda peering in to Nell's bedroom as the ten-year-old tended to Jumbo, Nell wiping the slime from the sides of his plastic terrarium, Lucinda chirping a synthetic "Hi there!" while the look on her face was one of pure disgust. A later memory of piano lessons with David, Lucinda hovering like a hungry mosquito, offering snacks and distractions, her voice the tonality of elevator Muzak, when real music was all that should have mattered. Mozart, for god sake, not cheese sticks and orange juice.

While Nell had sensed a shift in Lucinda's aura when she'd seen her at the Towne Meeting, there were no guarantees this woman wasn't still, basically, a dimwit. Consigning Pepe to an uncertain fate at the hands of this woman was a choice so painful Nell could feel the walls of

her heart rip in deep, muscular misery. Lucinda Leibowitz might still be a fool, but what else could Nell do?

They met at the train station. Nell wrapped herself in
layers, hid her face so as not to risk recognition. If the
woman uttered another fabricated "Hi there!" Nell would
abort mission and scurry back to the compound with
Pepe. For her part, Nell kept the conversation at a bare
minimum. All she wanted to do was grunt and moan.

At first the dog was undone, running in frantic circles
between Nell and his former enslaver, caught in a whirl-
pool of sense memories—new senses, old senses, good
memories and bad. Eventually the Balthazar memories
won out. The dog settled contentedly by Lucinda Leibowitz's fluffy snow boot, a boot that looked to Nell as if it
had been made from the hide of another woebegone dog.
There was a brief moment when Nell thought Lucinda
recognized her, but it passed in a flash. She pocketed the
ten crisp $100 bills and walked away at a feverish clip.

It was blood money. A betrayal. Poor Pepe. Nell rode
back to the remaining dogs through the torrential storm,
keeping her bike in the tracks made by the Towne snow-
plows, blinded by the whiteness, but also by grief. She arrived home in sodden shambles. To make matters worse,
when Nell returned to her brood huddled and whimpering on the cold living room floor she knew instantly; Eduardo and Boris were also gone for good. Not just
outside, snuffling for bugs under the boxwoods. The two
dogs were smarter together than they were separately. Together they formed one superior canine brain. They knew
this was the beginning of the end. Eduardo, driven by
hunger and survival instinct, had gone back to where he'd
come from, and his lover Boris would not be left behind.
In her mind's eye Nell imagined Eduardo leaving the way
he'd come, pushing open the flimsy front door, digging
a massive hole under the fence and bounding through

the snowstorm, but not so fast that Boris couldn't keep apace. The two of them were most likely back by now at Eduardo's former home. Back to being Angus and Barney. Warm, well-fed, celebrated. Better off.

Nell wanted to sink to the floor and allow the remaining dogs to lick her salty tears. She wanted to sob. But she was their rock, their keeper, their beacon. She was their savior. She needed to keep her shit together. She took a deep breath and smiled her first ever fakey-fake smile. She tried to console herself with the upside of three fewer mouths to feed.

Lucinda: Caught

The call came in around ten am. Lucinda was in the den, which she'd transformed into a full-fledged home office. She was at the computer, playing around with possible logos for her design business. She planned to launch a website, do all the requisite social media pizzazz, and market the hell out of LouDesign in the coming months. She'd put out a few feelers with her old contacts and a smattering of friends and neighbors. Already she had one or two small job possibilities percolating: a guest room redo for an old friend from Pilates class, and a master suite overhaul for the retired couple three doors down.

It was all good, because her work at the Kearny Mansion needed to stop. She'd been drawing certain projects out to justify the money Brady was paying her. Money for David, funds to jumpstart LouDesign and help her break free of her dependence on Dan's meager child support and even stingier alimony. She felt terrible about it, knew she had to pull the plug. She was living a double life. In one she was a loving and generous mother. In the other, she was a manipulative user. But it wasn't all her fault. Brady wouldn't let go. More and more lately, he'd been dropping unsubtle hints, talking about "the sanctity of marriage" and "the freedom in monogamy." He'd even added a new verse to that terrible song, a verse that stunk of commitment. Lucinda froze when he'd sung it to her the night before.

> I placed it in her hand,
> A gold and precious band,
> Lovely Lou,
> This is for you.
> So forever we can be,
> Not just her and him, but we.
> Lovely Lou,
> Say I do.

"You're speechless," Brady said as he lay the dulcimer across his lap and leaned over to kiss her cheek. "Overcome with joy?"

"I suppose it is a bit overwhelming." Lucinda quickly rose from the couch. "Sorry Brady, but I have to go. David has a Spanish assignment I promised to help him with." Spanish? David didn't even take Spanish. He was a Francophile through and through.

Sometimes she felt pity for Brady. Other times she felt smothered by him. Often she felt indifferent. Whatever the situation, it had to end. There was only so long Lucinda could tolerate her own deviousness.

When the landline rang, she almost had a heart attack she was so deep in her LouDesign reverie. Barely anyone called that number anymore, it was mostly robocalls and solicitations. Lucinda didn't recognize the number on the caller ID, so she let it go to voicemail and waited to listen.

"Um, hi? I'm calling about your dog? Balthazar? I found him. So, ah, I can give him back to you sometime? And get the reward? Soon? You can call me back at 516-482-5347."

It was a woman's voice. Or a girl's. No name, though. That was suspicious. And mentioning the reward was also a bit weird, or maybe just rude. The whole thing gave Lucinda pause. Balzy had been gone for over three months. While David and his new group of friends continued to poster Towne with their LOST DOG posters, it seemed to be more an excuse for the Puppy Pals to socialize. They were all a bunch of misfits, so just plain "hanging out" was a stretch for them. With his identity exploration and new set of friends preoccupying David, Balzy was more an after-thought. For her part, Lucinda was quite used to not having the dog around. The house looked better, smelled better. Her floors were free from chewed-up, saliva-gunked rope toys and the occasional incontinent gift. Once again she could sit on her couch without a crinkled sheet cover and feel the high-end linen silk blend against her skin.

But then again, this was Balzy. A member of the family. Lucinda felt a heart pang when she imagined his ugly little mug, his smooshed up, grizzled terrier face. She didn't miss his mess, but she did, surprisingly, miss him. And so she called back immediately.

"Hello?" a woman, or girl answered. Her voice was barely a whisper.

Lucinda could hear dogs barking in the background. She wasn't sure, it had been so long, but she thought one sounded like Balzy. "Hi. This is Lucinda Leibowitz? You just called about my dog Balzy, I mean Balthazar."

"Oh," said the whisper-voiced person, molasses slow. "Yes. Balthazar. You want him back, I suppose?"

"Of course we do," Lucinda said. "How is he? He's okay, right?"

"He's fine. I just, I just, just wanted to make sure he'll be okay if I get him to you."

"Excuse me? Of course he'll be okay. He's our dog. We love him."

It sounded as if the woman on the other end of the line was crying. There was a pause and then she said, "I guess we should arrange a pick-up."

"That would be great." Would it be great? Balzy back? It would be as it should be, but that didn't mean it would be great.

"Maybe in an hour?"

"Fine." An hour would give Lucinda time to finish up her LouDesign related chores.

"I'd like the thousand dollars in cash please."

Cut to the chase, why don't you, thought Lucinda. "Can't I write you a check?"

"No."

Sketchy. But then again, maybe the woman didn't trust Lucinda. Lucinda could write a bad check just as easily as the caller could con Lucinda. She'd have to go to the bank and deal directly with a teller for that large a withdrawal. Luckily she had the funds now, needed no extra help from Dan. All thanks to Brady Cole. "Alright. I'll give you a call once I'm back here with the money."

"Ah, I can't really bring him to you. I live outside of Towne and I don't have a car."

Lucinda's suburban snobbery took full hold. She refused to go to some trashy house in the backwoods, full of toothless addicts with a pocket full of cash. Luckily she was saved from that fate.

"I can meet you at the train station. Inside the waiting room. It's heated."

And public, thought Lucinda. "Sounds good," she said. "At eleven?"

"Yeah. Sure." Click. The caller was off.

Lucinda was driving to the bank when she got a text alert from David's school: DUE TO THE SUDDEN IN-CLEMENT WEATHER AND BLIZZARD WARNING, SCHOOL WILL BE SUSPENDED AS OF NOON TODAY. PLEASE MAKE THE NECESSARY ARRANGEMENTS

FOR YOUR CHILD. The sky was a gray slate, and the air had that feeling of a heavy load about to come. But blizzard? Really? The last she'd heard was a light dusting expected after dark. So much for reliable weather reports.

No worries, though, because Lucinda would be home by noon, or shortly thereafter. It was worth it, all of it. The inconvenience, the cost, the interruption to logo designing.

Lucinda got the money and headed to the train station. She parked the car and went into the waiting room. The place was empty. A radiator spat and sizzled in the corner. It was chill and damp and smelled like raspberry air freshener tinged with stale cigarette. Lucinda was acutely aware of the worn out, dirty plastic benches, and the sticky linoleum floor. The ticket window was shut with a handwritten sign taped to it reading, ALL TRAINS CANCELLED UNTIL FURTHER NOTICE DUE TO THE STORM. The overhead fluorescents lit the place like a movie set, and big glass windows facing a busy street. Nothing bad could happen in such an exposed location. But still Lucinda's imagination ran wild. Instead of the slurry-voiced woman on the phone, some hulking man would come without Balzy and rip her off at gunpoint. Or, he'd stab her without hesitation and while Lucinda bled out on the waiting room floor he'd wrench her bag off her shoulder and take not only the money, but all her credit cards, her car keys, and her favorite embroidered change purse from Guatemala.

"Don't be a weenie," Lucinda said out loud. She took out a few tissues from her bag and laid them on the bench. Then she sat upon them and waited.

A bit past eleven, in walked a waif of a girl, or maybe a young woman, in a childish red raincoat, matted russet-hued hair poking out from the sides of the hood, her long bare forearms and spindly hands extending from the cuffs, exposed and reddened from the cold. Her legs were bare also, her knees dry and scaly above old-fashioned men's galoshes.

The girl-woman seemed familiar, what Lucinda could see of her, as her alarming blue eyes rimmed with pale lashes and tears were all Lucinda had to go on. She had a pink wool scarf wrapped around her chin, loosely covering her nose and mouth. Like a bandit. She was so wispy, so small, the effect was more like a bundled up gypsy-nymph than dangerous thief. Where could Lucinda have ever encountered a person like this before? Had this odd creature checked Lucinda out at the Whole Foods in the Towne Mall, or filled her prescriptions for estrogen cream at the pharmacy, or waxed stray hairs from her crotch at Lotus Blossom Day Spa back in the day when Lucinda attended to such things?

"Do we know each other?" Lucinda had to ask.

The girl-woman shook her head. "Here's your dog."

And there he was, Balzy, on a leash, standing at attention by the girl-woman's side in his lopsided arthritic way. Lucinda had to admit, he looked good. Or as good as a thirteen-year-old dog could look. He'd lost weight—something the vet had always harped on—and when he barked at Lucinda, the sound was strong and happy. His eyes were clear, his coat bristly and clean.

"Hey Balzy," Lucinda cooed. "C'mere boy!"

The creature-girl let go of the leash and Balzy skittered towards Lucinda. He ran around her legs barking then returned to the girl and attempted to jump up on her, his stumpy little front paws pulling down the rubber tops of her galoshes, exposing a mis-matched pair of crew socks. The girl stood like a statue, attempting to ignore the dog, a dejected testament to the forlorn, her shoulders hunched forward, her arms lank by her sides, her brow furrowed, her gaze at a spot on the floor in front of her.

Balzy circled around both women a few times, then

finally, thankfully settled by Lucinda's feet. "How long have you had my dog?" she asked.

"I just found him," the girl-creature-woman said without moving.

"Are you sure we've never met? I've lived in Towne forever. My name is Lucinda Leibowitz," Lucinda said, even though this girl must already know her name from the poster offering the money she wanted to get her little grubby hands on, "And you are?"

The creature paused then blurted, "Clara Schumann. I'm not from around here."

"Oh. So then where did you find Balzy?"

"I can't tell you. He's back though. Isn't that enough for you?"

The snow was falling with fury. Lucinda wanted to get back home before David. "Not really, but okay."

"Where's my money?"

Lucinda took out the envelope of cash. Clara Schumann shuffled forward in her too-large galoshes, her tiny little elf feet shifting forwards and back inside. She grabbed the money and said, "Balthazar's a really dumb name. You should call him Pepe." Then she shuffled out the door and disappeared in what was quickly turning into a torrent of whiteness.

"Pepe? Not on your life, you fucked-up little weirdo," Lucinda called after her, knowing Clara Schumann was long gone. Balthazar looked up and whined. "Okay. Sorry. That was harsh. Come on, whatever-you-want-to-be-called. Let's get home before it's too late."

Brady: Caught

Morning chants: Check
Morning dance: Check
Morning music: Check

Fresh Direct order in: Check

Amazon browse for Tamago-approved books: Check

Google Alert search for new Brady Cole, B. Cole, or *Signet* links: Check (none)

Binge watch first three episodes of Cal's new show: Check (Blows chunks. Don't see what all the hype's about, but whatever.)

Pace in agitation afterwards, while accessing feelings of rage, envy, insecurity, depression, and panic: Check

Repeat the dance, the chants, and playing the goddamn dulcimer to rid self of masculine negativity to no avail: Check, check, check, check, check, check, check, check, check.

If Brady was honest with himself he'd have admitted the Beauteous rituals were starting to reek of bullshit. But honesty had never been his forte. The only thing, the only person, the only miracle that helped Brady feel better was Lucinda. His feelings for her were all the proof he needed to know he was on a better path. Being with her was all he needed. Watching her putter around the mansion. Making love to her. Talking about their future—or at least trying to, Lucinda was still a bit skittish about too much what she referred to as "happily ever after bullshit," and seemed more stoked when conversations focused on window treatments or rug placement. But a happy Lucinda made for a happy Brady, so he'd talk about home decor until the cows came home. She was due over later that morning, so he just had to sit tight.

Brady tried to keep busy. He picked up the needlepoint project Tamago had assigned him during their last one-on-one. A floral design that demanded intricate little stitches. The thing was driving Brady insane.

"Manual labor, using fine motor skills, paying attention to detail," Tamago said. "All things you need to do, Brady. You've lived your adult life like a pampered prince. Now you must feel what it's like to be a lady-in-waiting."

Brady's mother had done tons of needlepoint when Brady was in grade school. She'd sit in the kitchen, muslin and threads spread on the sunlit table, her thighs spread so she could lean forward enough over her rolled stomach to see which minuscule hole to poke the needle through. Brady would find her there when he got home. Back then, Connie Cole looked beautiful to her son, with tiny glasses perched on top of her chubby baby-pink cheeks, her naturally blonde curls pulled back in a ponytail, her lips pursed in concentration. The way her fingers worked the threads, plucking and pulling just so. It impressed Brady's younger self. It wasn't often he saw his mother so focused.

They'd ended up with little throw pillows all over the house. Each one had a cornball slogan stitched in. Home is where the heart is. Love is all you need. Peace to all God's children.

Eventually Brady would become his father's son. Plenty of girls, mothers, teachers, and strangers would be diminished and dismissed, wise-cracked at, led on, teased. But back when little Brady watched and admired his mother's needlework he'd yet to develop corrosive disdain for the opposite sex. And still, never would any be directed at Connie. He was, and would always be her little sweetie. He even had his own pillow to prove it. He'd carried that pillow everywhere for years, from house to house, film set to film set. Then Brady lost it, along with other bits and pieces of his past he'd been negligent about holding on to. But he'd always remember the inscription:

For Brady
My Little Sweetie

Almost forty years later, here was Connie's own little sweetie plucking and pulling his own little sampler. Brady had newfound respect for his mother. Needlepoint was pure torture. His fingers were covered in tiny scabs from pinpricks. This sampler was supposed to say, Beauteous Before Bravado. Brady considered edits: Beauteous Bites Big Time, or perhaps Beauteous Or Bullshit.

Maybe he'd call his mother later that day.

By noon, Lucinda still hadn't shown up. Brady went over to the front window and pulled open the curtains. He kept them drawn, out of habit, fooling himself that by now paparazzi might have discovered where he lived and would drive by to snap photos. It was wishful thinking. Brady Cole was in cold storage. Obsolete. There'd been no calls from Lois for months. No offers. No prospects.

Giant flakes, some as large as golf balls, were pummeling the circular driveway. Lucinda's car was gone from her driveway, but there were lights on in her house, so she was definitely home. Maybe the car was in the garage, because she'd told Brady she never wasted electricity. She'd lectured him about shutting his own lights when Brady left a room, something he'd never thought about before. She had so much to teach him. Why hadn't she come over? Why hadn't she called?

He had waited long enough. It was time to break his self-imposed house arrest. Brady couldn't remember where he'd stored his regular clothes and shoes when he'd first moved into the Mansion, but he did keep a snow parka out by the back door for when he wanted some fresh air and a walk around his large, still-gnarly, soon-to-be-landscaped backyard. Brady grabbed the parka and slipped on his only accessible footwear; fur-lined booties that were really just glorified slippers with guard rails. He walked out the front door and off the property of the Kearny Mansion for the first time since moving in months and months earlier. The snow felt like a giant Slushy thrown at his face. The wind whipped around his calves. Icy wetness seeped through the seams of his useless booties. Brady trudged out into the storm and made his way across the street, braced against the elements, feeling extremely masculine, like Shackleton at the Pole.

He rang the doorbell, but no one came running. He knocked. No answer. He tried the knob, it turned, so he went in.

"Ta dahhhhhh!"

A girl bounded down the stairs towards Brady in a long white gown. Too young to be hot, at least for Brady's taste, but super cute and obviously related to Lucinda. The same freckly skin, and sleeker, shinier version of Lucinda's strawberry blonde hair. Brady knew some supermodels who would've died for this girl's upturned nose and plump lips, they would've starved themselves for her naturally thin, flat-chested, androgynous appeal. Brady figured her for a visiting cousin on holiday break from a distant school.

It hit Brady when she reached the bottom of the stairs and looked up at him with gorgeous green eyes. Green like Lucinda's. This was no visiting cousin. This was David. The same kid he'd seen scrambling around to the backyard with piles of pink clothes in his arms. The same kid who rode off at times on his wobbly bike. The same kid Brady had imagined tossing footballs with. The same kid Brady had been desperate to meet and make a good impression on.

David stood like a stone statue. His mouth wide in a frozen grimace. Brady could see glints of silver bands around his teeth. He looked Brady up and down as if estimating whether Brady might fit in a cannibal's cooking pot.

Brady was at a total loss for words. The next few minutes were awkward agony. Normally able to smooth-talk himself out of any iffy situation and into anyone's good graces, Brady found David impossible to woo. Brady might as well have been there to read the electric meter for all David seemed to care. Yet the kid, all girly get-up and critical confidence, exuded something so impressive Brady was agog. Eventually David seemed to soften, especially after delivering a few cutting remarks about Brady's caftan. And then came the offer that sealed the deal: "I can make grilled cheeses, if you want," said David.

"Cheese is always good," It was true. Cheese was always good.

"Well, follow me," said David. He sashayed past Brady with the confidence of a hostess at Per Se. Brady didn't know if this odd kid would eventually take the world by storm, or get buried in an avalanche.

Brady sat at the breakfast bar while David made the sandwiches. He was nervous, so he rambled on about Beauteous Man crap. As he spoke, it became ever clearer to Brady how pretentious it all sounded. Dulcimers, and dancing, and the terrible outfit. Meanwhile, here was David, completely at ease in his white gown. Sure, he was a geeky teenager playing around with a really bad English accent and a walk that was a bit too fey. But David was something else. Something ageless. Something pure. No trying to be beauteous. He just was. His mere presence, his confidence, his aura. Maybe there wouldn't be any macho bonding in their future. But maybe there could be something even more profound. David could show Brady how to be authentically beauteous. If Brady could hang out with this little guy, everything would be awesome. Everything would be complete. Everything in Brady's twisted up, wrongly directed life would be righted on a brave new course.

Then things got really weird. And horrible. Lucinda came home calling, "Davey! Come here…"

Brady heard a rattling that reminded him of the Beauteous Men's retreat; the incessant tsk-tsk-tsk of shaky eggs in a robotic, relentless pattern. But it wasn't eggs. It was a dog. A runty dog running and huffing and puffing like an asthmatic. And whoa, did the beast ever stink.

"Balzy!" cried David. "You're home!" He lifted the dog up and they had a lovefest, all slurpy licks and slobber. So adorable. Brady could get used to all this kindhearted authenticity, all this goodness.

"Brady," Lucinda said as she walked in the kitchen. "What are you doing here?"

The love of his life looked at Brady as if he were some creepy relative she couldn't stand who'd shown up for a surprise visit.

"Hey, Lou." He got off the stool, put his arms around her and kissed the top of her head. She cringed, and his heart sank. Brady pretended not to notice. He blundered forward, doomed, but still trying to channel Shackleton at the Pole. "I came over to make sure you were alright in this blizzard."

Brady could tell by the way David stared at them that Lucinda hadn't told her son a thing about their relationship. Brady's heart sunk even further.

Then right on cue, as if the director gave the sign, Balzy started to growl.

Dogs. They get it. They know when something's wrong.

Chapter Twelve

Abe: Coming Clean

Abe could only pace for so long. Chilled by his nearly naked state and emotional tumult, he sat on the couch in his towel, shivering as if in a fever. Finally, at five o'clock, Claire came out of the bedroom and stood at the other side of the living room. She stared at Abe, enraged and wary, as if Abe were a hostile alien life force. Abe told her the truth: he'd lied; he hadn't written a word in over a year; instead, he'd watched lots of ESPN.

"But that's not all I've been doing," Abe stammered. "I've been running. Running is good for me. I've been releasing endorphins. I've been losing weight." Abe grabbed at his stomach, which was slightly smaller than it had been, but not that much smaller. "And other good stuff has come from the running." Did he dare tell Claire about Gordon and Freaky Sting Ray now? Would it do any good? No, he thought. It would only make things worse. It was a lie which once revealed, would lead to bad things. Claire would make the appropriate calls and close the canine sanctuary down in a hot second. The girl would never forgive Abe, and he'd never forgive himself. No, the truth about the dogs and the girl and the sanctuary combined would be protected. Abe's sin of omission for the greater good. "You have to believe me."

"One good doesn't undo a big fat suck-ass wrong, Abe. I've been schlepping to the city, sleep-deprived, half brain-dead, working my butt off to pay for this fucking house and all you've been doing is watching sports on TV?" Claire shrieked. "I don't give a shit about your endorphins. I could care less if you've lost some weight. And news flash, Mister 'maybe I'll train for a marathon': three miles a day is very average. Don't kid yourself."

"Sometimes I run more." Actually, that day it had been a record-breaking seven.

"Big whoop," Claire made an air circle with her right middle finger. "You run to escape. You run during Milo's nap time. On the weekends you're out the door as soon as you and I might have a chance to connect. When I try and talk to you there's no there there. It's all so obvious now. I figured you were focused on Milo, focused on your work. I've been cutting you emotional slack. But you're checked out, Abe. You're in another zone. And your mother," Claire shook her head side to side like she was trying to shake off fleas. "Don't get me started on that."

"What's wrong with my mother?"

"Nothing's exactly wrong with Barbara. But she was supposed to be here so you could write, Abe. Not so she could indulge your avoidant behavior. Jesus, you've been wasting everybody's time. Your mother's. Mine. Milo's."

"I'm sorry, Claire. Really, I am."

"Sorry doesn't cut it Abe. This is almost as bad as if you were having an affair."

"That's a little extreme."

"Maybe. But, why couldn't you be addicted to goddamn porn like most new dads? TV Sports? Really? And all the lies about how productive you've been. So, you tell me: how am I supposed to trust you again?"

Abe shrugged. "I dunno. You just do?"

"Oh gimme a break. You're like your deadbeat father and his cockamamie Ponzi schemes. But I am not your mother, prancing around, pretending everything is fine. Everything stinks, Abe. Thanks to you."

Claire stormed to the kitchen grabbed a jumbo bag of tortilla chips from the cabinet, and a six pack of beer from the fridge. On her way back to the bedroom she warned, "Don't even think of knocking on the door. You're in deep enough shit already."

Claire stayed in the bedroom for hours. With his ear to the door, Abe could hear the crinkling of the chip bag and the suck and zwip opening of numerous cans. Otherwise all was silent. No muffled sobs, no desperate phone calls to friends or family. It was as if his wife had disappeared and all that remained were the sounds of snacking.

Abe didn't know what to do. He didn't dare turn on the TV. He was too distraught to read anything. He made a sandwich, ham with mayo and mustard on rye. He ate it. He washed his plate. He paced. He ate an orange. He stared out the window. The snow was falling with furious assault.

Abe remembered the day, back when they had first moved to Towne, when he'd stood at this very same window with his tiny baby boy in his arms. The yard had seemed to stretch before them like an endless field of promise, not just a half acre of flat suburban sod. Abe himself had been full of grand artistic schemes. Fictional worlds brewed in his brain, a fuzzy mishmash of ideas yet to make their way to the page. Milo's diaper was filled with pee, a tiny fart was yet to make its way to the air. Everything and nothing. And look at things now, Abe thought. Milo continued to pee and fart and poop, but now he also walked and talked his gibberish. Barbara had her new friend Paddy. Clearly there was something creepily amorous and flirty going on there. Claire was moving up the food chain in corporate finance in spite of hating her job and everyone she worked for. And Gordon! Gordon had his deliriously happy new life. But Abe? Where was he going? What had he figured out? What had he done?

Abe made another sandwich. Cheddar and tomato on white. He put his ear up to the bedroom door again. Nothing.

At 5 pm, while buckets of whiteness assaulted his roof, Abe's mother called.

"Abie? Milo and I are going to stay here at Paddy's tonight. It's too dangerous out there. Paddy will drive us home in the morning once the roads are cleared. Tell Claire Paddy's got plenty of the foods Milo likes right here in his cupboard. Milo will be fine."

Everyone was moving forward, everyone but Abe. Who was Abe to question his mother's decision? Paddy cake, paddy cake, baker's man, thought Abe. Barbara Kaufman is your biggest fan. "Whatever you want to do, Ma," he sighed. "I'll tell Claire."

This sleepover situation seemed a legitimate reason to knock on the bedroom door. "Claire?" Abe called through the hollow wood. "I thought you might like to know that Milo and my mother are staying at her friend's house tonight. A guy. His name is Paddy. Can you believe it? I think he's like a boyfriend or something."

Nothing.

Abe waited a beat and added, "should we be worried?" Nothing.

It grew dark. Snow pummeled the house from every angle. Abe was a pale, hairy mound of misery. Eventually he dozed off on the couch in his towel with Milo's shredded but still-beloved baby blanket wrapped around his feet for extra warmth.

He dreamt he was slalom skiing down a precarious mountain path. Evergreens towering over his head, sunlight slicing through the branches like shards of glass, the snow oblivion white, Abe schuss-schussing around random obstacles: a suitcase, a refrigerator, a podium, an inflated punching bag clown.

Abe had never actually skied in real life. Too dangerous for Abe, according to his worrywart father. Mort forbade it. Ironic, really, as he was a man who took stupid risks all the time. Gambled, invested poorly. But never the physical kind of risk. Abe hadn't even ever seen Mort so much as run for a bus. Meanwhile, in his alpine dream, Abe was a daredevil wunderkind, humming "I Gotta Feeling (That Tonight's Gonna Be a Good Night)" as frosty air kissed his cheeks.

Another obstacle was ahead on dream-Abe's path. Something dark and hulking. He expertly glided towards it planning to veer leftward like a stealth missile when close enough.

The dark and hulking thing was Mort, in that awful gray overcoat he'd worn for years. He was hatless, his big, hairy ears bright red from the cold, his bulbous nose a dripping mess. Abe's notorious father, dead ahead, his shoulders hunched, his perpetual scowl, his aura of disappointment. His hands clenched in fists at his sides.

Abe couldn't turn. He shook side to side as he beelined towards his father. He couldn't stop. He headed straight for him. Mort's bloodshot eyes grew bigger as Abe approached.

His fists raised towards Abe, each hand grasping a grenade.

Abe startled awake, his heart pounding. It was 8 pm, and Abe could tell by the lack of any illuminated lamps, chargers, or once beloved TV remotes, that the power was out. This also seemed a legitimate reason to knock on the bedroom door a second time.

"Claire? The power went out."

No answer.

"You okay in there? I'm just checking because, like I said, the power is out."

A moment and then, "I'm fine Abe. I was sleeping. Leave me alone please."

She'd talked to him. He took it as a good sign. "Good night, Claire. I love you."

Nothing, then: "Whatever."

The house was a dark, cold prison. No light, no heat, no nothing. If Gordon had been there, they would've snuggled together for warmth. But sticking around Abe had been a road to nowhere, even for a dog.

Gordon, Gordon, Gordon. He imagined his buddy and his buddy's buddies enduring this stupid snowpocalypse with that odd, though actually wonderful girl with snaky hair. A waif who dressed in pink and red who lived among dogs. Who was probably half-dog herself. How had she become what she'd become? So feral and so fierce. Who formed her? What propelled her? What was that freaky saint's story after all?

Something interesting dwelled in the murk of it all, among the musty fur, unbridled love, and admirable insanity. There was something juicy in it that might lead to more. Abe opened his laptop and let the cool blue glow shine its challenging light upon him. He had nothing better to do, nothing to lose, and three hours of battery power. He went to the title page of *The Gist* and realized he finally had exactly that: a kernel of a purpose, the beginning of a story. He erased those two words, the real gist now inside him, and tapped out something new:

DAWG TOWNE, the story of a saint

As Abe sat there, the power came back on. The proverbial lightbulb. Abe gulped. He felt nauseated. It was a start.

Paddy: Unfurled

They smooched like a couple of teenagers packing as much in as they dared before curfew. Milo played in the kitchen, oblivious to their saucy goings on, his happy babble a sound score for their geriatric lust.

Paddy was mighty aroused as Barbara—who'd started it all—attempted to weasel her tongue between his lips. When his brain tripped to the memory of Gloria in the garage, Paddy had to pull away.

"Everything okay?" Barbara asked.

This is different, thought Paddy. "Sorry." Just like riding a bike. Take it slow. Paddy ran the smoother back of his hand across Barbara's cheek. "Everything is fine. Just had to catch my breath."

It was strange and sad and nice to kiss this way. Mariah hadn't been one for the French stuff, but kissing her had still always been a treat, like pressing his mouth against cool rose petals. How he missed those lips. And now, here were Barbara's lips, warm and slightly chapped, spreading as if to infer another kind of opening was also on offer.

Barbara was on a mission. She grabbed Paddy's hand and placed it on her breast, while she gamely reached her own hand to his cock. Their respective body parts, not the firmest or pertest, responded as they should, kneaded and stroked through layers of sensible clothing. Everything operational, if a bit flaccid.

When Milo's babbles became ragged and maniacal,

Barbara pulled away and said, "Hold on. Nap time." She rose from the couch to attend to her grandson, leaving Paddy aroused and befuddled. It wasn't that this was all some big surprise. But he hadn't quite expected things to advance so soon. And while Barbara was a gal with strong convictions, Paddy hadn't expected her to be quite so assertive.

Paddy heard kitchen cabinet doors open and shut. The microwave running.

"Can I help you in there?" Paddy called.

"No, no," Barbara called back, "I've got it under control."

I bet you do, thought Paddy.

Barbara came back carrying a sleepy Milo in her arms, a bottle of warmed milk plugged in his mouth, his pudgy fingers gripping the bottle at the right angle for ultimate sucking. "I suppose we could let him sleep there..."

Paddy could tell by the way she looked at the mussed cushions, the way she proposed it, the last thing Barbara wanted was to have Milo usurp them from the couch.

"Why don't we let him sleep in the den instead?" Paddy suggested.

Not one for hyperbole, Paddy admitted a bit later on that this blizzard was a doozy. Already the drifts covered the boxwood hedges and his mailbox was totally swallowed in white. It was decided that Barbara and Milo would stay the night. Paddy made up the sofa bed in the guest room, one side for Milo with a nest of bolsters to keep him from kerplopping to the floor, the other side for Barbara.

There were two doors, a hallway, and one toddler between them, but still things progressed in the wee hours of the night when Barbara snuck into Paddy's bed. And then, there they were, going the whole nine yards. Again Paddy fought against the memory of Gloria's blowjob. Paddy hadn't been sure the old hose could blow when it was he who wanted it to blow. He was pleased to find out it still worked just fine.

Afterwards, as they lay spent and languid together, Barbara reached between the pillows. "What's this?" she asked.

Paddy remained quiet as Barbara uncurled Mariah's bumble bee blouse from the tight wad it had stayed bunched in for months. The fabric slipped over Barbara's age-spotted forearm as she sat up in bed and smoothed the blouse lovingly, as if she were petting a dog. He could've stopped her. Reclaimed his special pillow. She would've understood. But he didn't say a thing. He felt something being smoothed inside himself as well.

"This is gorgeous," Barbara said. "Mariah's?"

Paddy nodded.

"How unfortunate it was lost down there. I wonder how it got there."

Paddy shrugged. "Dunno. Mariah had lots of blouses. Hard to keep track. She made that one herself."

"She made this? How incredible," Barbara smiled. "It should definitely be aired out and steam ironed in the morning." Barbara rose from the crumpled sheets, buck-naked and unashamed. She found a hanger in Paddy's closet and hung the blouse off the closet doorknob. She stepped back to admire it. "There you go, gorgeous," she sighed.

By morning, the snow had ended. The plows came out and the streets became passable. Paddy dug out his car, with the help of a couple of teenagers going door to door with shovels at the ready, eager to make a few bucks. Barbara ironed the blouse and a few other things while Milo played with Paddy's Tupperware. When Paddy finished, they all had some hot cocoa.

He drove them home midday. Barbara sat in the back with Milo on her lap.

"Don't tell my daughter-in-law I let Milo have chocolate," Barbara said. "She'll have a conniption."

"Your secret is safe with me. It's in the vault. Along with a few other events."

"Events?" Barbara laughed. "Is that what you'd call what we did?"

"Momentous events?"

He could see Barbara nodding in his rear view. "Much better."

As soon as they pulled up to the house, Barbara's son Abe opened the front door. There he was, the slightly pudgy, bearded 30-something-year-old dad who'd almost lost his kid in Paddy's store. That meant Milo was Mouse, the boy who'd almost been buried in Diet Coke cans. Paddy turned and examined Milo, snug as a bug on Barbara's lap, sucking his thumb. "You little devil," Paddy laughed. Milo looked up at him, unplugged the thumb and gave Paddy one of his signature scrunch-waves.

As Abe approached the car it was obvious he recognized Paddy as well. The younger man's expression indicated this might not be such a good thing. Paddy understood. No way Abe had told his conniption-prone wife that he'd let their son wander off in a convenience store and that the kid had nearly died under a mountain of carbonated beverages. And while Paddy already found it easy to tell Barbara most things, he could see by the way Abe looked at his mother with the blood-curdled panic of a man about to get a lethal injection, Barbara could also never know about that day in Paddy's store.

The two men shook hands warily.

"Nice to meet you, Paddy," said Abe.

"Same here, Abe," said Paddy. He gestured for Abe to lean close. For the second time that day, this time in a low whisper, Paddy said, "Don't worry, bud. Your secret is safe with me. It's in the vault."

By then Barbara had made her way around the car to join them. "So I see you've already made your introductions?"

"We did," Paddy and Abe said at the same time.

Barbara handed Milo to Abe. "Are you alright Abie? You look exhausted."

"I'm good Ma," Abe said. "I've been up all night. Writing, actually. Good stuff, I hope."

Barbara patted Abe's cheek, "Ah that's my creative genius!"

Abe pulled his face back and turned to Paddy. "Thanks for taking care of my family."

"Any time," Paddy said, "any time."

Abe glanced back at the house, where a slight and beautiful dark haired woman scowled at all of them, or maybe just Abe, through the picture window. He turned back to Paddy and said, "That's my wife Claire. She's having a moment. But really, we'd love to have you over for dinner sometime."

"That would be swell. I'd like that."

Abe walked away, trying to maintain his balance while Milo poked his face, kicked him in the sides.

"Nice boys," said Paddy. "Both of them."

"I could *kvell* for days." Barbara smiled, then she stood up on her tiptoes and grabbed Paddy's face to give him a big smooch right on the kisser, right there in public. "Let's do it again, Paddy, shall we?" said Barbara.

"We shall. We shall indeed," said Paddy.

It was a glorious sight, to see her face crinkle and wrinkle with joy. Would he ever tire of it? Of her? Quite possibly. But at that moment Paddy was grateful for this woman. He was grateful for her son who needed her help and brought her to Towne. He was grateful for her lousy sense of direction and her grandson, who'd brought her to his store. He was grateful for this snowstorm that kept them both with him for the night. He was grateful to not be alone. He was grateful for the way life went off course, sped up, circled around, stalled, then kicked back in to gear. Calm, cruise-controlled—at least for now.

David: At Last

A total stranger had seen him in a dress and David had survived. In fact, he'd thrived. Dressed in a dress. Dressed for success. Wait until he told Thomas.

David wasn't stupid enough to think that from then on he'd be able to wear whatever he wanted, wherever he wanted. That he'd feel comfortable in his own skin. That he'd feel comfortable in the world. That he'd never feel the urge to steal again. That comfort with himself was as easy to come by as a head-to-toe cream velour gown. That his cheese sandwiches would forever after be accepted. But the shift felt seismic. The rumbling in David's tummy wasn't hunger or panic. It was thrill.

Lucinda: Men in White

The look on Brady's face said it all. He was so happy to see her when she walked in to the kitchen. On the other hand, she was appalled to find him there.

Brady didn't fit. She didn't want him. She didn't love him.

It was cruel. It had to end.

David, on the other hand, looked adorable. Also happy to see her. Extremely happy to see the dog. She'd never stop wanting David. She'd never stop loving her son. She'd always need him. Or her. Or them.

The blizzard had forced Lucinda's hand. She had to do the deed. She would miss Brady's puppyish attention, would even miss the below-average sex. She'd miss having a reason to be in the Kearny Mansion, to run her hand along the impeccably restored woodwork, to admire the pitch perfect wall colors, to walk barefoot on the newly grouted and brilliantly lacquered tile floors and think all this beauty is restored because of me.

"David, would you mind taking Balzy upstairs for a moment?" she said, trying to keep her tone even and calm. "I want to talk to Brady about something."

"No prob. Later." David swished out of the kitchen cradling the old dog like a baby.

"That is some kid you have, Lou," said Brady. "I was kind of taken aback when I first saw him. How long has he—"

"Brady. It's over." Lucinda blurted.

Brady smiled. "The storm?"

"No, Brady. Us. We're over."

"Over what?"

"I'm breaking up with you. I can't see you any more."

Brady squinted at her.

"I'm sorry. It's just, well, I'm not in love with you. And I can't keep sleeping with someone I don't love. Who I will never love."

Brady's face went through painful looking contortions before settling in a wide mouthed, startled state of disbelief.

"Brady, let's face it; you don't really love me either. I'm just some weird aberration in your line of conquests. I made sense for the moment, for your Beauteous whatever."

"You're not an aberration, Lou."

He was not making this easy. "Can't we just agree we were the right thing at the right time, but the time is over?"

"But I don't want the time to be over," Brady whined. He reminded Lucinda of David at age three, harrumphing with his arms crossed over his chest and a grumpy scowl.

"You don't have to pay me the remaining fee on the mansion. I am so grateful to you for giving me that opportunity. I can't tell you what a recharge it's been."

"I can't believe this is happening," Brady cried.

Lucinda stayed strong. On point. "I would like to use the photos I've taken of the project for my website, if that's okay."

Brady dropped his arms to his sides. He stared straight

into Lucinda's eyes with unnerving steeliness. Brady took a deep snort of air in through his nose, flaring his nostrils like a bull, then exhaled out his mouth. He huffed and he puffed in a blow your house down manner before turning to race out the front door, coatless, without shoes, a hulking white spirit battling the storm.

"Well that's that, you heartless, manipulative bitch," Lucinda said to herself as she watched him disappear.

Brady: Abominable

Brady was heaved across the street by near-hurricane strength gusts. Snow and wind shoved mercilessly at his back, catapulting him back to his pathetic, single life, exiling him from a warm, cozy, familied future. He was so miserable he didn't feel his bare and frozen feet or the icicles forming on the hairs of his exposed calves. Brady was oblivious to the tears coating his cheeks, to his clucking wails, to the mournful howls instantly consumed by punishing winds.

Nearly blinded by his own gushing tears and the snow pellet assault, Brady stumbled towards his mansion through a series of thigh high snowdrifts. He pushed open the ponderous, carved and recently varnished front door, slammed it shut, and collapsed on the tile floor. Snow melted around his shivering body. The drenched white caftan clung to his body, transparent, like a membrane. Water pooled around his fetal form. Brady nearly swam in it.

Puddled, Brady shook and cried for a good long while. Eventually exhausted, he lay in silence but for the whoosh of blizzard wind, barely audible through the mansion's new triple-paned windows.

After an hour of solid moping, Brady rose from the floor, ready for a hot shower and a stiff drink, or three. But before he did anything else he pulled off his stupid caftan and ripped it to shreds. If it hadn't been sopping wet he would've burned the rags in a very non-beauteous ceremony. He would have doused the remains in lighter fluid and watched them go up in violent flames. He would've cursed these months of wasted folly, blind passion, and unrequited love. He blamed Tamago for this uniform of stupidity. This outfit of bullshit. As it was, he took the bogus pile of wet, useless cotton to the kitchen and shoved the rags deep in the belly of the trash can.

"Lot of good you did me, stupid piece of crap," he said.

Brady was about to leave the kitchen to head for the new burled wood, climate controlled combination liquor cabinet and wine cooler in his study when he heard a sound coming from the back door. A familiar repetitive pattern. A Hey! Hey, you! It's me! It's me! bark.

Brady opened the back door and there he was, Angus. The dog was dry, had been protected from the elements by standing under the very large retractable awning Lucinda had insisted Brady install. And with Angus was a tiny poodle who looked up at Brady with an expression that seemed to say, "I've got your number, Mister." In tandem, as if they had one brain, the dogs jumped upon Brady, happier than happy to see him.

Maybe at some point in the future Brady would feel grateful to Lucinda for installing that dog-saving awning. For now, however, she was in the proverbial dog house; the perfect place for a heartless, manipulative bitch.

Angus and his little friend pushed Brady to the floor and slobbered him with wet, warm tongues. Brady took it in. Brady received. Brady, licked all over, like a newborn pup.

Nell: Forsaken

Feeding the remaining twenty dogs, caring for all their bodily needs, heating a cavernous house, and buying the occasional pizza was still a money-sucking venture. By February, all 1,000 Leibowitz dollars were gone. Nell and the pack huddled in a furry heap by the hearth in her father's study, sleeping away most of the gray, chilly days. Sticks that would normally be tossed for games were now collected for kindling. The hatcheted kitchen chairs provided warmth for a day, a brightly painted armoire burned with quease-inducing toxicity for another two.

The low point came when Nell took an axe to her cherished Steinway baby grand. The last music it made came from the crackle and hiss of North American Sitka Spruce in a legato fade behind the fireplace screen.

By March Nell had to make another gut-wrenching choice. And then another. And then another. Some returns brought cash rewards, some only grateful hugs. Some dogs weren't wanted back as their owners no longer had room in their callous hearts or their homes. Boris' owner, that gruff old man from the Gas n' Go, hung up on her when she called. Nell kept the last three, Ziggy, Pandora, and Dash as long as she could, but with no food or hope left, she was eventually forced to give them up for adoption. WoofWorld, a sketchy organization that asked no questions, sent an unmarked van in the dead of night to collect the last of Nell's beloveds, taking them away to uncertain fates.

For almost nine months the dogs had known a better life. Nell had to believe that their superior minds would hold on to memories of their respite at her retreat. The swims, the games, the songs, the hugs, the licks, the rubs, the food. The freedom. She prayed they remained forever soothed by effluvia, whiffs, high-pitched tones never forgotten.

One special friend would never leave her. Raphael, her first, her best, her most-loved, would always remain by her side. All Nell had to do was look in his trusting eyes to know what she had done had been good and just. Maybe it had even been holy. In moments of doubt Nell recalled her conversation by the frozen pool with Abe Kaufman, who'd told her she was lucky and the dogs were too. That what she'd done was a wonderful thing. A *mitzvah*.

Once the pool had thawed and tender green nibs unfurled on bushes, plants, and trees, Nell would clean for days. She would open each and every window in the house. All traces of her rich, furry life would be scrubbed from the floors, washed from the down pillows, vacuumed from the upholstered furniture. When she was done, she would lay down to rest. Her parents would return from their year abroad to find their emaciated daughter barely conscious, in a sleepy drift on the cold linoleum tiles of the kitchen floor, her head resting on the belly of a well-fed congenial pit bull. They would wait a few hours before waking the two of them up. After all, the professor and the artist needed to unpack and have a bite to eat.

Conversations

David:

"Where did you get this dress, Danesha? I love it."

"I think my mom got it at H &M. Or maybe Forever? I can't remember. It looks super good on you, David."

"Thanks."

"You want it?"

"For real?"

"For real. I never wear it anymore."

"Ohmygod. That's, like, so cool of you, Danesha."

"David, do you think you'll ever wear any girl stuff to school?"

"I dunno. Maybe one of these days. But it still seems dangerous. Kids can be so mean."

"I hear you."

"For now, I'm cool to just dress up at home. And maybe here at your house also?"

"Mi casa es su casa."

"Merci."

"Listen to us, D. So international."

"True, D. So true."

Lucinda:

"LouDesign, Lucinda Leibowitz speaking."

"Oh hello, Ms. Leibowitz. This is Anabelle Carlson? We just bought an old farmhouse outside of Towne?"

"Professor Delano's house?"

"Yes! That's the one."

"I had no idea it was on the market."

"It was a private sale. My husband works at the university with Professor Delano. He and his wife Beverly decided to move to Spain. I believe she's an artist of some kind?"

"I suppose you could call her that. I know that house. I worked on it years ago."

"Oh good! Then you're already familiar with the property. The place is, well, it's in a shambles to be quite honest. We're considering a gut renovation and everyone we've talked to said you did a fantastic job on a famous mansion in Towne, and that you were the go-to designer for us."

"Wow. That's so nice to hear."

"Mrs. Leibowitz?"

"Call me Lucinda."

"Of course, Lucinda; would you be willing to come take a peek?"

"Sure! I'd love to."

"Yay. Does Wednesday afternoon work for you?"

"Wednesday works for me, Amanda. Around 1 pm?"

"Perfect."

"Oh, and Amanda? One last question; do you have any idea whatever happened to the Delano's daughter? I haven't seen her for years."

"They never mentioned a daughter to us. Though there was a girl's bedroom still in use when we first saw the house. Canopy bed, boy band posters, an old turtle terrarium. And we noticed one of those retro-Sting Ray bikes leaning against the porch. You know; banana seat, pink streamers off the raised handle bars. But no sign of a girl. Go figure."

"Hmm. Yes. Go figure."

Brady:

"It's the only offer you've gotten in a year, Brady."

"Lois, really? An accountant? I'm playing a fucking accountant?"

"Now's not the time to get all prima donna. The casting assistant didn't even know who you were when I first suggested you for the part."

"Whoa, Lois. That's harsh."

"Harsh, and true. So do I tell them we have a deal or not?"

"Where does it shoot again?"

"Somewhere in Romania. I don't remember. Why does it matter? A job is a job, Brady. And you need one, bad."

"Whatever. Tell them yes. But only if I can bring my dogs."

"Dogs? Since when do you have more than that one big mush-ball sweetie pie Angus?"

"Since earlier this winter. He's a toy poodle. His name is Beauty Boy."

"You with a toy poodle named Beauty Boy? Seriously?"

"Don't give me any shit about it, Lois. These dogs are the only things keeping me sane right now, so fuck the producers if they say I can't bring them to Bumfuck Whereverville, Romania."

Paddy:

"That Barbara really is something else, Mort. Or should I call you Morty, like she does?"

"Let's go with Mort, Paddy. It is a bit more dignified. And yes, Barbara can be quite a piece of work."

"Don't get me wrong. I adore her. It's just that she can be a bit bossy."

"That's an understatement."

"I'm not used to a woman being quite so opinionated. My Mariah was much more, shall we say, demure?"

"Ah, the good old days, right Paddy? When a broad acted like a broad, and a man could just be a man."

"Well, I'm not sure I agree with you on that Morty."

"No Paddy? How so?"

"It may have been simpler back in our day, but maybe not better. I like the way things have changed. Girls, boys, everything in between. Everyone should be what they wanna be, be with who they wanna be with, and do what they wanna do as long as it doesn't hurt anyone else or this goddamn beautiful, dying world we're living in. Oh, sorry to mention the 'd' word, you being dead already and all."

"That's okay, Paddy. It's impossible to hurt the feelings,

*or anything else really, of a dead person. We're impervious
to pain. It's one of the upsides of this death thing."*

"Have you run into my Mariah? A gorgeous woman
in her mid-seventies? Tall and curvaceous, long curly
gray hair, turquoise eyes, and a smile that could turn a
barren field to flowers?"

*"Nah, can't say I have. But from that description, I
hope I do soon."*

"Well, if you come by the house, you'll meet her.
Barbara and she have their own thing going. At first it
gave me the heebie-jeebies, Barbara talking to my dead
wife, me standing there, hearing only Barbara's side of
the conversation, but now I'm used to it."

*"Barbara and her spiritual stuff. It used to drive me
crazy. But now that I'm a spirit myself, I see that she
was right all along. I guess that's the thing with Barbara. She's a pain in the butt, but usually she's a correct
pain in the butt."*

"Amen to that. Ah—someone just drove up to the full
service pump. Gotta go, Morty. It was swell talking with
you. Come back and keep me company another time,
okay?"

"You got it, Paddy. It would be a pleasure."

Abe:

"Hi, Abe. Charlie Burnow of Burnow Literary here.
Thanks for taking my call."

"Are you kidding me? Of course. I'm thrilled you've
reached out to me."

"Well, like I said in my email, we adored your
manuscript."

"I can't believe I'm hearing these words—"

"*Dawg Towne* is such a marvelous story. Truly. Congratulations."

"Thank you Mr. Burnow. Coming from you, this means the world."

"Thing is, Abe; before we can offer you representation, there are a few changes we'd like you to make."

"I can handle that, I think."

"A lot of our concerns have to do with the character Joe. He's just not believable. A blocked writer who takes full advantage of his hard working wife and helpful mother, who watches sports all day, and then—big whoop—his big move is to take up running when his incredible dog gets stolen? I mean, really? He's such a selfish prig."

"Okay…"

"We think you should take him out of the book entirely. We don't need him. He's useless."

"Useless. If only it weren't true…"

"Excuse me, Abe? I didn't quite hear you."

"I said, I'll see what I can do, Mr. Burnow. Honestly? I've been trying to get rid of that guy for a long, long time."

Nell:

Dear Mother and Father,

The last few weeks have been difficult, to say the least. Your behavior is deeply unsettling to Raphael. The way you both run away from him when he comes near you, the looks you give him, the whispers behind his back. You are typical humans who think dogs have no feelings. Well, I have news for you: Dogs are the most creative and intelligent creatures on the planet, and Raphael is above all others. Smarter than you, Father, with all your fancy, useless degrees. More resourceful than you, Mother, with your silly art projects that look like kindergarten rejects.

You've been treating me in a similarly suspicious manner. I can tolerate this, but Raphael cannot. I will not put him through any more of your prejudice and venom. So we have left.

I've learned much in the last year. I know now what truly matters. Don't try and find me. I don't want to be found. I'm a full-fledged adult now, so you can't force me to do anything I don't want to do.

Don't worry. I will be fine. Better than if I stayed in the house surrounded by your toxic energy and empty values.

Your daughter,
Nell

spring

*I*t doesn't get much better than this. Warmth without discomfort. Breeze without destruction. Growth without invasion. Birth without crowding. Cohabitation without exile or murder. Air, sky, sun, earth, plants, animals, humans. Everything in a contented buzz.

Come to the part of me called Allenwood Park. Here humans have let things be, more or less. Some of these trees took root in my soil centuries ago. Some of these species of insects have been around even longer. No seeds planted by human hands. Everything "native." These are my babies.

Look how people love to be here. They walk through this forest and look up at the branches. They sigh with wonder and respect. They bend and collect fallen leaves. They cup newts and frogs and ladybugs in their hands, and let the tiny creatures go once sensing distress.

Look who's walking up the path now. An older couple, man and woman, holding hands. Large and strong once upon a time, the man now bears the crooked frame resulting from hard physical labor. There's a slight catch in his gait. He's smiling, something he does more these days than in the recent past. The woman is spindly, like a cricket, moving in rapid herks and jerks. Her hair is cut short, like a man's. She doesn't stop talking, but he likes to listen. Back at the house they now share, there's a cat, a fat, aloof creature who spends most of his time sleeping on a needlepoint ottoman. Occasionally the cat goes out back to crouch under an apple tree, making half-hearted attempts at hunting mice and birds. He does this to prove to me he still has some carnivorous feline instincts left so I won't use my pull with the larger powers that be and doom his kind to extinction. He needn't worry. I've grown to appreciate the importance of pets.

Further north there's the playground. Here my humans have cut down hanging vines, trees and natural pools to make space for bright, synthetic structures on which to swing, climb, slip, and slide. Irony or progress? You decide. Look at the little boy climbing up a purple slide. He's going up the wrong way. He ignores the stacked red steps at the rear, instead sloughing his way up the slippery incline on hands and knees. When he gets to the top the boy turns around, lays on his belly with his arms stretched forward to careen down the way he's come. His squeals scare off crows picking foodstuffs out of a nearby trash bin, but the grown-ups with him—his parents—laugh in delight. They stand on opposite ends of the bottom of the slide. The father on the left is hefty and unkempt. He attempts to keep his appearance tidy, but can't help but have food stains on his shirts, or shoelaces untied. He'd have been better off in the Stone Age when all my humans were hairy and a bit chaotic. The mother is as upright and sturdy as a bamboo stalk. Her dark hair looks like a helmet. Her shoulders don't know how to relax. The parents don't look at each other. All eyes are on the boy. They are ready to catch him before he falls.

Studying it all while straining at the end of a securely fastened leash, is a puppy, a mishmashed little mutt with more genes in his gene pool than even I can keep track of. He already loves the little boy unconditionally. Maybe even more than the parents do. The puppy will protect the boy fiercely in the future. More, I expect, than the parents will.

Watch the parents watching the time. In a little while they will meet up with the crooked old man and the spindly old woman at a picnic table and leave the son and puppy in their care. The parents must go to "couples therapy," which means they will sit in a quiet room with a woman who will take notes as they talk. The parents hope she is wise. They will not be sure if she is helping them. They will hate and admire her.

A bit to the east of the playground, two women sit side by side on a bench under one of my most magnificent trees. They're not quite in the center of things, and by the way they sit I sense an air of hesitation. They resemble each other. Mother and daughter. But no. When I look closer I see that the younger one is maybe not a woman after all. Whatever they are, this youth is filled with promise, hope, and pure beauty. Both mother and child are looking towards a flat wide field where other juveniles run around in frantic circles kicking a ball or trying to stop others from kicking it. These youngsters chatter like monkeys, screech like blue jays, laugh like themselves. Every now and then one tumbles as if mortally wounded, writhing on the ground as the others surround them. Once the fallen one has gotten the attention they sought, they rebound, stand with assistance, and valiantly start galloping again.

On the bench, the beautiful child turns to their mother and says something. The mother nods in return, reaches up to the child's long hair and combs caring fingers through the lustrous curly mane. Once upon a time she had hair just like this. The child rises and smooths the skirt that billows like an upside down tulip in the slight breeze. Their bare legs are like willow branches, white, smooth, perfect. They slip their feet out of buckled pink shoes and into a pair of springier silver lace-ups. After kissing their mother on the cheek, the young one races down the hill in their swirling skirt and metallic shoes to join the ball-kicking frenzy. The mother looks on, her face a mosaic of concern. I don't blame her for her worry.

Look there, at one of those god-awful airplanes flying high above Allenwood Park, making an incessant rumble, spewing smoky dirt into the clouds. On the plane is a man who spent a short period of time inside a large house on my southern border. Now he's reclining on a large and comfortable bed in the noxious flying machine while the others in the rear of this horrible, polluting contraption are upright in seats and smooshed unhappily close. In spite of his relative comfort, this man feels used and abused. He's deep in a cavernous stew. He may have lived upon my soil once upon a recent time, but he never quite fit in. He's a restless soul, always has been, always will be. He's on his way across the ocean searching for something he's never going to find. He's got a glass filled with fermented potato juice and ice resting on a tray near his elbow. This is his fourth such beverage. He stares blankly at a small screen filled with moving images; people running to and fro, faces smeared with dirt and blood, weapons everywhere, automobiles and houses in flames. There's a miniature version of this man himself on the screen, gesticulating with broad arm sweeps and a furrowed brow, a shiny ring on his finger as he points threateningly at a woman's nose.

On the reclining seat next to the man is a dog. A wonderful creature. He's a big yellow thing whose love is boundless, whose enthusiasm is infectious. He stares at the sullen man as the man stares at the screen. The dog is waiting for affection. A scratch on the head. A tummy rub. It will come, eventually, once the man is out of his cavernous stew. In the meantime, the dog is endlessly, faithfully patient.

Spiraled up in a tight brown ball, sleeping soundly by the yellow dog's haunches is another dog. This one is not so easily distracted by insatiable, canine needs. He'll gets what he wants when he wants it. The larger dog and the despondent man will take care of that. It is hard to tell which one of them loves this little curly nugget more.

Before you leave Allenwood Park to go home or to the store, to nap or eat a sandwich, take a closer look around. Do you see her? My girl? She's unassuming, blends in with the trees, her hair like the vines, her skin as green and pebbly as the ground. She's crouched in a corner, behind the dog run, next to a forgotten stream, back where no one bothers to venture. She and her block-headed, bejowled dog-friend have it to themselves. The dog is alert, available, ready for everyone and everything. The girl looks like she's sleeping, but she's got one eye out for those dogs who still need her. They sense her, lift their snouts and muzzles in the air and feel her, *if only for a distracted second. She hasn't stopped. She's still got her purpose. She'll never stop being a savior.*

Does she really exist? To me she does. I live off her purposefulness. All her guided and misguided energy. Her mania. Her love. Her passion. Her sloppy mistakes. I love her like I love all my humans. They make me who I am. They will have a place in me forever. For as long as my name is Towne.

ACKNOWLEDGMENTS

This book could not have happened without many walks through my Brooklyn neighborhood, where I'd often see dogs tied to street signs or benches outside cafes, bars, and bodegas, waiting patiently for their humans to return. The dogs got me thinking; "what would happen if someone came by and in a fit of spontaneous desire, took all you guileless, adorable creatures away?" Thus was born the story "Gifted and Talented" about Nell, published in *Hobart*. Thanks to Elle Nash and Aaron Burch for giving that seed story a home.

The characters of Abe, David, and Paddy also first appeared in story form; "Stages of Man" in *BULL: Men's Fiction*. So thanks to Benjamin Drevlow over at that fine magazine as well.

I am incredibly grateful to Leland Cheuk, Rachel Lyon, and Amy Shearn for their generous, blurb-tastic words about *Dawg Towne*, and to Kristin Eliasberg for giving this shaggy story a proof-reader's grooming.

Hugs and kisses to the friends and family who read earlier versions of *Dawg Towne* and offered frank feedback and encouragement when I needed it the most. I adore you all.

My deepest gratitude to the fine folks at word west: David Byron Queen, publisher/founder, who wrote me a love letter about this book, and made me an offer I couldn't refuse. Joshua Graber, my incredible, perceptive editor; so discerning and a complete joy to work with. Jesse Motte for giving David's sections a youthful read through. Julia Alvarez who designed the gorgeous cover I hope you, dear reader, are not smudging with dirty hands right now.

And then, of course, thanks especially to the dogs, each and every one of them. It was the pups who truly inspired this tale with their boundless affection, wet noses, and stinky breath. With their stupidity and their smarts. My heart throbs with love, and I'm so much the better for it. Woof!

Alice Kaltman is the author of the story collection STAG-GERWING, and the novels WAVEHOUSE and THE TANTALIZING TALE OF GRACE MINNAUGH. Her writing appears in numerous journals including BULL, Hobart, Joyland, Lost Balloon, and The Pinch, and in the anthologies THE PLEASURE YOU SUFFER, ON MONTAUK, and FECKLESS CUNT. Alice lives, writes, and surfs in Brooklyn and Montauk, NY.

CPSIA information can be obtained
at www.ICGtesting.com
Printed in the USA
FSHW012031191021
85601FS

9 781733 466349